Last night, as I was falling aslee[p] for a couple weeks, and that I'd had no problems, no serious systems failures, plenty of warning when something needed attention . . . and I thought, *It's not the ship's fault, is it, that I don't want to be here . . .* So I decided to give the ship a name, *Alice*, and I decided to be more grateful for everything this little vessel does for me. The logical, rational part of me—that part of me inculcated by years of training—naturally considers this anthropomorphizing as so illogical as to be bordering on the ridiculous. But I am not solely the product of my training.

I am so very alone.

The hours I spend alone here—with *Alice*—give me ample time to reflect upon my past. Where I have come from; how I have ended up here. I have barely had time to consider what it means that my mother did not die. My mother did not *die*! I learned this, and then she was torn from me again, and yet I feel, I feel so sure, that she is here in this time, and yet she's out of reach again.

I *feel* . . . Again, I hear Sarek's voice in my mind, chastising me for such self-indulgence. That I should not be tempted by such irrationalities. That I should discipline my mind. But I am adrift, and everything that I have used as an anchor is long gone. No ship, no crew, no Starfleet. Who am I, without these things? And I wonder—will I always feel as if I am bobbing around, directionless? Will I always feel that I am made up of disparate pieces? Will I never feel complete?

Will I always be this alone?

**DON'T MISS THESE OTHER THRILLING NOVELS
IN THE UNIVERSE OF**

STAR TREK™
DISCOVERY

DESPERATE HOURS
David Mack

DRASTIC MEASURES
Dayton Ward

FEAR ITSELF
James Swallow

THE WAY TO THE STARS
Una McCormack

THE ENTERPRISE WAR
John Jackson Miller

DEAD ENDLESS
Dave Galanter

DIE STANDING
John Jackson Miller

STAR TREK™
DISCOVERY

WONDERLANDS

UNA McCORMACK

Based on *Star Trek*®
created by Gene Roddenberry
and
Star Trek: Discovery
created by Brian Fuller & Alex Kurtzman

G

GALLERY BOOKS

New York   London   Toronto   Sydney   New Delhi

G

Gallery Books
An Imprint of Simon & Schuster, Inc.
1230 Avenue of the Americas
New York, NY 10020

First Gallery Books trade paperback edition May 2021

GALLERY BOOKS and colophon are registered trademarks of Simon & Schuster, Inc.

For information about special discounts for bulk purchases, please contact Simon & Schuster Special Sales at 1-866-506-1949 or business@simonandschuster.com.

The Simon & Schuster Speakers Bureau can bring authors to your live event. For more information or to book an event, contact the Simon & Schuster Speakers Bureau at 1-866-248-3049 or visit our website at www.simonspeakers.com.

Printed and bound by CPI Group (UK) Ltd, Croydon CR0 4YY

10 9 8 7 6 5 4 3 2 1

Library of Congress Cataloging-in-Publication Data is available.

ISBN 978-1-9821-5754-8
ISBN 978-1-9821-5755-5 (ebook)

To Matthew,
capable of at least six impossible things before breakfast

"Would you tell me, please, which way I ought to go from here?"

—ALICE, *ALICE IN WONDERLAND*

HISTORIAN'S NOTE

In order to defeat the artificial intelligence Control's plot to seize a treasure trove of information about the future, Commander Michael Burnham used the "Red Angel" suit to guide the *U.S.S. Discovery* from the year 2257 to beyond Control's reach (*Star Trek: Discovery*—"Such Sweet Sorrow, Part 2").

The ship should have arrived at the planet Terralysium, but something went wrong. Burnham arrived in the year 3188, but the *Discovery* is nowhere to be found (*Star Trek: Discovery*—"That Hope Is You, Part 1").

This novel takes place during the year where Burnham is learning to adapt, endure, and survive while searching for her ship, hoping to find the crew she calls family.

Some time ago . . .

Starbase 906

Sometime after the Burn

The base's long-range sensors had not been functioning for some time. The defense grid wasn't in much better condition either and as for weaponry—forget it. To all intents and purposes, then, the ships had come from nowhere, and, from the firepower currently directed at the base, they meant business. The kind of business that ended in people getting killed.

Commander Marshak, senior ranking officer on Starbase 906, gathered her small staff together. They knew the score. There was no help coming—how could help come? They were on their own. That was what they'd signed up for. This was why they'd stayed. Looking at the tired, scared faces of her staff, she said, "We have a decision to make. We can surrender and throw ourselves on their mercy . . ."

A ripple went around the room.

"No," said Marshak. "I didn't think you'd like that. Our other option is to negotiate."

The ripple, this time, was even unhappier. "What, exactly, do we have to negotiate with?" said her security chief.

Marshak, leaning back in her chair, said, "The project, of course. What else?"

Now the consternation in the room was in danger of getting out of control. Marshak lifted her hand to call for order—and enough respect remained for her rank for that simple gesture to calm people down. She was grateful for her insignia. The chain of command had kept them going through some difficult times. "One at a time, people, please."

"It's not safe," said her science officer, who surely knew

better than any of them. "It's nowhere near safe. Honestly, I would rather destroy the project files than hand it over to a bunch of damned pirates."

"Could we work with them in some way?" said the chief medical officer. "Could they help bring the project forward in some way?"

"How?" said the science officer. "What could they possibly have that we need?"

"Resources, people, ships—I don't know. Is it worth trying to come to some sort of deal? We must have something they want—"

"What they want," said the security chief, bluntly, "is this base."

Marshak sighed. This was, she knew, the truth of the matter. Starbase 906, a prime piece of real estate in troubled times. So far, they had been lucky. There was an occasional raid from a small and usually desperate ship. It was mostly dealing with refugees, people trying to get away from poverty or collapse on their homeworlds. Doing whatever they could with what they had to hand. But they were not placed to hold off a concerted attack.

And, in the space of a second, the decision was made for them. The lights flashed. Alerts sounded. *"Commander,"* said a frightened junior from the command center, *"they're pushing the attack."*

Marshak stood. Her staff stood with her. She laid her hands down on the table, palms flat, and looked at each one in turn.

"Whatever happens here, today," she said, "I want you to know that you are—you have always been—the best of Starfleet. We've been on our own for so long now. We've kept the lights on, and we've kept the faith. We've kept going. We've held on, and we've done our best to give help to whoever has come to us in need. Today we can only do what we've always done—give our best, for each other, for the people who depend upon us, and for the Federation."

"For the Federation!" her people said.

On the wall, the old flag was still hanging. By the end of the day, it was gone.

1

Sometime later . . .

Mother . . .

Michael Burnham has fallen down a rabbit hole

Mother . . .

a red figure with wings

Mother . . .

what was her name again?

Mother . . .

gabrielleamandaphilippawhatwasyournameagainmichael

Mother . . .

angel or devil

Mother . . .

are we there yet?

"Mommy?"

Michael Burnham opened her eyes and saw gray. She hovered in this place for a moment, caught in some liminal state between past and future, between dreaming and waking, between then and now. Like an angel with arms outspread—she tried to push both memory and waking away. If she could exist here, only in this gray eternal moment, then she would not have to choose.

Silver bells rang. She shut her eyes—but no use. The present was undeniably here, the past pushed entirely away, and however irrational this world was in which she now found herself, she must get up and live in it. She must resign herself to swallowing a whole heap of impossibilities before breakfast. She opened her eyes again. She began to murmur.

"*Commander Michael Burnham, science officer.* U.S.S. Discovery. *Serial number SC0064-0974SHN.*"

She sat up. "*You are Commander Michael Burnham . . .*" She reached out and, with a wave of her hands, she stopped the bells from ringing. Here—this was one impossible thing. Programmable matter. Wave your hand and the thing required appears and/or disappears. "Any sufficiently advanced technology is indistinguishable from magic." Where had she read that? Somewhere else, once upon a time, a very long time ago, in a different world, a world to which she belonged that was not this world in which she found herself now. The silver bells did not exist either, other than as a wake-up. She had programmed a nanocube—clumsily, inexpertly, her first attempt. The bells replicated the ones she heard each morning at the Vulcan Learning Center. They were the call to meditation before the start of the day's work: the solitary process of ingesting and digesting fact after fact, of reading and processing problem after problem, until the mind was so well trained that superior-level functioning became automatic, like blinking or swallowing . . .

. . . *science officer.* U.S.S. Discovery . . .

Michael Burnham pictured the skill dome, the 360-degree holographic information display, the constant flow of data. If she wanted, she could conjure up a skill dome here on the station. Her own mind palace. The idea seemed, suddenly, entirely preposterous. She thought, *Did they really take a bunch of kids and stick us in solitary confinement and force-feed us facts? They may as well have stuck us all on treadmills.*

Burnham got out of bed and began her morning stretches. She was having more and more thoughts like this. It was as if sometimes she found herself hovering above her old life and looking down on it with an objective and critical eye. Logic suggested that this was because she was spending so much of her time these days struggling to understand even the simplest of facts about the world around her, and having to explain even the simplest of facts about the world she had come from. Everything—*everything*—was suddenly open to question. Everything she had taken for granted was up for grabs, and— now that she thought about her education on Vulcan, there really was something *weird* about the way they did things there . . .

. . . *serial number SC0064-0974SHN* . . .

She stood by the wall of the room and again waved her hand. A mirror appeared. Blue rows of light passed down her, cleaning her body, changing her clothes. She opened her mouth in a rictus grin. Clean teeth. She should get herself a cat. A programmable cat. It could leap on her belly in the mornings and stick its virtual tongue in her face and demand virtual feeding and then disappear, leaving only a huge smile behind. She said, "You are Commander Michael Burnham, science officer. *U.S.S. Discovery.* Serial number SC0064-

0974SHN." But that seemed like one more impossible thing to believe too.

Michael Burnham's smile faded. She was now ready for a brand-new day in a brave new world. A week ago, she fell down a rabbit hole. Every morning since, she awoke calling out for her mother.

Communications Officer Sahil's office
Former Federation Spaceport Devaloka

Every morning, for years, Aditya Sahil would come into this office and sit and wait for the impossible to happen. One day, a week ago, the impossible happened. A very scruffy young woman walked through the door, announced that she was a Starfleet officer, looked at him in sheer bewilderment when he said the word *Burn*, and that told him she was a time traveler.

Aditya Sahil, on receipt of this news, tried to maintain as composed a demeanor as possible. Inwardly, he was trembling with shock, with excitement, with *joy*—as if someone had reprogrammed him upward from the molecular level. Within seconds, the whole world around him had been, in a small but very definite way, entirely reconstructed. Now, his morning rituals came with the promise of fulfillment. Now, instead of acting the part, he was commissioned. Now, instead of lying folded in its case, the Federation flag hung from the wall. Old, but well preserved. Sahil, going about his daily business, would sometimes find that he had stopped completely, and was standing in front of the flag, in awe, and in gratitude for the presence in his life of Commander Michael Burnham.

That Commander Burnham had come in the company of a courier was eminently forgivable. Sahil did not, in truth, approve of couriers. They had many uses—and he knew that the spaceport in all likelihood could not survive without the traffic and supplies that they brought his way—but he knew that their values were not his. What was needed in these dangerous times was stability, respect for what was left of law and custom. Couriers, on the whole, lived their lives at the very edge of legality. They also, Sahil suspected, liked it this way. Still, they were courageous, and they were often the only thing standing between some worlds and complete collapse. Take Cleveland Booker, for example, whose career Sahil had observed over many years. He was surely one of the more ostentatiously freewheeling of his kind, but Sahil sensed there was something more about him. Intelligence, yes; energy, yes—but also there were depths to the man that were kept well hidden. Born into a different time, perhaps, that restless energy could have been focused, brought into the service of a greater good, and thereby the individual promise could have come to its fullest fruition. Born into these times, Cleveland Booker was unlikely, Sahil thought, to be able to do more with his life than fly a beaten-up ship from contract to contract, working out his frustrations at these limitations by getting himself into fistfights. Sahil pitied him, but he hoped he didn't take Burnham down with him.

After bringing Burnham to the spaceport, Booker had thankfully departed not long after, leaving the commander in Sahil's care to grapple with the enormity of her current situation. Sahil quickly came to understand the quality of the young woman who had come into his life—her courage, her dedication, her sacrifice. He would never forget the report she gave him. She stood, back straight, hands clasped behind her back, explaining in a clipped, objective tone the sequence of events that had brought her here.

Red Angel . . . Seven signals . . . Section 31 . . . Control . . . Mother . . .

Sahil listened with great care as she explained—Sahil did everything with great care—trying to understand in full what had happened and what this meant, not for his own time but for the officer who stood in front of him. His sorrow grew greater as she spoke. She had thrown herself into the future and saved the universe. She had given up everything. The world she knew, the people she knew. Home, family, friends— everything.

After she finished speaking, he sat for a moment, considering what to say. It came out all in a tumble. "But Commander! Your brother . . . Your *mother* . . . This must all be terribly hard for you!"

He would never forget her face in the split second afterward. She seemed almost to crumble, like a nanocube that had been misprogrammed and could not bear the strain of the demands being put upon it. He realized, in that moment, that she was not used to hearing such a personal response to such briefings. *Ah,* he thought, *a misstep. Not how a Starfleet officer would reply.* He did not regret it. She would get nowhere if she denied the enormity of all that had happened to her. He would tread more carefully in the future on such ground. She would need time. "Well," he had said, "you are here now, for which I am very grateful—not only because that means that your mission was successful, and that you saved us all from extinction, but because of . . ." He smiled, and gestured at the flag, and watched her take a deep breath, as if that sight restored a little of her courage. That was its purpose, was it not? To remind them all that they were not alone. To remind them all that they were part of a greater collective endeavor.

Over the next few days, she had spent much time in his office, quizzing him about this new place. She arrived punctually at oh-nine-hundred, station time, and they would drink tea together. After a couple of hours, she would carry on her explorations of the spaceport. They met again, in the early evening. He explained the many projects under way to create successful methods of recrystallizing dilithium—all failed. Other attempts to find alternative warp drives—all terminated. And then they came to the Burn. From the files, he showed her the starfield grid—and the moment when the ship icons winked out and disappeared.

"*Puff.* The Federation was blindsided . . ." Gently he explained what this meant. Two lifetimes to Earth. More to Terralysium. And she did not even have a ship.

From the corner of the room, a little red bird sang and told Sahil that it was almost time for his morning visitor to arrive. She was as punctual as he was. He appreciated this. The birdsong had barely died away when the door chimed, and Commander Burnham came in. He smiled at the sight of her—this joy-giving, hope-affirming miracle. She was looking much better than she had when he first met her—cleaner, tidier, more rested. But he had detected, over the last couple of days, a growing brittleness about her, a light in her eyes verging on the feverish.

"Good morning, Commander," he said calmly. "How are you this morning?"

"Fine," she said. "Good. Yes. Thanks. Fine."

"You slept well?"

"Yes, I guess."

Sahil was not sure he believed this, but he pressed no further. He nodded and waved up a chair for her. He waved up tea. He sat. Throughout this, she prowled the room. Occasionally she threw glances at the flag. Eventually, she fell into the chair opposite him. Michael Burnham—Sahil knew— might be the stuff of legend, but she was also a woman in a great deal of pain.

He sipped his tea and left her the opening to speak on her own terms. At last, she bent forward in her chair, fists upon her knees, her whole body clenched. "I . . . I don't even know why I'm asking this . . . I have to ask . . . Is there anything yet?" she said. "Any signal? Any sign? Any response at all?"

Sahil put down his cup. He brought the display to life. Thirty sectors—the limits of his domain. Two Federation ships in flight, both subwarp, both carrying out routine supply runs around a handful of systems. The tattered fragments of an interstellar civilization. He knew that she understood, intellectually, what this signified for the Federation. He knew too that she had barely begun to grasp, emotionally, what this meant for her. Earth unimaginably far away. Terralysium, her mother, and the most likely point where her ship, *Discovery*, would arrive—even more than that. Before she had even slept on that first night here, she had co-opted a comm channel to send out further signals from her communicator and had also made him send out her message to Terralysium. Every morning since, she had come to see him and ask whether there had been any reply.

There had been, of course, no reply. He said, "You understand our message has been out for only a week?"

She stood up from her seat, resumed her prowling. "I know . . . I know . . ."

"Commander," he said, very gently, "I'm not sure that you do. Our communication may take months to reach Terralysium. And any reply—should there be anyone there—may take months in turn. Do not expect to hear anything back before a year is up." He thought of adding: *Do not expect to hear anything back at all*, but he could not see how this would help.

Besides, it seemed that this was enough for the time being. She turned to look at him, and her expression was one of such pain, such despair, that he had to stand and walk over to her. Carefully, as if handling a treasured and yet very fragile object, he steered her back toward her seat. She put her face in her hands.

"I can't bear this," she said, her voice thick and muffled. "I gave everything to save the Federation. Everything! Friends, family, crewmates . . . My whole life . . . Nine *hundred* years! And the Federation still fell . . ."

Sahil drew up his own chair beside her. He put his hand upon her arm. He thought she might weep, but she didn't. There was a shell around her, he had observed; it did not make her hard, but it did make her to some extent impermeable. He wondered how thick that shell was; how much more stress it could take before cracking. Quietly, he said, "For what it is worth, Commander, your arrival here transformed my life. Years, I waited, for someone to walk through that door. And here you are. You are living proof that hopes and dreams come true."

"Years," she said, from behind the shield of her hands. "I could be here *years*."

"You have come to a slower time. The noontime of the Federation is long gone and you find us fumbling around in twilight."

"It feels like midnight."

"I'm sure that it does," he said, and gave a small laugh. "I'd like to think we are not so unenlightened. Perhaps dawn is closer than we think. In the meantime, all I can advise is that we wait—and that you continue sending out your messages to *Discovery*." He could see from her face that this was little consolation, and he fumbled for some other idea that might help her. "Perhaps we can look around here, at the spaceport, for a means to boost that signal, or to target it more accurately. Perhaps there might be some technological solution—"

She leapt on this with greater alacrity than he had intended.

"What?" she said, immediately. "What solutions?"

"Well . . ." He hesitated, trying to think of something

that might help. "You have seen how we are fixed here. The spaceport is operational, yes, but not exactly in the first flush of youth."

Ah, he thought, *the first makings of a smile.*

"That's a polite way to describe the huge hole in its side," she said.

With great dignity, he said, "We do our best with the facilities available."

Now the smile was full, and her eyes were warm. "You do an incredible job, Sahil. I don't want to pull resources from what you need here to carry out your work. But if there's anything I can use to improve the speed or the range of the messages I'm sending, I'd be grateful. Have you gotten anything from the data chip I gave you?"

This was the chip from the tricorder, which she had lost at Requiem City Mercantile Exchange. He regretted never seeing this—a mark in the debit column for Cleveland Booker. She had kept back the chip and had trusted this to Sahil when she arrived. But the truth was, he hadn't known where to begin getting data from it. The thing was so remarkable, so precious, he could barely bring himself to touch it, never mind try to work with it. It was like being asked to prize open the Ark of the Covenant with a rusty knife.

"I . . . no, not yet."

She gave him a sharp look. "It's not a holy relic, you know."

"Commander Burnham," he said, "that is exactly what it is."

She jumped up from her seat. "I need to keep this moving along," she said. "I can't hang around doing nothing. I have to find my people . . . My mother . . . My ship . . ."

He caught the rising note of anxiety, and said quickly, "There is somebody here on the spaceport who might be able to help."

"Who?"

"A courier—retired courier, I should say—he hasn't done a run in nearly three years. One of our few residents here. His name's Jeremiah. He has a great deal of experience with old technology. He might be able to help us get something from the data chip."

"Jeremiah," she said. "Good. Where do I find him?" She was up already and heading toward the door. The speed with which she swung between despair and action. She was so quick, so focused, so determined—and so very alone.

"You want to find him now?" he said.

"Yes, Sahil," she said, with a smile. "I want to find him now."

"He has a workshop on level nineteen. I could . . ."

"If you took me there," she said, "that would be very helpful. Do you have the chip?" He passed it to her, watched faintly as she tossed the precious thing casually into her pocket. "Coming?"

She seemed to be in a state of perpetual motion. Perhaps it was simply that she was much younger. Or perhaps it was something to do with the culture in which she had grown up— one in which everything was possible, if you had the information, the training, and the resolve to act. His own world—well, the years had been one long slow watch over a long steady decline, hoping against hope that enough light could be kept flickering so that if help ever did come, there would be a few embers still glowing to bring back a bright flame. He loved her energy, her determination, her belief that if she worked hard enough, she could achieve whatever outcome she desired. But he knew that this was not her world, and that she might find that all she could do was wait.

Aditya Sahil knew something about waiting. He knew how the long years took their toll; how easy it was to fall into performing ritual without hope, with it daily becoming harder to see why the effort was worthwhile. He also knew that in his case, the wait had not—in the end—proven fruitless. More than anything, he wanted this to be true for Burnham. But the days had a habit of passing, and becoming weeks, and becoming months, and becoming years . . . before someone walked through the door.

"Yes," he said, following behind her. "I'm coming."

Former Federation Spaceport Devaloka

A week at the spaceport had been more than enough for Burnham to learn the main geography of the place, but she knew there were corners yet to be explored. For one thing, she would need a spacesuit to be able to visit some parts. That hole in the side of the spaceport meant that sections were out of bounds. Some of them were barely shored up. "Keep away," advised Sahil. "Who knows what will happen if we open some of those doors."

She had begun, too, to recognize some of the patterns of life about the place. What struck her most was its sleepiness. She had, over the course of her career, visited so many space stations of this type and size that she could no longer keep count. They were waystations, busy, full of life, color, and people. Alive with the bustle of activity: dozens of ships passing through, stopping for repairs, supplies, or a little rest and recreation. Countless species, from countless worlds. The flow of traffic and people that was the lifeblood of the Federation. And all of it—all of it—dependent on a reliable and universal method of traveling at warp speed. Which had gone . . . What had been Sahil's word?

Puff!

And now this was what was left. Empty corridors. Whole levels and sections sealed off for decades. Maybe a dozen or twenty people living here permanently, Sahil had said, when before there would have been fifty or so dedicated spaceport staff, and perhaps another dozen or so visiting. In what had once surely been a busy concourse, Sahil had shown her the small bar (well, there was always a bar) where the handful of couriers and other travelers who were passing through stopped to get a drink and a bite to eat, trade news and information, and catch their breath. And every so often, behind everything, Burnham would catch sight, in the gloom, of a Starfleet symbol, a ghostly image from an almost-forgotten past. The station, she thought, existed permanently around closing time.

And yet at the same time, all around her, she saw marvels. The couriers, carrying out their ship repairs with gravity belts. People zipping between ship and station using personal transporters. And everywhere, the sheer wizardry of programmable matter, conjuring what was needed as if from nowhere. She wondered what else she might have seen, had the Red Angel suit brought her to a point only a few hundred years earlier. What else had Federation scientists and engineers achieved in those centuries? When she was younger, she recalled, she had been given a gift by another officer (trying to win her heart, she suspected now)—a book of Anglo-Saxon poetry. There had been one that she read that she had dreamed about afterward, a man walking through the ruins that the Romans left behind. *This ruin is a wonder . . . Fate has broken and shattered it . . . the work of giants falls . . .* She felt as if she was walking through this dream now. All around her, the marvels left behind by people now lost; a world slipping from memory; new life fumbling around in the cracks and crevices, using whatever was to hand . . .

I walk through the ruins left by giants.

And this had been true for Sahil all his life, she thought, watching the man as he walked quietly beside her. He lived in this permanent twilight, in a spaceport so cut off that they could not complete major repairs. No, not twilight, she thought. *Dawn*, that was what he had said. Because he looked at her and saw the start of something new. He looked at her and saw the Federation flag flying again—not hidden away, gathering dust. He saw the lights coming back on.

Burnham took a deep breath. She didn't feel much like a lantern bearer these days. She felt like a woman who had fallen down a rabbit hole and couldn't make sense of anything around her. She clenched her teeth. *Focus on what you can do, not what you can't,* she thought. She couldn't rebuild the Federation overnight. But she could get the data off this chip—or find someone who could.

"This man we're going to see," said Burnham. "You said he was a courier?"

"Yes, but I don't hold that against him," Sahil replied, although with a twinkle in his eye. "Jeremiah and I go back many years. He was a regular visitor here, when he still took on courier work."

"Why did he stop?"

"Commander, he is older even than I am, and this life—as I think you have seen already—rewards faster reflexes than either of us have these days."

Fair point, thought Burnham. "Why don't you like couriers, Sahil?"

"I like many individual couriers, Commander, but I do not mistake them for allies. Courier values are not Starfleet values. It's best to assume they have their own particular interests at heart."

Burnham didn't reply. She felt a sudden stab of protectiveness toward Book. Sure, the man was exasperating, and he had indeed sold her out—but there was much more about him than met the eye. He'd helped her escape. He'd brought her here. And he'd risked life and limb to save that beautiful creature, the trance worm. There'd been no profit in that.

"I can't say," said Burnham, honestly. "I haven't seen enough. But will Jeremiah help, in that case?"

"Yes, I think he will, for my sake. I don't charge him much in the way of rent. But we should tread carefully, Commander. For one thing, we should not advertise your story—and your origins—too widely. While I may have elected not to enforce regulations about temporal displacement, your knowledge of the past may make you of interest to many unsavory people. It is best if you do not get into the habit of telling your story."

"Book knows," said Burnham.

"That cannot be helped," he said.

Level nineteen proved to be only two levels below Sahil's office, but Sahil had described the turbolifts as "erratic, on their best days," so they took narrow access stairways. Burnham was glad of the exercise, although her side was still twinging from her sudden fall to earth. Coming out on the level, they walked along a rather sorry-looking corridor, the walls scuffed and grubby, the lights running at three-quarter power. She tried to picture what it must have been like. Bright, busy, almost brash. Then she tried to forget the image. It did not help.

The workshop was easily identified by the steady hum coming from behind double doors. Jeremiah also seemed to have a warning system set up, since the hum stopped as they approached, and the doors opened. Burnham was confronted with a large space filled with a vast amount of spare parts, components, tools, and other bits and pieces. The first impression was overwhelming, but it rapidly became clear that the place was in fact ruthlessly well organized. There was a worktable to one side, filled with tools and parts (a little potted plant was perched rather incongruously upon it too). At the far end of the space there was an airlock, beyond which, Burnham was to learn, couriers docked when they wanted Jeremiah to work on their ships.

Behind the worktable stood a lean man, waving his hand to dissolve the visor he was wearing, revealing a lined and weather-beaten face. Back in her own time, she would have put his age well past one hundred, but that was with advanced medical techniques and a much higher standard of living. She reckoned he was probably in his early seventies. The man, Jeremiah, presumably, raised his palm in greeting. "Aditya. Is this your guest?"

"Yes, this is Michael Burnham."

"Huh." He came around the table and sat on the edge, folding his arms, as they drew closer. "Aditya said you were brought here by that rogue Book? That you'd lost your memory?"

So that was the cover story. "Yes," said Burnham.

"You remember your name, though?"

"And a great deal about my personal past. But when I try to put it in context—no good. Things seem to shade to gray."

"Huh." Jeremiah looked at her keenly. "I've seen bumps on the head do all kinds of strange things to people. I suppose that's no stranger than anything else."

"One of the interesting side effects," said Sahil, a playful gleam in his eyes, "is that Burnham sometimes believes she is a Starfleet officer."

"Now that," said Jeremiah, "is more like delusion than memory loss."

"Perhaps a historian of some kind," Sahil said. "You certainly seem to know a great deal about Federation history, don't you, Burnham?"

"With some curious lacunae, yes."

"And that would also explain how you happen to have this data core. If you had an interest, I mean," Sahil concluded, calmly.

"That would certainly be one explanation, yes." Burnham turned to Jeremiah. "It's a long story, and hazy in parts . . ." Surely a little white lie wouldn't do any harm. "I know that I was on board a ship. I know that ship is trying to contact me. What I don't know is where that ship is right now—or even if it's within hailing distance."

The old man looked at her steadily. He wasn't entirely convinced by all this, she could see, but he was trying to weigh the balance between what he needed to know, and what he wanted to know. "Your business is your own business," he said at last. "What do you want from me?"

"I'd like to get the data off this chip," she said, and offered it.

Jeremiah took it and looked at it closely. "This is *old*," he said.

"Too old?"

"Possibly. But then I like a challenge. Leave it with me."

"All right," she said. "Mind if I take a look around?"

He looked like he did mind. "Don't touch anything."

"You know," said Sahil, "you could learn a lot in here, Michael."

"One of my gaps in knowledge," she said, "is about the technology I find around me."

"Oh, yes," said Jeremiah. He glanced at Sahil. "I did a run up to level four yesterday, brought back a pile of components—"

"Jeremiah," explained Sahil, "has been dedicating his energies to going through the spaceport from top to bottom, to see what remains that we can use."

"I can help sort that out," said Burnham. "Perhaps we might find parts of a communications system—"

"To help you contact your ship," said Jeremiah.

"If you wouldn't mind," said Sahil.

The old man eyed them both. Burnham tried to look as innocent as possible. Sahil simply smiled.

"I suppose I wouldn't mind the company," said Jeremiah. "Welcome to the Back Forty, Burnham."

The Back Forty
Former Federation Spaceport Devaloka

Burnham spent a lot of time with Jeremiah over the next couple of weeks. The Back Forty was an endless source of fascination, for one thing, a real magician's chamber. To begin with, he set her tasks that he clearly considered simple—identifying key parts and components—but which for her, a thousand years adrift, were harder than they seemed. Gradually, she began to understand some of the principles behind programmable matter, and Jeremiah was helpful about shoving manuals and information sources in front of her. She had a feeling he had written some of these. He knew she was particularly interested in communications technologies, so he set her the task of taking apart and putting back together a subspace relay via holographic images. "Again," he'd say, when she was done. "Again, again, again. Now try it with gloves on." It was all humbling for someone used to such a high degree of competence, but gradually she appreciated the apprenticeship she was getting—and appreciated too what Sahil had done bringing her here, giving her the opportunity to equip herself for the long haul. One day, Jeremiah took her up to level two, and, systematically, they took apart a small section of control panels, looking for usable parts. *Like carrion*, she thought, *picking over the bones*. Throughout the day, the old man didn't have much conversation, being far too absorbed in his tasks. Burnham didn't mind—she had too much to think about. But late in the afternoon, station time, a little holographic bird would trill (an idea he'd got from Sahil, presumably), and he would put down his tools and drag Burnham down to the bar for a drink and something to eat. And then—then she got the real treasure. His traveling tales.

At first, Burnham only kept half an ear open. Her mind was on other things: sifting through the components and routers she had looked through that day; trying to map her own understanding of flight engineering and communications technologies with these vastly different systems. Jeremiah would talk on beside her. After a couple of evenings, she realized that she was missing out on gold. He was, as she'd guessed, in his seventies. ("Not a bad age," he said, "all thing considered.") He'd left his homeworld—he didn't say much about that—when he was a very young man and had been traveling up and down the twenty sectors around here ever since. She had a strong suspicion that he wasn't sure exactly how old he was.

That in particular struck her as bizarre. Federation citizens were logged, tracked, traced, and all with some form of data recording. You could probably find out where you had been down to the minute. Still, for all his vagueness about the details of dates, his knowledge of the area around the spaceport was encyclopedic. One evening, with a holo-stylus and a programmable cube, he drew a map for her, sketching a rough plan of the immediate systems around them. The major worlds in each system, where to go for rich pickings, where to avoid. He marked up a handful of mercantiles, and what he called "boneyards." When he was done, he shoved the map across the table toward her.

"I'm guessing," he said, "that this will come in useful. When you decide to leave."

Leave. Burnham considered that. The plan had been to bring *Discovery* to her; to locate her ship and her friends somehow. She had assumed she would be able to find ways to boost the signal, make it more efficient—but her days in the Back Forty were starting to show how limited her resources were. And this was a frustration. She had always, throughout her career, managed to find rapid solutions to her problems— even (particularly) under extreme duress. But there were no solutions here. She was stuck, and she was barely equipped to manipulate even the simplest of technologies around her. The past few days, she had been waking from bad dreams, staring at her gray and formless quarters, and truly grasping how desperate her situation was. She could be here for the rest of her life. She could be old by the time she heard anything from Earth, or Terralysium. Was she really prepared to spend the whole of her life in this gently decaying place? Did she have the nerve to go out there?

"Leave," she said.

"If you're trying to find ways to establish contact with your ship, then you're going to want to lay your hands on more and better technology than I have here. If it's broken, I can probably fix it. But I can't fix things I don't have."

"Where would I go?"

Jeremiah tapped the map. "There's a whole rotting empire out there. Take your pick."

Most evenings, Sahil came to find them, and she would watch these two old men engage good-temperedly in a quarrel that they had surely been having for many years: the old courier up against the old Federation man. Tweedledum and Tweedledee, she thought, affectionately. "If your Federation was so magnificent," Jeremiah said, "how come it fell apart so quickly?"

"If I knew the answer to that," said Sahil, "I would try to piece it together again, and we would be Federation citizens once more."

"Huh," said Jeremiah, unimpressed. "Different universe

now. I don't think anyone would be buying what you'd have to sell."

"But it's a good question," said Burnham, suddenly, one night, and both men turned to her, surprised to have a third voice enter their ritual exchange. "Why did nobody come? Why did nobody try to reconnect all the worlds that were suddenly left behind? I know," she said, seeing Sahil begin to answer, "no dilithium. So shortsighted . . ."

"You saw the files," said Sahil. "People tried for a long time—everyone knew that this was a weak point. Project after project after project. All failed. All terminated. They couldn't do it."

"And for some reason," said Jeremiah, "they didn't prepare for it. So when it came . . ." He held up his hand, spread the fingers out, like a firework. *Puff.* "So much for the Federation."

"But the Federation isn't—*wasn't*—only starships and supplies," Burnham persisted. "It was an idea. A set of values. A bond that held worlds together. How did that fray?"

"Like I told you," Jeremiah said, "nobody wanted what they were selling."

But that Burnham found impossible to believe. Who would not want the Federation, when the alternative was this? Who would want to live in darkness, when the alternative was the light?

One night, after Jeremiah ambled off to bed, Burnham sat for a little longer at the table with Sahil. Suddenly, he said, "What was it like, Commander?"

"Hmm?"

"The Federation—at its height. What was it truly like?"

Burnham looked around the almost derelict station. "Oh, Sahil," she said. "If I could tell you that, I think it would break your heart."

"My heart was born broken," he said softly. "There have been a few small repairs in recent weeks, mind you." He smiled at her. "Tell me what it was like. What this place would have been like."

So she did. She told him what a spaceport like this would have been like, in the time she came from. The color, the light, the sheer *diversity* of people and ideas and cultures . . . How strange, she thought, that sights that had been so commonplace to her that they had barely registered at the time had suddenly become precious memories. She was a lost archive, brought to life.

"Ah!" he said, when she had finished, and he shook his head. "Do you think we shall ever see the like of it again?"

She was so caught up in the images she had conjured. Not memories! This had been her *life* less than a month ago. Quickly, almost recklessly, she said, "Why not? Earth was in ruins when the Vulcans made first contact. And yet from that moment came the greatest interstellar civilization that has ever existed! We have so much more at our disposal than they did back then. All of this"—she gestured around—"all the technology that they left behind. Think how long you have kept this station running, on next to nothing."

He ducked his head. "I have certainly tried."

"And succeeded," she said, warmly. "If you can do this here, then this will have happened in other places. And think about what must have happened back on Earth, where there were more resources, more ships to hand. Around the other major planets—Vulcan, Tellar, Andor. The transmissions we sent out—the ones we'll be sending out, when we can improve our comms—maybe we'll contact others like you, like us. Maybe they'll be more advanced than us. Maybe they'll have access to resources that we don't have. All we have to do is connect with them."

Sahil sighed. "You make it sound so easy."

"It's not impossible. But we have to come up with ways to do it."

"What we lack," he said, "is dilithium, or a workable alternative."

"But what we *have*," said Burnham, "is a shared vision. And that transcends distance." She looked around her at the relics of the past. "Hey, maybe we should dust off some of those Federation logos," she said. "Display them more prominently."

"Oho!" Sahil laughed. "I don't think Jeremiah would like that! You must surely have realized by now that he has little love for the Federation!"

"I don't understand that," Burnham said, shaking her head. "An interstellar civilization, with travel and trade across hundreds of worlds, a secure life for every Federation citizen, the chance to thrive and grow and live the best life possible. What's not to like?"

"I suppose he never really saw any of that," said Sahil, equably. "Only the aftermath, which was not always pleasant, to say the least. Everyone has their own story, Commander. And, of course, the Federation would never have allowed him to operate the way he did over the years." He gave a snort of laughter. "I think he thinks he would have lost all his earnings to tax."

"We don't—we didn't—have taxes—"

"I doubt he believes for a second that was possible. I can scarcely believe it myself. He's a courier. They have their own ways."

Another voice chimed in.

"Did someone mention couriers?"

Burnham looked up—and her heart jumped. "Book!" she said in delight. Then she cleared her throat. "Hi."

"Hi, Burnham. How are you?"

"I'm okay. How's Grudge?"

"She's good. And so am I."

"Good."

"Mr. Booker," said Sahil. "I wondered if or when we would see you again."

"It's Book," said Book. "Thought I'd drop by."

Burnham's quarters
Former Federation Spaceport Devaloka

Burnham perched on the edge of the bunk. Book was sitting in the single chair, looking around the room. "Love what you've done with the place."

Burnham looked around in bewilderment. "There's literally nothing here."

"That's what I meant, Burnham."

"Oh. Okay. Yes. I see. So how's Grudge?"

"Still good. You know, not everyone asks about her."

"Then they're fools, and impolite."

He grinned at her. She grinned back. He stretched out his legs and got comfortable. "How's everything going?"

"Fine."

"You're still here."

"Yes." She raised an eyebrow. "That's not a problem, is it?"

"Not for me. And I doubt for Sahil either. That man looks at you like you're a unicorn or something."

She smiled. She did feel sometimes that Sahil treated her like she was some kind of legendary figure. Achilles, perhaps, or Hercules. No. Odysseus. Someone lost and trying to get home. She didn't feel like a legend. She felt like a small girl who had fallen down a hole into a world where nothing made sense.

"How are you living, Burnham?"

"What do you mean, how am I living? I eat and breathe and sleep—"

"No, what I mean is—what are you doing for money?"

"Money?" She stared at him. Money. Tokens representing economic units that functioned as a generally recognized medium of exchange for the purposes of transactions. How societies outside the Federation operated. She hadn't *thought*. "Money . . . I don't know—"

"Thought not," he said. Was he smirking?

"Do you have to sound so—"

"So what?"

"So damn smug!"

His eyes opened wide. "Sorry," he said, more quietly. "If I did, I didn't mean to. You've . . . You've been on my mind, that's all. I wanted to know how you were getting on."

"Not as well as I thought," she shot back. She wondered now how things were working. Did this room she was in have to be paid for? She had absolutely no idea. Was Sahil covering the bills? If there were bills?

Book was still talking. Damn the man! "All I thought," he was saying, "was that you might want some help to establish yourself—"

"Establish myself?" she said bitterly. "How, exactly? The technology I know—obsolete. The organization I served—nonexistent. The civilization I come from—on its knees. What am I going to do, exactly?"

"You'd be surprised. Anyway, I think you'd make a great courier."

They stared at each other.

"Are you out of your—?"

"No, listen!" he said. "You came in really handy on Hima. Yeah, okay, so you were also a complete liability that got me into trouble in the first place and then we ended up jumping off a cliff—"

Burnham shuddered at the memory.

"—but you were also a quick learner and at the end of the day neither of us is dead."

"Book, that's not exactly a commendation."

"Actually," he said, "that's quite a *big* commendation." He seemed completely in earnest. "And, besides, what else are you going to do? Sit around twiddling your thumbs for the next few years waiting for someone to answer your calls? There's only so many hours in the day you can spend taking that flag up and down again and folding it, you know."

She glared at him. That did look a lot like smirking. "What do you think I should do?"

"Get yourself a ship. Have a look round. That's more . . . Michael Burnham, wouldn't you say?"

"What do you know about what counts as being Michael Burnham?"

"When someone lands on your head," he said, "it makes a special bond."

"Only in your imagination," she shot back, tartly.

He shook his head. Definitely smirking. "Come on, Burnham. Let's go and find you a ship. Time you got your wings again."

Sahil's office
Former Federation Spaceport Devaloka

Burnham went, the following morning, to Sahil's office for their usual meeting—only this time with Book in tow. Sahil was standing before a console when she arrived, deeply engrossed in some file, and did not turn to greet her immediately.

"Is everything all right, Sahil?"

"I'm not sure," he said. "I'm somewhat alarmed at news I'm hearing from a world called Atalis."

"Atalis," said Book. "I've been there. Took some parts out for an irrigation system."

Sahil swung around. His eyes widened. "Mr. Booker," he said. "To what do I owe this pleasure?"

"Er . . . courtesy call? And it's Book."

"Book, yes."

He wasn't offering tea this morning, Burnham noticed. "What's this world, Atalis?"

"It's four sectors—" Book started, as Sahil said, "Four sectors from here—"

They both stopped. Dryly, Burnham said, "Well, one of you tell me."

Book nodded at Sahil. "Your office."

"Yes indeed. They are struggling to find parts again for their water-reclamation plant." Sahil eyed Book thoughtfully. "Do you think you might be able to help again?"

"Maybe. The mercantile at Requiem City was a good source for that kind of thing." Book gave Burnham a pointed look. "I'm *persona non grata* there these days."

"That's not entirely my fault," said Burnham.

"Debatable," said Book.

"But if something comes up," urged Sahil quietly. "They seem to be increasingly desperate."

"If they're desperate," said Book, "how are they going to pay?"

Sahil looked at him sadly. "Drought, Mr. Booker, is a terrible thing. There'll be children there—"

"It's Book. And I'll keep my eyes open, okay?" Book turned to Burnham. "Are you ready?"

She nodded. "I guess."

"Er, do you need to pack?" he said.

"There's nothing to pack," she said.

"What?" said Sahil in confusion. "Are you going some-where, Commander?"

"You must have some assets." Book shook his head. "For-get it. We'll sort you out."

Things, thought Burnham, were suddenly moving very quickly. Was she really leaving? Now? "Sahil . . ." she said, opening out her hands in a gesture of apology.

"Commander," he said. "May I have a word?" He looked meaningfully at Book. "In private?"

"Secrets, Sahil?" Book feigned offense. "Surely not be-tween us!"

"Michael," said Sahil, urgently.

"Book, please," Burnham said quietly. "This is my friend. My colleague. I want to speak to him in private." She smiled at Sahil, who smiled gratefully back.

"Ah, I see," said Book, watching this pass between them. "It's a Starfleet thing, so I won't understand. I'll wait for you outside, Burnham. But I'd like to get moving soon—"

"I won't keep you long," she said. "I promise. Just—go wait outside, will you!"

Book left. Burnham, before Sahil could speak, lifted her hand. "I know what you're going to say," she said. "He's a courier, he can't be trusted—"

"All true."

"But he took good care of me when I arrived. Brought me here. He didn't have to bring me here."

"I like the man," said Sahil. "No—truly, I do. I think he is personally very charming, and I am sure he is the kind of rogue that has a heart of gold. But you have a base here, Mi-chael. A command, of sorts. This is where your messages origi-nate from. This is where your ship will come looking for you, if they receive those messages—"

"Which might be *years*, you said so yourself," she replied.

"I've done all I can here for now. The message to Terralysium is sent, all we can do now is hope they get it and reply in our lifetime! As for *Discovery* . . ." She threw up her hands. "Where do I start working out where they might arrive?"

"Isn't Jeremiah working on the data chip? Isn't there something he can do for you?"

"There is," she said, "and he's doing it—but it's not enough. I could spend the next five years sifting through what he's got, and the right components would never turn up."

"We could send couriers to look for what we need—"

"I'm sure we could, but I'd rather be out there looking—"

"Ah," said Sahil, "so that's not the only reason you want to go, is it?"

"I can't . . ." She took a deep breath. "I can't remain stationary. I need to be moving *forward* . . . I need to understand more about where I am now. You and Book, you've both in your own ways been trying to get me to understand that I'm here for the long haul. And if that's really the case, then I need to see more of what's around me. Find out what *happened*."

Why the Federation fell so quickly, she meant—and she knew he understood. "I can't exactly stop you," he said, with a wry smile. "I should, I suppose, remind you that your presence in this time is in violation of all kinds of laws and treaties. I assume that you won't return to your own time and change the future?"

"This was a one-way ticket, Sahil," Burnham said, quietly. "And that means that I wait here. Not for a lifetime. I have to find something to do! Something *worthwhile*. Make contact with more people like you, reach out into other sectors. But I won't be doing it sitting at a desk here." She stopped herself; gave him a guilty look. "I didn't mean to offend—"

"And I am not in the least offended, Commander," he said. "It has been my observation, over the years, that some people are always in motion, while others are in place."

" 'They also serve who only stand and wait,' " she said.

"Exactly. Even when I was as young as you are now, I knew that my task was to be here when others needed me. And I *was* here, wasn't I?"

She reached across to touch the back of his hand. She gave him her most radiant smile. "You were indeed. And now your flag is flying again—and we'll see it flying in other places. I know we will."

"Then I will wish you safe traveling, Michael, and hope you will return soon, with a good ship, and the means to fly her." He patted her hand. "Ah, I'd like you to take something with you on this first trip away." He moved toward the console, and with a gesture, conjured up nanocubes, which he began to program. She watched, wondering when this would stop seeming like wizardry, and become second nature to her. Would it ever?

"Your journeys these days will take much longer than perhaps you anticipate," he said, and he handed her a small handheld device. "I imagine this will give you plenty of time to keep a log, and perhaps you might enjoy listening to some diaries stored on here." He tapped the little device, and a voice began to speak. A woman's voice.

"Councilor Priya Tagore. Personal log . . ."

Sahil tapped the device again, and the voice stopped. "My great-grandmother," he said. "She kept a diary from when she was a girl—ten years old when she started, and she barely missed a day!"

"Councilor?" said Burnham.

"Yes, she was a representative from our home planet to the Federation Council. It was good luck that she was back home when the Burn happened. You will hear, if you listen, her account of the day that it happened, and the days directly after. You might find something of interest."

Burnham was deeply touched. "This is a wonderful gift," she said, clasping his hand between hers. "Thank you."

"I hope it helps in some way," he said.

The Burn, and the days directly after. And also, what came before. A voice from a past closer to her own. A voice from her own civilization, or where it was, before it fell. She thought of this and was comforted. "I know it will," she said.

They left together, finding Book kicking his heels in the corridor outside.

"Ready?" he said.

"Ready," she replied, with a brisk, firm nod.

"Good luck, Michael Burnham," Sahil said. "And do be careful. Couriers aren't always to be trusted."

"I'm standing right here," said Book.

"I know," Sahil said quietly.

"We do have our uses," said Book. "Even if we're not true believers."

"Yes, Mr. Book," Sahil said, with a sigh. "But what is your price going to be?"

"Book," said Book. "I'll think of something."

Command Center
Starbase Vanguard

Several sectors away, out of the purview of Acting Communications Officer Aditya Sahil, lay another former Federation installation. This one, however, was in a very different condition. It was larger, for one, and had, at the height of the fallen empire, been a significant waypoint in this part of space. Great ships of the mighty fleet had stopped here; two had been docked here when the Burn occurred. They had remained here ever since, dark and useless. Their crews were long gone; their descendants were gone too. The shuttles had been retooled and taken away decades ago. As for the rest of the base: much of it was sealed off and empty, but the sections that remained operational were in good shape. This was thanks to the base commander, all those years ago, who understood quickly the ramifications of what had happened on that terrible day and began to organize for the long haul. Perhaps some credit could be given to the current owner-occupiers. They were not Starfleet, by any means, but they maintained Starfleet standards that would not have put the former staff to shame. The current owner of the base, who went by the name of Remington, preferred things orderly.

She stood now, in the command center of what was now named Starbase Vanguard—it had been Starbase 906—and watched her staff at work. They were young, in the main (she found younger people less set in their ways, and more eager to fit into the set structure she offered), and very hardworking. More often than not, their upbringings had been desperate. These were the kind of people who liked the safety she offered, and the kind of people she looked for when recruiting. They wore gray uniforms that, while not military, had a military flavor. The titles she bestowed on them were not military, but made clear that this was a hierarchy, with a chain of command. There were cadets, and junior officers, and senior officers, and chief officers. She used the title "chief executive officer."

This morning, there was the usual bustle. Remington liked to watch her people go about their duties. There was a beauty to quiet collective activity that she would never take for granted. Her childhood, like those of many after the Burn, had been troubled in ways she preferred to forget. But the marks had been left: an overwhelming desire to create a peaceful environment, one that would be safe and secure. Remington, born with more assets than many others living after the Burn, had made the most use of what she had to hand. Over the last fifteen years, she had worked steadily, and now she found herself in possession not only of a starbase but the means to defend it. Behind this starbase lay four sectors of space, patrolled by her ships, covering fifteen systems. On three of the worlds within these systems, the industrial replicators left behind by the Federation were up and running again; a fourth, on the planet above which this base was located, was due to go online by the end of this year. Resources were stretched, not thin—she didn't take unnecessary risks—but she was certainly keen to encourage other worlds to join.

"Ma'am," said the young woman at comms, "there's some babble on the courier channels."

"Interesting babble?" said Remington, making her way toward her.

"Some kind of fracas at the Requiem City Mercantile Exchange."

Remington came down to listen. The Requiem City mercantile was beyond the sectors that were her immediate concern, but they did supply several systems that could be considered as falling within her sphere of interest. If there was trouble there, she wanted to know—because it could be heading their way. She programmed herself an earbud and listened in on the courier chatter. A couple of names kept coming up.

"Booker," she said, thoughtfully. "Burnham." She took a mental note of the names—Remington didn't forget much—and sent instructions to one of her people placed with the mercantile regulators to send her any relevant information. "Maybe we should send someone over there," she said, thoughtfully. "See what's happening."

"There's a ship half a sector away. It could get there quickly enough, by tunnel."

"Let me think about that. I prefer to use them sparingly." Remington looked at the display. "Have we heard anything more out of the Atalis system?"

"A drop-off in traffic in that area, ma'am."

"Good."

Atalis was on the edge of her area of interest, but she had known for some time from the reports coming in from her scouts that the world was blessed with many mineral assets—the kind of thing necessary to supply industrial replicators. She also knew that for all its mineral resources, it was very short of water. There was opportunity here, surely; Remington wasn't quite sure what, nor how best to press her advantage—although she was starting to see what she might do next. Once she committed to this action, however, there was no going back, and she wasn't sure, yet, whether she was ready to make the move. But she knew that she was not content to stay on the edge of this part of space forever. Her scouts all reported back that this area of space was chaotic, to say the least. Many different players, all haggling for work and for advantage. A courier network of solo operators. A damaged spaceport, which kept running more or less because the elderly man in charge was a better bet than anyone else around him. She knew that she had the capacity to be a real player here. There were many worlds in this part of space that would benefit from the structures Remington had in place. Security, stability, resources. These were the kinds of things that people wanted these days, and that Remington could supply.

"Let's move a couple more ships that way," she said. "Just in case."

"And the mercantile?"

Remington thought a little longer. "Maybe we will take a closer look."

Book's ship
In flight

Burnham sat cross-legged on the floor, head down, listening to a dead woman's voice. About two feet away, Grudge sat, a huge puddle of fur, glaring at her. She couldn't tell what mood that was. Fury, jealousy, rage, interest, boredom. "Hey," she said, softly. "I'm not here to steal your man."

Grudge blinked. *Like you're in with a chance.*

Book came to join them, scooping up the beast and gathering her to him, pressing his face into the folds of fur. "Hey, lady," he said.

"I hope you're talking to the cat."

"There's no way I can answer that and not offend," he said. He caught sight of the device she was holding, and the earpieces she was wearing. "What are you listening to?"

"A diary, from before the Burn."

He gave her an odd look. "Really? Why?"

"Isn't an interest in history sufficient motivation in itself?"

"Sure, but you have a whole new world out here to explore. I could give you half a dozen files that would be more directly useful to you."

"Not if I want to understand why the Federation fell, I suspect."

"I was thinking more maybe a couple of textbooks. *Barter Economies for Dummies.* That kind of thing."

"Dummies," she said. "Thanks. Do you have something like that?"

"Not to hand. I could probably find something somewhere."

"Don't worry," she said. "I found some books on economics in the ship's databanks yesterday. I've gone through them."

He laughed. "What, and you're an expert now?"

"I was trained from a very young age to be able to take and assimilate large amounts of information," Burnham said, almost wearily. "By the time I was fourteen, my daily reading list contained research papers on advanced astrometrics, theoretical physics, and of course xenoanthropology."

"And what did you read when you were reading for pleasure?"

"I read poetry."

"Of course."

"Anyway, I can assure you that a couple of sophomore texts on economics didn't cause me any trouble. Although I do find the whole idea of a money-based system illogical, inefficient, and irrational."

"Illogical and what now?"

"Of course, I imagine that the ability to accumulate fictional wealth seems extremely rational from a certain perspective. More—the ability to *inherit* fictional wealth must be extremely attractive. I also find a great deal interesting in models which assume that humans are rational decision-makers. Mostly I find them interesting because of how much they get wrong about human nature. I'm sorry, am I going into too much detail?"

"No," he said. "Yes. But anyway—you still don't have anything to sell."

"I'll think of something," she said. She closed her eyes and went back to listening to the quiet, calm voice speaking to her from a long-lost paradise. After a minute or two, Book said, "You know there's a visual display with that?" said Book.

"Huh?"

"You can see her as well as listen to her."

He touched the handheld device, and images appeared before Burnham's eyes. A beautifully appointed office, with a neat desk and a polished wooden floor, filled with greenery. A woman in a cream-colored loose linen shirt, leaning back in her chair. She appeared relaxed, intelligent, witty. She looked like someone that Burnham would like. She was like her great-grandson.

"Whoa!" said Burnham.

"Thought you didn't know," he said smugly, and left her to it.

COUNCILOR PRIYA TAGORE
PERSONAL LOG

Since this is my personal log—sealed, coded, and unlikely to be heard until well after my death—let me record here for posterity that Councilor Ibithan Th'rhaven is a blithering idiot.

Burnham, listening, could not prevent a snort of laughter, which did not disturb Book but earned significant side-eye from Grudge.

Councilor Ibithan Th'rhaven! History knows your name now, and will forever remember you as—

"A blithering idiot!" murmured Burnham in unison. Poor Th'rhaven. He couldn't have imagined. But why, she wondered. What had the man done?

I am trying hard not to take his actions personally, but when one has spent months securing the agreement of seventy-seven worlds about the equable distribution of eighth-generation nanocubes across the entire Federation only to have one's carefully worded resolution blocked by someone who has taken umbrage at the phrasing of a minor codicil—it is very hard not to feel the failure most keenly! Months of work—literally months of work— brought down over a minor matter of procedure. I hardly know what to say. I am unlikely to be able to build this coalition again, and therefore the nanocubes will pass quickly throughout the core worlds and not make their way as rapidly to the worlds upon the edge. How ridiculous!
Sometimes it seems to me that the Federation Coun-

cil has become too unwieldy. That it is no longer able to operate in the way that it is supposed to operate. Yet even saying this seems somehow sacrilegious. Are we not, after all, the inheritors of the greatest interstellar civilization ever to have existed? Are we not the beneficiaries of hundreds upon hundreds of years of wisdom, experience, and expertise from hundreds upon hundreds of worlds? What would I prefer in its place? I remember, from my studies, how the Temporal Wars might so easily have brought the Federation to collapse. We should cherish what we have— I am told. These structures, these ways of operating, held the Federation together during those wars. Why would we want to change them now?

And to these people I would say—if I felt able to say it, if I did not feel that saying it was somehow a betrayal—that these ways of operating no longer work. Because if one man, a man who is too caught up in the notion of procedure and precedent, can stop technologies from being made available throughout all the Federation—then the Federation surely is not as unified, and not as functional, perhaps, as we would like to believe.

Ah, but who will listen to me, a junior councilor from a far-flung world! The council is now, blessedly, out of session, and I am returning home—not victorious, as I would have liked—but with the small consolation of knowing that at least I tried my best.

Burnham stopped playback. *Fractures*, she thought. *Were there fractures there already?* This required further consideration. But for now—her eyes were closing, the engines of Book's ship were humming, and a huge cat was sleeping at her side. Burnham surrendered to her own sleep, and for once, she did not dream of her mother.

2

COMMANDER MICHAEL BURNHAM

PERSONAL LOG

It is now a little over three weeks since I arrived in the future. What do I know? What have I learned? Let me set out my position as clearly and logically as possible, in the hope that a period of considered reflection will clarify what moves I should next make.

1. Our mission was successful. I did not arrive here only to find desolation. I try to keep that in mind. What we set out to do— we achieved. I must not forget this. When my spirits are low, I must remember this. There was a future here to receive me. We achieved what we set out to do.

2. I have done everything I can so far with the resources to hand. With Sahil's help, I have sent a message to Terralysium. I cannot make this message travel more quickly. I can only let it fly and live in the hope that it will be received with recognition and with love, and a desire to make contact in some way. For *Discovery*— I am hampered by the fact that there is limitless space (and time) in which she might arrive. Therefore, I must find a way of predicting where and when she might arrive. I have the data chip from my tricorder, and I have someone working on access-ing the information on it—but that is now so old that we may as well be trying to decipher Linear A. I would like to say that I have a team working on this problem. In fact, I have an elderly rascal who owes me two weeks of back pay. Related to this . . .

3. The world in which I find myself is one that I am badly equipped

to navigate. I am caught between knowing far too much and far too little. I am able to manipulate the new technologies that I find around me—such as programmable matter—but I have limited understanding of their underlying principles. This I can correct with study. My other areas of ignorance are not so easily remedied. In day-to-day interactions, I am likely to make simple but revealing mistakes. I cannot offer the truth of my presence here by way of explanation, since my presence is illegal. While nobody is likely to enforce these laws, it gives people a reason to mistrust me, a hold over me, and may arouse interest in what knowledge I have of the past. I must therefore begin each new relationship with a lie. This is unhelpful, and may become problematic, should my stay here become longer than I would like.

4. I cannot rely on the kindliness of strangers. I must reskill myself as a matter of urgency. The time that I spent working alongside Jeremiah has given me some grasp, at least, of known unknowns. I have some sense now of the parameters of my ignorance. The databanks on Book's ship are proving helpful. I am applying myself to these diligently.

5. These are the practicalities of my immediate situation. But I must not ignore the bigger picture. I must not ignore or deny my need to *understand* . . . What happened to the Federation? Why did it fall apart, in the end? Does anything remain—back on Earth, or the other core worlds? Why have they never come to these lost and lonely outposts like Sahil's spaceport? Behind everything I do are these questions—what, if anything, is left, and why did it not endure? I ask myself these questions, because if I can find answers, find people who can provide answers—this information might form the basis of some kind of *restoration*.

6. Not everyone, it seems, would welcome the Federation's return. Not everyone would be happy to see ships commanded by Starfleet officers arrive. Is this simply a mistrust of the unknown? Is there more behind this? I must know. I must, as ever, understand.

SOME HOURS LATER . . .

[Not numbered.] I am lost. I am more lost than I have ever been in life. My mother at least had an anchor between past and future, now and then, but I have nothing . . .

TEN MINUTES LATER . . .

Such thoughts are irrational, and therefore unhelpful. Let me list the friends that I have to guide me through this time:

> Sahil
>
> Jeremiah
>
> Sahil's great-grandmother
>
>
> Grudge
>
>
>
> Book, I guess

Cler Mercantile Exchange

They were standing just outside the mercantile, looking in. There seemed to be a holdup about gaining entrance. Burnham, stirring the toe of her boot in the dust, said, "Is there a problem, Book?"

"Yes," replied Book.

"What?"

"Requiem City is the problem. Word gets around, you know. We live or die by our reputations. Dammit!" He slammed his hand against the console. "I enter my code, and I get thrown out. Must have got onto a blacklist somewhere . . ."

She looked at him anxiously. "Is this going to be a serious problem for you?"

"A serious problem? No. A major irritation? Yes. I have

other codes I can use, but the ratings on those aren't as good. That means my pay won't be as good. So it looks like I'll be bringing home less latinum for a while."

"I'm sorry for whatever part I played in that," she said.

"Apology accepted." He gave her a sly look. "This is where I suggest you can make it up to me by giving me twenty percent of your takings."

"All right," Burnham said. "If that will help."

Book looked at her for a moment in disbelief. Then he leaned his forehead against the console, and banged it gently against the surface, several times. "Burnham. Don't take the first offer. Get me down below twelve percent at least. Aim for single figures . . ."

"But my presence on Hima must have cost you a lot of money—"

"Just try haggling with me." He grinned. "Trust me. You'll enjoy it. Play the part!"

She leaned one shoulder against the console. "Mister, you'll be lucky to take home five." She gave him her best dead-eyed stare, the one she usually reserved for Georgiou. "The rest comes in broken bones."

He moved back an inch or two. "That was . . . actually pretty good."

"That was better than good."

"I forget that you were, well, you know . . ."

A Starfleet officer. A war veteran. Not to mention a jailbird. "Don't forget," she said. "Did we settle on five percent, then?"

"We're settling on fifteen."

"Seven."

"Twelve."

"Nine."

"Ten—for pity's sake, Burnham, let me have double figures!"

"Nine point five it is."

"I didn't mean—"

"Nine point five and no broken bones." She blinked at him. "Do we have to . . . I don't know, shake *hands*, or something?"

"We can skip that part." He turned back to the console, muttering something that might have been access codes and might have been *"daylight robbery."* Burnham watched him. *I guess that's a deal. I hope it keeps.* What, really, did she know about this man? A crook, certainly, but one who had gone miles out of his way to do good for that beautiful creature . . . Charismatic, double-dealing, sharp talking. If she had any sense, she would walk away right now, find a way back to the spaceport, and knuckle down to help Sahil do whatever he could for the few sectors of space around him.

But as well as all those other things, Book was *here*, helping her—and had gone out of his way to help her. That counted. That counted a great deal.

With a grind and a whir, the doors to the mercantile slid open. "Oh!" said Book, staring at them in amazement. He hadn't thought that was going to work, had he? Burnham sighed, and followed him inside.

———

The floor of this mercantile was busier even than the one at Requiem City, the massive faces of the holo-vendors and holo-sellers looming high above, the steady stream of information flooding past. Burnham heard names for currencies she had never known existed, not just the familiar *latinum*, but *leks* and *vetusti* and *ultarian dollars* and did someone *really* just say *ningi*? What made this different from the other mercantile she had visited was that there were more actual people present. And, she had to say, this place was as diverse as any starship or starbase she had visited. Orions, Andorians, Trill . . . Was that a Kelpien over there? Had they joined the Federation? Not to mention a myriad of species she couldn't immediately identify. There had been hundreds of years of exploration since. Who knew what worlds had been encountered in the years since she had left? Burnham thought about how freely species had traveled in her own time; how far away from home people could be. What had happened when the ships stopped dead in space? People must have been stranded, away from their own worlds. Realizing they would never see friends or family or beloved places ever again. Just like her.

Firmly, Burnham drew her attention back to the present. Her eye fell on a small group of people gathered around a holographic display that was showing various types of Starfleet insignia. They were dressed—bizarrely—in a variety of Starfleet uniforms.

"Now that isn't right," she said to herself.

"What?" muttered Book.

"The insignia that one is wearing. The delta isn't right—it's too broad. Who are these people, Book? I'm assuming they're not Starfleet, otherwise you would have mentioned it."

Book, with some irritation, looked around. Burnham pointed over to the group. Book shook his head and went back to work. "Reenactors."

"What now?" said Burnham.

"Reenactors. They dress up in uniform and go around pretending they're in Starfleet."

"Really?" She boggled at him. "That's a *thing*?"

"Yep, that's a thing."

Burnham watched them walk past. "I like them," she said. "I mean, isn't that exactly what we're all doing at the start of our careers? Dressing up in uniform and going around pretending we're in Starfleet? It's just that it becomes habit. Second nature. As if the uniform seeps into the skin." She saw his expression. "You don't like them?"

"I don't dislike them—"

"They're not doing anyone any harm."

"Mostly harmless." He laughed. "There are worse epitaphs, I suppose." He shrugged. "You know, these are most likely rich kids with too much time and money on their hands. Who has time to go around looking at pieces of old junk? Who has the *money*? Most of us are too busy scratching around trying to make a living—"

"At least they're preserving the past when everyone else is just raiding it," Burnham said. "It's often a source of real regret for a civilization that goes through a period of contraction. People grab whatever's to hand and make use of it. Later, when things stabilize and people are in a position to value and venerate their past again, they regret what's been lost."

"A 'period of contraction'?" Book shook his head. "You have no idea."

"And perhaps wearing the uniform signals something."

"It signals that they've got too much time on their hands."

"It might also act as a reminder that a better way of life is possible."

"You know, they can dress up in costumes from dawn to dusk and stand on their heads singing the Federation anthem, as long as I can sell them something." He looked at her thoughtfully. "If only you had brought more with you."

"More what?"

"More, you know, *stuff*."

"Oh no!" She shook her head firmly. "No way. There are ethical issues surrounding the transference of technology from one time period to another—"

"Yes, I'm sure there's a regulation for every occasion," Book said. "Just as I'm sure there are ethical issues surrounding the transference of personnel from one time period to another—"

"In my defense, it was either that or allow the end of all—"

"—all sentient life," he finished. "I know."

"Next time I might not bother. Then you'll be sorry."

"And I'll be sure to scream my apologies from whatever plane of nonexistence I've been consigned to." He went back to scanning through the job openings. "I still wish we had something to sell them."

"Do you think I should tell them?" she said.

"Tell them what?"

"About the insignia. It's close, but it's just not right—" She watched them pass. They were young, and in good spirits. They were pleased with how they looked. "Maybe I could set myself up as a consultant. Do you think there's money in that?"

"Probably best if you leave it," said Book. "Too many questions." He glanced at her. "Are you going to help me with this or not?"

She moved into place next to him, glancing back over her shoulder to take one last look at the reenactors. One of them, seeing her looking at him, lifted his hand in a Vulcan salute. She couldn't stop herself. She lifted her hand and gestured back. His face cracked into a broad smile—somewhat ruining the overall effect of his performance—and for some reason that was what hit her hardest. It was all so close to being right, and yet subtly and completely wrong. These people weren't Starfleet. They were playing a part. There was no Starfleet anymore. Only one lonely commander, lost in time, and a gentle and patient liaison officer, flying a solitary flag. Burnham brushed the hand she was holding up against her eyes and focused on what Book was doing.

Watching him work, she felt humbled. He navigated the interfaces effortlessly, rapidly discarding jobs that he consid-

ered not worth the trouble and seeming to find easily the ones
that were paying fairly. "It's all a balance," he said. "Those
high-paying jobs—there's always a catch. You sign up and then
find it's in some far-flung part of the sector and you've ended
up spending more getting there than the job actually brings
you. But piece together some of these smaller jobs, get yourself a good itinerary across a couple of months—you can make
a living."

If you knew the region, and the people who were good to
work with, and how not to make simple mistakes that made
you an easy target. Burnham was beginning to feel disheart-
ened. A lifetime of study, and hard work, and discipline, but
how much of that knowledge could be transferred to this
world, to this life? She bit her bottom lip. *You're smart*, she
told herself, *and you're a quick learner. That's a start.*

She watched over his shoulder as the data flew past. She
saw the word *Atalis* come up—a plea for assistance to bring
out parts for their water-reclamation plants. "Hey," she said,
"wasn't that the place Sahil mentioned?"

"Yes."

"And?"

He snorted. "No chance."

"Why not?" she said. "Sounds like they really need the help."

"I'm sure they do. But the word on the ground is that
they've pissed off some serious players, and I don't want to get
involved."

"That sounds like they *really* need help."

"Not when I have an inexperienced crew member with
me, hey?" He glared back at the console. "Can I carry on?"

She kept close watch, soon detecting other patterns in his
selection process. "There's one name you keep skipping over,"
she said. "Gartilaa. It's like the job is right, and then you check
to see who's offering it, and pass. What's the deal there?"

He was clearly impressed. "Well spotted."

"Did you make them mad?"

"Not this lot."

"So why are you passing over work from them?"

"You know, there are a lot of not very nice people out there. Lots of small operators, trying to get bigger, trying to steal territory from each other. These guys are particularly unpleasant. I don't think they'll pay us. Also"—his face hardened—"I don't trade in flesh."

She shuddered. Slavers. "No. You know what? I think we should keep away."

"Nice to have your stamp of approval, Burnham." He shut down the data feed. "All right," he said. "That'll keep us busy for a while."

"What are we doing?"

"There's some messages to run out to the Lecksitt system, and also I've got a decent gig with a shipfitter who needs a pile of parts. The good thing about that is that it takes us past a big graveyard where we can scout out a ship for you."

"A *graveyard*?" She had visions of tombstones, mausoleums, pyramids . . .

He gave her a pained look. "A *ship* graveyard, Burnham."

"Of course." She rallied; tried to laugh it off. "And I thought you were taking me sightseeing."

"Oh, I promise you that you'll see some sights."

"What's this place called?" she asked.

He grinned. "The Necropolis."

The Atalis system
Nearing Atalis IV
Iliana Pa'Dan was in trouble again. She'd been in trouble many times over the years that she had been a courier. The difference was that this time she knew she wasn't going to make

it. The nearest of the three raider ships sped past again, strafing her little vessel. An alarm went off. Pa'Dan, swearing, switched this off. It wasn't as if she could do anything.

Pa'Dan had been making the run to Atalis IV for nearly a year now and, as far as she could tell, she was the last courier bothering. For the last couple of months, entering local space around Atalis IV had become dangerous. Raider ships, coming from nowhere, shooting down couriers making the run to the planet. Everyone else had pulled back. Pa'Dan—for reasons she couldn't quite fathom at this moment—had carried on, bringing the parts they needed to keep their water-reclamation plants going. Up till now, she had been lucky. But what was the old saying? She needed to be lucky every time. They only needed to be lucky once, and today fortune was smiling upon them.

The ship rocked again, more violently this time. Did they have to be so dedicated? Another alarm sounded, which Pa'Dan quickly curtailed. She needed just a little more time, just to bring her close enough to the atmosphere so that she could launch her escape pod. The raiders knew what she was doing, and were trying to bring her down before that.

The planet loomed closer and closer. Another ninety seconds, and she would switch to automatic pilot, and hope that the ship would hold out long enough for her to transport to the pod and launch.

Sixty seconds. She reached out with one hand and grabbed her bag, slinging it over her shoulder. What really rankled was that she couldn't bring most of her cargo. That was all going down with the ship.

Thirty seconds. How soon *were* they going to run out of water down there? Because Pa'Dan reckoned nobody was getting through after her.

Fifteen seconds . . . If she in fact got through . . .

Ten . . . nine . . . eight . . . seven . . .

"Bye, then," she said, patting the ship, holding back tears. They'd been through a lot together, over the years. "Thanks for everything." She thumped the button on the personal transporter and arrived in the small pod of the life capsule. She hit the controls, and the pod was thrust out, small and swift, speeding past the raiders, and plunging down toward the surface of Atalis IV.

Various points around four systems

They journeyed up and down the sector, and as they did, they quarreled like old friends.

"So you *don't* like Sahil," Burnham said, as she helped him check a shipment of nanocomponents they were shuttling off Lecksitt.

"I didn't say that," he said, and sent one crate back to the vendor to check again. "That is exactly not what I said."

"You think he's deluded."

"I think he's in denial."

"That the Federation will ever come back?"

Book glanced over at the Lurian vendor, whose patience was clearly wearing thin.

"Burnham, I've had enough quarreling with that one for today, never mind with you. Can we pick this one back up on the ship?"

They picked it back up on the ship.

"I'm not saying," he said, once they were in flight, and Grudge was back in his arms, "that I don't like Sahil. He's plainly a decent and honorable man."

"But deluded," she replied, from her place on the floor, where he had set her the task of individually testing nearly two hundred and fifty self-sealing stem bolts. "This batch don't seal, by the way."

"Burnham, I know how much you've lost. But it's never coming back. What do you mean they don't seal?"

"The seal doesn't seal itself."

"But it does seal?"

"Not by itself. That's not self-sealing. That's just sealing."

"Still seals."

"The Federation might still be going in other sectors. If Sahil has kept that place up and running for this long—"

He was staring at her.

"What?" she said, passing him one of the unsealed stem bolts. "I just think if we pass them off as self-sealing, then we're opening ourselves up to a world of—"

"I don't mean damn stem bolts! I mean Sahil's place! It has a hole in the side the size of a trance worm."

"But it's still functioning."

"Just about!"

"All it needs is resources—"

"Burnham," he said, firmly. "You must realize that it's surely a matter of time before the place is overrun by some gang or other. Sahil's not a young man, he can't last forever—"

"He's in his sixties—"

"Oh, and of course *you* all lived well into your hundreds." He caught her look. "Oh, so that bit was true." She nodded. He sighed, and passed the stem bolt back, offered her a probe. "Try them with that."

"Yes, that bit was true." She began work, as instructed. "But what do you mean he can't last forever?"

"Look," he said, "you need to understand how things stand around here. Sahil is able to survey thirty sectors, yeah? And he can communicate with two ships. Do you think that counts as a defensive capability? The spaceport is in a good location. It's a known waypoint; it's on several well-known routes. Sahil has been left alone because he keeps things tick-ing over and it's helpful to have somewhere to stop and get repairs. Everyone knows he's not as young as he used to be. You think the sharks aren't already circling? There are half a dozen people working these sectors who could put together enough firepower to take the place within days. And once they control the station—they control access to all those sectors. They go from local small fry to main warlord. *That* is what I mean."

She sat back, aghast. "Does Sahil *know* this? He's never said anything—"

"You know, you present to the world as a woman with a lot on her plate. He probably didn't want to bother you with his troubles. But I bet he was gutted when you said you were looking for a ship. He probably thought his successor had turned up. Someone young, to take over the spaceport. Not to mention a bona fide Starfleet officer." Book stopped. "Are you okay?"

"I guess," she said. She turned on the probe. "I suppose I'm just beginning to realize how little I know about the *politics* here."

"There's no politics," he said, firmly. "There's economics. Things have changed. It's fine by me if you and Sahil want to believe that the olden days are coming back, if you put up some flags and wear some badges. But this is the real world, Burnham—and you've got to learn to live here. Because . . ."

"Because time travelers don't come falling out of the sky every day," she said.

"Let's say it's only happened once. And that's not a trend. That's a . . ." His lips twitched. "That's a *happening*."

She offered him one of the stem bolts she'd been working on. "I think this one will seal under its own steam now."

"Good. Now do the other twenty-four."

She obeyed. This was not Starfleet—but Book sure knew how to give orders.

The Necropolis

The Necropolis turned out to be a ring of wrecked ships dumped around an empty planet that had, over the years, begun to form an asteroid belt around the world below. Burnham stared at the sheer extent of the detritus floating there. Book, sitting beside her, looked pleased. "What do you think?" he said. "We'll soon find you something here, I'm sure."

"The Necropolis," she said. "The city of the dead. You know, I think my heart has broken all over again."

"Impressive, isn't it?"

"That's one word for it." She looked at the wrecks and ruins, spreading out farther than she could see. "Who *owns* this place? Who *operates* it?"

"I don't know what you mean," Book said. "Nobody owns it."

"But someone must be keeping an eye on how the whole thing is run . . ." She frowned. "You're laughing."

"It's just when you say things like that, you show that you're not from around these parts. Nobody is keeping an eye on things, Burnham. Nobody. There's no police force, there's no health and safety committee, there's nobody dropping by to make sure that people are maintaining standards—there's just people like me, and other couriers—and you soon, coming by when they need to, seeing if there's anything of value."

"But how do the ships get here? Who *brings* them here?"

"They get dumped," he said. "Someone might come here hoping they'll find something to fix their ship, then find something they like more, and go off in that instead. Some people drag things here because they're cluttering up the main routes and causing us all trouble." He shrugged. "People have been doing it for decades—long before I started operating. I guess it's a self-regulating system."

She shook her head. "All that effort," she said. "All that work. And not even to build anything constructive. Just dragging rubbish to the middle of nowhere . . ."

"Well, Starfleet, I'm sure it looks that way to you," said Book. "But we didn't make the rubbish. We just . . . curate it. And it works. More or less. Sometimes. Mostly."

Book came in slowly, sending out hails as they made their approach. A voice came through the comm. *"Cleveland Booker, have you come all this way for those eight strips of latinum I owe you? That's petty even by your standards."*

"Who is it?" said Burnham. "A friend?"

"An acquaintance," Book said. "But a friendly acquaintance. Not an actual bona fide enemy. Not yet, at any rate."

"Do you think of all your friends as enemies you haven't made yet?"

"Not all of them," he said, and opened a comm channel. "Hey, Brodie. Just passing through. But I'll take the latinum if you have it—or any dilithium you've got to spare."

"Fat chance. What are you here for, Book?"

"Looking for a ship. New courier on the block."

"Oh yeah? You know we're all struggling to get by—"

"Her name's Burnham and she's sitting right next to me."

"She, huh?"

"That a problem?" said Burnham coolly.

"Not my problem if it is. Anyway, Ms. Burnham, I saw a Nirvana-*class flyer over in the second quarter that might suit you. It'll need some work."*

"They always do," said Book. "Thanks for the tip, Brodie."

"Yes," said Burnham. "Thank you."

"You're welcome. Can I take that off the tab?"

"Dream on, my friend!" Book, laughing, cut the channel and began to steer the ship around the edge of the graveyard.

"Second quarter," he said. "May as well head that way. Pick up the other parts we need too. Two birds, one stone."

He brought his ship to a halt above a big vessel with a huge hole in the side and a pair of sorry-looking shuttles still more or less attached. "This should have most of what we need," he said. "Let's try this one. You take the shuttles."

They suited up and went to work. She had spent a large part of the journey giving herself a crash course in recent starship design. There was only so much of several hundred years of innovation you could learn about in a short space flight, but anything that was part of a matter-antimatter propulsion system was hardly worth looking at, except for scrap metals. What everyone wanted was dilithium, but there would be none of that here.

"Jobs like this," said Book through the helmet comm, *"they're all about looking for the small stuff, lots and lots of small stuff, and building up a living from that."*

It was slow work, tiring, even with the personal transporter that let her move quickly from one shuttle to another. When she had gone through these, Book gave her a list of other ships in the area to investigate. Entering one of these, she was startled nearly out of her skin when she heard voices and saw a ghostly figure up ahead. She almost screamed—and then laughed when she realized what it was.

"Burnham? You okay?"

"I'm okay," she said. "Holographic system fired up."

"Oh yeah," he said. *"That can happen. The ghosts in the machine. See why we call it the Necropolis?"*

She went across to the figure, which was pale blue, a species she didn't know, wearing a uniform she didn't recognize. Not only Starfleet was affected by the Burn. From the urgency in its voice, and the way it moved, she thought she might be seeing those last moments. She found a control and turned the figure off. Rest in peace, she thought, and went tiredly back to her salvage task.

Part of her exhaustion, she thought, as she worked, came from the double filter behind which she seemed to be living permanently these days. She was two people, at the same time: Commander Michael Burnham, a Starfleet officer, supremely competent; and this other person, who was confused, lost, deskilled; who understood only the basics of the world in which she was now working. Sometimes these two worlds collided in the most sudden and upsetting ways. Like today, she had found herself again and again working in the crumbling husk of a ship covered in Starfleet markings, and her heart cracked a little more. Just a few weeks ago, she had been on board *Discovery*, the most advanced starship that the Federation had as yet produced—and now she was scrabbling around in the ruins of the civilization that had built that ship. At least she had skipped the actual apocalypse, she thought. She was just living with the consequences.

The enormity of this hit her at last when she transported onto the bridge of what was plainly an old science vessel. Even this far into her own future, something of the basic design remained familiar. The curve of the bridge, the various stations, the captain's chair. Every console was dark, every system was dead. All the great work that this ship had done, brought to a halt, in one tragic, brutal moment. She found the ship's dedication plaque on the bulkhead: the Starfleet symbol engraved at the top, name, number, and place of construction below.

U.S.S. Maryam Mirzakhani. *Named for the first woman mathematician to win the Fields Medal. New Utopia Planitia Shipyards.* Suddenly, she grasped the full scale of the collapse. Not just supplies, not just communication, not just these beautiful ships, but everything had stopped. Manufacturing. Defense. Education. Healthcare. Science. All stopped. She put her hand against the plate, and, standing on the dead bridge, began to cry.

"Burnham? Are you okay?" Book's voice came through the mic.

"What? Yes, I'm fine!"

"Your breathing sounded rushed, that's all. Check your oxygen."

"You know, Book, I have used a spacesuit before. I was wearing a spacesuit when you met me, remember?"

"I'm not likely to forget."

"I'm fine." *But thank you for caring,* she thought. *Because I'm more alone than I ever thought I would be.*

"Good. Now back to work."

Burnham smiled. That moment had sure passed. But again, somehow, he had brought her back to reality—back to the present—and that, after all, was where she had to learn to be. She looked up at the visual display, telling where she should go next, and what to look for. But before she went back to work, she laid her hand upon the plaque once again. *Could I? Should I?* Was it a kind of sacrilege? Or a kind of rec- lamation? Quickly, she made her decision. She detached the plaque from the bulkhead and carried it away with her.

———

A couple of hours later, they rendezvoused back at Book's ship. As she ate, he went through the parts she had scavenged.

"Some good work here," he said. "Although you've also picked up a lot of junk . . ."

She looked at the pile of memorabilia she had collected. More ship dedication plaques. Once she had started, she couldn't stop. "I couldn't leave them there to rot," she said. "They have a history. They have meaning. Value."

"History—definitely. Meaning—perhaps. Value—well, we'll see."

"I didn't mean financial value."

"What other kind of value is there?"

She opened her mouth to reply, then saw the gleam in his eye. "I'm not going to quarrel with you, Book."

"No? I thought you enjoyed it."

"I enjoy the part where I get to break your nose."

"I . . . enjoy that less." He sifted through the plaques. "I don't blame you wanting to take some of this with you, but you do realize there's a lot of it out there these days, don't you? You might need to be choosy about what you bring with you, what you leave behind."

She had, she thought, already begun to see that. What could be saved? What had to be cut loose? *I'm Starfleet,* she thought; *that much is not negotiable.*

"Anyway," he said. "I think you've earned your keep today. And the good news is that I found the ship Brodie thought might suit you. It'll need work, but I think we can do it. Do you want to come and see?"

"What? Of course!"

"Finish up your dinner, then."

Ten minutes later, they were suited and helmeted, checking the charge on the personal transporters. And then—

Burnham found herself inside a dark tomb. "What the hell is this place, Book?"

He waved his flashlight around. *"What do you think?"* he said. *"I think it has potential—"*

"The potential? It's a damn coffin."

"It's solid. It's reliable. It's in unbelievably good shape. These little flyers—they built them properly. Look, can we do this back on my ship? Without helmets?"

They went back to his ship.

"I'll be in that thing for days at a time! Weeks! Why can't I have something the size of this?"

"Because you can't pay for the upkeep, Burnham."

"Oh," she said. "I see."

"Look, it's well made. It doesn't need much fixing up. I'll help. I promise—you'll love it."

She took a deep breath. "Okay," she said. "Okay. Let's go and have another look."

They were reaching once again for helmets when an alarm sounded. "Hang on," said Book. "Ship incoming."

He summoned up the visual display. Burnham saw, in holo, a small ship, sleek and well maintained, with white marks across the black hull, as if someone had put their palm down into paint, and then laid their hand across the vessel. Book, easing into his chair, opened a comm channel.

"Hey there," he said. "Who are you?"

"We're here to look after our property?"

"Your what now?" said Book.

"This whole area is under our jurisdiction. It's time for you to move on."

Burnham whispered, "I thought you said nobody owned—" but quietened when she saw Book lift his hand to stop her from speaking.

"Now, you guys know as well as I do that nobody owns this place," said Book. "We're all free to come and go here, as we choose. It works well, and I don't see any good reason for that to change—"

"We can think of a good reason. Our weapons are targeted onto you. So we'll say again—leave. And don't come back."

Book cut the comm.

"That seems a fairly persuasive argument," said Burnham. "I'm guessing you don't have the firepower to take them on?"

"No . . ."

"So?"

"So they can go to hell," said Book.

"Is this a hill you're willing to die on, Book?" said Burnham. "I mean—look at what you're squabbling over. It's a heap of junk."

"Yes, but it's not *their* heap of junk."

"Courier ship. You're not moving. Soon we start firing."

Book reached to open the channel again. Burnham stayed his hand. "This isn't worth dying over!"

"This isn't theirs to claim!"

"So we back off, we find out more about them, we regroup, and we come back—"

"I'm not surrendering this to them—"

"This is one *hell* of a time to discover your principles," said Burnham.

"What do you mean by that?" said Book. "You think I don't have principles? Listen, Starfleet, you don't have the *monopoly* on right action!"

"That's not what I'm saying," Burnham said, patiently. "But—I don't want to die defending a heap of scrap. Can't we at least try *talking* to these people, whoever they are?"

The comm chimed again. Book, opening the channel, said, "I told you, I'm not leaving!"

"All right, Book. No need to snap!"

It was Brodie. Burnham took a deep breath.

"I picked up another ship heading your way and came over to check everything was fine. Is everything fine?"

"Yes," said Book.

"No," said Burnham, quicker and louder.

"So which is it?"

"These guys think they can stake a claim on this place," said Book. "You see my problem?"

A low laugh came across the comm. *"Yeah, I do."* They

heard a few thumps and curses, and then Brodie spoke again. *"Unidentified vessel—you've threatened a friend of mine, and I don't like that. I've scanned your ship, and I know I've got more firepower here than you do. Yes, that's right, scan my ship . . . See? So I suggest you back off, and go back to wherever you came from, and don't come this way again. Nobody owns this place, and we like it that way."*

There was silence. Then the ship with white markings began to move—away from the scrapyard, and off into the deep of space.

"Thanks," said Book.

"Has that cleared the tab?"

"That has at most cleared a small but not insignificant part of the tab."

Brodie laughed.

"Have you upgraded your weapons capacity since we last talked, Brodie?"

"What? No! Scrambled their sensors."

"Of course . . ."

"Anyway, work to do. Take care of yourself, Book. Ms. Burnham—that ship is a good ship and you'll be a fool to pass. Brodie out." His own ship began to move slowly away.

"I wasn't expecting that," said Burnham. "I wasn't expecting anyone to come and help."

"We're not just on the make, you know," said Book. "We look out for each other."

"But what if you want the same thing?" she said.

He gave her a crooked smile. "Well, like all relationships, you work your disagreements out."

"I'm sure you do." She looked around. "What do we do about my ship?"

"Your ship now, is it?"

"Brodie," she said, "was very insistent. Who am I to ignore a recommendation like that? Anyway, what if someone comes in the meantime?"

"We have our ways round that," he said. "We'll set up a marker. It'll let people know we're staking a claim. That we're coming back for it."

"And people *honor* that?" she said incredulously.

"On the whole, yes, they do."

"But won't the marker draw them in? Won't it tell people there's something of value?"

"Right now, this is chiefly of value to us. We could find another half dozen ships like this around here, no problem. Why bother taking this one? At some point they'll want to do the same thing. They'll find some scrap they want, but they won't be able to move it, and so they'll want to leave and come back. So they pass over this, and let us get on with our business." He gave her a sharp look. "Starfleet might have had the monopoly on regulations, Burnham, but it didn't have the monopoly on collaboration."

"I just don't see how this works without anything to back it up," she said.

"Firepower, you mean?"

"I didn't mean that, although it certainly comes in useful."

"Well, I guess we'll find out when we come back from the exchange." He nodded toward her bag of ship plaques. "Are you bringing that heap of junk, or leaving it?"

Cler Mercantile Exchange

Book had said that the reenactors would be rich kids with too much time and money on their hands, and he was not wrong. Their taste was for the shiniest of memorabilia, and Burnham was glad that she had taken the time on the flight back to clean up the various pieces she'd salvaged. Give them their due, they had a good eye—and their pockets were satisfyingly deep.

Burnham, seeing a group of them gathered around a vending console, walked right up and said, "Don't look at that stuff on-screen. Look at what I have for you here."

She put her bag on the ground and opened it up, spreading out her wares. The whole group gasped. They gathered around her, the holo-images forgotten.

"Where did you find this stuff?" said one, reaching out to touch, but stopping when she lifted her forefinger. *Careful with the relics*, she thought. He was a young man, dressed as a Vulcan, with a *Kol-Ut-Shan* brooch on his jacket.

Burnham pointed to it. "Did you find that?"

"This? No, I made this."

"It's *good*," she said. The proportions were perfect, and there was a real diamond at the heart. No mistakes here. She felt a tear form in her eye.

"Thank you," he said. "I think . . . I think it's the most beautiful of ideas too."

She smiled. "So do I!" One of the first ideas from Vulcan philosophy she had embraced. Infinite diversity in infinite combinations; that celebration of the sheer variety and difference of the universe.

"I guess . . . that's why you got into this stuff," he said. "You don't often find couriers interested in this stuff."

"Well, I am interested," she said. "And I guess that's good news for me as a vendor!"

He laughed. "Yeah, I guess it is!"

One of his friends was holding up the plate from the *Maryam Mirzakhani*. "Is this genuine?" he said. "How can I be sure?"

"Not that one," she said, hurriedly. She couldn't give up that one. "How about this one. I can show you the footage from my helmet when I was on board, if that would help," she said. "I guess I could always have faked it—but that seems like a lot of effort when I just go and get the stuff. Here." She began to play back the holo-images from her suit. "Look, here I am arriving on the vessel. And here I am removing the plate." Even now, it felt slightly sacrilegious. But then she heard the thrilled murmur passing through the group around her. They were at least as enthralled by the glimpse inside a Federation vessel as they were by the actual merchandise. She tried to put aside her qualms at selling them these pieces. They loved them, she thought. They would take good care of them. And she remembered enough from her archaeology classes to know how important antiquarian collections could be. They had lost the context, yes, but something had survived. "You should take this footage," she said. "Not just for provenance. Maybe one day someone will want to know about the context in which it was found."

One of the young women in the group—she was dressed, charmingly, in a space station uniform from the 2220s—looked at her in awe. "You really know your stuff. It's just . . . I guess you're not like a courier."

Burnham had to smile. She didn't *feel* like a courier either. She was just dressed up in the costume and pretending. "I guess we're all different," she said. "Everyone has their own story. And I . . ." She looked down at her collection again, with a pang of loss and grief. "I really love this stuff."

"I wish I'd lived back then," the woman said. "It all seemed so . . . *peaceful.*"

"There would have been scary moments," said Burnham. "They still had wars."

"But they tried to solve things *honorably,*" she said. "I've read a lot about this, you know."

"I'm sure you have."

"These are so beautiful . . ." She was looking at the ship plates once again. "I wish I knew their stories. The worlds they'd seen. The voyages they'd taken. The people on these ships—the distances they traveled. They were so *brave* . . ."

"They would have had some wonderful tales to tell, that's for sure," Burnham said, unable to keep the sadness away from her voice. She had some stories of her own to tell. What would she do, this young woman, if she realized she was talking to someone who knew this past intimately? What would this group do? Would they want to hear about the Federation as it truly was, or would they prefer to keep their own versions intact, untainted by personal account? The Federation—a mythical time of great heroes and adventurers. *Sing, O goddess, of the wrath of Achilles.* No, not that hero. *Tell me—O Muse!—of the one of many wiles, the wanderer, lost for many years.*

They sat and talked for a while longer—and she sold them almost everything she had. When they left, the young man took off his badge and offered it to her. "Would you take this?" he said. "I've got another."

"I'm not sure I can afford—"

"As a gift. Moneyless society, yeah?"

Gratefully, she accepted. They saluted their good-byes, and she went to join Book. She showed him what she'd earned. "How's that?"

His eyes went wide. "That," he said, "is not bad for a pile of junk."

"Not junk," she said, firmly. "It has meaning—and therefore it has value."

He saw the badge in her hand. "What's this?"

"A symbol," she said. "A star to guide me home."

The Necropolis

Once again, as they made their approach to the ship graveyard, Book sent out a few tentative hails. There was no sign of either friends or foes. They proceeded to the ship they had selected and found their markers still in place.

"See," he said. "Nobody touched it."

"Honor among thieves," she said.

"Honor among couriers," he said. "They're not the same thing. You'll get the hang of that eventually."

They suited up and used personal transporters to take them over to the ship. Her ship. It was smaller inside than Burnham remembered. Darker, more cramped. Her heart sank to think of the hours that she would be spending inside this little space.

"You'll soon make the space your own," said Book. He couldn't have seen her face through the visor, through the gloom. But he'd known. He'd known how she was feeling. It wouldn't take an empath to guess, surely.

"I suppose," she said.

"But you'll never get there if we don't get started."

So they got to work, using the matter patches they'd bought at the mercantile with her money from the sale of the memorabilia, sealing up the damage to the hull. She thought about the ships she had plundered to be able to fix this one. She hoped that mending it went a little toward counting as reparations for her theft. Once the hull was solid again, they got to work on getting key systems online. Before the first day was over, they had life-support up, and could work without their helmets. That helped. About an hour later, full lights came back. "See," said Book. "It's looking better already."

Burnham, bone weary, half closed her eyes so that everything around her became blurred. If she looked at her surroundings this way, she thought, she might almost persuade herself that this was a Starfleet vessel. A shuttle perhaps, although it was smaller than most standard shuttles. Book, watching her, said, "We'll stop soon. We'll go back to my ship. Get something to eat. Some sleep. Grudge will be wondering where we've got to."

"Yes," she said. "I'm pretty tired."

"Hey," he said suddenly, "I've had an idea!"

"Yes? Should I be excited or alarmed?"

"Excited, I hope. You should look for the black box."

"The what now?"

"The black box." He leaned back against the nearest surface. "All Federation starships constructed after the twenty-sixth century had navigation and flight-control recorders—"

"Oh, the flight recorder!" she said. "We had those too, you know!"

"Yes, but these were a step up in terms of how robust they were. Practically indestructible. It will tell you the story of the ship."

She smiled at the echo of what the young reenactor had said. *They'd have some wonderful tales to tell.* "So I'd find out what brought the ship down?"

"I didn't say it would make cheerful reading."

She looked around, the gears in her clever mind shifting. "What if it went down as a result of the Burn?"

"It's about the right age. No reason the black box wouldn't be recording."

She stared at him. "So if this ship was in flight during the Burn, there might be a record somewhere of what happened in those final moments?"

"If you can find the black box. Might be interesting."

"Book," she said, "it's more than interesting!" She could feel the elation growing within. "Don't you see? This means that every vessel destroyed by the Burn will have stopped recording at the same microsecond! Find the black boxes, see what they contain—there's a real chance we can work out what happened!" She almost clapped her hands together in delight. "Have you ever done this?" she said. "Does it *work*?"

He shrugged. "Have to say I've never gone looking for one. Not even sure what it might look like. I'm sure Sahil would know where to find it, what to do with it."

She fell back, deflated. Another obstacle. She'd been ready to rip the thing out now, open it up, learn all its secrets, discover what the *hell* had happened.

He caught her look. "What? What have I done now?"

"I can't believe you wouldn't go and look—"

"Burnham, it's ancient history! Nobody's buying!"

"But how can you not even be *interested*? If it gave even the faintest clue as to how the Burn happened, logic dictates that it might contain the germ of a solution!"

"Maybe, but it doesn't keep me in space!"

She stared at him. She said, "Don't you want the Federation back?"

He threw up his hands. "What do I know about the Federation? Starfleet, UFP—this is all old news—"

"But everything was better!"

"Was it? Was it really better?"

"You wouldn't be trying to save beautiful creatures like Molly from becoming food under the Federation!" That, she saw, hit harder than she intended. "I'm sorry. Low blow. That wasn't fair—"

"No, not really. You know, there are a lot of things I wish were different, Burnham, but I don't live in a fantasyland."

"Is that what the Federation is to you? A fantasyland?" She could see that he was biting his bottom lip. He was trying not to say something that might offend. "Look, don't hold back. I want to understand."

"All that I'm saying is . . . Well, what did the Federation ever do for me? It's just a shadow, Burnham. A rumor from the past. I bet half the things that people say about it weren't even true. Like not having money. How does that even work? And whole planets dedicated just to going and having a good time?"

"Those things were true."

"Okay, bad examples—but why should I be bothered either way?"

"Because it matters!"

"It matters to you, Burnham," he said, gently. "To Sahil. To a few rich kids playing dress-up."

Burnham closed her eyes. She knew, just from Jeremiah, that people had mixed feelings about the Federation. That they couldn't see how it would work. But she had assumed that all she would need to do would be to *explain* . . . The obvious benefits. The joys, the pleasures, the quality of life. Sure, she could see that some people benefited from the status quo; those with local power bases who were doing well out of the chaos. That kind of opportunism she could recognize, even if she found it reprehensible. But this was something else. Book simply didn't *care*.

"I'm sorry," he said. "I don't mean to offend, but . . ."

"You haven't offended me," she said. "I'm just . . ."

"I know it matters to you," he said. "I know—it's a big loss. But I can't make myself feel that way about something I never knew."

This loss, she thought, this all-encompassing loss. How could he not feel it? How could he not see how his life was *shaped* by it? His whole way of life was built around the empty space where there had once been order, peace, enlightenment. How had people come to feel this way? How could people not *care*?

"It's late," he said. "We've been working hard. Let's go and see how Grudge is getting on. Let's come back to all this in the morning. I think we'll have you in flight by the end of tomorrow."

"All right."

"Friends?" he said. He sounded worried.

She managed the ghost of a smile. "Friends."

I guess.

Sahil's office
Former Federation Spaceport Devaloka

Sahil's office, Burnham decided, had a remarkably calming effect. The colors were muted, the space clear and uncluttered,
but a substantial reason for the overall air of tranquillity was
surely the man himself. Perhaps it was something to do with
all the waiting, day after day, year after year, for someone from
Starfleet to arrive. Perhaps patience like that taught you serenity. When Burnham walked through the door, he greeted her
with gentle excitement.

"Ah," he said, "in time for morning tea."

She settled back into their old routine happily. He kept on
smiling at her as he summoned up the cups and the rest of the
paraphernalia. His pleasure at seeing a Starfleet officer once
again had obviously not worn off, but there was something
else there now. He was genuinely glad to see her, for herself.
She began to relax in the chair, watching his careful actions.
She had observed him perform this ritual many times, but she
found it very soothing.

"And how was the journey?" he said, pouring out the tea
at last. "A success?"

"We salvaged some spare parts. Did some supply runs. I
found a ship."

"That's excellent news, Commander! A good ship?"

"Let's say it has potential."

"Ah," he replied. "I understand. Where did you go?"

"I think Book called it the Necropolis. It was something of
a shock," she admitted.

"I can imagine," he said. "We who were born to these
times are used to living with it—the sense of loss, of living
among the ruins. But to come from where you have come . . ."
He looked at her, shyly, wonderingly. "It is still a marvel to

me, Commander, that you walked through that door. I am so very glad you are back."

She smiled. Sometimes she worried he expected more from her than she was able to give. But it sure was nice to be wanted. "I wish I understood more about what happened."

"The Burn happened, Commander."

"I know, but that alone shouldn't have been enough to make the Federation collapse. The Federation withstood many shocks over the centuries. Why this?"

"But this struck at the core. One cannot maintain an empire if one cannot reach its most distant regions."

"I take exception to your description of the Federation as an empire," said Burnham, "but I understand what you mean. But it wasn't technology that held the Federation together. It was a sense of shared purpose. It was a set of common values. This should have made those distant regions pull together. But they didn't. So what happened? Not to the technology. To the *will*."

"It might still be there."

"Yes—there was you, wasn't there? And while you're unique, I think, Sahil—"

He smiled at her.

"—perhaps there are others like you, keeping the flame alive. Perhaps back on the founding worlds—Earth, Vulcan, Tellar, Andor." She saw a hazy, almost romantic, expression pass across his face. Her voice faded away. She was speaking to him, she realized, of fantasylands. She might as well be talking to him about Narnia. These were places he had never visited; could never visit. "I can't believe they didn't try to do something. I can't believe they're still not trying to do something."

"That has always been my hope, Commander. In the meantime, I try to hold as much together as I can in this little part of space. Try to keep the couriers in order."

"Try to keep the warlords at bay?" she said.

He looked at her carefully.

"Book," she said, "explained the strategic value of this spaceport."

"Ah," he said, and frowned. "That, perhaps, is my greatest fear. That something will step into the void left by the Federation's fall. That something or someone pulls together and fills the gap. And that what we end up with shares nothing of the values of Starfleet, or the Federation. For the moment, we keep the balance here, but . . ." He gestured upward with his hands. "We ought not to imagine ourselves into trouble."

No, she thought, *but they could think more about their defenses . . .*

"Did you start the journal?"

"I did," she said. "I'm very grateful. I'm starting to put together a picture of what was happening just before it all. Oh yes, and Book had an idea of something I might pursue."

Sahil raised an eyebrow. "Did he."

"He said that you might know where the black box was on my ship. That if we found it, we might be able to find out something about the moments leading up to the Burn."

"That . . ." said Sahil, "is not a bad idea. Finish your tea, Commander. Let's see what your ship can tell us."

Burnham's ship

"I see what you mean about potential," Sahil said, looking around. "But as I understand it, these were very good ships in their day. One of the most reliable designs. Perfect for what you'll be doing with it, Commander—if you do decide to take on work as a courier."

He still didn't like the idea of that, she could see. His beloved Starfleet officer, working as a courier. But she needed to be doing *something*. She suspected that if she offered to stay with him, take on his role, he would leap at that. But she wouldn't find the answers that she wanted here. She would be waiting for them to come to her.

"So where do we find this black box?" she said.

He gestured that he wanted to come past her. She pressed herself back to let him through. Damn, this ship was small. "Generally, they're kept near to the main console. Well protected there." He bent and pressed lightly against the panel, which popped out with ease. "Ah."

"What?"

"Nothing."

"*What?*"

"It's not there, Commander—"

"Not there? Why would anyone take it? Book said nobody would be interested in that kind of thing—"

"I cannot answer that," Sahil said. "There are many reasons why someone might take it. Perhaps the pilot took it with them when they abandoned the vessel. Perhaps they had the same idea as you. But it's gone, Commander. I'm sorry."

"*Dammit!*"

He stood up and reached to touch her hand. "This is not the only ship. There are many, many more out there. They'll have what you're looking for. Think of it as . . . as a quest."

But the despair had fully overwhelmed her now. "What's the point?" she said, bitterly. "Chasing around for a couple of black boxes?"

"Information is never a waste of time—"

"But what will they tell me that I don't already know? I know the Federation is gone, I know that! I've spent the last few days picking over the bones, selling the last bits and pieces. And all I have to do is look around me—look at this ship! And say I did find a couple of these boxes—and they tell me when the Burn happened. As if everyone doesn't already know when the Burn happened! As if everyone doesn't know why!

But they can't tell me what I need to know. They can't tell me how to set things right! Because there's no way of doing that. Starfleet's gone. It's never coming back!"

He was shaking his head. "You came," he said. "After all those long years, and the flag is flying again, here. Why might it not fly again elsewhere?"

The words of the true believer. *Sahil is in denial.* Book's voice, in her mind—not taunting her, no, he wasn't cruel—but bringing her a cold dose of reality.

Wake up, Michael.

"It's all gone, Sahil," she said. "It's never coming back. We can pick over the ruins and scavenge for pieces, but we'll never put those pieces together again." Reaching up, she pulled off her delta shield. "Here," she said, shoving it into his hand. "Take it."

"Commander, please—!"

"What good is it? Just another useless relic. And I can't bear to see any more."

"Don't give up, Commander. Things can change very suddenly. Answers come—unexpectedly." He folded his hand over it, keeping it safe, as he had with so much over the long, sad years. "I'll look after this for you," he said. "I'll have it ready for you—when you're ready to receive it back."

———

After he left, she sat for a while on the bunk, head in hands. Eventually, she lay back, thinking of trying to sleep, but something in her pocket jabbed at her side. Reaching in, she brought out the *Kol-Ut-Shan* brooch she had been given by the young man at the mercantile.

She twisted it around in her fingers. A facsimile, not the real thing, but still so very beautifully made: the copper circle gleaming, the jewel flickering, the silver triangle holding them together. Did it matter that it wasn't real? The sentiment was as valid as ever. She swung up to a sitting position, still looking at the brooch. Sarek had often worn one like this. Memories of her childhood on Vulcan came back to her: Sarek's distance, and yet the bond they shared; Amanda's warmth and care. She thought of her brother, the cruelty of having come to an adult understanding with him, and then being ripped away. She thought of the child she had been on Vulcan—not one thing, not another—and she wondered: *Will it always be this way? Will I always be caught halfway between worlds? Will I ever feel whole?*

She looked around her ship with a sinking heart. Potential, Book had said—but all that did was show his poor standards. It was bad. It was a wreck, a mess, a disaster zone. She would spend hours trying to put it right, to make it safe, to turn it into somewhere she could live and work. And for what purpose? To drag herself from mercantile to mercantile, picking up odd jobs here and there. Michael Burnham, who had traveled to a mirror universe, and through time, who had fallen about as low as it was possible for a Starfleet officer to fall— and then dragged herself back up, through guts and determination. And for what? So that she could find herself having to start all over again.

Suddenly, it all became too much. The loneliness, the distance from anyone that would count as a friendly face, the shabbiness of the ship, which was supposed to be the basis for a whole new life. Burnham slid to the deck. She wrapped her arms around her knees, bent her head, and wept for everything she had lost. It was all gone—friends, family, *Discovery*, yes, all of that . . . But more than that. Starfleet was gone. The Federation was gone. The worlds and institutions she had served with such love and reverence, that had been the bedrock of her life, had turned out to be fragile, easily broken. All it took was one random mischance, the work of a few moments, and the whole edifice had tumbled. Had it always been so frail, so slight? Had her life of service and duty been a waste of time? That was a hard thought, almost too hard to bear.

Terror gripped her; a dark, trembling fear that rocked the very foundations of her sense of self. She thought, *What shall I do? What should I do now?*

And the other part of her—the dogged part, that had survived a terrifying childhood, and then the aftermath of her mutiny—spoke back, *What do you think, Michael? You get on your feet, you pick up the pieces, and you start all over again.*

But how many times would she have to do that?

She knew the answer to that.

As many as it takes.

"Get up, Michael," she said. Wearily she pulled herself back to her feet. She went over to the ship's main console. She stood the brooch up there and thought, *We fake it until it becomes real.* She gritted her teeth, and stretched, and cleared her mind. Centered herself. Slowly, she began the forms. *Suus Mahna.* Focus. Attention. Precision. Living in the moment. That would have to do for a start. When she was finished, she fell, exhausted, on the bunk, and waved the lights to darkness. Sleep, she knew, would be hard to come by. So she went back, once again, to immerse herself in the past.

COUNCILOR PRIYA TAGORE

PERSONAL LOG

I have now been home on Prithvi for two months, and the memories of my extended period on Earth have almost entirely retreated. The occasional dream, perhaps, where I attempt to pack all my possessions into a very small suit-case while all the time aware that the departure of my shuttle is imminent. Well, it would hardly take a fully trained psychoscoper to interpret these little nightmares, would it?! Those final few weeks at the Council were, after all, dispiriting beyond measure.

Let me put that behind me! I am enjoying a well-earned vacation from Council business. I have timed my arrival home, as ever, for the summer. I spend the mornings meeting with my constituents here on Prithvi, and the afternoons in the garden. The orchids have been particularly successful this year—at last we have persuaded the moon-flowers to bloom! Joshi and I sat up late one night together to watch them. He fell asleep before the first one unfurled, dear boy, and I must confess that my eyes too were drooping, but then I forced them open, and I swear I saw the petals move. "Joshi!" I called and shook him awake, and we sat together for another hour. He spent the next day making a holo, and now whenever I wish I can see those petals unfold at speed, violet and dark blue, and the white flash inside, like moonlight in the heavens.

Bright orchids. Moonlit gardens. Burnham looked at the grubby gray walls of the ship, and felt a sudden hunger for vivid color.

We have had great fun as a family this holiday, which makes me even more keenly aware that this summer—like all summers—cannot last forever. In three weeks, I must return to Earth, where, I hope, I can begin to pick up the frayed shreds of my work, and start the process of mending the consensus I had so carefully stitched together. And I fear that I must turn my mind seriously to addressing the underlying problem, which is—that the vast expansion of member worlds prior to the Temporal Wars has left the Federation's governance structures unwieldy, leaving us with a cacophony of competing voices. This means that the strongest voices are more easily heard, and the newer, less powerful ones are drowned out. Increasingly, we fail to represent the diversity that is our lifeblood. This is, I believe, the greatest challenge for the Federation over the coming years—but this challenge must be met. We cannot ignore these voices—it is not right, and, in time, I believe it will prove self-defeating. Who will want to stay in a Federation that sees them as unequal?

But I have a month yet! Tomorrow I'm taking a full holiday, and we will be walking in the mountains . . .

"Stop playback."

More than a century later, sealed in the tiny space offered by a small, slow-moving ship, Michael Burnham could no longer bear to hear this voice, so thoughtful, so reasonable, so tragically oblivious to the disaster that was about to overcome her.

Burnham lay on her side on her bunk. The past brought no solace. The future was beyond her reach. There was only this hopeless present. She lay for a while, watching the lights flicker on the flight console, before falling, at last, into fitful sleep, waking at last from a nightmare in which her limbs grew too large and popped out of the sides of her little ship.

3

COMMANDER MICHAEL BURNHAM

PERSONAL LOG

When I woke up today, I felt for the first time at home on this little ship. I looked around, and I was pleased with what I saw. The lights were warm, orange; the space felt almost cozy! I have begun to acquire personal possessions. I have the map that Jeremiah drew for me up by the main controls. I have the dedication plaque from the *Maryam Mirzakhani*. I have a belt that I borrowed from Book, which I probably ought to return. That reminds me that I know people here; that I have made friends, or . . . How did he put it? Friendly acquaintances. I have work. I have money. It's all a start.

Last night, as I was falling asleep, I realized I'd been on board for a couple weeks, and that I'd had no problems, no serious systems failures, plenty of warning when something needed attention . . . and I thought, *It's not the ship's fault, is it, that I don't want to be here* . . . So I decided to give the ship a name, *Alice*, and I decided to be more grateful for everything this little vessel does for me. The logical, rational part of me—that part of me inculcated by years of training—naturally considers this anthropomorphizing as so illogical as to be bordering on the ridiculous. But I am not solely the product of my training.

I am so very alone.

The hours I spend alone here—with *Alice*—give me ample time to reflect upon my past. Where I have come from; how I have ended up here. I have barely had time to consider what it means that my mother did not die. My mother did not *die*! I learned this, and then she was torn from me again, and yet I feel, I feel so sure, that she is here in this time, and yet she's out of reach again.

I *feel* . . . Again, I hear Sarek's voice in my mind, chastising me for such self-indulgence. That I should not be tempted by such irrationalities. That I should discipline my mind. But I am adrift, and everything that I have used as an anchor is long gone. No ship, no crew, no Starfleet. Who am I, without these things? And I wonder—will I always feel as if I am bobbing around, directionless? Will I always feel that I am made up of disparate pieces? Will I never feel complete?

Will I always be this alone?

Enough of this, Michael. You have shipments to deliver. You have latinum to earn. You have dilithium to acquire. And your signals are out there—sent with hope and love. To your mother. To your crew. To your *friends*.

I'm looking for you. I'm waiting for you. Come and find me. I'm hoping to find you.

Six kilometers outside Freya City
Atalis IV

Five days ago, the last industrial replicator in Freya City stopped. There was a dreadful finality to the silence that followed. Every so often, someone tried to look on the bright side, and say how you could hear birdsong again, but when Iliana Pa'Dan listened, all she could hear was the cawing of birds. Living with technology like that was like being on board ship; you might forget the background noises, you might get used to them—but when they stopped, that was when you needed to be afraid. One morning you woke up, and the soft, steady *thud thud thud* of the plant was no longer there, and that lack of steady industry was terrifying, because it meant that this world could no longer sustain itself, and it meant that without help from someone, from somewhere, people would soon be thirsty, and not long after that, people would start to die.

On a sunburned hillside overlooking Freya City, Iliana Pa'Dan sat back wearily on her heels, and listened to the ominous silence. It was just over three weeks since she had abandoned ship and sent her escape capsule down through the atmosphere. She had landed fifty-five miles west of Freya—the main settlement—in desert so inhospitable that even she, with her Cardassian physiology, could not bear to be outside for more than a couple of minutes. There had been just enough charge on her personal transporter to get her to the city. She'd reached out to her contacts on the governing body, regretfully showed them the little she had been able to bring from the ship, and then tried to help as best she could. This morning she was out with a colleague trying to fix key components in a sewage-treatment system that had broken down earlier in the week. The sun had risen less than an hour ago, and already the heat was becoming too much. Beside her, her colleague, Ajud, was suffering, sweating and swearing and fumbling with the tools in their hand.

The truth was, Atalis was in a desperate situation. Pa'Dan had been the last courier willing to make the run here, and now she was grounded with the rest of them. The raiders now in control of local space had been clear: *Surrender control of this world and its resources or die of thirst.* That, Pa'Dan thought, was pretty unequivocal. But the governing body seemed paralyzed. Some wanted to surrender, at once. Others believed they could hold out. They couldn't even agree whether or not to call for help. Who would come? Only Pa'Dan had been stupid enough to try her luck with the raiders, and she was stuck here. The problem was that the people of Atalis had, in the past, made others pay for what they had to sell them: a vast number of rich and rare minerals key to di-lithium recrystallization. Some of the couriers, Pa'Dan knew, used to grumble that the people of Atalis had been holding them for ransom. She imagined that, far from being willing to come and help, they were happy to see them on the other side.

Pa'Dan scrubbed a hand across the ridges of her face, smearing them with streaks of dirt and sweat. If she thought back to a couple of years ago, when she first took this run out to Atalis, she could dimly recall that she had been attracted by the high and increasing pay rate. Now she came to think about it, she hadn't been paid at all yet. And what exactly would she buy, here on this barren red rock? Atalis was a desert. There were lizards. A great number of small and vicious insects. Some succulents. She might accept these in payment. They might soon be the only source of water left on this benighted planet . . . Pa'Dan, a product of the Cardassian diaspora, didn't mind the heat, but even Cardassians needed to drink.

Hey, everyone! Time for our daily drop of cactus juice!

Beside her, Ajud swore, emphatically, and slammed the hatch closed. "It's broken."

No shit, thought Pa'Dan. She said, "So we have to find a way to fix it."

"What with?" said Ajud. "The power of our minds? I can fiddle around with the programming in here, but ultimately the problem isn't in the computer. The problem is mechanical. The pump is busted. It needs replacing. We don't have a replacement because we're not making those parts any longer because the industrial replicators aren't working any longer either." Ajud sighed. "Sorry. Sorry. I know that you know."

Pa'Dan leaned back and closed her eyes. Three years ago, she had been a courier taking on jobs across half a dozen systems in this sector. One morning, she turned forty-five years old; waking up and looking at gray streaks in her hair, she thought, *I can't keep on living this life forever. I must have a plan.* So she called on her networks, and went out of her comfort zone, and found a handful of big jobs that put some decent money her way. All was going well, until she took on that first job to bring components to Atalis.

The problem with being rich in minerals but not much else—even succulents—was that worked best when there was an interstellar civilization bringing you everything you needed on regular supply ships. The last century or so? Not so much. Infrastructure was decaying. Water-treatment plants, the sewage works, the careful irrigation projects—all falling apart. They'd kept things going this long by keeping the mining operations going and charging vastly inflated prices. But it wasn't sustainable. More and more of their efforts had gone into simply keeping the water supply at subsistence levels. The mining had more or less stopped, which meant the money stopped. Now Atalis was without friends, and choking on dirt and shit.

Pa'Dan had done a few runs here, swearing each time that this trip would be the last. When she realized that she was literally the last courier bothering to come this way (and why would anyone else come, they weren't paying any longer), she knew she'd saddled herself with a responsibility she couldn't ignore. She kept somehow finding the parts they needed, and she kept somehow finding herself in this area of space, and she kept somehow ending up landing at Freya City and handing over what she'd found and saying, "That's fine, don't worry, we'll stick this one on the tab too." Then some adult holding hands with a snot-faced kid would start crying, and Pa'Dan would think, *I'm going to do this again, aren't I?*

But as the couriers withdrew, the black ships moved in. White Palm, they nicknamed them on Atalis, because of the markings upon the ship hulls. Pa'Dan had adopted the name. At first, they seemed like good news: they had seemed to be offering the same deal as Pa'Dan. *Don't worry, we'll stick this one on the tab.* Pa'Dan had misgivings, but that was the business of the people of Atalis and, besides, it freed her up to go off and do some other jobs. Jobs that went into her retirement fund. She didn't come to Atalis for a while. And then—about six weeks ago—a call had come out for help. She thought, *I've done my duty there*. And then she thought, *I hope they're all okay . . .* She took her little ship past.

And hit the blockade.

She got a message through to friends in Freya City, and heard the news. The White Palm raiders had decided it was payday. Their price, it turned out, was the planet.

Help, said her friends in Freya City. So Pa'Dan helped.

No good deed goes unpunished. Now she was stuck here, waiting until the planetary defense grid stuttered and collapsed, or the governing body decided they were thirsty enough—or help came.

Nobody thought that help was coming. But Pa'Dan—new to the siege—was ready to trust that someone out there was listening. "Put calls out," she said. "Ask for help. Someone will come, eventually." Six weeks on, as yet another piece of infrastructure broke off in their hands, even Pa'Dan was finding it hard to believe that anyone was coming. And Ajud was right. You couldn't mend something with wishes and thin air. Atalis was abandoned. Drought was coming. Disease was coming. Surrender, surely, was inevitable.

Pa'Dan pushed out a breath. *I'm too old for this game*. She looked at Ajud, sitting on the ground, cradling a driver.

"Are we done here?" she said. "Are we finished?" She meant the general as much as the particular, and Ajud knew it.

"I think we're getting there," Ajud said.

"I don't like losing," said Pa'Dan. "Also—if those raiders get their hands on me, they're going to string me up."

"I think they're going to string us all up."

"Like I said, I don't like losing." Pa'Dan stood up and

looked across the orange plains. "But I like dying of thirst even less."

The Alice
Nearing the Atalis system

Burnham opened her eyes. She had been dreaming again, of Vulcan, the place that was both home and not home. She was caught, she thought, in a permanent state of half-being, of permitting access only to certain parts of herself at any given time. The Vulcan self, all logic and stoicism, who had made some terrible miscalculations; the human self, of intuition and care, who had fallen disastrously in love with someone equally divided. Was that what had pulled her to Ash Tyler? she wondered now. That sense that here was someone as much split in two as she was?

"Burnham," said an increasingly familiar voice. *"Are you sleeping on the job?"*

She rolled out of her bed and hit the comm. "Book. What do you want?"

"Sahil said you were heading for Atalis."

"Yes, I am. Why are you asking?"

"Because as far as I know, it's a ball of dust up to its neck in debt. What do you know that I don't know?"

"They sent out a general distress call. I saw from Sahil's logs that they've been trying to get parts for their water-filtration infrastructure for ages now. It sounds like things are getting desperate."

"And how are they paying you?"

She didn't reply.

Book sighed. *"Burnham, we've talked about this—"*

"I can't ignore a call for help."

"That's very noble of you. But when you work for free, you bring down the price for the rest of us. It's not rocket science."

No, she thought. Rocket science had some basis in reality. Economics? It was all one great mass delusion, as far as she could see. " 'Each of us must decide,' " she quoted, " 'whether to walk in the light of creative altruism or the darkness of destructive selfishness.' "

There was a pause. *"Did you just go Vulcan on me?"*

Sometimes being half one thing, half another had its benefits.

"No, Book," she said, "I went *human* on you."

"Did you just call me selfish?"

"If the shoe fits, Book—"

"Yeah, well, you know what I say to that?"

This should be good. "I'd like to hear what you have to say back to one of the most revered philosophers from a world renowned for its philosophical thinking."

" '*Help someone, you make a friend. Help someone too much—you make an enemy.*' "

" 'It is in giving that we receive.' "

" '*Give too much of yourself, you end up with nobody.*' "

" 'Pay it forward.' Look, is this why you took the time to contact me? So we could throw *bon mots* at each other? I mean, it's fun, but this is time that I could be using sleeping."

She thought maybe she heard him laugh. *"Okay. I was just checking in. You're an adult, and you can make your own decisions. Just . . . make sure you have the full facts, yes? You might be missing something without even realizing it. Book out."*

"Bye, Book," she said, to thin air, feeling strangely bereft. She hadn't assumed he would offer to help, surely? Why would he, after all? What did the people of Atalis have to offer him? But still it was something of a shock to realize that she was on her own. Still, perhaps she should be encouraged by this. Perhaps she was beginning to look more competent than she felt. She tweaked the collar of the leather jacket slung on the back of the chair. Wear the uniform long enough, she thought, and it will seep into the skin.

"All right," she said, to the little space around her. "Let's show him. Let's make this a success."

The Alice
Approaching Atalis IV

Entering the Atalis system, Burnham began to pick up encrypted comm signals. Putting her standard decryption routines to work, she set about contacting the people on Atalis. Using the frequency on which she had received the distress signal, she sent out her own message. "This is the independent freighter *Alice* calling Atalis IV. We got your distress call. We're here to help. Can you let us know the problem?"

That *we*, she used instinctively. Always better to let people think you were legion.

"Atalis IV. Is there anyone down there? Can you hear this message? Can you signal in some way that you're there?"

Nothing. And then—from nowhere, a ship. Sleek and black.

Where the hell did that come from?

Scrabbling at the controls, Burnham was deeply conscious of how vulnerable her little ship was. Limited weapons capability. Shields solid enough to protect her against the usual wear and tear of space, but certainly not against a concerted attack from even one other ship.

"Courier ship, state your business."

"Hey," she said, scanning her sensor readings with increasing alarm at the firepower currently pointing at her. "I'm just answering a call I got for assistance—"

"The situation on Atalis is under control. You can leave."

Then she saw the markings on the ship. White, like a handprint. She took a deep breath. "I guess," she said, "I'd like to hear that from someone on the planet's surface?"

The ship hung there. Silently. Burnham thought, *And the most irritating thing is that Book told me not to come here.*

And then, *"We've opened a channel to the surface. Go ahead, courier ship."*

Burnham found the transmission. A voice came through. *"This is Soce Foy of the Governing Body of Atalis. Who is this?"*

"Atalis IV, it's good to hear from you. This is Michael Burnham, on the courier ship *Alice*. I'm answering a call I received."

"We've put out no call for help in some weeks."

Yet she had received one only a couple of days ago. Burnham thought quickly. Perhaps they were using channels the raiders knew nothing about. Perhaps this person she was speaking to knew nothing either. So she didn't want to reveal too much over this channel. She said, "You sent a message a while back, asking for components for water-reclamation systems."

"You find us short of ready cash right now," said the person on the ground. *"And, in fact, you find us in the middle of trying to settle the bill with our friends here."*

Burnham was watching the display in front of her. A signal was coming through, on the same channel that had sent the distress call a few days ago. She set her decryption protocols to work and stalled for time. "So our friends here want to be paid?" she said. "I'm guessing—dilithium?"

"What else," said the person on the surface. *"I don't suppose you happen to have any?"*

"Not today. What if I came back with some?"

There was a brief pause.

"Dilithium," said the voice from the raider ship, *"would go a long way to reducing the debt."*

"And what's in it for me?" said Burnham.

"We don't blast you out of the sky?" suggested the raider pilot.

"That would be nice," said Burnham. "All right. Can I go now?"

"You can go," said the pilot. *"Don't come back empty-handed. Better still—don't come back."*

"So long, Burnham," said the voice from the ground. *"Thanks for swinging by."*

Carefully, she steered the ship away. The raider ship did not move, but her sensors showed how carefully she was being monitored. As she moved farther out of range, the console chimed to let her know the files were decrypted. She read through.

"The people of Atalis IV request help. The planet has been subject to a blockade from raider ships for the past six weeks. The White Palm ships had, until recently, been supplying essential components for water-reclamation and sewage-treatment plants. They are now demanding full payment, or else the surrender of this world and its resources. Atalis is in no position to pay. The situation here is deteriorating rapidly. Water is severely rationed. There are outbreaks of disease in several settlements. There may soon be insufficient power to maintain the planetary defense grid. Help is needed. Urgent help. Please—help."

Burnham listened to the transmission several times. *Help*, she thought. *Who else was there? Who else was going to come and help?*

The Alice
Beyond Atalis local space
"So . . . it didn't all go according to plan?"

Burnham glared at Book. At least he wasn't smirking.

"There's a blockade around the planet. Nothing's getting in, nothing's getting out. Communications blackout too, pretty much. I picked up an encrypted transmission. I don't know how long they've got, but it can't be very long. The raiders are asking for payment in dilithium."

"*You know that's most likely a con, don't you? You bring them dilithium, they take it and then blow you out of the sky?*"

"Yes, of course," she said, impatiently. "But at least it will allow me to get close again to Atalis—"

"*Why would you ever want to get close again to Atalis?*"

"Book, are you listening? There's a quarter of a million people down there. They've already got outbreaks of disease. They're facing drought—"

"*Then they shouldn't have gouged everyone for their goods and they definitely shouldn't have done deals with pirates.*"

"They put out call after call for help. I was there! In Sahil's office! You heard him talking about it!"

"*Burnham, I can't help everyone! It's just not possible. I can't conjure up what they need from nowhere. Somebody somewhere along the line has to pay.*"

"Your system is insane. It's cruel."

"*I didn't make the rules.*"

"Nobody's making the rules! That's the problem!"

"*Yeah, I know, I know—everything was better back when the flag was flying. Three cheers for Starfleet! Long live the Federation! Oh no, wait, that didn't happen. Because the Federation isn't around any longer. And you know what—maybe the people of Atalis need to face up to the reality of that. Maybe they need to understand what the reality of their world is—*"

"What do you mean by that, Book?"

"*What I mean—is that their world can't sustain their way of life any longer. They've been living on borrowed time since the Burn. So either they let someone come in and run the place for them, or they realize they're done and they move on.*"

Burnham sat back, shocked. "You think they should leave their *home?*"

"*If their home is about to become a plague-infested desert, then yes.*"

"These people didn't choose to settle there. They were born on Atalis. That isn't just! That isn't fair!"

"No, I never said it was fair. Nothing's fair about this, Burnham—"

"There's a quarter of a million of them—"

"Yes, I know, and they should have started on this years ago. What kept them there? They were greedy. They wanted to keep their hands on the mineral deposits."

She shook her head. "It's their home."

"Maybe, but they kept raising the prices. Well, you can't eat rocks, and you can't buy goodwill, and they're learning that now the hard way. And you need to step away. You can't get involved."

"I'm already involved."

"It isn't your problem!"

"They can't do this alone. They need help. They need *somebody* to help!"

"But why does it have to be you*?"*

"Who *else* is there, Book? Who else cares?" She gripped the console. "You said it yourself. The Federation is gone. Starfleet is gone. But who is going to fill that gap? I'm all there is." Her voice faded away. She was gripped, suddenly, with doubt. Was she fooling herself? Imagining herself as some sort of paladin, the last defender of a set of values that everyone else had set aside. "Somebody has to help these people."

"True believer, huh?" He sighed. *"Well, I guess I'm not going to be able to stop you. But do you know exactly what you're getting yourself into? Do you know anything about these raiders? If they're lone operators? If there's someone bigger backing them?"*

"Is that likely?"

"It's possible. And if you keep taking these kinds of jobs, Burnham, you're going to attract the wrong kind of attention.

Couriers fly below the radar. Take the job, get the job done. They don't try to clean up the sector while they're at it."

"You mean like you didn't, when you risked yourself to save Molly?"

He raised an eyebrow at her. *"All right,"* he said. *"What do you need from me?"*

"You know what I need. I need what everyone else needs."

He sat back in his chair. He glared at her. *"Dilithium, huh?"*

"Dilithium. Enough to save a planet."

"You don't ask for much, do you, Burnham?"

"I set my sights high, that's true."

"Trouble is, I've seen you plunging from those heights."

"Book," she said. "We have to help."

He stooped to pick up Grudge. *"All right,"* he said. *"I have an idea. I'm sending you some coordinates so we can rendez-vous. But you should realize, Burnham, that the people of Atalis probably won't thank you for your efforts on their behalf. Book out."*

"We'll see," she murmured to herself. "We'll see."

Radok Sien Mercantile Exchange

Outside the Radok Sien mercantile, two scruffy couriers, each in black leather, greeted each other less than enthusiastically. "Hi, Book," said the woman.

"Hi, Burnham," the man said back.

"Thanks for coming," said the woman.

"Well, someone has to fish you out of trouble," said the man. "Last time you got a full dose of pento-spray and told everyone you were a time traveler."

"As I recall, that was because you'd just sold me out—"

"I hope," said Book, "that we're not keeping score. Because you caused me a lot of trouble that day."

"I'm not keeping score," said Burnham. "I'm . . . remembering the good times we've had."

He gave a snort of laughter. "You're a troubled woman."

"Never denied it," she said. "You said you had an idea."

"Yup. There's a cargo coming through today. A cargo that is most certainly relevant to our interests."

"Oh yes?" She looked past him across the street. "And how did you hear about this?"

"I have contacts."

"I dread to think. So how do you intend to *pay* for it?"

He didn't reply. Burnham, turning her head to look directly at him, saw that he was grinning. The damned Cheshire Cat again. "I don't intend to pay for it, Burnham. I intend to steal it."

"Oh," said Burnham, looking back across the street again. "What could *possibly* go wrong?"

———

Planning a heist, as any connoisseur of the genre can tell you, requires planning, precision, and chutzpah. Book, it transpired, had brought only one of these to the operation, and this, in large part, was one reason why he and Burnham found themselves, a few hours later, sprinting through the streets behind the Radok Sien mercantile, pursued by armed guards.

"I thought you said you had a plan!" yelled Burnham.

"I said I had an idea! That's not the same as a plan!" Book yelled back. "You're the one who wanted to come here and get this damn stuff!"

To be fair to Book, Burnham thought, as they sped through a crowded marketplace that reeked of fish and the gamier sort of meat, at least they had laid their eyes on the dilithium. Or, more accurately, the crate in which the dilithium was being transported. And then—Burnham assumed some kind of virtual trip wire had been, well, tripped, since a whole bunch of alarms started sounding, and huge people brandishing big weapons started heading toward them at a speed you would not expect given their size.

"Wrong code!" Book yelled, as he dragged Burnham. "We shouldn't have caused all that trouble at Requiem City!"

"If only I knew how to go back in time!" she yelled back at him.

"I'm touched you'd come to help me!"

"I meant—I'd go straight home and leave you here, you damned idiot!"

Leaving the stink and confusion of the market, they sped around a corner and hit a wall. Literally, in Book's case. He grabbed his nose and Burnham saw blood. "*Shit!*" he shouted. "*Shit!* That *hurt!*"

"Book," she said, in quiet and urgent tones, "shut up."

"It fucking *hurts*, Burnham!"

"Of course it hurts. It's broken. Now shut up."

"*Mmph*," he said, from behind his hand. She poked her head around the corner. Two heavies, coming past the nearest stall, saw her, and shouted out.

"Shit!" she said, and ducked behind the corner. "Personal transporters, we've got to get out of here, now!" She pulled hers out. Full charge. "Book, where's your transporter?"

He pulled his out. It wasn't fully charged. He grinned at her—and slammed the button on her transporter. "See ya later, Burnham!" she just about heard, as the beam pulled her away. And she revised her criteria for successful heists—planning, precision, chutzpah, and a damn sight more luck than either of them was accustomed to.

Book's ship
Radok Sien docking area

Burnham collapsed into Book's usual seat in front of the flight console. Grudge, jumping up in front of her, stalked across the display and gave an interrogative, "*Mnao?*"

Burnham reached out and ruffled her fur. "I know. Just me on this occasion. Sorry about that. The damn regulators have him."

"*Mkgnao!*" said Grudge.

"No, I've no idea what to do. What do you think I should do, Grudge?"

"*Mrkgnao!*" she replied, which could, Burnham figured, be some really good advice or else just a request that food be supplied immediately. She fed the beast just in case, which seemed to make Grudge happy. At least that was one of them. She opened the comms and found local police channels. She soon heard reports of a man matching Book's description being detained and found out where they were taking him. She hunted down the specs of the detainment facility inside the regulators' zone at the mercantile. *Dammit! What do I know about jail breaks? Last time around, Lorca got me out!* She suspected she was going to need help this time too, so she started looking hurriedly through Book's most recent logs. *Assistance,* she thought. *Who can I call on for assistance . . . ?* If that meant calling in a few favors, then so be it. The trouble was finding someone to help. People weren't near enough, or were caught up in their own problems, or wouldn't respond. Eventually, she managed to reach Brodie, whom she had met, of a fashion, at the Necropolis, and whom she knew had at least owed Book enough of a favor at one point to put himself in the firing line. But Brodie shook his head.

"Radok Sien is bad news these days."

"Bad news?"

"It's under Leavitt's protection. You don't mess with him."

"But Book's in trouble."

"He shouldn't have gone to Radok Sien. And if he wasn't up on that piece of news, then maybe he should spend less time showing off to beautiful new couriers—"

"Doing what now?"

"—and more time out there on his business. Brodie out."

The holographic image winked and was gone.

"Creep," said Burnham to the space left behind. Grudge looked up from her supper.

"Mnao."

"You and me both, queen." Burnham began to make her own plan.

Radok Sien Mercantile Exchange

In the end, the plan was nothing more complicated than heading over to the regulators' zone in the exchange, triggering the fire alarms with a few smoking flares, waiting till the prisoners were evacuated, then swinging a few punches, dodging the ones that came her way, and running like hell into the warren of streets outside the mercantile. One of the punches (in the haze, Burnham could not entirely be sure it wasn't one of hers) landed on Book's nose with a *crunch*.

"Dammit, Burnham!" he howled, as they pelted away. "Is this how they taught you to fight in Starfleet?"

"You can go back to your cell if you prefer!" she shouted back.

"I'll take what's on offer!" he squawked. Behind them, someone fired a shot. They ran down the nearest alley, and dived for cover behind a huge gray container, trying to keep their breathing quiet. After a moment or two, they heard people running past, voices shouting, heading off into the distance. Burnham rested her head against the container. There was something familiar about it.

Laughter bubbled up within her. She suppressed it, but she pulled the sleeve of Book's jacket. "Book," she whispered, and gestured to the container. "It's the dilithium."

He gave her a look that said: *You're kidding me.*

She shook her head.

He smiled.

She smiled. She reached into her satchel and pulled out the extra personal transporter that she'd brought for him. She handed this to him. She boosted the range on her device, like he had shown her, and watched him do the same. Then they gave each other a contented look.

Payday!

Book's ship
Leaving the Sien system

They fell, laughing, into the seats in front of the flight console of Book's ship. "Ow . . ." he said. "Mustn't laugh. Ow!" Grudge, trotting toward them, took one look at his face, and ran to hide under the bed. He scowled and winced. "Heartbreaker," he muttered.

"Shall we get this boat up in the air?" Burnham said.

"I guess we should."

They used her courier codes to get permission to leave local space, but not before Book showed her a neat trick to shield a cargo of dilithium. "Might give the game away," he said, holding a cloth to his face. "And I'd hate for us to attract any passing pirates."

Once they were out of local space and heading out of the system, they sat simply staring at the container. "Will you look at the size of this thing?" Book said. His face was beatific.

"You keep looking at it like that and Grudge is going to leave you," said Burnham. Grudge, hearing her name, poked her head out from under the bed and hissed.

Book looked at her lovingly. "Never anyone but you, sweetheart," he murmured. "Think of the kibble this will get you." He looked at Burnham. "What are you going to do with your half?"

Burnham leaned back and twisted a braid of hair between her fingers. "You really want to know?"

"Yes, actually, I do," said Book, swinging in his chair. "What does a thousand-year-old time traveler yearning for better days do with the amount of latinum that will shortly be coming her way?"

"You won't like it."

"I'm sure I won't."

She took a deep breath. "All right, then. I'm going to give some to Sahil to help maintain the ships he has in flight."

He gave a snort of laughter. "I knew you were going to do something *good*."

"I'm going to keep some for a rainy day."

"I'm glad to hear that. And what about the rest?"

This was the part he was really going to hate. "You know what I'm going to do. I'm going to hire half a dozen ships and end the blockade of Atalis."

He stared at her. His face was a mess. "With *all* of it?"

"Yes, with all of it," said Burnham. "Can I interest you in a job?"

"No way am I going anywhere near Atalis."

"I'm not asking you to go anywhere near Atalis. I want you to be my middleman. Broker the deals. Help me get the ships. Your contacts are better than mine." She wouldn't mention, she thought, that none of them had answered the call to help break him out of jail. But then she hadn't been waving dilithium in their faces when she asked.

Book looked at her through narrow eyes. "That's all?"

"That's all," she said.

He turned around back to the console and began to busy himself. Grudge, seeing he had turned away, crept out from under the bed and sidled toward them. "You," he said, "are off your trolley."

"My what now?"

"Off your trolley. Not right in the head."

"Oh, I see," she said. "Perhaps. You'll do it though, won't you?"

"Burnham," he said, "what do you think I'm doing right now?"

"Did we discuss a fee?"

"I was coming to that."

Grudge had jumped up onto her knee. She clasped her arms around the beast, bent to hide her face in the soft fur, and smiled.

The Alice
Entering the Atalis system

Burnham made her rendezvous with the other courier ships outside the Atalis system and briefed them on the mission. Their main concern was how they would get paid.

"When the raiders are gone, and we've visited the surface, we'll meet Book at the Cler mercantile. The dilithium is there." There was some displeasure about this—as if she had brought them out there under false pretenses—but she cut through the complaints. "If you want to go—go now. I don't have time to waste with anyone who is not entirely on board. But stay, and help me, and you'll get your share of the biggest stash of dilithium that Book has ever seen."

One of the couriers decided against, leaving Burnham with eleven ships, including her own. Their encounter with the raiders was short and bitter. Burnham took point—announcing herself to the raiders, offering the promised dilithium to draw them out. After that, it was a matter of who was overwhelmed first. The others used a combination of courier tricks: manipulated sensor readings to give the impression of vastly more powerful weapons systems; faked comm chatter to give the impression that more ships were on the way. And there was some honest-to-goodness crisp flying and sharp shooting. Burnham's little ship proved ideal here: swift, maneuverable, and with just enough firepower at close enough range to disable ships for long enough for someone else to move in and finish them off. By the time the raiders began to withdraw, the couriers were two ships down to five of the black raider ships. It was enough. "Keep away from Atalis," said Burnham, as the last ship pulled back. "This world is defended."

There was quiet after that. The courier ships regrouped and took stock. Repairs began; assistance was given. Burnham hailed the planet below.

"This is Michael Burnham on the courier ship *Alice*. The blockade is over. Repeat—the blockade is over."

She got no reply. She tried the secure channel that had been used to contact her before, but, again, there was nothing. Brodie, who had come along on this trip—the promise of dilithium had swung it—spoke to her. *"What's going on?"*

"Nothing from down there."

"Perhaps their comm system is busted along with everything else."

"Perhaps." Burnham began to suit up. There was only one way to find out. Five minutes later, she was standing in the central plaza of Freya City, and raising her hands as a troop of armed police raised their weapons at her.

Freya City
Atalis

"You know," Burnham said, "all things considered, this is not the welcome I was expecting." She kept her hands up, palms out, showing she was no threat. "Any chance I could speak to someone in charge?"

Burnham heard a whirring noise—a skimmer, large but past its prime, was descending into the plaza, throwing up red dust all around. Her eyes were quickly full of dirt and grit, but she didn't dare bring her hands down to cover her face. At last, the skimmer landed, with a grinding noise, and the hatch opened. Three figures, civilians, Burnham thought, came out. One came marching up to Burnham. They looked furious.

"Who the hell are you?" they said to Burnham.

"Michael Burnham. And in case you hadn't noticed, I just ended the blockade around your planet—"

"I know you did, you damn idiot," they spat back.

"Excuse me? Who are *you*, exactly?"

"I'm Soce Foy," they said. "I'm the head of the Governing Body of Atalis, and I was about an hour away from making a deal with the leader of those raiders. What the hell do you think you're doing here?"

Burnham, lowering her hands, looked back in horror. "We spoke before—"

"We did no such thing," they said, and then called around. "Pa'Dan! Someone find Pa'Dan! Get her here." Soce Foy swung their attention back to Burnham. "Do you realize what you've done today? The deal I was making would have secured this world's future—saved people's lives. But not only that— those raiders are going to think I've double-crossed them. When they come back—and they will come back—they'll want more than I was offering today. If I'm lucky. If I'm not lucky, they'll come in shooting."

Another skimmer was landing. Burnham shielded her mouth, and, when the skimmer landed, rubbed some of the grit from her eyes. The hatch opened, and a woman—gray skinned, and with ridges on her face and neck—was more or less thrown out. Soce Foy, turning back to Burnham, said, "Here's your associate."

"My what?"

"I assume you and she came up with this together. I don't know what your intention was, and I don't know who is paying you, or why. But you've both caused a great deal of damage today. The White Palm don't take double-dealing lightly. Leave Atalis now," said Soce Foy, "or you won't be leaving at all."

Pa'Dan had made her way across to Burnham. Turning to her, she mouthed, *Help?*

Burnham sighed, and shook her head. What else was she supposed to do? Reaching into her satchel, she pulled out her spare transporter. "Thank you," muttered Pa'Dan.

"Don't say a word," said Burnham.

"Go now," said Soce Foy. "Both of you. And don't come back."

The Alice
Leaving the Atalis system

"Sit over there on the bunk and don't speak," Burnham said to Pa'Dan, who obeyed. Burnham took her own seat at the flight controls, contacted the other ships and gave them the details to rendezvous with Book, and then began to chart her own course away from Atalis. Once they were under way, she sat staring at Jeremiah's map for a while, collecting her thoughts. At last, she turned around in her chair.

Pa'Dan was slumped on the bunk, chin upon her chest, clearly exhausted. Hearing Burnham move, she looked up. "Sorry," she said. "I'm sorry."

"Do you want to explain to me," Burnham demanded, "what the *hell* just happened?"

There was a pause—and then Burnham listened as the whole story came tumbling out. Pa'Dan's repeated trips to Atalis. Her last trip, losing her ship. The weeks under blockade, out with the engineers, trying to patch together systems long past their breaking point.

"What happened?" said Burnham.

"I found out the governing body was cutting a deal. And that I was part of the deal. So I sent out a call for help." Which Burnham had answered. Pa'Dan shook her head and went on, "I'd pissed off those raiders too often, I guess. Still— you'd think there'd be a little gratitude. You know," she said thoughtfully, "I never did get paid."

"Well," said Burnham, after Pa'Dan finished. "I feel a little less bad about breaking up their deal with the raiders now."

"Me too," said Pa'Dan fervently. The two women shared tentative smiles.

"I'm inclined to cut you a little slack," said Burnham, "but I'll be honest and say that given the losses I'm facing, I'm not particularly inclined to take you wherever you want."

"There's nowhere for me to be," said Pa'Dan. "Where are you heading?"

"Cler Mercantile Exchange. You know it?"

"I know it well," said Pa'Dan. "That's as good a place as any. If you don't mind."

"I don't mind," said Burnham. "Glad to have company." She nodded at the shower. "Clean up. Get some sleep. I've got some things to do here."

Pa'Dan nodded, and stood up, swaying slightly.

"One question," said Burnham. "White Palm? Is that what they're called?"

"It's a nickname we gave to the raiders. Because of the markings on the ships. You know?"

"Oh yes," said Burnham softly. "I do know."

Cler Mercantile Exchange

It turned out she was right about having company. Pa'Dan was smart, dry, and certainly knew her way around this part of space. "More than twenty years a courier," she said. "And there I was, thinking of retirement. Oh, I loved that little ship," she went on, regretfully. "But you shouldn't get attached to anything in this life, should you?"

Burnham had to agree.

They fell into a comfortable pattern; sharing the small space, swapping out to use the bunk, but also spending time in conversation. At some point, Burnham decided to trust Pa'Dan with her own story.

"Well," said Pa'Dan. "What can I say? I hope you find your ship. Your friends. I mean, I don't know what your chances are, but I hope you beat the odds."

"So do I," said Burnham, softly.

At length, they reached Cler, and Burnham made contact with Book, confirming that payment had been made to her little fleet.

"Sorry again," said Pa'Dan, who knew now exactly what the cost had been. "I'd say I'll pay you back but . . . Not likely, is it? But you've got a friend."

Burnham smiled. "That'll do for now."

They transported down to the mercantile and made contact with Book. He'd heard part of the story—not all, Burnham wanted to steel herself to tell him that—and greeted

Pa'Dan with interest. "So you're the reason Burnham raised a private army and took on a pack of raiders?"

"And you're the man who keeps breaking his nose?"

"Touché," said Book, with a smile.

Pa'Dan looked around the mercantile. "No place like home." She sighed and hoisted her pack onto her shoulders.

"What are you going to do next?" asked Burnham.

"Find a ship. Start again." She looked exhausted saying it. "You know, Atalis was just a job. It wasn't my world. I'd never been there until a couple of years ago. But I'd been hoping to do a world a favor and call it the place where I was going to settle, slow things down, move toward retirement."

"The courier life doesn't come with a pension plan," said Book.

"Let me tell you two right now, you're going to want to think about it," said Pa'Dan. "Because one morning you'll wake up and you'll be tired just at the thought of rolling out of bed. And you won't be as sharp, and you won't be as quick and it will all come on you so fast that you won't know what's hit you—" She stopped herself. "Anyway. Those are my problems. You two have done enough already. You didn't have to bring me here, not after . . ."

"I chose to come to Atalis," Burnham said softly. "I wouldn't have done anything else. I *couldn't* have done anything else. You'll stay in touch, yes?"

"I will," said Pa'Dan. "And with luck, one day I'll be able to pay back some of what I owe you." She raised her hand, held it up palm outward. Seeing Burnham looking at it in puzzlement, she said, "Cardassian greeting. We press palms."

Burnham smiled and put her palm against the older woman's hand.

"Wait," said Book. He was pulling something from his bag. "Here's something that will help you get back on your feet."

He handed over a little box. Pa'Dan, opening it, said, "Dili—"

"Yes, yes," he said, gruffly. "Don't go shouting out about it. Someone will have it out of your hand."

Burnham's eyebrows shot up. This was, surely, his cut from ending the blockade of Atalis . . . She caught his eye. *Thank you.*

I must have lost my mind, he seemed to be saying back to her, but with a rueful smile.

Pa'Dan stashed the box away, looking considerably more cheerful, and went on her way. Burnham, watching her go, felt overcome with sadness. Was this where the courier life led? Did good people, after years of hard work, find themselves without anything? Was this where she might be, twenty years from now?

She felt a hand upon her shoulder. She turned to look up at Book. "You didn't have to do that, you know."

"Yeah, I think I did," he said. "Anyway, I've got something to show you."

He led her over to a console and fired up a hologram. The picture was poor quality. She peered closely. "What am I looking at?"

"Take your time," he said.

She looked back at the holo. A black cylinder, maybe eight inches long, an inch in diameter, with gray caps at either end. Four dull orange panels on the side—lights, perhaps, when powered up? She altered the setting to zoom in, and saw numbers and letters scratched on the surface. Not all clear, but enough to make sense of the whole.

NC*4*7*-E

They sent a jolt through her. "Oh my," she murmured. "Oh my."

"Do you know what it is?" said Book.

"It's a black box."

"It's a black box. Do you want a closer look?"

"Of course I do!" She turned to him, eyes shining. How had this come up? she wondered. Of all the things he could have been checking out, how had this come to his attention? "Book," she said, "have you been looking out for these?"

He was faintly embarrassed. "I couldn't believe how much you got for those ship plaques," he said. "I thought I might start a sideline in memorabilia."

"So purely selfish motives," she said.

They stared at each other. "Well," he said, "what other motives are there?"

That line won't wash forever, mister, she thought. "You've certainly hit the target with this."

"Just to point one thing out, Burnham," he said, "but the longer we spend gawping at the damn thing, the more the price tag goes up. Because they can see you're interested."

Damn this money economy, she thought. She was constantly getting caught out by these kinds of things. "Doesn't there come a point where they price me out of the market?"

"There does," he said, "but the algorithm is pretty good at working out where your breaking point is. The price is still going up, you know."

She stared at the box, at the partially decipherable set of letters and numbers. She thought of asking him what she should do, but she knew his answer: *Let the past go, Burnham. The Burn happened a long time ago. Everything has moved on. You have to live in the present. Live in the moment. Looking back will only bring heartbreak.* She thought of Sahil, waiting patiently for a messenger from a lost world—who finally arrived.

"I want it," she said. "I want to know what it has to tell me."

"Just so you understand," Book said, "that it's going to

cost you almost everything you've got left of your unbelievably dwindling supply of—"

"I understand," she said, and cut the deal.

Later, when she'd collected the merchandise, she brought it back to show Book.

"Success?" he said.

"Yes."

"Can I see it?"

She looked at him curiously. "I thought you weren't interested in relics from the past?"

"Show me the damn thing, Burnham."

Carefully, she lifted it out, and cradled it in her hands. Tough, durable, and so very small.

"Well," said Book, quietly. "Look at that."

"I know," she said, tears in her eyes. She felt something close to awe, like when she had visited the temple on Mount Seleya or at Delphi. Fragments of a lost and glorious past, that seemed somehow hallowed by the very fact of their unlikely survival. "What do you think?"

"What do *I* think?" Book laughed. "I think they saw you coming!"

"You don't feel it?" She looked up at him—preparing to be disappointed. But she saw that whatever he'd said, his face too was full of awe.

"I feel it, Burnham. I really do."

The Back Forty
Former Federation Spaceport Devaloka

Burnham timed her arrival for morning tea, and Sahil welcomed her with quiet delight. When she showed him the black box, he was enchanted. "What a miraculous find!" he said. "I know you were so disappointed that your own was missing, Commander. I am so glad you have found this."

"Can Jeremiah help get the data off it?"

"I should imagine that if anyone can help us, it will be him."

They finished the tea and headed down to the Back Forty. "He's had no luck yet with your data chip," said Sahil. "I believe the thing has become something of a matter of honor now."

The old man, when they showed him the black box, was fascinated. "I've never seen one before," he admitted, turning it around in his hands. "Clever of Book to think of this."

"He's a man of hidden depths," said Burnham. "Well-hidden depths."

Jeremiah was already at work, with a bunch of sensors and a scanner, hooking the cylinder up. He found a panel, attached it to the sensors, and said, "If there's anything on it, we'll see it here."

Burnham and Sahil watched him work. "What did this cost you, Burnham?" asked Sahil, quietly.

"Let's say that I didn't make my fortune on that last run," she replied. She looked him straight in the eye. "There are too many questions unanswered," she said, quietly. "And . . . I do not like unanswered questions. No Starfleet officer does."

He smiled at her. It was like a warm glow emanating from him. She felt comforted, after the disastrous time she'd had. Perhaps it had been worth it, to bring this back to him. "I'm very glad to hear that," he said. "I have many unanswered questions too. And I appreciate you using all that you earned to help answer them."

On the panel, data was starting to scroll past. "Now we're getting somewhere!" said the old man, with satisfaction.

Burnham and Sahil leaned over the display. She stopped the text scrolling; went back to the start.

"The *U.S.S. Yelchin*," Sahil said. "NCC-4774-E." He sighed. "Well, now we know something about them."

It was strange, Burnham thought, how a string of numbers and letters could sound almost like poetry. To hear him rattle that off . . . Everyday language, once upon a time. Now he might as well be reading something out to her in Latin or ancient Greek. She wondered what the ship had been like; who had crewed her; the story behind its name. She touched her heart, saluting what had been lost.

More data was streaming from the box. Details of the ship's last flight, routinely collected from all the ship's sensors, more information than she could process at once. She would have to set up some kind of analysis. She would eventually, she guessed, know as much about the *Yelchin* as its long-lost captain. And then, abruptly, the stream of data stopped.

"Hold on," she said. "Go back. Was that it?"

Sahil scrolled back up. She saw what she was looking for. A stardate. She read off the numbers. "81986-mark-272129. That's it," she said. "That's the moment it happened. The Burn."

All three of them stood in silence, looking down at the display. They all, Burnham thought, lived with the reality of that event, but to see the moment of its happening laid out so starkly. What must they have felt, on this ship? Did they fully understand? Had they grasped at once the enormity of what had happened, or was it too much? Could they have foreseen where the Federation would be, where Starfleet would be?

"More of these," she murmured. "We need more of these." She was aware of Sahil smiling at her. "What?" she said. "What is it?"

"Your mission, Commander," he said. "You've found it at last."

She shook her head. "I don't need a mission, Sahil. I have a living to earn."

"You've been spending too much time with Mr. Booker, I think," he said.

"Book," she corrected him, automatically. "And maybe you're right. But I have a lot to learn from him."

"I think," he said softly, "that he has at least as much to learn from you." He turned back to the data stream. "Look," he said. "Personnel files. The last crew of the *U.S.S. Yelchin.*"

She looked back down. Names were scrolling past on the display. Captain Namid Hacquin. Commander Iryi Roala, XO. Commander Reiko Kamada, Chief Medical Officer. Lieutenant Commander Grace Kavanagh, Chief Science Officer. On and on the list went, right down to the officers who ran the ship's day care. She wiped her face and thought of *Discovery.* Her crew, her comrades, her friends. Saru, Tilly, Detmer, Stamets. They, too, were caught in the crossfire of a terrible disaster. They had promised to come after her . . . to find her. She'd sent her signal to guide them through, but she had lost them. She thought of the flight recorder on *Discovery.* Would she want somebody, finding that, to ask questions? To find out about their mission? To remember them, even after they were gone? She would, of course she would. She would want their actions honored, their bravery remembered, their names turned into a blessing. She touched the black box. Perhaps she did owe something to these people. Perhaps she could find some answers to the question of what happened on that terrible day, in that dreadful moment.

Surely, that was all she could do. She could not restore what was lost. She could not, alone, awaken a dead civilization. All she could do was lay the ghosts to rest. Say good-bye. And move on. Move on. *I have so many to grieve for*, she thought. *All of my own—and all of these. All of Starfleet.*

She felt a hand upon her shoulder. "Don't give up yet, Commander," Sahil said softly. "I believe—I truly believe—that you will see them all again, one day."

True believers, she thought. *Are we the last?*

Command Center
Starbase Vanguard
"A *heist?*"

Silence fell around the command center. People busied themselves at their consoles, hoping not to attract attention, relieved not to be the bearer of this bad news, sorry for the junior officer to whom the unlucky task of telling their chief had fallen. Remington did not realize exactly how formidable she could be. Often this was inspirational; sometimes it could be terrifying.

This purchase of dilithium from a vendor operating through the Radok Sien mercantile had been, they all knew, one of the many quiet incursions that were under way in the sectors of space opened up by their recent acquisition of this starbase. Ships, scouts, informants—all out around multiple systems. Gathering intelligence; making contacts; doing business. Establishing—well, a vanguard.

"What happened?" said Remington, at last. "Do we have any idea?" Her tone of voice, everyone was relieved to hear, was measured, thoughtful. The shock of the news was clearly beginning to wear off. She was now in pursuit of information, which meant she was now trying to decide her next move.

"The shipment had reached the mercantile when a fire alarm was set off. The whole exchange was evacuated. Someone must have moved the shipment." There was a brief pause as the young officer took a breath. "And when everything died down, it couldn't be found. More than a dozen ships had left by then, none of them showing any sign of a cargo of dilithium." His voice died away.

"A fire alarm was set off?"

"Yes, ma'am."

"And that fooled local law enforcement?"

"Apparently so, ma'am."

"I see. Any names?"

"Someone was arrested earlier in the day for entering the mercantile with an amber-flagged courier code. A man named Cleveland Booker, ma'am."

"Booker," said Remington, thoughtfully. She never forgot a name. "Is he still there?"

"He seems to have escaped custody."

"Well," said Remington, at last. "It increasingly sounds as if these sectors are even more chaotic than we anticipated, and local law enforcement is not entirely up to the task." Her staff watched her surreptitiously. Remington did not like chaos. She liked order. "Which should make our presence here more welcome, I imagine." She gave a rather chilly smile that made some of the staff avert their eyes. "In some quarters, at least."

The storm clouds had passed—or headed in another direction. Everyone quietly returned to work. After a few minutes, another junior officer—taking a deep breath—came forward to speak to her.

"Ma'am, there's news from Atalis."

Remington eyed the young woman thoughtfully. "Go on, Raud."

"There seems to have been some activity in local space—"

"Activity?"

"The blockade is over."

"*Is* it? And to whom are the people of Atalis indebted now?"

"It seems that an alliance of courier ships was formed. There's some haziness about the number of ships involved—they seem to have very effective ways of scrambling ships' sensors. It could be anywhere between ten and twenty-five."

"That's something of a margin of error," said Remington.

"Yes, ma'am."

"Something we'll need to bear in mind if ever we're dealing with couriers." Remington paused for a moment's thought. "There was a courier on the ground on Atalis, wasn't there? If our intelligence was correct?"

"That's right, ma'am."

"Do we have any names?"

"The name Burnham keeps coming up."

"Burnham," said Remington—who did not forget a name. "An alliance of couriers. Interesting. I didn't think they were so well integrated."

"All our intelligence pointed to a much looser network, ma'am. But we've observed several examples of mutual aid now."

"Yes, we have," said Remington. "Well, perhaps we should find out a little more about the couriers. Let's get some jobs out onto the mercantiles. Money will draw them here, I'm sure."

The young officer nodded and went on her way. *Couriers*, thought Remington. Could they hold the key? She preferred to make use of existing structures. The alternative was messy. *Couriers. Burnham. Book.*

COUNCILOR PRIYA TAGORE
PERSONAL LOG

We are back from our week in the mountains refreshed and relaxed, and we have, it seems, timed the holiday to perfection. Last week the heat in the capital reached its peak and we would have had to stay indoors for much of the afternoon. No particular hardship, but instead we were able to enjoy cool mountain air, hike up into the hills. We have visited the Northern Peaks every summer since Joshi was born, but this year was the first time he has attempted Mount Keru with us, and the first time I have attempted it since he was born. Ravi took holos of us just after we reached the summit, and I have that here now: Joshi is smiling, thumbs up, a very proud young man! I look . . . knackered! And how I ached the next day . . . I spent the rest of the holiday back in the hotel, sitting on the balcony overlooking the lake, reading trashy holo-novels. I am addicted to a series about a scholar of literature who investigates murders.

I come back to an overflowing desk, and requests from colleagues on the council for meetings as soon as I return to Earth. Anita and I will sit down with my diary tomorrow to schedule my first week back—ugh! In truth, it looks like this will take up the best part of the second week too. In addition to which, I have agreed to speak at a meeting of councilors who represent smaller worlds, about voting reform, and I will need to start preparing that speech very soon. How quickly this holiday has gone! And it will be the best part of a year before I am back on Prithvi. Joshi is already planning our attempt on Mount Sirivithin, and while I'm not sure how many more mountains I have in me, but I hate to disappoint him in any—

—pause entry

COUNCILOR PRIYA TAGORE
SUPPLEMENTAL
Thirteen hours later. There has been a significant incident, and we do not as yet know how serious. An Eden-class vessel, en route between Delacroix and Prithvi, has exploded while coming out of warp, near local space. All lives lost, a terrible tragedy, almost beyond belief. While our planetary communications net remains operational, there appears to have been damage to at least two of the

subspace relays serving Prithvi. We are, temporarily at least, on our own. A team of engineers has been sent out to fix the damage. In the meantime, with Governor Mahmut away at a meeting on Trill, I am the face of the Federation here on Prithvi—

—pause entry

COUNCILOR PRIYA TAGORE
SECONDARY SUPPLEMENTAL
The relays are fixed. But we seem unable to reach the rest of the subspace communications network. Our engineers have no explanation for this. This is a very frightening time. I am doing my best to speak as calmly and as positively as possible, urging people to go about their day-to-day business. It will only be a matter of time, I am sure, before relief arrives.

I must sleep. Tomorrow will surely be exhausting.

Burnham, reaching this point, stopped the recording. She could not bring herself to listen to any more right now. *Poor Priya*, she thought, her heart going out to this warm, kindly, civilized woman. *She still has no idea what's coming next.*

Because there would be no relief ships. There would be a few more communications. Governor Mahmut would not return from Trill. All the burden of caring for this world and its people after this terrible catastrophe had fallen upon Priya Tagore, and she had no idea that her world as she knew it had ended.

At least I knew what I was going into, thought Burnham. *I knew there was no going back.*

4

COMMANDER MICHAEL BURNHAM

PERSONAL LOG

I have been reflecting upon my experiences on Atalis. It is of course
evident that I made mistakes—or, rather, I entered the situation with
a set of expectations that did not in the end prove wholly helpful. In
cases such as these, I have found it useful to examine the counter-
factual: what if I decided not to answer Iliana Pa'Dan's distress call? Let
us go logically through the steps, assessing negatives and positives.

1. I would now be in possession of considerably more latinum.

2. The people of Atalis would have brokered a deal with the White
   Palm raiders, presumably allowing them and their paymasters—
   whoever they may be—exclusive access to mineral deposits,
   at reduced rates, but gaining access to medical supplies and
   other resources necessary to maintain essential infrastructure.

3. With Book's aid, I formed an association with a dozen couriers
   that, while short-lived, was mutually beneficial. I offered a job; I
   paid quickly and in full. This, I hope, has earned me credit with
   the couriers operating in this area. I would not have this otherwise.

4. Iliana Pa'Dan would most likely be dead.

It is this last point that decides the case for me. The needs of
the many cannot outweigh the needs of the few. It is true that Pa'Dan
went to Atalis looking to make money from a dangerous and volatile
situation; it is also true that she put herself in considerable personal
danger in order to fulfill her side of the bargain, well beyond anything

most couriers would have done. She did not deserve to be sold out by the Governing Body of Atalis. For this alone, I am glad that I went to Atalis. I have accrued a debt; more importantly—since I shall continue to resist reducing all my associations to the transactional—I have made a friend.

On balance, I cannot say that my intervention was wholly mis-guided, nor wholly without gain. But the truth remains that I have not made anything—and that I need to earn latinum if I want my ship to stay in flight. The best way to make it is to trade in the most valuable, most coveted resource—in other words, dilithium. Dilithium channels matter-antimatter reactions, which allows warp flight, which in turn enables the spacefaring species to, well, go into *space*. My own crystal will last a while yet, but to earn latinum, getting dilithium is the best way to go about it. To stay in flight. To be able to continue my search for . . .

For more black boxes. For subspace relays to extend my communications capabilities. For anything that can help Jeremiah access the contents of my data chip.

For answers to my questions.

So now I must take on whatever jobs I can and make whatever associations that I can. But—whatever Book may advise—I must not and I shall not refuse to answer calls for assistance. Or else . . .

Or else what is left of me, now that Starfleet is gone?

Reef City
Ikasu

Sometimes, on warm summer evenings, Binye would lie on her back in the garden rockpool, looking down across the city waters, and she would feel content. They had been on the move so much in recent years, she and Mamma, and this new place, on the northern edge of Reef, was the first place that she had dared to call home for some time. Mamma was always restless, always looking out and on to the next place. Binye had longed for somewhere to call their own. This little coral house up on the hills suited them both.

Binye spread her limbs out in the warm pool water and looked down upon the city. Reef was built around a huge lagoon, spreading out and up into the hills around three sides, the sea stretching out eastward. From this vantage point, she could look straight toward the southern districts, the layers upon layers of coral houses that made up the most populous residential parts of the city. Bright colors—blue, pink, yellow, orange—all sparkling in the last light of the day. She sometimes imagined living there; imagined having the life of an ordinary Ikasun child. A big coral house through which an extended family ranged. A family broadboat to get around. Sitting with friends on the bridge between the streets, legs dangling over the canals, chattering, laughing, gossiping. Being nothing out of the ordinary.

Binye lowered her transparent eyelids against the sun's glare. To her right, on the west, obscured from view by the bend in the shore, were the towers and gardens of the central administrative district. The big council offices. The governor's mansion. The hall of representatives and the Senate building. Glass and steel, these buildings, beautiful in their own way, but not quite Ikasun. They spoke of the world's connection to an older culture, one which was no longer present in any meaningful way, but still shaped some of this world's ways of going about its business. Behind her, in the north cove, could be found the least prestigious part of town; the sandstone and shell-covered tenements, hunkered down around the salt water, cut off from the sea air by the long, thin peninsula that sliced into the lagoon.

The water was sluggish there, with a salty reek. They had lived alongside it briefly, she and Mamma, when she was small. She remembered crowded streets, heavy heat, the overwhelming stink of fish. She shuddered, and, as if to cleanse herself of the memory, slid completely beneath into the rockpool, switching to breathe through her gills. Lying on her back, looking up, she watched the sun set, and felt safe.

Then she saw the shadow of Mamma passing by. She came back to the surface, to say hello, and saw with dismay that Mamma had brought out some nanocubes. Binye felt a flutter of anxiety. She was afraid that she knew what was coming next. The anxiety turned into a small surge of anger. Why did Mamma always have to do this? Why, whenever Binye thought they had found somewhere to be safe, would Mamma start this all over again?

"Mamma," she said, "do you have to do that this evening?"

"But the sky is so clear tonight!"

"I know. It's just . . . It was all so *peaceful*."

Mamma didn't reply. She frowned and kept on programming the nanocubes. Binye watched with an increasing sense of despair. Soon enough, the telescope was fully constructed. It looked, if possible, even bigger than the last one, the one which had been big enough to get impounded and precipitate their most recent move. The reason why Binye was here right now, by herself, swimming in a rockpool on the north side of Reef, and not sitting gossiping with her friends around the southern canals, and swimming together in their family waters. Watching Mamma pull up a stool and sit before her telescope, Binye felt her anxiety turn into a sick fear. "Mamma!" she said. "That thing is *massive*! Remember what happened last time! Someone is going to see!"

"Who is there to see?" said Mamma. "We made a good decision coming up here. Not so many prying neighbors around here. Besides, I'm not doing anything wrong."

Technically, this was true. There was no law, as such,

against the practice of astronomy. But the hobby was considered at best curious, and, at worst, in extremely bad taste, bordering almost on the obscene. Why would someone be so interested in looking upward and outward? Nothing good was out there. Nothing good could come from there. Here on Ikasu, everything was beautiful. The sea was beautiful. The weather was beautiful. The people were beautiful. Life was beautiful. Looking up was a waste of time. More than that—looking up was dangerous. It was the sign of a disordered mind.

Mamma turned to Binye and smiled. "We should be able to see the moons of Alla tonight," she said. "It's rare you get to see them both. I'd really like a closer look."

Binye was enough her mother's daughter that something stirred at the thought. Alla, the planet nearest their sun, was a regular visitor at dawn and sunrise, but the moons were not visible to the naked eye. Binye had first seen them as a very little girl. Telling her friends at school the next day had brought about the very first move of her life. One of her friends had gone home that night and told their mamma about the big rocks in the sky and that Binye had been looking at them through a big glass, and that parent had complained to the school. Mamma had come back fighting—but it was a losing battle. And when the other kids were banned from playing with her, swimming with her, diving with her, it was time to move on. Binye, remembering now her confusion and shame, pushed down the bubbling of excitement that she felt, and said, harshly, "Why? Why do you want to look at some stupid moon? It's just a huge rock in the sky."

Mamma kept adjusting the telescope. "You don't need to come and see, little one," she said. "But remember to speak with kindness and respect."

Binye went hot with shame. She hated when Mamma did

that kind of thing—turned Binye's perfectly reasonable anger back onto her. She slid into the pool again for a moment, almost imagining she could see the steam rising, and then came up again. "You didn't answer my question. Why are you so keen to look at the moons of Alla tonight? You've seen them before."

There was a pause. "Like I said, you don't often get to see the second one."

"I know that you saw it eight weeks ago."

"Ah, so you do pay attention!"

Because I need to be on the lookout. "What do you think you're going to see this time that's going to be so special?"

Mamma took a while to respond. Eventually, she said, "Remember that subspace relay I found?"

"Yes?"

"I sent a message."

Binye went cold. "Mamma! You *promised*! Looking only!"

"I know, I know. I'm not entirely sure the thing is working properly. I don't think anyone will reply."

"Yes, you do! You're looking for a ship, aren't you?" Binye felt tears gathering in her eyes. "Mamma, this isn't fair!"

"No, little one, it's not fair. It's not fair that we have to pretend that there's nothing out there. It's not fair that I have to hide away the only real talent that I have. It's not fair that I'm punished and sidelined and ostracized simply for asking questions!"

Binye was crying now. This argument—it happened more and more often, and Binye couldn't see why she was always the one at fault. Mamma was the one at fault! Why couldn't she just leave this all alone? Why couldn't she be happy? Ikasu was beautiful! They could be happy here if Mamma would only let all this go. But she was never going to let it go, was she? Binye was never going to be free of this.

Binye slid once again into the pool, under the surface, salt tears mixing with salt water. She waited for a while, looking up, in case Mamma's shadow appeared overhead, but no. Of course not. Mamma would be completely absorbed in her studies by now—looking up, looking out, looking into danger. Binye closed her eyelids fully and hoped that the stars would stay exactly where they were.

The Alice

Another day over, another job done. Michael Burnham, tired and grimy, set a course for the spaceport. Although she was mostly on board her little ship these days, she kept the spaceport as her main base and returned there as often as she could. Jeremiah was still working on cracking open the tricorder's data chip, in the hopes that they would be able to find something that would give them a clue as to where and when *Discovery* might arrive. Part of her time was spent looking for the oldest scraps of technology she could find, anything that might bridge the technological gap between now and then. She was, by necessity, becoming more adept, spending hours on flights constructing simple nanoprograms, but she knew she had a great deal to learn. Like having to make the leap from making a household fire to illuminating a whole city with sustainable power sources, with one hand tied behind her back.

The main draw back to the spaceport was, of course, Sahil. The fixed point behind her, the still point in a whirling and still often surreal universe. Navigating busy and often unpleasant mercantiles, or sitting alone hour after hour in the cabin of her ship, she would often find herself thinking of the quiet little office with the teacups and the flag. The small, calm room where the Federation still existed. Sometimes, when she stepped into that space, nine hundred years seemed to slip away, and she could pretend that she was home again, in her own time, and that her friends and her loved ones were only the touch of a communicator away. These days, she found herself thinking of that office more than she thought of the cabin she had shared on *Discovery*. Only one of those places was accessible.

Burnham stood and stretched, joints cracking. She looked around the tiny cabin, about as far from Starfleet as it was possible to be. It was somewhere between a studio apartment and storage unit. Crates and boxes piled up everywhere. Her uniform thrown on top of one of these. She reached out to retrieve it. She spread it out across the bunk, folded it properly, and wondered when she might get a chance to get the creases out. Not here; not now; not in this place. This place was the home of someone who was very busy, someone who was very harassed, who was often leaving places in a hurry. Someone with no time to get the creases out of a uniform. Still, she should take more care.

Unbidden, an image flashed into her mind of the quarters she had shared with Tilly back on *Discovery*. Tilly didn't countenance mess, not really. It was not that she made you feel guilty about a stray coffee cup or a discarded and sweaty T-shirt from a morning run. No, scratch that, thought Burnham, with a smile. It was *exactly* that she made you feel guilty about all these things, and it was therefore fortunate for both of them that Burnham's Vulcan upbringing had instilled habits of sparseness and orderliness. They had been well suited to sharing accommodation. She thought of Tilly, seeing this place.

Oh, Tilly!

Suddenly, Burnham was almost overwhelmed by loneliness. Sweet, brilliant, funny, impossible Tilly—how she missed her! She hugged her uniform to her chest; almost forgotten a moment ago, it was suddenly the most precious thing she possessed. How she missed Tilly! How she missed her constant and—it had to be admitted—occasionally infuriating chatter. She could almost hear Tilly's voice, keeping up her running commentary on these new surroundings: *Okay, well, um, I don't know if you've noticed, but actually getting past each other is going to be something of a challenge? There's not really enough room for one of us to get through, never mind two, and that's something of an issue when it comes to personal space? I mean, I like you, Michael, but that doesn't mean I want to be pressing against you all the time—not that you're unattractive, I mean, I'm not attracted to you and you're not not attractive but I'm not . . . Um, perhaps I should shut up now?*

Burnham closed her eyes. She held her uniform against her cheek, feeling the sensation of the familiar material once again. She tried to stop the flood of memories; the sound of a friendly voice that she might not ever get the chance to hear again.

"Michael," she said, out loud. "Michael. Stop this." Her voice sounded dry, hoarse—almost harsh. "Keep your mind on the present. Keep your mind on *now* . . ."

The comm chimed. Gratefully, she went over to respond to its summons.

"Burnham."

"Hello, Commander. Sahil here. Good to hear your voice. When are you back?"

"Another three hours, I think, maybe a little longer at current speed. Why, have you got another job for me?"

"It's . . . a little more interesting than that. Come as quickly as you can, Michael."

Well, she thought, as she cut the comm. It wouldn't be *Discovery*. He would have told her that straight out; the same with a message from Terralysium or Earth. What could it be? She put the uniform to one side. The present had overtaken her again—blissful relief.

Sahil's office
Former Federation Spaceport Devaloka
"This is Ikasu calling. We are here. Is there anyone out there?"

The voice was clear, direct. The speaker was reaching out. Making contact. Still, though, the message was so brief and practically contentless. Burnham said, "Is that all there is?"

"I hope I didn't raise your expectations too high," Sahil said. "But this is genuinely one of the more interesting transmissions I've received in some time. I had no idea that this particular system was inhabited, for one thing. And—as you can see from the time stamp—whoever sent this message seems to be using an old Federation subspace relay."

Burnham was interested: very much so. A communication from a system that had hitherto been silent. An old subspace relay . . . "How old is the message? Any idea?"

"From what I can tell, no more than a few weeks."

"Oh," Burnham said. She took her usual chair. She was conscious that she had come straight from her ship; that she was grubby and untidy in this crisp and painfully well-kept space. But he didn't seem to mind. He seemed—as ever—simply very glad to see her, and his growing excitement was mirroring hers.

"Do you know what Ikasu is?" she said. "Is it a planet?"

"I'm assuming so." Sahil gestured around somewhat helplessly. "Again, we are confounded by the gaps in the databanks. It's not a name with which I am familiar. My father or grandfather might have known; my great-grandparents certainly. It could even be a ship, of course, traveling through that part of space—but then ships more usually announce themselves as such." He gave her a shy smile. "I hoped you might have some information, Commander."

"If it's a world, it's not one that I've heard of," she admitted. "It was a big Federation even in my time, and from all that you've told me, it had expanded vastly even farther before . . ." Before imploding. She left that unsaid, merely waved her hand. He understood. "This could be a world that was contacted or settled long after my time. But the fact that they're using a Starfleet relay . . ."

"This relay is of considerable interest," he said, hope rising in his voice. "It may be connected to others that we have not hitherto been aware of. Perhaps they are in contact with many others."

Castles in the air. Gently, she said, "I don't think we should set too much store by this, Sahil. One world, sending out a message. It could be decades old—"

"Not from the time stamp—"

"Sure," she said, "I get that—but really all that tells us is when it was sent from the relay. Not when it was sent up there." She watched his face fall. He was so kind, and always so full of hope. A combination that was impossible to refuse. Burnham sighed. "I can go and take a look, if you'd like me to."

He brightened. "That would be most kind of you."

"Could I at least get a shower first?"

"I believe that would be a wise decision, Commander."

———

She gave herself a couple of days before leaving. She made some repairs to the ship; she even tidied up a little—and she got the creases out of the uniform. It lay now on the shelf beside the console where she stored her few treasures, folded into a regulation-neat square. Who knew, after all, when Tilly might drop by. If there was any reason to believe, after all these months, that *Discovery* might put in an appearance, it would be because Tilly could no longer bear the state of Burnham's ship. As if the mess would draw her, across time and space: *I get that you're busy, Michael? I mean, I get that? I really do, but perhaps you could remember that some people are more sensitive to dust particles in the air? Also, given that the ship is sooooo reconditioned, I guess it's not a great idea to have so much potential for dirt to get into the components?*

"Oh Tilly," Burnham said, as she eased her battered little vessel on its way once more, "I'd give anything to have you here right now, nagging me to clean."

About thirty hours later, and in the middle of a deep sleep, she was woken by a gentle chime on the comm. "What?" she grumped.

A holo-image of Book's face appeared a few feet away.

"Hey," said Book. And then: *"Oh, hey. Did I wake you? Sorry if I woke you."*

" 'S okay," she mumbled. "What d'you want?"

"More what you want. I happened to be near the port. Sahil told me where you were heading. I was . . . curious . . . Wait, hang on a second."

She saw the top of his head as he bent over. Next moment the holo of a familiar furry face came into view. "Hey, Grudge," she said and waved. Book lifted the cat's right paw to wave back at her. The cat glared at her with the kind of supremely focused contempt that only cats find it possible to achieve. Burnham envied that degree of centeredness. Grudge jumped away, and Book's grinning face was back. "I see she's forgiven you for breaking your nose again."

"Our love is eternal. A bond that cannot be broken."

"You said you were curious," she prompted, before he could get onto the subject of Grudge. They'd be here for hours. It would be like listening to Tilly complaining about the mess.

"A whole world I've never heard of before? You bet I'm curious."

"If it is a world. It might be a ship. It might be nothing more than a decades-old message burped out by a malfunctioning relay."

He pulled a face. *"Thanks for that image. Well, whatever it is, I'd like to know more."*

"What you mean," she said, "is that it might be a business opportunity. Am I right?"

"Gotta pay the bills."

"They might not have money," she said, mischievously. "If they've been out of touch since the Burn. They might still be operating by Federation standards. There was no money in the Federation—"

"Yeah, you keep telling me that, and I still don't really believe you."

"Even knowing how hopeless I am with my finances?"

"That is perhaps the most convincing argument I've seen that a moneyless economy ever existed. Because you really are hopeless—"

"Thank you."

"So can I tag along?"

"Why should I let you 'tag along' with me on what might be a significant moment reestablishing contact with a lost Federation world just so you can . . . speculate?"

"Because I bring the fun?"

She laughed out loud; a pure laugh straight from her core, a sound she rarely heard herself make. Damn the man! How did he slip past her defenses?

"You know, you might not be welcome."

"What do you mean?"

"Some places have gone to some lengths not to be noticed."

"They sent a transmission asking who else was out there."

"And you have a tendency to wander in talking like . . ."

"Like a Starfleet officer?"

"I was going to say like someone not entirely informed about

how things work these days, but I guess it amounts to the same thing. Think about what happened on Atalis. They weren't exactly thrilled you dropped by, were they?"

Burnham leaned back in her bunk and suppressed a smile. "Book," she said. "Are you *worried* about me?"

"I'm worried about your ship," he said. *"It's a nice ship. Bit of a mess inside—I'm surprised to find out you're so slovenly, by the way—easily tidied. And I went to some lengths to help you fit it out. It would be a shame to see all those parts all over the place."*

"Thank you. I'm truly touched."

"You're welcome. Get the rest of your beauty sleep. I'll see you in a few hours."

His holo-face disappeared. She rolled over. She still thought she could see his grin.

Ikasun system

They rendezvoused just outside the Ikasun system and traveled together to the subspace relay. Book had no problem with the design—he had salvaged many similar ones, and she was able to follow his explanations and quickly work with its systems. "Well," she said at last, "the signal was definitely sent up to the relay recently. I've tracked it back to somewhere on the second world in the system, but I can't find any other local communications traffic . . . No sign of a local planetary net. No other chatter."

"The second world. Let me scan. Looks like it could support life. Shall we take a closer look?"

"We've come a long way not to."

Entering orbit around the system's second planet, Burnham saw a blue and white swirling surface that reminded her painfully of Earth. "Still no comms," she said. "It's like the whole world is under some kind of blackout."

"Maybe there aren't many of them. Hold on, I'll check for life signs."

She heard him whistle. "What is it, Book?"

"Two million of them down there, Burnham!"

"Two million?" She checked her own readings. He wasn't wrong. "Why so *quiet*?"

"Maybe they've only just got comm systems back online."

"Maybe they don't want to be contacted," she said, doubt creeping into her voice. "Book, perhaps we should go."

"What? Where's your Starfleet sense of adventure?"

"There are rules about first contact."

"But this isn't first contact, is it? That's a Starfleet subspace relay they were using. It was even a Federation channel. Isn't this the kind of thing you've been hoping to find?"

"They didn't announce themselves as Federation. They barely announced themselves as anything at all."

"I still don't see why this would count as first contact."

She took a deep breath and started to explain. "We know from historical studies how quickly societies forget—sometimes even when there are still eyewitnesses to events. It's been over a hundred years. There'll be nobody left alive who remembers life before the Burn. We have no idea what happened on this world. It's long enough that their civilization might count as something distinct. Something new."

"Are you done with the xenosociology lecture?"

"I'm sorry if my ethics *bore* you."

"On the contrary, they have led me into all kinds of interesting and exciting situations. All I want to say is that if we leave now, we'll have come a long way for nothing."

"This isn't a business opportunity, Book," she said, with some irritation. "We don't have the right to turn up on their world and announce ourselves."

There was a pause.

"Book?"

"That wasn't actually what I meant."

"So what did you mean?" she shot back.

"I . . . just want to know what's down there."

Burnham felt bad. She tended to assume he was always on the make, but there was that other side to him—well hidden but undeniable. The side that saved beautiful and endangered creatures. The side that had come to help her. "I'm sorry," she said. "I'm just trying to be careful, after what happened on Atalis. But . . ." She thought of the message. "They did reach out, didn't they?"

"They did. Look, I've located the source of the transmission. Do you want me to go and take a look? You stay on the ship?"

"If this really is a first-contact situation, I should probably be there. Unless you've been studying the regulations in your spare time?"

"Not very likely, is it? All right. I'll send you the coordinates. But—just don't announce yourself, okay?"

"What do you mean 'announce' myself?"

"Don't go talking about Starfleet to the first person you meet."

"But I come in peace, Book," she said dryly.

"Yeah, well, they might not see it that way. Just . . . don't go in flying the flag."

"Like I'd do that—"

"You've got that look about you, that's all."

" 'That look'? What look, exactly?"

"The look of the true believer."

"I just want to make friends."

"Yeah," he said. *"That's sort of what I meant."*

The Reef
Ikasu

Book had traced the transmission back to a location in what, from the readings they were getting from the planet's surface, seemed to be a large but dispersed conurbation situated around a lagoon. At his insistence, they made planetfall well outside the city, up in the hills to the north. He was already there when she transported down, standing with a hand up to shield his face from the bright sun.

"Hey," he said. "It's a bit of an uphill hike."

"Could we not have come down on the other side of the hill?"

"Are you losing your edge, Burnham?"

"Do you want to test that theory firsthand, Book?"

"Not today. Here," he said, handing her a small black metal disk, "we'll use these."

She turned the disk around in her hand. "What does this do?"

"Personal holoprojector," he said. "A simple way of blending in. It scans the immediate area for life signs and builds up an image so that we can project a similar appearance. We don't want to attract attention by not having horns or a tail or something."

"You'd suit horns," she said.

"You'd suit a tail."

"I couldn't compete with Grudge."

"I'm glad you know your place. Anyway, I've set them up. All you need to do is stick it on your pocket or your bag or something, and let it get on with things."

"What if it turns us into the local equivalent of a cat or something?" she said.

"Then we will surely be treated as a king and queen among lesser beings, and that is only our due. You coming?"

She nodded.

"Let's see how you cope with the walk, then," he said.

"Let's see," she replied, and set off at a brisk pace. They bickered cheerfully for a few uphill miles, until they crested the summit, and Burnham caught her first sight of the city below, the city that she would learn later was called the Reef.

The lagoon lay below, brilliant blue, with the wide sea stretching out to the left. Around the other three sides of the lagoon lay a settlement of bright primary colors. The impression of life—teeming, vibrant, joyful *life*—was almost overwhelming. She saw skimmers and aircars zipping around and between each other; their warm hum filled the air. Looking to her right, she saw a sight that brought tears to her eyes—the high shining towers of a city built by a great civilization.

"*Oh . . .*" she whispered.

"Burnham?" Book turned to her. "Are you okay?"

"It's here," she said. "I'm sure it is!"

"What's here?"

"The Federation!" The moment the words were out, she regretted them, afraid of what his comeback might be. She was not sure that she could bear listening to his scorn. But he didn't reply straightaway. Instead, he stared down at the city.

"It's impressive," he said, at last. "It looks like they held things together better here than in . . . Well, pretty much anywhere else I've seen."

"I could be on Earth," she breathed. "I could be on Trill, or Betazed . . ." She hurried on, eager now to enter the city itself. About twenty minutes later, they reached a main road. She was slightly ahead. Turning to look back at him, she began to laugh, quietly.

"What?" he said. "What is it?"

"You've got gills," she said, gesturing at her own throat. "And webbed hands."

He looked down and waggled his fingers. "Sheesh," he said. "You've got . . . is that *fur*?"

She held up her hand: soft down covered her wrist and forearm. "No tail?" she said, twisting around.

"Not one that's showing. Gills," he said thoughtfully. "Underwater?"

"Partially, I'd guess," she said. "The fur would help with insulation."

"Grudge would love me even more."

By the time they reached the city, her sense of coming home was so strong she was almost overwhelmed. Book was impressed, staring around at the busy streets, the traffic, the sense of wealth and comfort, of ease and plenty. She felt like someone coming from a desert, parched with thirst, finding fresh water.

"Is this really what it was like?" said Book quietly. "In one of your cities?"

"Everywhere was different . . ." said Burnham. "But this is very like Earth . . . San Francisco or Shanghai . . . Maybe Geneva or Venice . . . Even the *air* smells the same." She breathed deeply. Scent triggered memory. She felt the ache of loss.

She looked at the people passing by. Yes, they breathed air, but they had gills too, and not only their hands, but their feet too were webbed. And they did indeed have fur—a thin layer of sleek fur, like a seal might have, on each one. Otherwise, they had the looks and diversity she might expect from any Federation colony. Had they settled here? Were they engineered for the environment? Had that been allowed, in the later days of the Federation? Or were these people the indigenous species? She wondered how she looked, appearing as one of them.

"What do you want to do?" he said. "We can't exactly go up to someone and say, *Take me to your leader*? That's not the Starfleet way, is it?"

"No, not exactly. We'll go to the source of transmission. That at least will presumably be someone expecting offworld visitors. If it's someone in authority—that's fine. If not—we'll work with what we've got. But I'm hoping we'll find someone like Sahil."

"A true believer?" he said.

"Someone who has been waiting for us to come," she chided him gently. "Someone who wants us to walk through the door. Oh, Book!" she said, and grasped his arm. "Could this really be what I've been hoping for? Could this be a place where the Federation still exists?"

He gave her an anxious look. "The Federation's been gone a long time."

"Maybe it hasn't! Maybe the sectors we know were just unlucky. Maybe everywhere else is more like this—"

"I don't think that's the case."

"But this is how it *was*! No—this is more! It's as if everything that I knew is still alive, but has grown better, become *better*—"

"All right," he said. "But tell me when you see a Federation flag."

"Excuse me?"

"That flag that you and Sahil put out with such ceremony. Tell me when you see it."

She looked around, quickly. "You know, it's not like the flag flew everywhere."

"Okay."

"What?"

"I said okay."

"You said it, but you meant the opposite."

"I just think—if there's been something out there all along, if somehow, beyond our few sectors, the Federation is still much as it was . . . Well, why didn't they come, Burnham? Why did they leave all those people to suffer?"

She shoved her hands in her pockets and walked on. "There'll be an answer. I'm sure. There'll be a good answer."

"Yeah," he said. "I'm sure there'll be an answer too. I'm just not sure you'll like it."

They were walking along a wide boulevard, still high above the main city, with a view overlooking the water. The houses, although modest and single story, were spread out. Little streams ran between individual plots, tiny rivulets of clear water bubbling downhill. Children were playing in the open spaces. They looked at the strangers with curiosity, but only because they were new to the area, not that they were alien in some way. At last, they came to a pale coral house decorated with shells.

"Here's where the signal is coming from," murmured Burnham.

"Not the governor's palace, then," said Book.

Burnham tapped on the door. Nobody answered. She knocked again.

"There's definitely someone inside," murmured Book. "There's a life sign, anyway."

Burnham knocked again, more insistently. She saw a shadow move behind the nearest window. She waved. "Hey!" she called. "We're friendly!"

There was a pause, and the door opened, a crack. A girl—teens, were she human—peered out. "Who are you? What do you want?"

"We got a message to come here," said Burnham. "Is there someone else here? Are you alone?" She reached for culturally neutral language. "Is there someone here who cares for you?"

"Nobody," said the girl. She blinked rapidly—*adipose eyelids*, thought Burnham, *that makes sense*—and then tears began to run down her cheeks.

"Hey!" said Burnham gently. "Are you okay? Can I help? Please—let me help!"

Book, later, said that there was something about her voice when she made these offers. It made people reach out to her. Whatever it was, the girl nodded, and opened the door. Burnham, Book following behind, entered a wide, low house, sparsely furnished but neatly kept, with a breeze rushing through.

"Hey," Burnham said, "is there somebody we can get for you? Someone we can contact?"

She shook her head. "No. There's nobody. Please don't call for anybody—"

"Listen," said Burnham. "My name is Michael Burnham. I've come . . . I've come in answer to a message sent from here. Do you know who might have sent it?" Carefully, she reached into her pocket, and thumbed the button to turn off the holo. The girl stared at her. Then she burst into tears.

"Oh, Mamma! Why did you do it? Why did you put us in such *danger*!"

———

Her name was Binye. She wanted them to go—at once. No, she hadn't sent the message. Of course she hadn't sent the message. The telescope was bad enough, but sending messages like that definitely wasn't allowed—

"Not allowed?" said Burnham. "What do you mean? And the *telescope*—?"

"Burnham," said Book, "I think we should go."

"What?" She turned to him. "We've only just got here—"

"I've heard of worlds like this," he said. "They cut themselves off after the Burn. They haven't made contact before because they didn't want to." He turned to Binye. "I'm right, aren't I?"

She nodded. "It's not allowed . . ."

"But why not?" said Burnham.

"You've seen this place!" said Book. "Seen the resources they have. Self-sustaining. Not reliant on supplies coming in. I guess, when the Burn came, they knew what would happen next." He turned to Binye. "Am I right?"

She was nodding. "They knew back then that people would try to come here, take what we had. They withdrew. Set up a communications blackout. Cut us off."

"At least it kept your standard of living high," said Book, and Burnham detected a slight hint of bitterness in his voice.

"Did nobody come from Starfleet or the Federation?" asked Burnham. "Did your ancestors even reach out for help?"

Binye frowned. "I . . . don't know. The way I understand it—there wasn't a Federation anymore."

Burnham took the news with equanimity. The end of that particular hope. Ikasu was not some hidden gateway to a wider galactic community. It was a dead end. She took a deep breath and straightened up. She felt Book's hand come to rest, only for a moment and very lightly, upon her shoulder. "So nobody has come in and out of here for years," she said, flatly.

"There was a ban on space exploration too," said Binye. "Even stargazing. It became a kind of *paranoia*." She led them to the side of the house and stood by the window. "Look."

In the garden, Burnham saw the telescope.

"Mamma had to get a permit for that. It took her three years to get it. I wish she hadn't." Binye put her head in her hands and began once again to cry.

"Tell me about your mother," Burnham said, softly.

"She's obsessed with making contact with the rest of the sector. She thinks we can't go on living this way, that we have to come out of isolation eventually. That we have a responsibility to share what we have."

"I've got to say," said Book, "some of this might have come in useful."

"Most of all, though . . . she just couldn't bear it. Couldn't bear knowing that the universe was out there, and that she was forbidden to know anything about it."

"So she decided to bring the universe to her," said Burnham.

"I didn't have any idea. She sometimes talked about what it would be like, if visitors from beyond finally came . . ." Binye gave a wan smile. "And here you are."

"Well, where is she?" said Book. "We'll say hi before we go." He turned to Burnham, spoke urgently. "And I mean it, Burnham, we really should go. Because I have a feeling that we're not really welcome round here—"

Burnham raised her hand to stop him. "Where is she, Binye? Where's your mother?"

"She disappeared three days ago. I came back from the study center and she wasn't here. She hasn't come back . . ." The girl trailed off.

"Arrested?" said Burnham. Binye shrugged. She didn't know.

"Burnham," said Book, in a warning voice. "No. Don't get involved."

"But she called to us," said Burnham. "She asked us to come."

"Burnham—"

"Do you have *any* idea where she might have gone?" Burnham said to the girl. Book, frustrated, turned and walked back into the main part of the house.

"There's a place outside the city," Binye said. "Out in open country. She told me she used to go there before I was born—she would stargaze. Out in the marshes."

Book came hurrying back. "Listen," he said, urgently. "We

really do have to go. A couple of flyers have pulled up outside, and there are people getting out of them, and you know that look that regulators and enforcers and police have whatever the time and place?"

"Yes?"

"They've got that look," he finished.

Turning the holo back on, Burnham ran to the front window. He wasn't wrong. They *definitely* had that look. Their flyers had dark glass, for one thing. "Where?" she said. "Where shall we go?"

"Out of the city," he said. "Where we arrived."

Burnham reached into her satchel, pulled out her spare transporter, and set the coordinates. Then she shoved the device into Binye's hands. "Let's go," she said, and, before anyone could protest, all three of them were gone, the sound of hammering at the door ringing in their ears.

———

Later, when she was able to sit and take stock of all that happened to her over the next few hours, Binye would recall the whole episode as a series of shocks, of sudden changes of scene, of dislocation. She could most certainly not have predicted how this frightening and disorienting day would end.

One moment she was at home; the next she was on a hillside. She was used to personal transporters, but not someone else suddenly forcing a trip on her. "Where are we—"

"Dammit, they've located us," said the woman, Burnham, and Binye suddenly saw, two meters away, four enforcers appear out of nowhere.

"Stop!" one cried. "Stop right now."

"Move it," said Burnham—and they did, hopping to another spot. "Can we randomize our destinations?"

"We are," said the man, Book, after they'd shifted again. "But their tracking is on top of it . . ."

The enforcers arrived. They jumped again.

"Deflect the transporter traces?" said Burnham. Again, the enforcers arrived; again they jumped.

"Pretty tricky to do on the fly . . ." said Book, as they transported yet again. "But I'm doing my best . . ."

They kept transporting, to random places, Book working on the deflection of the transporter traces in the brief moments they had between arrival, their pursuers tracking them, and being able to transport again. At last, he said, breathlessly, "I think I have it."

They jumped. They waited for the time it took their pursuers to track them—and nobody came. They all stopped at last to catch their breath. "How long before they work out what we've done?" said Burnham.

"No idea," said Book. "But we should assume their technology is at least as good as anything I have access to. They've had an extra hundred years to innovate . . ."

Binye burst into tears; a wailing sound that filled the air with deep and shuddering sobs. Burnham put her arm around her. "I know you're frightened, Binye," she said. "I know how disconcerting this must be. I promise you—we'll speak to your mother, and then we'll go."

"It's too late for that, isn't it?" Binye said. "They must *know* that you're outsiders. Contaminators. It's over for Mamma, isn't it?"

"You said you thought you knew where your mother might be," said Book. "Can you tell us? Do you know the location?"

"Yes, yes," she said, through her tears, punching the coordinates into her transporter, sharing the information with them. She saw Burnham look at Book.

"Will they find us?"

"Almost certainly," he said, "given enough time."

"Then we should get moving," Burnham said. Again, she said to Binye, "I promise you we'll leave—but we won't abandon your mother. We'll do all that we can to help."

———

This time the jump took them from the hills into a flat landscape of reeds and rushes. *Salt marsh*, thought Burnham, breathing deep. She turned to the girl standing next to her, sullen and scared, her arms wrapped around her body, trying to bring herself comfort. "Binye," she said, gently. "Where now?"

"This way," said the girl, leading them along into the reeds. There was a banked-up piece of earth that formed a narrow pathway. To either side, the ground was marshy and soft. Insects buzzed around. "Nice," said Book, swatting them away.

They followed Binye for maybe ten or fifteen minutes. Burnham asked a few questions and got only curt answers— her mother's name was Zuka—but it was clear the girl did not want to talk to them. There were a few moments when the path went very narrow and treacherous; Burnham, losing her footing, slid into the marsh. Book had to wade in to pull her out. Once out, she began to scrabble furiously at his legs.

"What?" said Book. "What's the matter?"

Binye, looking back, said in the scornful tones universally perfected by adolescents of most species, "They're just *leeches*. Pull them off."

"I imagine," said Burnham, "that they're not so bad if you've got *fur*."

"I didn't ask you to come along," said Binye. "Are you coming or not?"

For the last part of the walk, the ground rose steadily, and the reeds began to thin. The air became fresher and saltier. They came out at last onto sand dunes. Ahead, Burnham saw a little wooden cabin. A woman was standing outside. When she saw the three of them, she raised her hand to shield her eyes, and then began to run toward them. Reaching them, she pulled Binye into her arms. Burnham noted that the girl did not return the embrace but stood stiffly as her mother held her.

"Binye! Are you all right? Who are these people?"

"They got your message," said Binye, bitterly.

Zuka turned to look at them. Suddenly, her expression changed to one of sheer joy. She reached out and grabbed Burnham by the hand. "Is it true? Are you really from—"

"We're not from Ikasu," Burnham confirmed, and the other woman's sudden cry of joy made her laugh quietly in turn. "It's true! Book and I—we're from worlds very different from this one."

"Although I kind of like it here," said Book. "When people aren't chasing me. Things *work*, for one thing."

"I knew if I tried hard enough, somebody would come," said Zuka.

"Well, you were lucky it was us," said Book. "But the problem is that I don't think we're very popular here. Burnham," he said, softly, urgently, "we can't hang around—"

Burnham nodded.

"Where are we going?" said Zuka.

"That's up to you," said Burnham. "We can take you to a place of safety here on Ikasu, or else . . ." She glanced at Book.

"Don't say it," he said.

"Or else we can take you offworld," she said.

"And she said it," said Book.

"Offworld?" Zuka's eyes were shining. "Oh please! Yes! *Yes!*"

"All right," said Book. "But it's going to take a while for these transporters to have enough power to get us back to the ship—"

"What?" said Binye. "Your *ship*?"

"Binye," said her mother in a warning voice.

"Mamma, I'm not going anywhere."

"We don't have time to discuss this, Binye."

"This is my *home*!"

From farther down the beach, they heard a cry. "*Stop!*"

"And here come the enforcers," said Book.

"Do we jump again?" said Burnham.

"No point. They can track us now. And we'll be wasting power. They'll run down before we get a chance to use them long distance." Book eyed Binye. "If that's the plan."

"I'm not *coming*!" said Binye. Any further dispute was delayed when the enforcers arrived—four of them, with weapons aimed at each one of them. "Zuka Baleso," one of them said. "You're under arrest."

Burnham moved forward. "Let me handle this, Book," she murmured. "You get on with doing what you need to do."

"Don't go Starfleet on them," he hissed back.

Burnham, raising her palm in a gesture of openness, addressed the enforcer who had spoken. "My name is Commander Michael Burnham of the Federation *Starship Discovery*," she said.

"And she immediately went Starfleet on them," muttered Book.

"I'm here on Ikasu in good faith," Burnham went on, but the enforcer interrupted.

"Federation?" she said. "You're *Starfleet*?"

Burnham squared her chin and her shoulders. "Yes," she said. "I am."

The enforcer laughed. "What, are you a *time traveler* or

something? If you're from the Federation, I'm the president."
Her colleagues laughed too.

"I'm a Starfleet officer," said Burnham. "There are still
some of us out there, you know. I'm here to make contact—"

"We don't want contact. Commander Burnham, if that's
really the name you want to go by," said the enforcer, "whatever's left of the Federation—we haven't needed it for generations now. We're doing fine here. All we want is to be left
alone. Unfortunately," she gestured with her weapon toward
Zuka, "not everyone is doing their part."

Zuka shook her head. "We can't live in isolation forever."

"Maybe not," said the enforcer. "But neither do we need
to advertise our presence." She turned back to Burnham.
"Commander Burnham. I hope you like what you've seen of
Ikasu."

"I have," said Burnham. "Very much."

"Because I'm afraid we can't let you leave."

"What?" said Burnham. "You can't hold us here against
our will—"

"We can," said the enforcer. "And we must. I'm sorry,
Commander—we can't allow knowledge of our existence to be
spread out farther across the sector."

"I won't be telling anybody," said Burnham. "I'll leave,
and I won't return."

"I won't be telling anyone either," put in Book. "Ikasu?
Never heard of it."

"We'll go back to our ship," said Burnham, slowly and
carefully. "We'll remove the subspace relay that Zuka used.
There'll be no further chance of communication with the outside world—" She saw the enforcer shaking her head. "You
can't detain us! We've committed no crime—"

"You violated our territory when you came to Ikasu, and

now you're subject to our laws. And our laws don't allow anyone to leave. It's a matter of self-protection."

"I've seen this place!" Burnham said. "You're as close to the Federation as anywhere I've seen. I don't believe that these are your values! I don't believe you think this is right!"

"We believe in protecting our way of life," said the enforcer. "And you're a serious risk to that."

Burnham said, "We just want to go on our way."

And found herself back on Book's ship. "Sorry," he said, as he ran over to the flight console. "But the transporters had fully recharged and I didn't see that conversation going anywhere."

Burnham looked around wildly. Standing just next to her were Zuka—and Binye. The girl was looking around in horror. "Take me home!" she cried. "Take me *home*!"

Book looked over his shoulder. "Sorry, kid," he said, and his ship pulled out of orbit.

The Alice

En route to Sanctuary Four

Burnham had insisted they keep their promise. They returned to the subspace relay, and Book, using the tractor beam, towed it back to Burnham's ship. When they were done, he looked at Burnham, and an unspoken agreement about their next destination passed between them.

"I'll go ahead," said Book. "Make sure they know you're coming."

"We'll see you there," said Burnham, and she, Zuka, and Binye went over to her ship. Soon they were in flight. She turned off the holo, to Zuka's delight, and explained the events of the last hour or so to a frightened Binye and an excited Zuka; Book had boosted the range of the personal transporters to take all four of them back to his ship, and that now they were en route to a world called Sanctuary Four. "It's peaceful," she said. "It's beautiful. You'll like it. You might want to stay—you might want to go on."

"I don't want to go anywhere," said Binye, "but home."

Burnham shook her head. "I'm sorry," she said. "That's a trip I won't make. I said I'd leave and never return—and that's a promise I intend to keep. Maybe one day you'll get back— but you need to decide whether you want to reveal to anyone where Ikasu is. I don't know many people willing to make a one-way trip. And I'm not sure that you want to tell people where your home is."

"So I'm trapped," said Binye. She looked bitterly at her mother. "I'll never forgive you for this."

———

Zuka had taken the bunk for a few hours. Burnham looked to where Binye was sitting, curled up on a makeshift chair made from boxes and blankets. The girl was exhausted, clearly, but unable to sleep. Burnham turned her chair around to look at her.

"Hey," she said softly. "I guess . . . the past few hours have been crazy."

Binye looked at her with tired eyes.

"I do know how you're feeling right now," said Burnham.

"If you knew, you'd take me back," said Binye.

Burnham shook her head. "That isn't going to happen, I'm afraid. We're taking you somewhere safe."

"Well, it is called Sanctuary."

"Yeah." She smiled. Binye did not return the favor. "Anyway, it's a good place. Quiet. Clear. Lots of water."

"I lived in a city of hundreds of thousands of people. Why do you think I want to go and live in the middle of nowhere? You shouldn't have brought me out here," she finished bitterly.

"We couldn't leave you. I honestly don't know what they would have done to you. Besides, your mother—"

"Had no right to make this decision for me. Sure, she wanted to go to the stars. But I didn't want to come, Burnham. I don't want to be here!"

"I know," said Burnham, sadly. "I know." She tried again. "I really do know how you feel," she said. "It's hard to explain, but I was very suddenly forced to go on a very long journey, and I had to leave everything that I know and love behind. I came . . . even farther than you'll be going."

Binye looked around the little ship. "I'm not going to ask whether everything came out all right in the end."

Burnham gave a rueful smile. "It's not much, I know. But it's mine. I've worked to pick up the pieces of my shattered life. And I'm still finding out how much can be put back together. It's not been easy, but it I think it can be done."

"How?" said Binye. "How can it be done?"

"I think . . . you have to be aware of what you still have. Your mother, for one, in your case. I came here alone." *And I can't find my mother anywhere.*

"There's Book," said Binye.

"He . . . sort of attached himself to me once I got here," Burnham said.

"Good to have a friend around."

"Yes, it is," she said. "I'm grateful for that. And I guess what I'm trying to say is—it's not been easy. But it can be done. And maybe this is the start of something, back on Ikasu. Maybe your world can start working toward looking outward again. Maybe that's something you both start, and one day you'll get home."

"Will you go home, Burnham?"

Burnham gave her a sad smile. "I'm not even sure that's possible anymore."

Sanctuary Four

Book was waiting for them on Sanctuary Four. To what extent he'd had to prepare the ground ahead of them, Burnham never knew, but then the people here were, on the whole, open-minded, and openhearted, and Zuka and Binye were made welcome. They stayed a few days, resting, and on the morning of the third day, Book took Binye and Burnham out onto the waters, to see the trance worms.

Their small boat slipped easily across the lake. Binye sat in the prow, looking small and lost. And then—

Then the trance worms came, their sinuous bodies curving up and out of the surface of the lake. Binye cried out to see them and, before Burnham knew what she was doing, the girl was up on her feet, and she leapt into the water—

And swam. She weaved her way between the trance worms, like she was in tune with them, and Burnham, watching, thought, *She'll be okay. In time, she'll be okay.*

———

Later, sitting with Book on the shore of the lake, watching the sun go down, she said, "I'm glad we went to Ikasu."

"Really?" he said. "I was just thinking that it was a complete waste of time."

"Not for those two," said Burnham. "Well, not for Zuka."

"I'm not sure. How are they going to live out here, Burnham? They've been protected all their lives, shielded—"

"Zuka's smart and capable. And Binye will be safe here, for as long as she needs."

"Huh. Still, that's days of my life I won't get back. Not to mention the resources I used up—"

Burnham looked at the beautiful sunset. "Book," she said. "Hush."

He hushed. They sat quietly, almost companionably, together. Burnham found her thoughts drifting back to Ikasu. She was glad to have gone there. She was glad to have seen a place so much like home.

Beside her, Book sighed. He said, "You know, this world we live in—it's not so bad."

She turned to look at him. "Are you doing your psychic thing on me?"

"Am I doing my what?"

She waved her hand up at her head. "Your psychic thing. The mind reading. I don't know! Whatever it is—don't do that!"

"Burnham, I was not reading your mind. It was pretty obvious what you were thinking."

"It was?"

"The deep sigh, the melancholy look."

"Go on, then," she said, almost dangerously. "Tell me what I was thinking."

"You thought Ikasu would be the answer. You thought you'd find some small outpost of the Federation, and that there would be . . . I don't know, some kind of *portal* you could fall through and find yourself back where you were—"

"In all fairness," she said, "falling through portals has happened to me before. I mean—you were *there* for the last one."

He laughed. "Fair point. But you were hoping for something more impossible, I think. That you would find the Federation there, just as you left it."

"The technology was amazing at least," she said. "But, no—that wasn't the Federation."

"Do you think it was ever like you picture it in your mind?" he said. "You have this ideal, don't you—the perfect society, peace and prosperity, living in harmony. Was it ever really like that?"

She sat and thought for a while. "Yes," she said. "Yes, it really was. There had been a war, yes, and people weren't always happy, all the time—people were still people. But there was a set of ideas, of values, that we shared, that we tried to live up to, in everything we did." She felt tears forming in her eyes. "And it's gone. It's all gone."

She thought about the world that was lost. She thought about what she had seen on Ikasu: that glimpse of what the Federation had become. It was like losing her home once again.

"I'm sorry Ikasu didn't hold the answer," Book said.

"You did try to warn me."

"Well, yes, I did. But I'm not trying to say I told you so. All I'm trying to say is—this time—here and now—it's not so bad, in its own right. And maybe . . ."

"Maybe what?"

"Maybe . . . you can learn to live a little with it."

"Huh," she said, and looked out across the lake. The sun had gone and the sky was getting dark. "Maybe."

Former Federation Spaceport Devaloka

"Commander Burnham!"

Burnham turned to see Sahil walking quickly toward her, a smile on his face. For the longest time, Burnham had been greeted chiefly with suspicion, if not with outright hatred. The woman who started the war. The traitor. It was even worse when it happened on *Discovery*, where people like Saru had known her. But slowly, slowly, she had earned back their trust. Showed that underneath it all, there was still the officer she had once been, whom they had respected. Nobody knew anything about her past here. Nobody knew her mistakes, her errors of judgment. But neither did they know her triumphs. Yes, they knew, in some indistinct way, that she had saved sentient life throughout the universe, but that was not what she meant. They did not know how hard she had worked, to make friends again, to earn trust and respect—even love—again.

They did not know *her*.

Sahil was glad to see her.

"I'm very glad you've come home safely," he said.

Home.

The word caught her completely unawares. Is that what this was now? A beaten-up spaceport? A shabby ship, limping around a handful of systems? Was this home? Burnham sighed and straightened up. Even if she was uncomfortable with the sentiment, she could at least recognize the spirit in which it had been given. "Thank you, Sahil."

"I have to say that I was worried you might find that new world more to your liking," he said softly. She had, in her last message to him, explained a little about what had occurred on Ikasu. The need for secrecy. The need to erase from his files any record of Zuka's communication with them.

"My liking?"

"More familiar than . . ." He gestured around the dilapidated spaceport. "Well."

They fell into step together, walking back toward his office. "There was a great deal to like there," she admitted. "You could see that their lives were peaceful, harmonious. Nobody's suffering or lacking anything. But . . ." She shook her head. "They don't want us. They don't want to come near us."

"Fear of what people might do?" he asked. "There are plenty who would like to take whatever resources they might have."

"That's part of it, yes," she said, "although I suspect they could put up a significant defense. No, it was more that they thought the outside world might *contaminate* them in some way. They have a good way of life, and they want to be left alone to get on with living it. They weren't interested in anyone else."

"They do not sound like the inheritors of the Federation to me," he said.

"No," she agreed. "No curiosity, no desire to explore, to learn, to meet anything or anyone new." She sighed. "What I don't understand is *why*. Why did they turn inward so quickly?"

"What do you mean, Commander?"

"I mean—if there was a general call for help, after the Burn. If Starfleet Command, or the Federation Council, or even the nearest starship called out for help—why didn't they respond? Why did they . . . give up? I know they were afraid of losing what they had, but was the Federation *so* easy to give up?"

He did not reply. She turned to see that he was lost in thought.

"I'm not asking the right person, am I?" she said. "I mean, if there's anyone around here who *didn't* give up, it would be you, right?"

He gave a self-deprecating laugh. "I could not have done anything else."

"You *could*," she said. "But you didn't. But—no. Ikasu was not the Federation. And I think it had stopped being Federation long before the Burn. What loosened those ties?" She sighed. "I guess I'll never know."

"But not an entirely wasted journey, I hope? The subspace relay . . ."

"There is that," she agreed. She had sent the specs to Jeremiah, who had told her that, with a little work, it would be more effective than the one currently serving the station. Send out its signals farther and deeper into space than ever before and find . . . what, exactly? *Discovery?* Terralysium? Starfleet Command? She sighed.

"Come and have tea, Michael," Sahil said gently. "Tell me your tale in full. You must have seen some sights."

COUNCILOR PRIYA TAGORE
PERSONAL LOG

I am aware it is some days now—no, almost two weeks—since I last had time to record my thoughts here. These have been difficult days, and it is my own belief that there are harder days ahead. I am aware that this opinion is not widely shared, that many here on Prithvi are certain that it is only a matter of time before contact is reestablished with the rest of the quadrant, and that life can resume as it was before. I try, gently, to seed the idea in the minds of my ministers and advisors that this may not be the case, that we must prepare ourselves for a longer period of self-sufficiency than perhaps they realize—but no.

And surely it is natural for people to want things to return to how they were before? We enjoyed—still are enjoying—a very good life here on Prithvi. Naturally, since we are members of the most enlightened civilization yet to encompass so vast an area of space! I can sit here, at my desk, recording my image and my thoughts on a holorecording device, which is a sheer marvel. I can wave my hand and nanotechnology will create for me whatever I need, at exactly the moment at which I need it. When I leave my office today, and go for my usual walk around the city, I will see groundcars and aircars and people out enjoying the good weather; they will return to homes built by industrial replicators whose infrastructure is maintained by self-correcting systems and their food, more often than not, is created by home replicators. Some will have traveled around this world several times today, using personal transporters. Some are visitors here, waiting for news of the starship that will be taking them out to the spaceport at Devaloka, from there to make connections with other ships, that will take them to many different parts of our far-reaching Federation.

What would we do, I wonder, if all of this were no longer the case? How would many of us manage? How would we live? How well would we adhere to the values that we claim to espouse? I am not prone to catastrophic thinking, far from it. But in my heart, I believe that something has gone horribly wrong.

Very quietly, then, I have begun to prepare for the worst. I take stock of our infrastructure. Our power reserves. How dependent we are on what comes to us from outside. I have recalled ships that were in local space. We shall, I think, be needing them. I have sent extra security farther out in the system to Devaloka. I want to be sure that we are . . . I hesitate to say "defended." Let me say "protected."

For I believe—for many reasons—that these are questions that we will surely be asking ourselves, concerns which we will need to address. Because I do not believe the Federation will come. I do not believe the Federation can come. Something has happened out there. Something terrible, from which we may never be able to recover.

5

COMMANDER MICHAEL BURNHAM
PERSONAL LOG

It's a while since I've added to this. I guess these days it's hard to know the purpose of keeping this log. Your professional log—the log I kept as specialist and then science officer on *Discovery*—that's part of the job. But these personal logs—they're a habit that Starfleet encourages. They serve a therapeutic function; simply describing events or emotions can go a long way to relieving stress or anger or frustration. Like talking to a counselor. And I did have a lot of stress and anger and frustration when I first arrived. Now . . . Now I'm *tired*. Keeping this ship flying is so much work. Not that I'm afraid of working hard, or incapable of working hard. But the energy that's eaten up worrying about money, worrying about supplies, worrying about resources. At last I fully understand what our moneyless society did for us. Freed us to concentrate on our higher needs. So while I might have had the time—some of these flights feel pretty long—I haven't had the energy, or the inclination.

There's something else too. Starfleet personal logs . . . we all know—*knew*, I should say; I must make myself start using the past tense for the *past*—we all knew that we might set out on a mission and not come back. These logs were there for our loved ones. A memory of who and what we were; what and how we were feeling. I know from the families of comrades what a comfort this has been. The black box on the *Yelchin* contained the logs of all the command staff. I know how Captain Hacquin was looking forward to her wife and son coming on board. That Commander Roala was in the middle of a messy breakup. That Commander Kamada was frustrated with the results from a recent experiment. That Lieutenant Commander Kavanagh was staying up late finessing techniques for dilithium recrystallization, and wished that more people listened when she told them that this was a serious problem that the Federation faced.

Perhaps we wrote for posterity. So that future historians could go through these records and find frank and immediate accounts of important events. Sahil said his great-grandmother had been keeping a diary since she was a girl. I don't know how old Priya Tagore was when she set her eye on the Federation Council, but at some point she must have been keeping that log with an eye to writing her memoirs. Bad luck, Councilor Ibithan Th'rhaven. Your name is still mud, more than a century later. And when it became clear that she was living through—well, the end of life as she knew it . . . Give Tagore her due. She kept up her logs.

I've lived through great times and events. That's true. The problem is—I no longer truly think that anyone will ever read this.

The Alice

The little ship was full of boxes: an errand to the Treylis system for some Andorians that Burnham had picked up at the Queen's mercantile in exchange for enough to keep her going for the next couple of months. The pay was sufficient that she wasn't asking any questions about what was in the boxes, other than to be sure it was nothing sentient, and that there weren't any local wars that she might be supplying. One newly honed skill was knowing when to ask questions, and when to stay ignorant. This didn't sit well, but then so many things didn't. She had struggled with hard decisions in the past—and had misjudged badly—but she had always appreciated the extent to which Starfleet regulations provided a safety net. A way of testing her immediate reactions. A kind of communal wisdom,

based on long years of experience, with tried and trusted results. Yet these regs, by their very nature, had not anticipated
the fall of the Federation. Each new encounter, she thought,
forced Burnham to think again about what was the best thing
to do. She was surprised to find how often she thought to herself, *What would Book do?* Sometimes she did that. Sometimes
she absolutely made sure she did the opposite.

Other aspects of this new way of life had been a real struggle. For example, the time alone on these long journeys. Too
long with her own thoughts, thinking about all that was lost,
and her helplessness in the face of it all. Meditation helped,
a little, but there were only so many hours one could sit still
and not think. Practicing *Suus Mahna* was better, although the
small ship was full of cargo, making workouts harder. Burnham found she slept more than she used to—deep, exhausted
sleep—and some days she struggled to get up. There had been
a couple of weeks where she would stay where she was, let
the hours drift past, and the ship's systems handle what was
necessary, until she fell back into oblivion. She had been doing
this more and more, until she almost slept through an alarm,
telling her there were asteroids up ahead and she needed to fly
manually. That frightened her. She got lucky that time; next
time, she knew, it could be fatal. She recognized this slump: it
had happened before, during her incarceration. The folding in
upon herself. The cessation of thought and action.

She did her best. She constructed routines. She made herself get up. She made herself exercise. She made herself medi-
tate. She kept up her regular checks for any signal that might
come . . . although she doubted more and more that this was
ever going to happen.

Were things getting better? Was her life here getting better? A little. She wasn't making as many foolish mistakes in her
day-to-day interactions, at the mercantiles, for example. She

was learning the customs of this new time—she balked at calling them laws. Sometimes she got messages from people she realized considered themselves her friends. Sahil, of course, with his air of gentle concern for her well-being. She had heard from Zuka, who was now traveling on one of the supply ships that ran regularly out of Sanctuary Four and was learning to be the ship's navigator. She got a message from Pa'Dan too; she had a ship again and was taking a job farther out in the next sector. She'd heard there was a base out there, a group of people looking for couriers to join them, well established and paying good rates.

"I'm going to go out there," Pa'Dan said, in her most recent message. *"Take a look. Let you know what I find. If it's not the usual cutthroats and gangsters, you might find it interesting."*

Burnham wondered about these messages. Were these people friends? Was she putting down roots, as far as you could in this solitary, fragmented place? Part of her pushed back against this: the people she thought of as her friends were on board *Discovery*; they might be out there right now, a little out of reach, but trying to find her. The days were passing, had long since turned from weeks into months, and who knew how long she might have to wait? Sahil had waited years. And for all her stoicism, the sense of detachment and self-reliance that marks those people who lose parents early, the fact was that nobody can be an island, not indefinitely. Everybody needs a network of some kind. Perhaps it made sense to lower a few defenses, let a few people inside her carefully maintained perimeter. She had done that on *Discovery*, part of what made the loss of those friends and comrades even harder to bear. Burnham's preference was always to keep some distance. The last person she had trusted fully was Ash Tyler. She wasn't eager to make that mistake again.

And then there was Book. Cleveland Booker: thief, rascal, liberator of beautiful and mistreated creatures, empath, and easily the most annoying person she had ever crashed into from a great height. Her guide, in the early days. He hadn't been in touch for weeks, damn him. Typical. He would turn up again from nowhere, she guessed, and they would pick up where they had left off, as if they were still in the middle of their last conversation, and she would be glad to see him. She was always glad to see him. Glad, and infuriated. He did infuriate her. He hadn't been exactly the first friendly face she had seen in this time—more the first *unfriendly* face—but he was the first, and that felt like an anchor. Besides, he tended to smile these days when he saw her, rather than scowl, and it was a nice smile. It was a smile worth seeing.

So when he did turn up on the screen, she couldn't help smiling back. He was, she thought, what passed for normality, these days.

"*Hey, Burnham,*" he said. "*How's it going?*"

"I'm fine," she said.

"*How's the ship? Still in flight?*"

She gestured around. "It's snug. But reliable."

"*I found you a good one.*"

"Hey! I'm the one that fixed up the damn thing!"

He shrugged. "*I guess that counts for something. Hey, how busy are you right now? Doing anything important?*"

"Right this minute I'm sitting here talking to you. So no, nothing vital." *But nice*, she thought. *This is a nice way of spending time.* She checked herself. *Or, at least, not entirely odious.* "Why? Are you in trouble?"

He grinned at her. "*How would you like a holiday?*"

"A holiday?"

"*Yes, Burnham. Did you have those in the Federation? Or was everything so perfect that you were always on holiday?*"

"You mean like shore leave?"

"*Shore leave?*"

She shook her head. "Forget it. Where? And what's the catch?"

"You know me well," he said. *"There might be some dealing in stolen goods."*

"Mr. Booker," she said, in faux shocked tones. "You know that it's a serious offense to try to corrupt a Starfleet officer?"

"You're about two hundred years too late to pin that one on me, Burnham. Besides, it's nothing you haven't done already."

Well, that could be all manner of things, some of which he didn't even know about . . .

"Trance worm," he finished.

"Where?" she said, instantly. "And when?"

Iliana Pa'Dan's ship

Pa'Dan was glad to be back in flight again. Once she was back in circulation, she'd called in a few favors from the old days, and found herself a decent ship. It was not in the same league as the one that had been destroyed above Atalis, which had been her home for over a decade. It was serviceable enough, and she supposed that eventually it would start to feel like home. But it was going to be a slog. Her plans to do a last couple of well-paying jobs and retire had not paid off. She had learned again a lesson from her younger days—don't get too invested in anywhere or anything, because you can lose it all in the blink of an eye. All that mattered, really, were the relationships you built; the people you could trust, more or less, to help you out when you were stuck. In this respect, Pa'Dan thought while the people on Atalis had been less than reliable, she might have lucked out in her savior. Michael Burnham was someone else who knew that everything could change suddenly; she was also clearly someone who would help a friend in need. Pa'Dan was grateful to Burnham for the part the woman had played in getting her off Atalis, for the help that had been given getting her started again. She wanted to find a way to repay some of these favors.

So, when she heard from a friend on her network that there were good opportunities a couple of sectors away, a sleek and well-run setup, it made sense to go and take a look. And, she thought, it would do no harm to let Burnham know where she was heading, and that there might be something for her there too. There was a debt to pay. And, at the end of the day, couriers had to look out for each other. Because nobody else was going to, and Burnham was even more out of her depth than Pa'Dan. At least Pa'Dan was *born* in this time.

On Burnham's ship, heading to the Cler mercantile, Pa'Dan had picked up almost immediately that the woman was, in some way . . . how should she put this? Starfleet-curious? There were stacks of memorabilia piled up at the back of the ship, for one thing. Burnham said she would be surprised at how much people would pay, but then you had to know about what you were selling, didn't you? Also there had been a uniform folded up in one corner; it was well kept, wasn't up for sale. Pa'Dan had tried a few conversational openings, but Burnham had never taken the bait. But there was something more there. Pa'Dan was sure she was more than a history buff with a sideline in selling to reenactors. Burnham often checked in with someone called Sahil at an old spaceport, for example, and sometimes he called her "Commander."

"Nice title," she remarked.

"A nickname," Burnham replied. "Private joke."

If that was true, Pa'Dan was a fully fledged fleet admiral, but everyone was entitled to their secrets, so she didn't push. She talked openly about her own life, when asked, and willed Burnham to reciprocate. Long flights in small spaces with near strangers encouraged the sharing of secrets. Long before they reached Cler, Burnham had confided in her.

"Well," said Pa'Dan, who hadn't seen *that* coming, "you have even less luck than me."

"On the contrary," said Burnham. "This was exactly the outcome we'd hoped for. Anything else, and you and I wouldn't be talking now. There'd be nothing. Nothing at all."

"But now there's just no Federation?" Pa'Dan's eye fell on the uniform. "I'm sorry."

Burnham looked tired and sad. "Maybe there's something, somewhere . . ." But Pa'Dan wasn't sure the other woman believed that.

Pa'Dan had never thought much about Starfleet and the Federation. These were distant names to her, relics of the past, a history that did not impinge upon her day-to-day life, beyond what she could use from the broken scraps of technology left behind. She'd seen images of gleaming towers of glass and steel, but these may as well have been make-believe. They looked nothing like her own homeworld. She was slightly hazy, in fact, about whether her own planet had been a member of the Federation. The population wasn't particularly diverse in terms of species—which was usually a clue to a Federation outpost—mostly Cardassians, like her. Still, as she understood it, colony worlds of member planets had been common too, and maybe that's what her own homeworld had been. Who knew? Pa'Dan had a feeling that even before the Burn, the Federation had been a hazy concept on her homeworld. A few supply ships, every couple of months; maybe a flag hanging in an office somewhere, a holo of whoever was president right now. If these superficial wrappings of empire had ever been present, they had long disappeared. That, she guessed, had left her world better able to cope with what had happened: the people there were already self-reliant. Starfleet, the UFP—these were distant ideas that, in the end, meant little, and were quickly forgotten.

Theoretically, Pa'Dan supposed she could see the point of something like the Federation. A shared set of rules and customs would be helpful sometimes, when you were perched on top of a piece of disputed salvage with a half-gone oxygen tank and staring at an angry Andorian who was the one making this into a dispute. In situations like that, it would be handy to say, "Hey, according to Starfleet regulation 9B underscore sixteen bracket 12 close bracket, this piece of practically useless junk is unquestionably *mine*." Which you *could* try saying, but you probably wouldn't get past the first bracket, never mind to the second. Even better was the idea that someone might be there to actually *enforce* these rules. That, she supposed, was what Starfleet had been for. Like the regulators, but . . . not corrupt? She could see the point of something like that. This made her think that this new setup a few sectors away was interesting. If someone was taking the time and trouble to establish a little local law and order, then perhaps it was worth finding out how well that was working out for them. Fifteen or twenty years ago, Pa'Dan had thrived on adventure. These days, a more peaceful and ordered universe was starting to have a distinct appeal.

The flight was uneventful. She fiddled with the ship's systems, optimizing them as far as she could. She sent out messages to friends, acquaintances, all points, just short of outright enemies, letting them know she was back in business, asking them for news, telling them where she was heading. She read too. For the first time ever, she looked up some history holos, tried to find out a little more about what the Federation was like. She was left pretty dazzled. She'd seen the ruins of ships lying all around, but she'd only ever looked at them for scrap potential. She hadn't taken the time to imagine what they might have looked like when they were operational. For the first time ever, she felt a strange, dull kind of ache about this lost Federation. She found herself wondering what her life might have been like, if she had been born a few hundred years ago, at the height of it. *What more could I have done with myself? What more could I be?* No wonder Burnham looked sad.

After about two weeks in flight, she realized that space traffic was becoming more frequent, more regular. Increasingly, she had the sense that she had crossed some kind of border into a new jurisdiction. There were more hails—polite but firm questions about who she was, where she had come from. She got the sense there was something coming up ahead. She started to feel jittery, but consoled herself that nobody had opened fire, not yet. Eventually, the inevitable happened. Three sleek black ships approached and hailed her.

"Courier ship. Do you have a permit to travel?"

Pa'Dan gaped. "Do I have a what now?"

She heard a quiet laugh come through the comm. *"Courier ship, you need a permit to travel through this system. Why don't you follow us, and we'll help you find one?"*

They were so polite, it seemed rude not to comply. Besides, a quick scan had revealed the extent to which they outgunned her, which was substantial. "Okay," she said. "I'm happy to comply with your wishes on that. Where are we heading?"

"Starbase Vanguard," one of them replied. *"Don't worry. You'll like it there."*

They weren't wrong. About four hours later, Pa'Dan, still trailing after her guides, came within sight of the starbase.

It was like something from one of the historical holos she had been consuming on her way here. Silver and glittering. Lights shining. Swift little ships darting to and fro, coming in to dock, on their way to new journeys. It was a glimpse of civilization. It was beautiful. It was tantalizing. It was beguiling.

"Oh," breathed Pa'Dan to herself. "Is this the Federation?"

Book's ship

The Luxiar system

"You know," Burnham said, as they sat together on Book's ship, "it strikes me that you could just as easily do this job by yourself."

"I suppose I could," he said. "But you came in handy last time."

"I thought I got in the way last time."

"That too. But I thought you might like to see another trance worm."

That was certainly true. But more than that—she had realized, on her way over to meet him, stopping to drop off supplies to a few worlds en route, doing a few errands for Sahil—she was looking forward to seeing Book. She had missed him. Not that she would say this to him in a million years. She said the next best thing. "I'd *love* to see another one."

That made him smile. Which made her . . . She wondered what the name for this feeling was. She decided that it was happiness. Seeing him smile that way made her *happy*. She wondered what this meant. She decided not to analyze it too closely. Perhaps it was possible to analyze things too much. Perhaps she should trust her instincts a little more.

At Luxiar, they received news from his contacts that the "merchandise" was safely in their hands, and ready to be transported to his ship. "Good news," he said. "No need for heroics this time." He caught her look. (Was it her look? Sometimes she thought he caught her *mood*.) "What?" he said. "Were you looking forward to getting into another scrape?"

"It keeps the reflexes sharp."

"I promise I'll rustle up a scrape for us soon. Or perhaps you could work on that?"

"Perhaps I will," she said.

At last, the trance worm—he'd called her Lily—was on board. When they were back in space again, she went down to the hold with him to take a look. She loved seeing him with these creatures. She loved to see him so relaxed. "Can't wait to get to Sanctuary," he said. "Can't wait to talk to her properly."

They were standing close to each other. There wasn't much room in the hold. Book cleared his throat.

"Are you okay?" she said.

"Yeah," he said. "Did you . . . Did you know that your hair is longer than it used to be?"

"I guess I did," she said. "Given that it's my hair. Why? Is that a problem?"

"No."

"Good."

"I like it," he said. "Is it okay for me to say that?"

"Yes," she said. "It's okay for you to say that."

They stood looking at each other. Burnham thought, *Is he about to* kiss *me?* Before she could decide how she felt about that, an alarm started to sound. She looked deep into his eyes and said, "Alarm."

"Yes," he said. "It is." They blinked at each other. Then Book said, "That's a fucking *alarm!*"

They sprinted back to the main cabin, where Grudge was yelling at them, *Where the hell have you two been?*

Two black ships, with white markings, heading toward them and firing on them. Book's ship lurched violently. The alarms became more strident.

"Bad news," muttered Book, grabbing for the controls and trying with limited success to steady them.

"White Palm!" said Burnham.

Book shot her a quick look. "You've heard that name too?"

"Can't seem to get away from it."

"I know," he said. "I don't understand where they're coming from. I don't know how they *move* so quickly!"

"Do they have a source of dilithium we don't know about?" she said.

"If I knew that, I'd tell you!"

"I'm conjecturing, Book!"

"And I'm trying to stop the damn ship from crashing!"

"You know what? I don't think you're going to succeed."

"I know that, Burnham! Take over flying for a minute, will you?"

"What?"

"Now's your chance to show me what you're made of, Starfleet."

I'll show you, you bastard, she thought, well aware that this was what he wanted her to do. "What are you doing in the meantime, Book? Clutching the cat?"

"Do not take Grudge's name in vain. I'm sending out a distress message. On my networks. If we *do* crash, we're going to need help."

She landed the ship, in a fashion. She sat for a moment, catching her breath, willing her hands to steady. Then she said, "That's okay, no need to thank me."

"I can't find Grudge—"

"She's under the bed."

"So she is . . ." Head under the bed, he said something muffled.

"What?"

His head came out again. "Jaffir. This world is called Jaffir. Shall we go and take a look?"

"We're going to have to," said Burnham. "Because power reserves are running low, and we'll need what we've got to keep Lily alive."

"Great," he said. "Well, that proves the old saying."

"What old saying?"

"Never trust a Starfleet officer with your ship."

Starbase Vanguard

Pa'Dan was increasingly feeling as if she had somehow slipped through a portal into the past. After docking her ship, she came out into a well-maintained docking bay, which made her little ship seem suddenly smaller and grubbier than ever before. She patted it on the side. "Don't worry," she said. "I imagine that I look even worse."

The words were barely out of her mouth when she heard footsteps behind her, and a voice called out, "Iliana Pa'Dan?"

She turned to see a crisp and cool young woman wearing a crisp and cool gray uniform. There was a badge on her left shoulder, a five-pointed black and silver star.

"Yeah, I'm Pa'Dan." She gave a little wave. "Hi."

"Welcome to Starbase Vanguard. I'm Senior Officer Nenee Raud. I'm the liaison for new arrivals. You were traveling without a flight permit, correct?"

Pa'Dan, suddenly conscious of being weaponless, said, "Is that going to be a problem? I've got to say I didn't know I needed one."

"Yes, we've found that a lot of people aren't aware of the new requirements to travel through this part of space. We'll arrange one for you straightaway—and don't worry," the young woman said, catching Pa'Dan's expression. "There's no cost. Not for first-time visitors."

"That's . . . good news," Pa'Dan said. At least the ship wasn't going to get impounded. Raud gestured to her to follow, and Pa'Dan fell in next to her. They came out of the docking bay and into a sparse but well-kept and bright corridor. Raud led her to doors at the far end of the corridor that turned out to be the entrance to a turbolift.

"Administrative wing," said Raud. "Block eleven."

The turbolift swung smoothly into action. Raud smiled brightly at Pa'Dan. The Cardassian smiled anxiously back. After a moment, Pa'Dan said, "Look, I'm sorry if this is a stupid question, but I have to ask you something."

Raud said, "There are no stupid questions, Ms. Pa'Dan. Please, go ahead."

"Are you guys . . . Federation?" It sounded ridiculous the moment she had said it, as if she'd asked this smart young woman if she was a Cardassian legate, or something. "I mean, this is sort of what I imagined a Federation base might look like . . ." Her voice petered out.

Raud smiled. "You'd be surprised how many people ask that when they first arrive here. This was a Starfleet base once upon a time, and in fact it remained operational after the Burn, for a little while. But no. We're not the Federation. The Federation doesn't exist any longer—or if it does, it's so far away that it makes no difference. But here and there, we've found, there are places where infrastructure remained in good working order. When we find this kind of thing, we try to put it to good use. I guess you can say that we're trying to fill some of the gaps that Starfleet left behind."

The turbolift halted. They came out into another bright and almost cheerful-looking corridor. There were green plants dotted along the way as they walked. It took Pa'Dan a couple of minutes to realize that these were for decorative purposes. The kinds of places she tended to visit didn't usually have potted plants. The corridor was busy too; other gray-uniformed people—mostly young—going past, looking purposeful, smiling and nodding to Raud, looking at Pa'Dan with interest and curiosity.

"Everyone looks busy," Pa'Dan said.

"There's quite a mess to clear up in this part of space," said Raud.

Raud stopped in front of a little door, which didn't say "Interrogation Room" on it, and waved it open. They stepped inside, and Raud programmed up a small office space: a couple of chairs, a desk, a computer console. Pa'Dan took the proffered seat.

"Tea?" said Raud.

This was getting increasingly surreal. "Do you have any red leaf?" said Pa'Dan.

"We have pretty much everything," replied Raud.

Pa'Dan almost asked for *kanar*, but said, "Red leaf tea would be great." About thirty seconds later, she was holding the mug between both hands, breathing in the scented steam. Raud, she saw, did not get a drink. The questioning that followed was straightforward, and Pa'Dan supplied answers readily, conscious of, but not really querying, what right Raud had to ask them, or whether she in fact had the right to record everything that Pa'Dan was saying.

"I'm a courier. I'd heard there was work out here, and I came out to look."

"How did you hear about us?" said Raud.

"Oh, you know, the usual."

"Which is?"

"Courier grapevine. Half of what you hear is rubbish, but sometimes it's worth going to have a look. And a friend said that they had done a few jobs out here and earned some good money."

"Your friend's name?" Pa'Dan hesitated. Raud smiled. "How's the tea?" she said.

"Er, yes, it's great. His name's Camjo Padim."

Raud seemed to check something. "Yes, we know him. So you decided to come out this way and see for yourself?"

"More or less." Pa'Dan looked around. "I didn't expect all this."

"This is just an office," Raud said, mild amusement in her voice. "Wait till you see the command center."

"I can't imagine."

"What were you expecting, Ms. Pa'Dan?"

"The usual. Some gangsters with big ideas about themselves. Bad décor. Strong vibe of underlying violence. Maybe some leather. It's not like that here, though, is it?"

"No," said Raud. "Not really." She turned back to her console. "Let me explain what happens next. We do a few background checks."

"Background checks?"

"We make sure that there are no outstanding warrants out on you from any jurisdictions on our borders. All being well—"

"Er . . . what if it isn't well?"

Raud smiled. "We'll escort you to the limit of our jurisdiction and ask you not to return until your record is cleaned up."

Pa'Dan, who couldn't think of anything immediately—not anything that hadn't expired, at any rate—said, "Okay . . ."

"Then we can issue you with the relevant permits and licenses to work within our jurisdiction. We probably ask for a little more latinum than is usual in these contracts, but you'll find that the more you work with us, the more latinum you get back."

"All right," said Pa'Dan. She put down her mug. "What's the catch?"

Raud looked up from the console. "I don't think there *is* a catch," she said. "We're just trying to make these few sectors a little more orderly." She sat back in her chair, mirroring Pa'Dan's own position. "How long have you been a courier, Ms. Pa'Dan?"

Pa'Dan snorted. "Longer than I would like. Twenty-five years? Nearly thirty?"

"And how is that working out for you?"

"What do you mean?"

"How much longer do you think you're going to be able to do this job?" Raud was looking at her compassionately. "You know, my parents were couriers. Both dead."

"I'm sorry," said Pa'Dan.

Raud shrugged. "I don't remember them. I don't hold it against them either. They were just trying to make a living. Trying to make a better life for me. But it isn't a good life, is it? It's lonely, and it's dangerous, and chances are you don't live to a ripe old age. I think you've been lucky to get this far—"

"I try to stay out of trouble," said Pa'Dan.

"But it's not always possible," said Raud.

Pa'Dan, thinking of all that had happened on Atalis, couldn't disagree.

"So when I saw what they were trying to do here, I knew it made sense. You're welcome to participate or not, as you like. There are no oaths, no swearing fealty or loyalty, just good work and decent payment."

"What's the goal," said Pa'Dan. "What's the end point?"

"Good questions," said Raud. "I guess . . . we're just trying to build a critical mass. Hope that this all spreads out a little farther, week by week, month by month, year by year. Life has been chaotic for too many places for far too long. People deserve a better future. That's all we're trying to do." She looked at Pa'Dan. "Look, you don't have to agree to anything at once. You don't have to agree to anything at all." She turned back to the console and entered some commands. "There's a room assigned to you now. You're welcome to stay. Spend a couple of days here. Look around. Take the contract away with you. If you want to join, you're welcome. If you don't . . ." Raud smiled. "We won't stop you leaving. You have the permit to travel back through our space and head back to your old life. We'd just ask you not to take on any work or cause any trouble while you're within our jurisdiction."

She rose from her seat. Pa'Dan drank the last of the tea, and then did the same. The young woman lifted her hand, palm facing front. For a moment, Pa'Dan thought she was about to spread the fingers apart in that weird gesture that she'd seen some reenactors use a few times. But no; the palm stayed flat, but she didn't move it forward, like she would in a traditional Cardassian salute. It was just an open-palmed salute.

"Tell the turbolift to take you to the accommodation wing, block two," Raud said. "Then take a look around. We hope you like what you see here."

And Pa'Dan, head spinning, walked out into the corridor, and thought, *Well, I've come a long way. I may as well see what there is to see . . .*

———

Pa'Dan's assigned quarters were small and functional while simultaneously one of the more comfortable rooms she had slept in over the past few years. There was one chair, for example, but there was a cushion on it. A cushion. This place was insane. After cleaning herself and her clothes, she went out for a look around. First stop was to check on the ship. A nice young man in dark gray coveralls was busy doing repairs—and a few upgrades.

"What's all this?" said Pa'Dan, anxiously.

"Your navigation systems were slightly misaligned," he said. "No charge, by the way," he added, seeing her expression.

"Then . . . great." She folded her arms. "Why?" she said. "Why are you doing this?"

He smiled. "Paying it forward," he said. "I guess you're trying to decide whether to sign up. Even if you decide not to—and that's fine by us—you'll at least say good things about us when you head back to where you came from."

"That's true," she said.

"We do a few small things for you that we can afford, and you say good things about us, and someone decides to take a look, and maybe they do come on board. Works for everybody, yes?"

Well, Pa'Dan thought, wasn't this exactly why she had come out here after all? On the young man's advice, she took the turbolift this time to the Center, stepping out into a small plaza filled with stalls and vendors and people passing to and fro. Some of these were clearly base staff, in neat gray uniforms; others, more variously dressed, she assumed were visitors, or perhaps even residents. She went looking for a bar, but there was, so far as she could make out, no alcohol for sale anywhere on the plaza, and she had to be content with red leaf tea. She took her tea to a table and sat watching people go about their business. Everyone seemed busy but content. She fiddled with the credit chip she had been given. They had even supplied her with a small but sufficient living allowance for her stay. Pa'Dan tried to work out what was going on here.

"Is there anyone sitting here?"

Pa'Dan looked up to see a human woman—short dark hair, middle-aged—looking down at her, gesturing to the spare seat. "Be my guest," she said.

The woman took the seat. "You're new, I think?"

"Visiting."

"Have you been given the sales pitch?"

Pa'Dan gave a small smile. "Pretty much."

"And do you like what you see?"

"Ye-es . . ."

"But?"

"But . . ." Pa'Dan leaned forward. "I keep trying to un-derstand—what's the *catch*?"

"The catch?"

"It seems too good to be true. And if there's one thing I've learned, it's that there's no such thing as free *kanar*."

The woman's mouth twitched. "That's true. But there really isn't a catch. What's the catch about living an orderly life?"

"I guess it might get boring after a while?"

"Maybe," said the other woman. "I don't know about you, Ms. Pa'Dan, but I'm getting to an age where boring seems an attractive proposition."

"Huh," said Pa'Dan; then: "How do you know my name?"

"Did I not introduce myself? My apologies. My name is Remington. I'm the chief executive officer here."

Pa'Dan gaped. "You're the *boss*?"

"In a manner of speaking. I certainly handle most administrative decisions—and I make it my business to know who's here."

Shit, thought Pa'Dan. "I hope I haven't said anything to offend—"

"Not in the slightest," said Remington. "You know, most people say similar things when they visit here. They want to know the catch. But there really isn't one. We're well organized, and tired of living hand to mouth. We want a little more order in the world. A little more certainty. We've all been dealt a rough deal, Ms. Pa'Dan, those of us who came after the Burn. But in my experience there are two kinds of people in this universe. Those who accept what they've got, and those who try to make life better for themselves—and those around them. I'd rather leave this part of space in better shape than it was when I was born. And I've found people who feel the same way."

"There are a lot of young people around here," Pa'Dan observed.

"Ah, you noticed that? Most of them have had a terrible start in life." She eyed Pa'Dan. "So many people have these days, no?"

Pa'Dan gave a noncommittal shrug.

"They've found that the steady sense of purpose we give has . . . Well, it's saved many of them," Remington said. "Many people find their place with us. And we take care of our own. The young, the old, the unwell. Those who need some care and support. You're welcome to go—if you like. But you're welcome to stay too. Work with us, for as long as you like or as long as you're able. Then find a safe place here, or on one of the worlds under our jurisdiction, when you want to stop."

Pa'Dan looked around the plaza. This place felt safe and bright—a long way from a lonely little courier ship struggling across unfriendly sectors.

"Are you sure you're not the Federation?" Pa'Dan said.

Remington smiled. "No," she said. "There is no Federation anymore." She stood. "Enjoy the rest of your stay, Ms. Pa'Dan. I hope you'll be back. From what I've heard, you'll fit in well. And perhaps you'll put a good word in for us with your courier friends. We've got plenty to offer them."

From what she's heard? Pa'Dan watched her depart. *What has she heard?* She finished her tea. As she began to stand up from her chair, the Trill at the table behind also stood up. They collided. "I'm sorry!" said Pa'Dan. "My fault—"

"It's fine," said the Trill, a woman markedly older than most people Pa'Dan had seen around here. The woman bent down to pick something up. "Here," she said. "You dropped this." She pressed a datarod into Pa'Dan's hand, and then went on her way.

Pa'Dan pushed the datarod into her pocket. Later that day, having taken on a few well-paying errands that would run her back to familiar space, she went back to her ship. Everything was in beautiful condition: mended, cleaned, reconditioned. The thing was a pleasure to fly. She left the starbase and went on her way. Only after putting a significant amount of space between it and her did she examine the contents of the datarod. There was a message on it:

"This place is not what it seems."

Yeah, thought Pa'Dan, *I think I kind of knew that already.*

The Sea of Jaffir

On the shore of a sea on a ravishingly beautiful and hitherto unpopulated world, a small but robust courier ship lay at an uneasy angle. Small creatures, on the upper limit of sentience as far as this planet was concerned, watched incuriously as a hatch on the ship popped open, and someone came out. They stopped briefly to put something to their face, and breathe deeply, and then turned to help someone else come out. This person was carrying a large bundle of fur.

"Is she all right?" said the first person.

"She's furious," said the other.

Burnham and Book—for this is who these people were—stood and took stock of their surroundings. Burnham had already flipped open a handheld device and was taking readings. "Oxygen levels are low," she said.

"Well, we'll have to stay for a while at least."

"Are you sure the distress signal got out?"

"I'm sure," said Book. "What I'm not sure about is whether it was received."

"When will we know?" said Burnham.

"When someone arrives to pick us up," said Book. He took a considered breath from the oxygen mask.

"I . . . am less than happy with the paucity of information that answer supplies."

"Suck it up," said Book, and offered her the mask.

They sat down on the pale pink sand. "That's a nice sea."

"I assume it's not toxic."

The whine of a handheld device. "We'll suffocate before it can poison us."

"At last some good news."

They watched the waves lap to and fro. Grudge, sitting in Book's lap, purred.

"Is that coming in or out?"

"What?"

"The tide."

A minute passed. "In, I think. We should try not to talk."

Another five minutes passed. "That might be a problem for us."

And another. "I think you might be right."

"We could go back inside?"

"All systems diverted to keeping the trance worm alive. Including life-support."

"So . . . climb onto the top of the ship is it, then."

"I guess so."

There were some further abbreviated exchanges. A cat was given oxygen, and then passed around, several times. With as much conservation of energy as possible, a man, a woman, and a pet cat were hoisted up onto the top of a spaceship. Burnham, lying on her side, and trying not to gasp, watched the sea approach, and thought that its gentle purple sway was one of the most beautiful things she had ever seen. "Not a bad last sight," she mumbled.

"Shush," said Book. "Not enough air for famous last words."

Ten minutes passed. The sea drew ever closer. Burnham heard the hard *tink* as it lapped against the ship's hull. There was a dark, oily reek. She wondered if it tasted as bad as it smelled. She drifted . . .

"High watermark," said Book, pulling her back. "Alleluia. Saved."

"At last some good news," she muttered.

"That's my line," grumbled Book.

"Shush," said Burnham. "Not enough air for complaints."

"At least we won't drown," said Book.

"Just suffocate."

"They'll come," said Book.

Burnham closed her eyes. A memory popped into her head, as vivid as if she were there again, lying in her bedroom in her second childhood home, curled up against Amanda, listening to her read.

"If we get out of this," said Book, "you should make a pact with yourself."

"Huh?"

"Put down some roots. Make some friends."

"I have friends . . . Tilly . . . Saru . . . Detmer . . . Struggling now, that's true . . ."

"I mean make some friends *here*—"

"Ash . . . Oh damn, Ash . . ."

A few moments, or maybe several hours, passed. Faintly, from a great distance away, Burnham heard the steady *whoosh* of a ship entering the atmosphere. Closer to hand, she heard a man say, with some considerable grievance to his voice, "Who the hell is *Ash*?"

A cat yowled. "White rabbits," said Burnham, with regret. Then hands lifted her up, and she fell into a hole.

Supply ship
En route to Sanctuary Four
Burnham opened her eyes. Something was licking her face.

"Book?" she said.

"Over here."

She sat up, slowly, struggling against the heavy weight in her chest, made worse by being in the presence of a large cat. "Are we alive?"

"I am, so I assume you are."

"What happened?"

Book, in clipped sentences, explained. A ship had come from Sanctuary Four to rescue them. They had been transported aboard, with Grudge, while his own ship was fixed and flown back. Lily, he was glad to report, was safe.

"We should take a trance worm with us wherever we go," said Burnham. "That way we know someone will always want to come and save us." She closed her eyes and thought about getting some more sleep. She heard movement across the room and, opening her eyes once more, saw that Book had come to sit beside her.

"Hey," he said.

"Hey."

"Not much of a holiday."

"Kind of what I expected a holiday with you would be like, if I'm being honest," said Burnham. She closed her eyes again.

"I didn't like those ships."

"Neither did I, Book."

"They seem to come from nowhere . . ."

"They sure get about . . ."

"White Palm. We should find out about them."

"I guess we should."

"Find out what's making them move so fast."

"Book," mumbled Burnham. "Shut up and let me get some sleep."

She thought she felt a hand touch her brow—feather-light.

"Okay, Burnham. Sleep tight."

On the edge of sleep, a memory flittered past. She

thought: *Did somebody mention Ash?* But sleep overtook her before she could remember more.

Sanctuary Four

They reached Sanctuary Four; it was autumn. The air was crisp, sharpening, and on the hillsides the gray of winter was encroaching. But, for now, the trees were still a riot of red, and creatures rustled in the undergrowth. Burnham went with Book as they released Lily into the wild. The creature leapt through the water. She turned to look at Book and saw him laughing. Burnham realized how much she loved to see him happy like this. Natural. Unconstrained. His best self.

They joined friends that evening; ate together. She got news of Zuka, still out on the supply run; and of Binye, who was out in the wild on a conservation mission. Burnham thought, *Maybe she's finding a place here after all.* She was glad that everything seemed to be working out.

In the cool evening, Michael Burnham went out to sit and watch the lake. She breathed deep, and she felt alive. She felt *present*. The trappings of civilization—of empires, of technology, of the cold eternal stars—seemed to have melted away. She was left with the wind upon her face, the rich scent of wet leaves, the fall turning into winter—and, beyond that, the promise of spring, and fresh growth. She thought, *I have never seen a place as wild as this, as lovely.* If this journey into the future brought her nothing else, it had brought her this—a moment of calm, of oneness with her surroundings, of serenity. She could not recall a time in her life when she had felt this way, when she had been free to feel this way. Detached from everything that had gone before, she had found a moment of peace.

She heard footsteps behind her. She turned to see Book, walking toward her, carrying mugs of something steaming hot. "Thought you might be getting cold," he said.

"A little." She took the mug he offered, gratefully. The drink was hot, sweet, thick. She felt her bones warm.

"Come and sit down," she said, and they sat together, side by side, on the deck outside the cabin, watching the lake. Slowly, behind the mountains, the sun began to set.

"Will you look at that?" he said softly, perhaps to her; perhaps to himself. "Isn't that something?"

"Thank you," she said.

He turned to look at her. "What for?"

"For this," she said. "For bringing me here. For . . . all your help."

She thought for a moment he was going to shrug this off, come back with some riposte, but instead he stilled himself, and smiled at her. "You're welcome, Michael."

The sky was turning gold. She said, "I miss my friends so much. I miss Tilly, and Detmer, and Owo, and Saru. I miss the ship, and my quarters, and the way the air is always still and warm. I miss the *lights*, you know? The blues and whites . . . I miss how the food tastes. I miss everything." Her eyes were clouding. "And I feel bad, because they're starting to become hazy, and when I sit and look at this sunset, and this sky, I think that I've seen nothing more beautiful in my whole life, and my chest starts to hurt. It hurts so *bad*, Book . . ."

She was crying. He moved closer to her. She leaned against him. "You know," he said. "It might help if you let yourself let it all go."

So she did. She sat beside him and wept. His arm was around her: solid; comforting. The dam broke. She told him everything. Her childhood; her parents; her move to Vulcan. Starfleet. Georgiou—the mother-mentor she'd longed for— and how she had ruined it all. Prison. The war. And Ash—Ash Tyler, whom she had trusted, and how mistaken she had been. It all came flooding out.

Book listened. Sat with his arm around her, listening to it all. When she finished, she cried for a little while, and he held her hand until she was calm again. Then he said, "Michael, that's really fucked up."

For a moment, she couldn't believe what she was hearing. She was about to get angry, and then the words suddenly sank in. It was a revelation to her—like a lightning bolt. Her life. Everything that had happened to her; everything that had *made* her . . . He was right. Her childhood—the deaths of her parents; the bewildering complexities of her adolescence on Vulcan; her career, and its unhappy first ending; her first real love, the horrible realization of the duplicity; Georgiou . . . Amanda . . . *Gabrielle* . . . She leaned against him; this stranger who now knew everything about her, who had no reason to judge her and no reason to lie to her . . . He was completely right. It was all *fucked up*. Burnham took a shuddering breath, and she felt some of the burdens she had been carrying for so long lift, and the wind take them away.

"Michael," he said, in a worried voice, "are you okay?"

"I'm okay," she whispered.

"Did I say the wrong thing? I'm sorry if I said the wrong thing—"

"You didn't say the wrong thing."

"I just . . . Everything you said . . ." His arm tightened around her. "Nobody should be dragging that much around with them—"

"Ssh," she murmured. "Don't worry. It's all good. Everything is good."

"Good," he whispered back. She felt his head rest, for a moment, on top of hers. Solid. Here. Now. In this moment; in this time. Something anchoring her to the present.

I have been so lost for so very long.

She closed her eyes. She felt something warm and heavy—

very heavy—thump into place upon her lap. She reached out to stroke the fur. "*Queen*," she murmured. Grudge purred loudly.

"Queen," said Book, quietly.

Burnham let her breathing fall into sync with the cat's. She felt muscles relax that she had not realized had become so tight. Stoicism, she thought, was all very well, and she had needed the discipline, the restraint, so often throughout her life, to hold her together, to prevent her from breaking into tiny pieces. But maybe it wasn't everything. Maybe there was some virtue to letting things go. What if she let everything go? Her past, her life, *Discovery*, the Federation, Starfleet, Gabrielle. What if she admitted it was all lost, and allowed herself to be fully here, in this present? This world, these people, this particular friend. A picture came into her mind: herself, standing upon the edge of a cliff, rocking to and fro. What would happen if she took that step forward? Would she find, after all, that she had wings? That she could fly?

She heard a soft chime on her handheld device.

"Don't check that," said Book.

"It might be important."

"Don't check it."

"I ought to . . ."

"Don't."

She did. Sahil's face appeared, a very small holo.

"Damn," muttered Book. He moved away, very slightly. Grudge, sensing the change of mood, jumped from her lap, surprisingly light-footed for such a giant cat. "Must you?"

"Duty calls."

"What duty? Starfleet duty?"

"I'm still technically a Starfleet officer, you know."

Book stood up. "I'm not gonna quarrel with you, Burnham. Not today." He moved away, but stood, watching over her shoulder, as she ran the message.

"Commander Burnham," Sahil said. *"I hope this finds you well. I have received exciting news. A transmission on what I believed was an obsolete Starfleet channel. It is old, but not so very old—twelve years since the message was sent."* His eyes were shining; he seemed to be almost trembling with excitement. *"The message is from an admiral named Senna Tal. They say they are waiting for people to join them on Earth. Commander, please come as quickly as you may."*

A wave of emotions swept through her. Some she recognized; some she did not. Later, alone on her ship, she would realize that one of these was disappointment. She heard Book, behind her, sigh.

"Twelve years," he said. "That's a long time."

"It's the best news we've had yet. Twelve years! It's hardly anything!"

"Burnham," he said, "you've come nearly a millennium into the future. You might not have the best perspective on this. Twelve years? It's quite a long time! The Federation fell apart in less than that—"

"Or didn't," she said. "Because now we know that something was still there, on Earth, not much more than a decade ago."

"Twelve years is not a decade."

"And if it lasted that long, why not a few years more? Maybe as this message went out, people received it, and went to join them." Her voice was rising in excitement. "Maybe they're stronger than ever by now!"

He didn't reply.

"I know," she said, "that you don't care either way. But could you be excited for me?"

"I don't want to quarrel."

"We're not quarreling. I'm not quarreling. Are you quarreling?"

"I'm not quarreling."

"I thought we were talking."

"We *are* talking."

"Then *talk*!" she said. "Talk to me! Tell me what the *matter* is?"

"Do you want to know the matter? The matter is—I don't think Sahil is being fair to you."

"Not being *fair*?"

"This message is *ancient*, Burnham! He's calling you back to chase phantoms! He keeps pulling you back to a past that isn't there any longer. That *can't* come back! That's what isn't fair to you. You have to put this behind you. Learn to live with everything that's around you. It's not all bad."

"I can't put it behind me, Book," she said softly. "I *can't*."

"I think I'm beginning to see that's true," he said.

After a moment, she said softly, "You have to understand. All my life—it's been blow after blow. My parents. Missing out on the Expeditionary Group. I never gave up! Not even after I was stripped of my rank, put in prison. I had to believe that it was not the end, that there was some light, some *purpose*—"

"Oh, Michael!" he said. "Don't you understand? There is no purpose to life! There's just who we are, now, right at this moment! Trying to do our best with what we have!"

She looked him steadily in the eye. "I don't believe that," she said. "I believe—I truly believe—that we know only a fraction of how this universe operates. I *know*—I know more than *anyone*—how deeply we are all connected—across time, across space, in ways that we can't yet comprehend! And that gives me *hope*, Book! Hope, that even if it's against all the odds, even if it seems like a dream that can't come true—I might still find something left of Starfleet, of the Federation. If I gave up on that—I wouldn't . . . I wouldn't be Michael Burnham any longer. And she's been too hard-won to give up on so easily."

He was holding Grudge close to his face.

"Book?" she said, uncertainly.

"I don't agree," he said, voice muffled in the cat's fur.

"I know you think there can't be anything left," she said.

"I don't mean that," he said. "I meant . . ."

"What?" she urged. "What do you mean?"

"Look, you told me that Starfleet cashiered you. Threw you out."

"In a moment of weakness, yes, I did tell you that." She regretted the first part of that the second it came out of her mouth.

"I see," he said. "Well, I don't regret that you trusted me. Because I know that despite all that, you remained Michael Burnham. And that proves that Michael Burnham can stand by herself. It's not Starfleet or the Federation that makes her who she is." He looked her straight in the eye. "You do that, Michael. All by yourself."

She got up and went over to him. She pressed her hand against his cheek. "I am grateful for what you have just said. For your faith in me."

"But . . . ?" he said.

"But I have to know for sure."

"Yeah," he said, regretfully. "I know you do."

Sahil's office
Former Federation Spaceport Devaloka

Sahil was always pleased to see her, but this time his excitement was palpable. "It was the subspace relay that you brought back from Ikasu," he said. "What a blessing it has been, Commander! Our range is steadily increasing. And I was able to find an old Starfleet communications channel."

The relay. Of course. Her trip to Ikasu was bearing unexpected fruit. "And you heard this transmission?"

"It isn't much," he admitted, "but it's something. Well, why not listen to it yourself?"

She sat in her usual chair. He waved up the display and a voice began to speak.

"This is Admiral Senna Tal. I will wait for any who would join us on Earth, anyone who still believes in us—the Federation lives on. But we need you—"

There was a hiss, and a crackle, and no more.

Sahil murmured, "A voice cries out in the wilderness . . ."

"Is that it?" she said. "Is that all there is?"

"I'm afraid so," he said.

"There's so *little* . . ." Burnham rubbed her hand across her face. Her heart was fluttering in her chest, as if all her uncertainties and confusions had returned, all at once. "Let me hear it again," she said. He nodded and played the recording back once more. As she listened, her eyes drifted toward the flag draped proudly upon the wall. One lonely voice, she thought, speaking into the void, hoping that someone was out there. Had anyone else heard this, before them? Were they first?

"The Federation lives on. But we need you—"

"It's so old," she said. "Could there really be anything still there?"

"Twelve years isn't so long in the great scheme of things," Sahil replied. "How long did I wait, after all?"

She thought of what Book had said to her; that Sahil was being unfair, asking her to keep on believing. She had pondered this on her way back here, whether she was chasing a dream. What had Book called it? A phantom. But hearing that voice now, calling out to them, calling out to *her*. She wondered who this admiral was; where they had been sitting when they sent this message. At Starfleet HQ, in San Francisco, with the sun sparkling silver on the bay? Or perhaps they were in

Paris, the city of light. She took a deep breath, which sounded ragged to her ears. She felt that deep pang of loss, and a profound desire to see Earth again.

"To think this has come to us all the way from Earth," said Sahil, reverently, as people once spoke of Rome or Athens. "Oh, how I wish that I might see Earth before I die!" He smiled at her. "The sights you must have seen, Commander! The Federation at its height!"

She was moved, profoundly, by his words. All her life, she had taken for granted the ability to travel vast distances, to shift as easily across space as she might walk down a corridor. She reached to put her hand upon his arm. "Maybe you will," she said. "I guess this proves we can't give up hope."

"I cannot begin to tell you how glad I am to hear you say this, Commander," said Sahil. "I know how hard this has all been for you. I know how you have despaired." He gave her a smile that was almost boyish. "I have something for you," he said. He took out a little box, which he passed over to her. Opening it, she saw her delta badge.

"I've kept this very safe for you," he said, almost shyly. "I knew that you would want it back. I knew you would find your way back, once again. Who would ever have thought?" he said. "That we would receive a communication from Earth? I would never have believed that, Commander. But then—you arrived."

Burnham looked down at the familiar delta emblem lying in the box. She thought, *I could be free of this; I could be free of the waiting and the doubt and the disappointment; I could be free to find out who I could be in this time, this place.* But she knew in her heart that what she had told Book was true: that if she gave up now, she would no longer be Michael Burnham. She picked up the delta badge—took back her charge—and put it in place above her heart.

"Whatever's still there," she said, "there's going to be a

lot of work to put it back together again. Everything frayed. People lost trust in the meaning. If there's going to be a Federation again, we need to understand what went wrong. Work out how to patch things up. The Federation now might have to mean something very different from what it did back then."

"One thing will not change, Commander."

"What's that?"

"It will still mean *hope*."

Later, back on her ship, she listened once again to the message from Senna Tal. How improbable, she thought, that Sahil would receive this signal—and yet he had. How improbable, that she would come falling from the sky, to find Book—and yet she had. She thought of Alice, falling down the rabbit hole, trying to believe six impossible things before breakfast. *Maybe I should keep believing the impossible for a while longer,* she thought. *That I might find* Discovery, *and Terralysium, and Senna Tal, and Earth, and that somehow the Federation will come back again . . .*

But the impossible didn't happen overnight. You had to build it. You had to *make* it. She opened a channel to the relay. She said, "*Discovery,* this is Commander Michael Burnham. My current base of operations is the Federation Spaceport Devaloka. I am including coordinates with this message. Please rendezvous with me there. You can trust the man named Sahil. He will know where I am. I'm waiting for you. I'm looking for you."

Then she let her message go, and she sat for a while, watching the flickering patterns of the console. They seemed like candle flames, a little light still lingering in the darkness.

COUNCILOR PRIYA TAGORE
PERSONAL LOG
My worst fears have been confirmed. No—beyond my worst fears.

A ship arrived at Devaloka, limping into port, and bringing with it at last news of what has been happening in the world beyond Prithvi. I could not have guessed how complete, how final, this disruption would be.

Dilithium. We knew we were overdependent. We have tried many other options, but the Federation moves so slowly these days. Decisions are harder to come by, priorities harder to establish. And we have left it too late. The Burn, they called it, on the ship. I imagine I will hear that word many times again over the years to come. More ships, I think, will find their way here—even a spaceport as small as Devaloka will draw people to it eventually. I wonder what other news we will hear. I wonder how hard some other worlds will be hit, cut off as they are now, from supply ships, from everything that has made their life possible.

I have always counted my blessings to live on a world as beautiful and bountiful as Prithvi. Now, more than ever before, I am filled with gratitude. We can, I know, with careful management and intelligent decisions, sustain ourselves here. But we will need to make sacrifices. There is only this planet, now, to depend upon. Ships may well come, but they will carry little with them. Infrastructure will have to be maintained more carefully, less casually. I will, I expect, be forced to make many unpopular decisions over the coming months—and it will, alas, fall to me to make these decisions. With the governor away, I am de facto governor here on Prithvi. We are of course still, theoretically, a member of the Federation, and so we shall hold elections in eighteen months, on schedule, and the citizens of Prithvi will be able to judge me on my record. We are, to all intents and purposes, now an independent world. But we can maintain our values. Our way of doing things. We can strive to keep some flame burning. One day, perhaps, the ships will return. But not in my lifetime.

In one other respect, I must be grateful. That I was here, at home, when this terrible disaster occurred. There must be many here on Prithvi who will shortly learn that their visit has been extended for who knows how long. The warp-capable ships that are out there will surely now be commandeered for life-and-death missions—and until we know the cause, we cannot blithely use warp drives in the way in which we have been accustomed. This leaves many people stranded here, and we must make provision for them. Ensure that there are homes, networks in place for them, physical and emotional support, and, should the worst come to fruition, the means for them to create new lives here. We must welcome them. And then there are those whose loved ones were not here. My heart in particular goes out to the governor's family, whom I must soon go to see, and explain to them that their loved one is not likely ever to return. How much harder, it seems to me, to have to live with the knowledge that someone you love is alive, but completely beyond reach. How does one even begin the process of mourning? Always there will be some hope, cruel hope, that a miracle may occur, and they will return. I thank the stars, and whatever fortune there is out there, that my family and I are together. This will be a great source of comfort to me in the months— the years—ahead.

6

COMMANDER MICHAEL BURNHAM

PERSONAL LOG

To say that the message from Admiral Senna Tal has shaken me would be an understatement. I think, because I was starting to become accustomed to my life here. To being on board this ship, and striking deals, and running errands. I was becoming . . . not comfortable, no, *accommodating* is closer. I was finding my way, at last. And now . . .

Now I can't put that voice out of mind. The images it conjures, of Earth, of Starfleet Headquarters, and the office of the Federation president. I know that a great deal must have changed in all the time I have been away, but there are many buildings on Earth that have lasted centuries. Why shouldn't these? Why shouldn't Earth still be much like I remember it. Why shouldn't *Vulcan* be much as I remember it? All I have to do is get there. Oh, Michael! Castles in the air, you're building castles in the air. And the problem with these—the foundations aren't strong.

I haven't yet spoken to Book. I don't know what to say. We were . . . we were connecting. I had told him . . . Damn, when I think of all the things that I told him.

And naturally this message makes me think—what else is out there? Who else is out there? How long did other places that were blessed with resources and facilities last? What starbases are still more or less operating? Outposts? Facilities that were as well placed as Sahil's but didn't suffer the ill fortune of a reactor breach? Suddenly, this time seems to be less hostile, but composed, potentially, of many little local pockets where the rule of law has been maintained. All they have to do is reconnect. Come together. Re-federate.

All *I* have to do is get there.

I should speak to Book. I can't speak to Book.

I have to put all this out of my mind. What, in fact, has the message done to change my day-to-day existence? I still have to keep this ship flying. I still have to find work, concentrate on the jobs at hand, try to keep out of trouble, try to establish friendships and connections and networks that will enable me to continue to survive. That will enable me to continue to look for answers . . .

What would I say?

The Alice

Zuka's message came through late one night, ship's time, when Burnham was completing her log for the day, and wondering how many entries she could produce that said no more than: *I flew very slowly through space.* She seized on Zuka's message as a chance to break up the boredom and routine. But the news was not good. Zuka's face, appearing as a small holo directly in front of her, was tired and very anxious.

"Michael. I hope this finds you well. I have a serious problem. It's Binye."

Michael fell back in her seat. "Oh no."

"I came back from my latest supply run, and she was gone. It seems she's taken a flyer and headed offworld. We've tracked her route, and we think she's heading toward the Eschis system. Burnham—if you're anywhere close, please, go and find her. Please. She's still so young . . . She's been so sheltered . . . We should have left Ikasu years ago . . ."

There was no question that Burnham would help. She was close enough, and her current job wasn't particularly urgent. She sent messages ahead warning there would be delay, and then she altered her course to follow Binye. She found the girl's ship drifting, but there was a single life sign showing. With a sigh of relief, Burnham opened a comm channel and hailed the ship. "Hey, Binye. It's Michael Burnham. Do you want a ride?"

Ten minutes later, the girl was huddled aboard *Alice*, and Burnham was busy laying in a new course to get her back on schedule, towing the flyer behind. "Whenever you're ready," she said, "I'd love to hear what happened."

Eventually, Binye sighed and said, "I wanted to go home."

"I know," said Burnham. "I understand." She understood much better than Binye could possibly realize.

"Mamma keeps saying what a sheltered life I've led. But I thought I could manage by myself. Turns out I can't. I just wanted to go back home."

She sounded entirely wretched. Burnham, her heart going out to the girl, came to a decision. She swiveled around in her chair and leaned forward. "I've not told you about my past, Binye, have I?"

The girl looked confused. "Aren't you from Sanctuary Four?"

"You know, you've trusted me today, coming with me, so I'm going to tell you some things about me. I shouldn't be here. In fact, it's not legal for me to be here."

"What, are you on the run or something?"

"You know, in many ways that would be preferable. But this . . . is more complicated." Slowly, as clearly as possible, she explained to the girl the circumstances of her arrival in this time. "I'm from a long time ago. I came to this future to . . . to make sure that the future had a chance to happen. By rights, I should be back in my own time."

"Your own *time*?"

"That's right. I was born more than nine hundred years ago." She saw the girl's eyes widen in disbelief. "I know it sounds crazy—ask Book. He saw me arrive. He talked to me right after. He can tell you exactly what a bewildered and newly arrived time traveler looks and sounds like. I remember the Federation, Binye. I was a Starfleet officer."

"You said that back at home," said Binye, thoughtfully. "I thought you were making it up. Later I thought maybe you were one of those people who just can't give up on a lost cause."

Burnham gave a small laugh. "Book would certainly say that's true! But . . . I was a Starfleet officer, back in my old life. A commander. These days . . . There's not much evidence that Starfleet is around, but I am. So is Starfleet. I'm here, and I can't find my friends, and I don't know if I ever will, and I don't think I'll ever get home again. So I do understand, Binye, and I'm possibly the only person you know who does—apart from your mom, and I don't think you want to talk to her."

Binye shook her head firmly. No, it was difficult, sometimes, talking to mothers. It was difficult, sometimes, even talking *about* mothers.

"So," said Burnham, "if you're running away from home, I'm going to say that's a pretty clear signal that you're not happy."

Binye, to her credit, managed to laugh. "Not really, no."

"But you do understand that it isn't safe for you to go back to Ikasu? That it's possible you might not be able to move freely if you went back?"

"What do you mean?"

"I don't think they'd want you telling people what you'd seen, Binye," Burnham said gently. "I don't think they'd want stories about space travel and trance worms and other worlds getting out." Burnham had gotten no sense that they would mistreat Binye, but she was pretty sure from the way that enforcer had spoken that the girl would be incarcerated in some way.

"No," said the girl in a small voice. "I guess not . . . It's not fair! I didn't want to leave—!"

"I know."

The girl sat with a mulish expression for a while. Then she began to look into one of the boxes she was sitting by. "Starfleet, huh?"

"Commander. Science officer."

"Was it . . . fun?"

Burnham laughed. "I guess by some definitions, yeah, it was fun! Mostly it was kinda . . . *terrifying*."

Binye laughed with her. "When did you know you wanted to be a Starfleet officer?"

"Mmm . . ." Burnham recalled the crushing disappointment of failing to get into the Vulcan Expeditionary Group, and the hastily arranged assignment to the *Shenzhou*. "You know, it wasn't the plan. The plan didn't work out—they often don't—and then it was the best thing that happened to me." Yes, she thought, even with all that had followed. Starfleet had given her two gifts: her self-respect, and Georgiou. She had squandered those gifts, but they had been given. She tried to find something positive to say to this lost girl. "Over the years, Binye, I've found that sometimes the things that seem like the biggest blows turn out to have been an undiscovered blessing. We don't know what the future holds, but we won't ever know if our eyes are always on the past. And the danger is that we can throw away our lives, hoping to put right things that can never be put right." As she listened to herself speak, she thought: *This is good advice. Perhaps I should listen to it.*

"I don't know what to do," said Binye. "I don't know what I can do, out here. It's . . . Home was *safe*."

"All right. Well, you're going to have to travel with me for a little while," said Burnham. "I have to finish this supply run, or I won't have enough latinum to get you and your flyer home. Come on this trip with me, see a little more of what's out there. I still think Sanctuary Four is a good place for you, but perhaps you'll find that there's more out here than you realized. Ikasu was beautiful, Binye, but it's closed, sealed off. There's a universe out here."

"All right," said the girl, ungraciously. Hearing how her voice sounded, perhaps, she added, "I'd like that. Thank you, Burnham."

"Michael."

"Michael," said the girl, and smiled.

"All right," said Burnham. "So—you can start earning your keep by helping me sort what's in these boxes. And I'll tell you a little more about Starfleet."

———

The next few days were uneventful. There really wasn't enough room for two on the ship, but Binye was surprisingly sensitive to this, and made an effort to do her part in keeping the place running. About forty hours away from their destination, while Burnham was catching some sleep, Binye came back to speak to her. "I'm really sorry to disturb you, Michael, but I think we've picked up a distress call."

Burnham jumped up and went forward. Binye was right: a slow, steady pulse, a mayday.

"Do we go and help?" said Binye.

"We'll take a look," said Burnham. "I don't want to get jumped by pirates."

"Pirates?" Binye looked fearful.

"Oldest trick in the book. Send out a fake distress signal, trap the unwary."

"Oh yes," said Binye. "I didn't think of that. I guess there was a lot I didn't think of, when I set out from Sanctuary Four."

Burnham altered course toward the signal, sending out

regular hails, trying to make contact, masking the route they were taking toward the source. About an hour away from the ship, she received the first message back.

"This is Michael Burnham of the courier ship *Alice*. I picked up your distress call. Are you people still in trouble? Can I help?"

A holo-image began to form: a humanoid face, rather thin and anxious. *"I'm speaking to you from the* Maildun. *We've been under attack from raiders for the past two days. We've held them off so far, but at significant cost to our power reserves. They've pulled back—but we think they'll be returning. Please help!"*

Raiders. White Palm? Burnham hadn't seen any of those increasingly familiar ships in this part of space, but it wouldn't surprise her to learn they were making incursions into this sector. "I'm on my way. I'm only a small ship, but I'll see what I can do."

The *Maildun* turned out to be a huge but antiquated vessel, like an ancient whale floating through space. Scans revealed nearly six hundred people on board, but limited weaponry. Slow moving, badly armed, but potentially valuable for scrap if nothing else, this ship was always going to be a target. Burnham reached out again to make contact, but this time could raise nobody. Odd. Perhaps their comm system had sustained damage . . . But she had little time to puzzle over this one. Her scanners were registering four small ships, heading her way, and rapidly, and of a type she had come to associate with the White Palm.

"Where the hell do these guys come from?" she muttered. "How do they turn up out of nowhere?"

"Michael," said Binye, uncertainly, "what are we going to do?"

Burnham took stock. Four raiders against one courier ship—it was hardly a battle, unless you happened to have some courier smarts. And Burnham, by now, had some real courier smarts, courtesy of a very smart courier.

"We thank my lucky stars that the first person I met was Cleveland Booker," said Burnham. "Watch and learn." Quickly, she initiated one of the defensive protocols she had picked up from Book—and watched in satisfaction as the White Palm ships wheeled around and began a hasty retreat.

"What happened then?" said Binye. "What did you do?"

Burnham smiled. "Courier trick," she said. "Scramble their sensors. Make them believe there's more of you than they'd like to take on." She breathed a sigh of relief. She didn't like to think what she would have had to do if they hadn't been fooled, but she was pretty sure she would have had to leave the big ship out there to its fate. She couldn't take on the White Palm alone.

"Were they White Palm ships?" said Binye. "The markings on the side . . ."

"You've heard of them?"

"Everyone on the supply runs back on Sanctuary has been talking about them. Mother said some of the couriers have been saying it's not going to be possible to operate soon."

"I think that's the general idea," said Burnham. "Drive the couriers out of this part of space. Move in to clean up afterward." She thought about a conversation that she had once had with Book. "I wonder if they have their eye on my friend Sahil's spaceport."

"And you're not going to let them do anything?"

Burnham shook her head. Not while Sahil was still there. Not while a little piece of Starfleet survived. "Certainly not today." She turned back to the controls. "We should try to raise someone on the *Maildun* again."

She checked the readings. All those life signs, still registering. She hailed the ship again but got no reply. "There are certainly people still alive on there," she said. "They might need help." Or perhaps this was one big bait and switch, sending out a distress signal, luring unwary couriers to their fate.

Burnham weighed up the situation. The most logical scenario was that the ship had sustained damage since that first communication and was simply no longer able to reply to her hails. That suggested that they needed help—which was the reason she had come here in the first place. With a sigh, she reached for the personal transporter.

"Can I come?" said Binye.

"No."

"I'm sure it's safe," said Binye.

"And I'm absolutely sure it's not," said Burnham. "Besides, I might need backup." She operated the transporter and found herself standing in a dim subsection of an old, old ship. About two seconds later, Binye appeared.

"Sorry," she said. "I couldn't resist."

"Binye! Do I have to *ground* you?" Wasn't that what you did, with teenagers? Burnham had no idea. Back then, she had not exactly gone through a rebellious stage. She'd been too busy in the skill dome.

"You could *try*." Binye switched to a wheedling voice. "Oh please? *Please*?"

Burnham, now way out of her depth, panicked. "All right! Stop that!"

"If it makes you feel better, it all *looks* safe," added Binye.

"Or not immediately dangerous," said Burnham. "There is a difference." She took stock of their surroundings. A small hold stacked with crates and various pieces of elderly machinery. Binye, going to investigate, gave a low, odd whistle that sounded like whale song.

"What is it?" said Burnham.

"These systems look *old*," said Binye. "I mean, centuries old."

Burnham came to see. All beyond her, technology not yet

invented in her time. Again, she experienced that odd sensation of double vision: being among things that were run-down
and elderly, and yet at the same time contained the shock of
the new. She studied some of the gauges closely. "I think these
are grain and seed stores," she said.

"Seed stores?" Binye ran her hands over an emblem on the
next crate. "Hey, is that the Federation symbol?"

Burnham came over to look. "No," she said. "Close, but
different. No wreath . . . And just the one star here in the center." She touched the emblem, and it came away in her hand,
as if it had been placed there, rather than embossed on the
surface. "How odd." She looked around the dim space. Now
she knew what to look for, she could see the symbol dotted
around the room: sometimes loose, like this, or else scratched
on cabinets, on the door . . . Like and yet unlike, as if someone who had never seen the Federation emblem had tried to
draw it from description. She ran her hand over the familiar-
unfamiliar symbol, and her heart quavered in her chest. Was it
too much to hope that this was a Federation ship? Was it too
much to hope that there was something or somebody here
that could answer her questions?

"Michael," said Binye, in a quiet and frightened voice, "I
think we have company."

Burnham stood up. Her hand strayed instinctively toward
her weapon, but she drew it back. The door to the little hold
opened, and two people came in. Burnham lifted her hand and
spread out the fingers in the salute she had learned in childhood.

"I come in peace."

———

They were led through the ship to a communal area where, at
Burnham's estimation, about two dozen people were gathered.

She took stock of them—they had the same long and hollow faces as the person she had seen on the holo, partly natural to the species, she suspected, but perhaps partly a result of ship life and artificial gravity. These grave people eyed Binye with suspicion, taking in her fur, the webbing on her hands. *I should bring one of those holoprojectors of Book's with me wherever I go.*

"Michael," Binye murmured, "have you noticed there's nobody young here?"

Burnham looked around. The girl was right. Everyone middle-aged, at least; many much older. What was happening there? Were there no children at all? She spoke, with a clear voice. "My name is Michael Burnham. I received a distress message from your ship and came to help."

"That call was sent out without permission," said a woman.

"Ah . . . We did not know that," said Burnham, uneasily, memories of what had happened on Atalis coming back to her. "But you were under attack?"

"We had defended ourselves against the raiders already. We were holding them off."

"With great respect, ma'am, I don't believe you could have held them off indefinitely. Those raiders seem able to call up reinforcements very quickly, and move about space very quickly, and they have proven themselves very determined in the past."

"If your arrival helped us in any way, we're grateful for that," the old woman said. "But we did not give permission for you to board our ship."

"I apologize for that," said Burnham. "I hailed you re-peatedly—"

"We received your messages. We did not reply in the hope that you would leave us alone."

"When I didn't get any response to my hails," Burnham

said patiently, "I was worried that people had been hurt, or that essential systems were breaking down. We came across to make sure everyone was safe and well. We're only here to help." She was reminded very much of the hostility with which she had been met on Binye's planet. The isolationism, the fear of strangers that bordered on the paranoid, like a fear of contamination. "We can leave, if you would prefer."

Binye, beside her, muttered, "This is like being back at home. Only this place is a *dump* . . ."

Burnham quietened her with a small gesture. "This is a generation ship, isn't it?" Her voice was clear and carried throughout the space. "Is there anyone here who set out from your planet of origin?"

"Nobody," said the woman. "The last of the first is dead. My name is Aoila. I am now the oldest here."

"What's a generation ship?" Binye murmured.

"A ship that sets out to settle a new world but doesn't have interstellar warp," said Burnham. "Each new generation is born on board, and then the next, then the next, as long as it takes to reach the destination."

Binye's eyes widened. "So these people were all born on board here?"

"And may well die here, if the ship is still making its journey." Burnham addressed the company, her eye on the woman who had spoken. "We don't mean you any harm. I found this in your cargo hold," she said, and held out the emblem she had taken from the grain store. "I wanted to ask about it."

The mood in the room had suddenly, dramatically shifted. The woman walked toward her and snatched the emblem from her hand. "Where did you find this?" she said, her voice trembling with . . . was that *fury*? Burnham looked at her in dismay.

"It was in the grain store," Burnham said. "Where we arrived—"

But the woman had turned around to speak to her immediate group. "This is getting worse," she said. "They're getting bolder—"

"I wanted to ask," said Burnham, "because it looks very like a symbol I knew well, once upon a time." She was aware of increasing disquiet around her, even rising anger, but she pressed on. "The symbol of the United Federation of Planets—"

She was not prepared for the reaction this got. A babble of voices rose up, and somebody yelled "*Shut her up!*" from across the room. Someone made a grab—Burnham blocked them easily. She called out above the growing melee, "Stop this at once! I am Commander Michael Burnham. I'm a Starfleet officer. Is this a Federation vessel?"

She was prevented from saying any more. Hands grabbed her—Binye too—and pulled them to the ground. The woman who had been speaking stood over them, looking down with barely contained fury. "Lock them up," she said. "Lock them both up."

They were pulled to their feet and dragged off. Struggling to break free, Burnham heard, behind her, the woman continuing to address the others. "I don't need to impress on you—not a word of what she said can leave this room. Not a single word."

———

"Well," said Binye, coming to a halt in the middle of the tiny room where they were being held, around which she had been pacing for the last fifteen minutes, "if you were hoping I was going to learn anything, Michael, my take-home message is that I should never, ever help other people."

Burnham, who was trying to practice mindfulness on her

bunk, breathed out slowly, counting to twelve as she did so. "No good deed goes unpunished."

Binye sat down on the other bunk. "Tell me if I'm missing something, Michael—but we can leave here, right?"

"The personal transporters, yes," said Burnham. "But I'm curious. I want to know more of what's going on here."

"I was sort of afraid you might say that."

"They've not threatened us—not yet."

Binye rubbed her arm thoughtfully. "They were pretty energetic dragging us here."

"But they could have killed us there and then. They didn't."

"They might be warming up to that."

"You can go back to the ship if you like, Binye."

"No, I'll stay. I'd just worry about you." Binye pulled her legs up to sit mermaid style on the bunk. "Go on," she said. "Tell me what you're thinking."

"I've read about generation ships," said Burnham. "Warp drives meant they were no longer necessary. There were one or two that set out from a pre-warp Earth. Who knows what may have happened to those?" That would be hard news, she thought, to learn that your long, brave journey had been rendered pointless by innovation. "Some ships put their crew into cryogenic storage. Others were like this—successive generations living on board, hoping that their descendants might enjoy a better life on a new world. It's a brave decision to make," she said, "although hard on the interim generations. I suppose each new generation has to decide whether to end or continue their voyage—if a suitable planet becomes available." She shook her head. "I guess none of us choose the world into which we're born."

"Do you think this one came from Earth?"

"They don't seem to be human, which would suggest

not," said Burnham. "Obviously they know about the Federation and Starfleet, or some of them do—"

"While others are kept in ignorance?"

"That seems to be a logical inference from what we heard as we were being taken away, yes," said Burnham, dryly.

"But why conceal that knowledge?" said Binye. "Is it about holding on to power?"

"It often is," said Burnham. She smiled. "You see now why I'm curious? We know we can get away whenever we like."

"If they're not busy cutting up your ship for parts as we speak—"

"A risk, yes. But I think they have questions for us too. I didn't sense that they were violent. I think they'd rather we were just gone. Which means leaving our ships intact. Which means . . . I think we should wait and learn a little more."

Binye considered her for a moment or two. "You're hoping they can tell you something about the Burn, aren't you? About what happened before, and after."

Burnham had to admit that was true. "My friend Book told me that after the Burn, some worlds knew their planets were not sustainable without Federation supplies. They gambled what they had on putting their populations on board ships like this. Tried to reach whatever was left of the Federation. Tried to connect."

"If that's the case," said Binye, "why the hostility when you mentioned Starfleet?"

"I said I still had questions, didn't I?" Burnham rolled onto her side. "I'm going to try to get a little sleep, Binye," she said. "They'll come and find us when they want to tell us more about themselves."

"Let's hope that all they want to do is talk," said Binye, lying back on her own bunk. She was soon asleep; Burnham could hear the odd breathing sound she made through her gills. But Burnham lay awake for a long time, contemplating the old ship in which she lay, and the strange sad symbol she had found—like a child's drawing of what the Federation might once have been.

———

Burnham woke, in the dead of night, aware that someone else was in the room.

"Binye? You okay?"

No reply.

She sat up quickly. "Who is this?"

"Please!" someone whispered. "Not too loud! We need to talk."

"Who is this?"

The lights came up dimly. She saw a young woman, surely barely in her twenties, with the thin face of her species made narrower by worry. "Can you come with me?"

"In the middle of the night? What's this all about?"

"Things here—they aren't what they seem. We need to talk to you—"

"We?" said Burnham. "What's going on here?"

"I'll explain—but please come with me."

Burnham slid out of bed. She pulled on her clothes and followed the younger woman out of her quarters. They moved quickly but quietly through the ship, along bare corridors and narrow metal stairwells. At last, they came to a small hold somewhere in the depths of the vessel. There were flashlights on the floor, and a dozen people sitting around them, talking quietly. Burnham's companion called out, softly.

"We're here. She's come."

Everyone looked up, straight at Burnham, and she was

struck immediately at how young they all were. Her companion was one of the oldest. They looked at her half in fear, and half in hope. As she walked toward them, her hand went up instinctively in the Vulcan salute. They shuffled to open up a space for her, and she sat down cross-legged with them.

"There's a story here, isn't there?" she said. "I hope you're going to tell me."

"Are you really Starfleet?" said one.

"It's a long story, but . . . Yes." She smiled around to see the pleasure that answer gave them. "For almost my entire adult life, I have been a Starfleet officer." That, she thought, was completely true, while avoiding lengthy and unhelpful complications. Her story could wait. She wanted theirs first. "Does that matter?"

But she already knew the answer to this. She caught the looks of pure delight they were sending each other, the murmurs of excitement. "What do we call you?" someone said.

"My rank was commander. You could always call me Michael."

"*Commander.*" The word was passed around, almost venerated.

"What you might not understand, Commander," said a young man who surely couldn't be more than seventeen, "is that arriving here and announcing yourself so clearly, so openly . . . You might as well have thrown a grenade."

"A *grenade*?" She looked around in deep concern. "But why?"

"Starfleet . . . I guess we all knew that it existed. Really did exist. But the older people—they deny it was ever real. That the Federation was ever real."

"I can assure you it was real," said Burnham. "Why would anyone want to deny that? It's hardly controversial."

"They didn't want to go back," someone said. "They wanted to leave, and they didn't want to go back."

"I don't understand," Burnham said.

"They say we're free from all that," said the young man. "But we're not free. They're not telling us the truth."

He got no further. Suddenly, the whole room was flooded with light—blinding light. Burnham closed her eyes, put her hand in front of them for protection. She heard footsteps, boots against the metal floor. A voice called out, clear and authoritative. Older. She reached out for the arm of the kid next to her, wanting to draw them under her protection.

"This meeting is forbidden," a voice called out. "Surrender yourselves at once."

She heard more people come in. She heard people being pulled away—some calling out, some crying, some screaming. She struggled to see what was happening, to stop it from going any further, but her eyes were still watering from the blast of light, and all she could see were shadows. She felt a hand upon her arm, maneuvering her gently but firmly away.

"Commander Burnham," said a voice in her ear, "for your own safety, you must come with me."

———

About fifteen minutes later, Burnham found herself back in the room where she had met the older people only a few hours earlier. Her inquisitors were back again, but now the mood was not so welcoming.

"Why have you made contact with the dissidents?" said Aoila. "Did you come here for this purpose? Had they made contact with you already?"

Dissidents? Calmly, Burnham said, "You know why I'm here. Because I heard a call that your ship was in trouble. I came to give assistance. Do you customarily treat people who have come to your aid this way? And, more to the point, do you customarily break up gatherings of people who have shown no opposition?"

"You know nothing about our life on board this ship. You're in no position to ask these questions."

"I can recognize a scream of fear," Burnham shot back. "Is everyone who was at that meeting this evening safe?"

"Of course!" said Aoila. "What do you think we are?"

"I think people find all kinds of justifications to stop people expressing their disquiet or voicing their opinions. But I swear I never thought I'd see the day when this was done under the auspices of the Federation."

"The Federation?"

Around the room, voices rose up. Burnham heard one or two rather bitter laughs.

"That's what's happening here, isn't it?" said Burnham, looking around. "You're trying to prevent those young people from having their say, from being part of the Federation."

"Oh, Commander," said Aoila, shaking her head. "You've got this completely the wrong way around. We're not part of the Federation. It's those children you want to speak to. Playing at Starfleet. Thinking they have the best interests of this ship at heart. A ship like this—we've been in flight so long. We are barely holding together. We can't afford these kinds of indulgences. They're going to destroy us!"

"I don't understand," Burnham said.

"No," said Aoila. "But I can show you."

———

The device Burnham was offered was, Aoila explained, a kind of holo-imager, but allowed the viewer a more fully immersive emotional experience. "You feel as if you were there," Aoila said. "You feel what people were feeling."

Burnham, deciding to trust the other woman for the moment, allowed her to attach a sensor to her temple, and then put on the visor she was offered. At first, all she could see was a gray haze, and the figures of Aoila and her companions behind—and then, with a blink, she seemed to fall down yet another rabbit hole, and she found herself wholly immersed in the fall of the planet Iolos.

Was this what happened after the Burn? she thought. *Did war come so quickly to worlds like this?*

She saw buildings explode. She saw streets turn into rivers of flame. She saw people turned to ash in seconds. It took no time—but it was enough. A few burning, searing hours—and Iolos was reduced almost to nothing.

And then the wait began. People saying: *They'll come.* Then, *When will they come?* And then, *Will they ever come?* And, at last, *We are alone.* She saw the betrayal, the fear, the loss— the realization that the Federation was not there for them. She saw them slowly start to sift through what remained. She saw them put together a ship—a ship that could carry what was left, and watched it set out, slowly, among the stars.

She saw the people left behind. And then . . .

A starship, in the skies above Iolos.

What? Burnham thought, bewildered. *How? I thought this was after the Burn* . . . And then she understood. It wasn't the effects of the Burn she had seen. *This was much earlier. This was the Temporal Wars.* She remembered, from Tagore's log, the impact of those wars, how the Federation had been rocked on its foundations. Had they neglected some of the smaller worlds? That seemed to have been the case with Iolos.

The images around her faded. She saw Aoila's face again. "Those were the last communications we had with Iolos. All our suffering, Commander. The Federation could have come to help us—but didn't. Not until far too late."

"I don't know much of what happened," said Burnham, slowly, "but there must have been a reason. Perhaps communications were cut off. Perhaps ships were scarce—"

Aoila shook her head. "We didn't matter enough," she said. "We'll find our own way now. Wherever that takes us."

"But you've told a different story to the children, haven't you?" Burnham said. "You've told them the Federation didn't exist."

She saw the looks passed around. "We want them to forget the past. We want them to make their own future."

"You've told them untruths, and they've found out. You've broken trust." Burnham held up her hands to stop the angry responses. "I understand why you might want to keep your ties to the Federation in the past. But . . . this was not the way to do it."

"Certainly your arrival has not helped," said Aoila. "Like someone from legend come to life. Like a second coming!"

"Or it's given you a chance to put the record straight," said Burnham. "Let them make informed decisions about their future. Otherwise"—she looked around at the aging vessel—"you said it yourself. Do you think this ship will survive civil war?"

The elders began to murmur among themselves.

"I'll help, if I can," said Burnham. "I'll go and talk to them. Explain all this. Perhaps one of them could come here—see what I've seen. You can try to make them understand why you did what you did. But you need to tell them the truth."

She listened to them talk, hurried, urgent whispers among themselves. She started to sense that they were coming to an agreement. Just as she thought a breakthrough was about to happen, the door burst open, and once again light burned bright around her. Arms grabbed her, pulled her away. She heard Binye whisper in her ear, "I wasn't going to leave you their prisoner."

———

"That," said Burnham, when at last she was allowed to stop and take her breath, "was not a helpful intervention."

The young faces around her—Binye included—fell measurably at the sight of her disapproval. "They had you captive," said the young woman who had first come to speak to her.

"I was talking to them. They were *listening* to me! I was about to persuade them to talk to you—"

"We have nothing to say to them. They've *lied* to us, again and again. They told us Starfleet was a myth! That the Federation never existed!"

"Bad mistakes. I think they can see that now." Burnham looked around the group of her young disciples. "It's time to meet them," she said. "It's time to sit down and talk, come up with a solution that makes everyone happy."

She heard the rustle of discontent pass around the room. "Why should we talk to them? They don't let us live the way we want to live."

"They have a share in this ship," said Burnham. "They've lived here, worked here, all their lives—"

"So have we. We'll be here longer, after they're gone! If anything, we should have more of a say in how things are going to be run."

"Maybe they have experience you can learn from," Burnham said.

"Look around you," said another one. "The ship's starting to fall apart. They've made a mess of things!"

"You've been in flight a long time," said Burnham.

"And who knows how long we have to go! The ship needs

discipline, routine—regulations. The ship needs to run as if we're *Starfleet*."

Burnham looked at the keen faces around her. She knew she had power over them—the strange power of an icon come to life. It was not a kind of power she wanted, but it was hers, nonetheless.

"You know," Burnham said, "joining Starfleet was one of the greatest achievements of my life." She saw the awe in their faces that someone had really been at that place. "I could not believe that I got to wear that uniform. That I got to continue that tradition of duty, and service, and honor. My career didn't always run smoothly"—something of an understatement, she thought, but that was not the point of this story—"but that uniform has meant more to me than anything else in my life. And what mattered most were the values that it represented. And those values are simple. Mutual respect. Tolerance. Infinite diversity, in infinite combinations."

She could hear the anger and disappointment beginning to bubble up around the room. She raised her own voice to counter it. "You need to sit down with your elders. You need to find a way through this, together."

Now she could barely be heard. So she switched voices. Her officer's voice.

"That's not a point for discussion, cadets! It's a damn *order*!"

The shock in the room was palpable. Beside her, she heard Binye say, "Now?"

"Now," said Burnham. They hit the personal transporters.

Control room
***The* Maildun**
The three-person crew in the command center was not prepared for their sudden arrival.

"Out!" barked Burnham. "*Now!*" She didn't draw a

weapon, but with her hand shoved into the pocket of her leather coat, she could give the impression that they were armed. They were out within half a minute. Burnham sealed the door behind them.

Aoila's voice came through a comm channel. *"Burnham, come out of there, now!"*

"Not until both sides can show they will come to an agreement—or ask me to help."

"This is blackmail—no, it's terrorism! You can't hold us hostage like this!"

"I can," she said, "and I will." She cut the comm and took stock of their immediate surroundings. The ship was old, but had been maintained with care and love. She considered the situation; weighed her responsibilities and her duties. She glanced at Binye—a young woman in her care, in the middle of an escalating situation. She should, for Binye's sake, transport them both back to her ship immediately. But she had responsibilities here, too, now. The situation on the *Maildun* had been a long time in the making, it was true, but it was surely her presence, her announcement of her name and rank, that had precipitated the present struggle. Binye, looking at her, said, "You're not thinking of leaving, are you?"

"I should take you back to my ship."

"I'd never forgive you, Michael."

Burnham sighed. The hotheadedness of youth, the absolutism—that was part of the problem here, surely. "All right," she said. "Well, against my better judgment, we'll stick around and try to help these people work something out."

"Do you think we *can* help?"

"We can try." Burnham lifted her chin and straightened her back, instinctively settling into the stance of a Starfleet officer. She might not have anything to support her, but she could speak authoritatively. She could try to resolve this conflict. She opened up a comm channel and spoke to the whole ship.

"This is Commander Michael Burnham. You all know that this situation cannot continue. You do not serve yourselves, your ship, your ancestors, or your descendants by fighting in this way. Put aside your differences. We can negotiate, not fight. We can find a peaceful resolution to this conflict."

There was a brief pause, and then weapons' fire. Someone was shooting at the door.

"Or not," muttered Binye.

"Wait," said Burnham. She addressed the ship again. "I know there are children on board this ship. Think how frightened they must be now. I know that each side in this dispute wants a different future for them, but surely you can agree at least that this uncertainty, this violence, is not what you want. Is that what you want them to see? Is that a place where we can meet in agreement?"

Aoila's voice came through the comm. *"We start when you give us back control of our own bridge, Commander Burnham!"*

Still using her title. A little authority remained, or perhaps an increased hostility toward Starfleet. "I can't do that," said Burnham, calmly and firmly. "Listen, Aoila—I can leave whenever I choose. Binye and I both have personal transporters in here. We can leave when we want. But we are prepared to stay and help you."

"Michael . . ." murmured Binye.

Burnham shot her a quick look and shook her head. *Let me finish this.* She continued, "I know that my presence here has brought long-standing differences to a crisis point. I want to help you get past those, if I can."

"Michael," said Binye, more urgently. "This is serious."

Burnham cut the comm. "What is it?"

"Those White Palm raiders—I think they're coming back. I think they've brought some friends."

Burnham looked at the display. Sure enough, half a dozen pinpricks of light were heading their way. "Well," she said. "I'm glad we stayed. If we'd left, most likely they would have picked us both off before coming back here. As it is—we might yet be able to defend this ship." She opened up the comm to speak again to the ship. "People of the *Maildun*. The raiders are back—and they've brought reinforcements. I can defend this ship, but I need a crew. Make your choice now. Help me fight your attackers and save us all. Or keep up your quarrel and we can all die together in the next hour. I'll give you five minutes to decide. If you choose to fight your common enemy, then each side send me your two most capable people to help. Burnham out."

She cut the comm.

"Will that work?" said Binye.

"Let's see," said Burnham. "You know, Binye—you should go back to my ship now."

"Not a chance!"

"Shall I make that an order?"

Binye laughed and shook her head. "I'm not Starfleet, Michael. And I'm not very good at doing what I'm told."

"Your mother's daughter, huh?"

"Low blow, Commander."

The comm chimed. Aoila said, *"You can open the door now. You have your crew."*

Burnham operated the control to open the sealed door to the bridge. Her new crew came in, two younger, two older. The pairs eyed each other warily. Burnham, from the command seat, said, "Names and specialties, please. I can guess already which sides you're on."

The oldest of them looked at her doubtfully. "We're not

made to fight battles, you know," he said. "The ship is old, slow. They're much faster than we are—"

"I don't intend to fight them," said Burnham. "I intend to outsmart them."

Quickly, she explained her plan, and what she needed them to do. They were unsure—she didn't blame them. She was fairly doubtful too. She'd tried this trick with her smaller ship; she had no idea how and if it would work with this big generation ship.

The raiders were coming about. They fired a few trial shots, leaving the *Maildun* shaking. "Shields?" she asked.

"Holding," she heard back.

"Good," said Burnham. She glanced at the two she had assigned to the sensors. "Ready?"

"Nearly there . . ."

"I want this ready by their next pass," said Burnham. Then she waved to Binye to stand next to her. "Binye," she murmured, "when I tell you—you're to go. Back to my ship. Get away from here—"

"Michael, no—!"

"This time," said Burnham, "you'll listen, and you'll do what I say."

Binye subsided. She stood quietly beside Burnham's seat, and watched as the White Palm ships turned, and came back for another pass.

"*Now!*" commanded Burnham. There was a split second, and then the raiders swung swiftly around and away, without firing a shot. "What they're seeing," said Burnham, "is four more of us—only this time, armed to the teeth. They don't know where the hell those ships have come from. They might suspect something—but they're not going to risk it."

"The nearer of the ships is hailing us, Commander Burnham," said the young man who had taken on comms.

"Let me hear what they have to say," said Burnham. When the captain's holo materialized in front of her, Burnham spoke before he could. "White Palm ship. Your attempts to board this ship have been unsuccessful twice today. I strongly advise you do not make a third attempt."

He gave a wry smile. *Don't worry. We know when we're beaten.*

"Good," said Burnham. "It's time for you to go home. And tell whoever you're working for—Commander Michael Burnham of Starfleet will not allow them to harm anyone in this sector. Tell them that something of Starfleet remains."

The captain gave a short, contemptuous laugh. *Starfleet? There is no Starfleet. We've seen to that. We're ready for you, Burnham.*" But the ships pulled back and were soon on their way. Burnham breathed out and leaned back in her chair. She felt Binye's hand come to rest upon her shoulder. "You really are Starfleet, aren't you?"

"I guess I still am."

"So now you get to play diplomat, huh?"

"What?"

Binye nodded around the bridge at the two pairs that comprised her crew, now eyeing each other again. "There's still a civil war to stop."

—

As Burnham had hoped, the fact that people had fought together brought them together—to some extent. There was still suspicion between the two groups, and mistrust, and the ship could, ultimately, choose only one direction. But the people on board could, perhaps, go separate ways.

"Here's my proposed solution," said Burnham at last, after hours of listening to opinions from, it seemed, just about everyone on board the ship, from Aoila down to a very opinion-ated and articulate six-year-old girl. "I'm hoping this means a chance for everyone to lead the kind of life they want to lead."

She drew a deep breath.

"Twelve years ago, a Starfleet admiral named Senna Tal sent a communication from Earth, advising anyone who was able to return to join him on Earth, where he would be wait-ing. Now this ship"—she gestured around—"is uniquely placed to make a journey like that. You were sent out as a gen-eration ship. Sent out to make a long voyage where only your children's children would reach the destination. Let me be clear"—and she wondered now to what extent she was speak-ing to herself—"the Starfleet you will find there—if you find anything—is unlikely to be the one that I knew, or that your ancestors back on your homeworld knew. But I know in my heart that if it bears any resemblance to my Starfleet, then it will be something worth both saving and aiding."

"Some of us never wanted to be part of Starfleet," said Aoila. "What about us?"

"Then it's time to make a decision," said Burnham. "You can stay on this ship—which is your home—and lead your life here, in peace, accepting the route the ship is now taking. It will not reach there in your lifetime. Or you can move on."

"Where?" Aoila asked. "Where can we go?"

"Binye and I," said Burnham, "will be returning to a world called Sanctuary Four."

She saw Binye roll her eyes, and then make a face that said *All right . . . all right.*

"It's a peaceful world, secluded. They've taken in people before, and they'll take in others. It's a good place to retire to. The *Maildun* can spare a shuttle or two. We can escort you there. And if you want to move on, there's a spaceport that I use as my base. It's Starfleet, but it's friendly. You can get sup-

plies there. Find a new destination. Move on. But this ship—
its next stop is Earth."

In the end, only a handful of people decided to leave. The
journey to Earth—as legendary a world as lost Atlantis—was
enough to sustain the Starfleet faction, and distant enough to
satisfy those who had wanted to leave the past behind. Burnham, raiding her memory for old Starfleet training sessions on
conflict resolution, helped them set up a new way of making
decisions. As a second coming of Starfleet, she had been something of a disappointment to many on board, she suspected.
Still, they had a resolution.

"Never meet your idols," said Binye, as they settled back
on board Burnham's ship.

"There's more heroism to making day-to-day life function
than people appreciate," said Burnham.

"Says the time-traveling savior of all sentient life," said
Binye.

Burnham felt laughter bubble up within her. "That's the
kind of thing I do on the odd days," she said. "On the evens,
I'm pushing paperwork with the best of them."

"To even days, huh," said Binye, "and stable government.
I told you I never wanted to leave Ikasu."

They watched the *Maildun* go on its way. "True believers," said Burnham. "So true that even the real thing wasn't
good enough for them."

Former Federation Spaceport Devaloka

Burnham returned Binye to Sanctuary Four, where a fran-
tic Zuka, caught between anger and terror, threw her arms
around her daughter, and promised there would be changes.
Binye seemed quite poised, Burnham thought. "Mamma," she
said. "I'm not going anywhere. Not for a while, anyway."

About half a dozen people from the *Maildun*, mostly the

oldest, seeing the beauty of Sanctuary Four, decided to remain there. Burnham escorted the shuttle from the *Maildun* with the remaining refugees back to Devaloka.

Sahil watched the new arrivals with his usual equable manner. "You seem to gather strays, Commander," he said.

"I know how they feel," she said.

"I am not complaining," he said. "I am very glad to see you. I don't see as much of you these days . . ."

"At least when I come, I have an interesting story to tell."

That evening, she, Sahil, and Jeremiah met at their old spot. Jeremiah had a gift for her. "I've started to get meaningful data off that chip of yours," he said.

"Anything to use to predict where my ship might arrive?"

"Not yet," he said. "But I thought you might like this." He handed her a little holoprojector. She pressed the switch—

—and was completely unprepared for the images that appeared. Her friends from *Discovery*. She remembered that she would file these moments away on her tricorder, transfer them later to her personal files. She saw Tilly, playing kadis-kot with Airiam. Airiam . . .

Burnham blinked back tears. She turned off the projector and put it in her pocket. Clearing her throat, she said, "Do you want to hear the whole story of the *Maildun* or not?"

Sahil and Jeremiah exchanged looks. Jeremiah took out a pack of cards and spread them out upon the table in front of him. "Fire ahead, Burnham."

Burnham told the tale. "What was fascinating about them was that their ancestors set out before the Burn," she concluded. "Their homeworld was cut off during the Temporal Wars and collapsed into chaos. Their ship was sent out before the Federation reestablished contact."

"An interesting period," said Sahil, "and one about which I must confess I know little. My own homeworld was not affected by the wars, and life there continued as usual until the Federation was able to reestablish contact."

"Other places weren't so lucky," said Jeremiah, laying cards down upon cards.

Burnham, considering this, nodded slowly. "The biggest question I have is how the Federation collapsed so quickly after the Burn," she said. "If there were stresses and strains dating back to the Temporal Wars—internal fractures caused by those wars—that might explain why the Burn was a fatal blow. The trust had been lost long ago. The damage was already done."

"I see," said Sahil. "Many of the worlds out on the edge already felt they had been abandoned. The fragmentation was already under way." He rubbed his brow. "As I say, my own home was lucky to come through those wars unscathed. But if other places had been left behind . . ."

"I've seen places that never recovered from the Temporal Wars," said Jeremiah, quietly. "Places where you'd think the Federation had never returned—long, long before the Burn. Out on the edge. Not one of the big or powerful worlds. No voice in the Council—"

Burnham shook her head. "That's not how it worked. Every member world had an equal voice—"

Jeremiah smiled. "That was the ideal, Burnham," he said. "But was it the reality? By the time the wars broke out?"

Burnham faltered. "I . . . can't say," she replied honestly. She thought about that. It was true that the Big Four—Earth, Vulcan, Andor, Tellar—held considerable sway. But to the extent that other worlds felt left behind? Surely not. And yet, something had gone wrong. For some reason, all these worlds no longer felt allegiance to the United Federation of Planets. There had already been cracks when the Burn hit, shattering the Federation for good.

"You know," said Jeremiah, "time travel is still a crime under interstellar treaties."

"Excuse me?" said Burnham.

"Yup. All these laws and accords and rules and so on came in afterward."

There was a pause. *Does he know?* Burnham glanced at Sahil, who gave a quick shake of his head. *I haven't said anything.*

The pause went on. "Still," said Jeremiah, after a moment or two, "who is there out there to enforce those treaties?" He looked at both of them. "The Federation doesn't exist any longer, after all. Whatever you two might like to believe."

"That's an interesting question," said Sahil, smoothly. "Is a treaty still a treaty if the parties concerned no longer exist?" He gave a small laugh. "I, for one, would hardly have the resources to incarcerate any time traveler who came this way."

Jeremiah finished his drink and gathered up his cards. "This is where the conversation gets too technical for me," he said, and, wishing them a good night, went on his way.

"Does he *know*?" said Burnham.

"I can't see how," Sahil replied. "I have been very careful."

Burnham, guiltily, thought of the people she had trusted. Pa'Dan. Binye—a girl, for pity's sake. "Do you think we should have told him?"

"That is your decision to make," said Sahil.

I should be more careful, thought Burnham, and decided against. She said good night and went back to the quarters she used here. An empty room now, more or less. She had never had the chance to make this room home. Home was her ship now.

She took out the holoprojector, and conjured them up, the ghosts of her friends. Tilly burbling. Saru, uncomfortable when he realized she was taking his image. Ash Tyler—

Clumsily, Burnham turned the device off. The past, she thought. There were some things that were better left there. Sealed away there. Forgotten.

PRESIDENT-ELECT PRIYA TAGORE

PERSONAL LOG

Well, we have won. I must say, when we started on this process, a year ago, of reconstituting Prithvi, there were times I doubted we could ever succeed. Hope springs eternal, the old saying goes, and that is surely a good thing. But when hope prevents people from recognizing the truth of their situation, of finding ways to move on into an uncertain future, while keeping what is best from the past, then it becomes a burden.

Although I do not have many examples to draw upon, I imagine that the people of Prithvi have not been unique in taking some time to come to terms with the realities of life after the Burn. I imagine there are many who still believe that Starfleet ships will appear from nowhere and we shall go back to how we once were. Some people are harder to convince than others. I have seen a number of conspiracy theories on the planetary net—some of them centered on me, no less! "The Burn" is all a lie, to usurp people's rights as Federation citizens, to establish me as dictator. Dictator! Frankly, that sounds like a great deal of trouble for very little gain.

In making our transition from federated world to post-Burn world, I have tried to tread a very fine line. We must keep to the principles and the values of the Federation—representative government, diversity, toleration, moderation—while at the same time leaving us room to respond to the very different times in which we find ourselves. One example might be maintaining . . . I hesitate to call it our "sovereignty"; perhaps "preferential usage rights" of our nearest spaceport, Devaloka. I foresee a time when we might have to defend Devaloka. I must therefore ensure that any leader who follows me has the power and the legitimacy to defend our interests in this part of space.

These, then, are some of the reasons behind my program of reconstitution. The leader of this world cannot rely on Starfleet for support, and, increasingly, I believe, will struggle to use the idea of the Federation as legitimacy for her or his power and authority. But I will not sever those historical ties. If, when Prithvi is able once again to participate in the wider galaxy, if the Federation exists, then we shall insist upon our rights as a Federation world. We must show that we remained, in a meaningful way, connected to that culture and values. But I will not hamper my successors in any way. Because the galaxy out there is very dark, and we will have to do many things differently in order to survive.

7

COMMANDER MICHAEL BURNHAM

PERSONAL LOG

I have spent the past three days deep in a series of complex calculations. Before I left Devaloka for my current run, Jeremiah came to see me. He had retrieved the rest of the data from the chip on my tricorder. This gave me a set of coordinates: I am extrapolating from these a series of best-case scenarios in order to predict where *Discovery* might potentially arrive in this time period.

My aim is to identify a dozen likely locations where *Discovery* might have arrived and to send my message there. If these prove fruitless, then I shall identify another dozen likely arrival points and send out my message, over and over again. The number of variables makes this a time-consuming and—I have to admit—not particularly gratifying exercise. In truth, I have no idea where or when *Discovery* might arrive. But I have to work on the assumption that my friends are coming to find me.

Again, I experience that sense of a duality: of pragmatically living with the reality that I am here, alone, for good; of deciding to live with the possibility of hope, and therefore trying to turn that hope into reality. Because *if* my ship and crew have made it to this time period, and *if* I can determine correctly where that might be, and *if* they have not traveled too far from the arrival point by the time my message reaches them—*then* I might perhaps make contact. You see how thin the thread is upon which all this hope hangs. The fact is that if I do not try to contact *Discovery* with whatever information I have to hand, then there is *no* chance that I will ever find my friends. You have to work to bring your hope to life. You have to build those castles in the sky from something concrete. And you must not trust a dream to keep you safe and warm. I will do all that is within my capabilities, all that is logically possible, to find *Discovery*. At the same time, logic dictates that I am here for good, and that I must make the most of the here and now.

Jeremiah, when he handed me the data, was a little more closed, a little less friendly. I recalled the odd exchange when he gave me the holos of my friends. I certainly had the sense, at the time, that he knew more about my circumstances than he was admitting. But he has said nothing. When he gave me this data, he only said, "Hope you find your ship." But all this serves to remind me that I must be more careful about whom I tell my real story. Who knows, exactly, who I am? Book, of course. Sahil, Binye, Pa'Dan. I trust the last three of these not to reveal anything about me. As for Book . . .

I have not spoken to him since our last meeting on Sanctuary Four. Our last *disastrous* meeting on Sanctuary Four. I cannot regret returning to hear the message from Senna Tal. How could I regret that? A message from Earth! Even if it leads to nothing, it proved to me that working to make contact could bring contact. We would not have received that message had I not brought back the subspace relay from Ikasu. No, I don't regret leaving to hear that message. What, then, do I regret? It's not that we quarreled bitterly. But did we quarrel irreparably? I regret, then, that we did not part on better terms. I am uncertain now, whether we are still friends . . . if we even were friends. What, exactly, were we? Friends? Acquaintances? Associates? Friendly enemies? Unamicable friends? I am not entirely sure what we were and what we are. Most of all, I am not sure what we *could* be . . .

Whatever it is, or was, or might be—I'd still like to hear from him. And I do trust him with the secret of my presence here. He was the first person I met. He is . . . my lucky charm.

Book's ship
Near Donatu VII

Burnham, if she had been able to directly access Book's thoughts, might have been surprised to the extent that they mirrored hers. After her departure from Sanctuary Four, to chase yet another phantom, Book had stayed awhile nursing his rather bitter feelings. Holding his Grudge close. He also found himself caught in two places at once. Regret that Michael Burnham—with all her ancillary complications—had ever plunged into his life, and with this regret came the firm decision to put her out of his thoughts. But this was coupled, entirely unexpectedly, with deep gratitude. She was, simply put, the most interesting person to cross his path in many, many years. Her strange, old-fashioned values. Her odd turns of phrase. Her weird tendency to act as if the Federation existed, and try to live according to a set of rules that might as well be the laws of a fantasyland, for all the use they had in the real world. She was smart, and sharp, and she could hit very, very hard.

But he was forgetting himself. After all, he was putting Burnham out of his thoughts, wasn't he? He had far more important things to worry about than a very strange woman with a Starfleet fixation. She could take care of herself—she could, after all, hit very hard—and chase after whatever ancient signals she wanted. Meanwhile, he was going to take care of himself—and Grudge—for a while. Mind his own business. In particular, he was going to find out exactly what the hell was going on with these White Palm ships. Where were they coming from? How did they get around so damn quickly?

Turned out these questions were pressing on the minds of many of his courier acquaintances. The courier channels were buzzing about the White Palm these days. Too many of them around. Soon nobody was going to be able to make a living in these sectors. Then, two days ago, Book received a message from his old acquaintance Brodie, asking Book to meet him at the country club. There was a little local difficulty there. Book, knowing exactly what this was courier code for, set a course immediately for Donatu VII, preparing himself for a fight. He arrived in time to see three White Palm raiders taking on a half a dozen courier ships. Brodie's ship was among them. Between swerving and dodging and helping to pick off the nearest ship, he pressed Brodie for information.

"Brodie! What the hell's going on?"

"Usual story. They came from nowhere yesterday. Seem to be able to enter the system without us picking them up. Trying to take control of local space."

"How have they found out about you?"

"Don't know. Could be they haven't got a clue what's down there. Maybe they've just tracked courier ships coming this way and decided to take whatever's there."

"They'll be disappointed."

"Yeah—and I'm not keen on a bunch of angry pirates reaching the surface."

Book agreed, and that brought renewed vigor to the fight. Soon enough, the three ships began to withdraw. *Now we'll find out something*, he thought. "Brodie," he said. "I'm going after them."

"What?"

"See where they go."

"They'll blast you out of the sky if they discover you—"

"I'm smarter than that."

There was no reply.

"I said I'm smarter than that! Hey, Brodie, how about *agreeing* with me?"

"On your own head, Book."

"Thank you, my friend." Book cut the channel and tracked

the ships as they sped away from Donatu VII, following them outside the range of their scanners, just keeping them in range of his own sensors. And then his own scanners went wild—like some kind of massive explosion had registered.

"What the fu—"

Wildly, he sped his hand across the display, trying to get some hard information. The three lights showing the White Palm ships were still there—and then one winked out of existence. Whatever had happened, it had got one of them. "Couldn't happen to a nicer pirate," he muttered. And then up ahead he saw what was sending his sensors wild.

It was as if the space ahead had been torn open, and beyond lay some vast and whirling hell dimension, or the maw of a hungry beast. Book's ship began to rock and sway. He steadied her, tried to keep his distance. He saw that, incredibly, the other two White Palm ships were heading straight for it.

The ship rocked more violently. Grudge howled. Book said, in as soothing a voice as he could muster, "It's all right! It's all right!" Grudge wasn't persuaded. She dived for cover. Book was tempted to follow. The mouth of this—well, what the hell was it? Tunnel? Wormhole? Whatever it was seemed to be drawing closer, exerting some powerful gravitational force over his own ship. He chucked every bit of power that he could at the engines, throwing his ship into reverse. But it was no good. The pull was too strong. He, his ship, and his cat began to tumble down into the rabbit hole.

Pernilla Mercantile Exchange

Burnham was glad to see Pa'Dan again. She looked happier, sleeker, and considerably less exhausted than the first time they had met—but then weeks on a drought-stricken planet trying to hold off blockading raiders and then getting thrown to the wolves by the people you'd been helping would surely prevent anyone from looking their best. Pa'Dan offered her palm in the traditional Cardassian way. Burnham pressed her own palm against it, and then they embraced, like old friends.

"You look *well*," said Burnham, with pleasure.

"I *feel* well," said Pa'Dan. "Amazing what being away from a desert hellhole does for you." She pressed her hand against Burnham's shoulder. "Thank you."

"No problem," said Burnham, softly. "Hey, let's get a drink and swap news."

"Yes, but first you have got to come and see my ship!"

They walked companionably down to the docking bays. Burnham gave her own news and brief, report-like accounts of her own adventures. Trance worms on Sanctuary Four. An encounter with the generation ship. The hazy events on Jaffir.

"Poor Grudge," said Pa'Dan.

"That cat," said Burnham, "has *nothing* to complain about." She talked about her constant, nagging worry—the ever-present and growing threat of the White Palm raiders.

"Any contact with Starfleet?" said Pa'Dan, softly, and Burnham sighed.

"I'll take that as a no," said Pa'Dan.

"Not quite," said Burnham. "We heard something. We're just not sure what to do about it." Quickly, she explained the message they had received from Senna Tal.

Pa'Dan whistled softly. "Twelve years is a long time. How did you get the message?"

Burnham hesitated, not wanting to reveal anything about Ikasu but knowing how uncomfortable it made her to conceal aspects of her life from Jeremiah. "That's a long story, and not all of it is mine to tell," she admitted, and was grateful when Pa'Dan nodded.

"Other people's secrets," Pa'Dan said. "I understand. But twelve years?"

"You see my dilemma," said Burnham. "Recent enough to offer hope. Long ago enough to promise disappointment. We laid our hands on a more effective subspace relay—that's how we received the message in the first place. And I've sent messages out again. I've got the data from my old tricorder and I'm trying to work out where *Discovery* might arrive. But . . ." She shook her head. "When do you give up hope?"

"I think the trick is never to give up hope," said the other woman. "But not to bank everything on that hope."

"Yes," said Burnham. "That's the conclusion I'm coming to. But also to make that hope happen, however you can."

"Which is one reason I sent those messages from Atalis. I knew I'd be part of any deal the governing body struck with the raiders. I wasn't going to sit back and let that happen. You could have, though. You could have let them take me, to buy your own release."

"I . . . hadn't even thought of that," said Burnham.

"No," said Pa'Dan, with a smile. "That's one reason I like you." They were coming to the docking bays now, and she brightened. "Anyway," she said, "that's all over now."

They walked on. Burnham envied her friend's capacity to put the past behind her, to say "that's done," and move on. Perhaps Pa'Dan's ties to her own past hadn't been strong. Perhaps her past was more easily put away. She realized how little she knew of Pa'Dan, what had made her, what moved her, what motivated her. She wondered what her homeworld had been like, who had loved her as a child, who in her life had cared . . .

"How's Book?" said Pa'Dan.

"He's . . . Book," said Burnham. "I've not heard from him for a while."

"No?" Pa'Dan frowned. "Huh."

"He'll turn up," said Burnham. "He usually does."

"Okay," said Pa'Dan. Burnham was relieved when she took the hint and asked no more.

Pa'Dan's new ship turned out to be a considerable improvement on the battered old ruin she had abandoned in orbit around Atalis. Inside, the cabin was much larger than Burnham's little vessel—not quite as big as Book's—and everything seemed so *new*.

"How did you *pay* for this?" said Burnham; the part of her that still lived in the past noticed how this had become her first question.

"It's all thanks to those people over at that starbase. They've got supply lines stretching out from there farther than I've ever gone, back to a world that's got manufacturing up and running."

Manufacturing, thought Burnham. She knew some places had an industrial replicator or two still working, but mostly these were given over to producing and maintaining essential parts. From what Pa'Dan was saying, this was something else. Manufacturing on that scale meant a certain amount of stability; it meant a society and an economy that was no longer scrabbling around using up what had been left behind, or fighting over the best of what was left, trying to eke out a living from this flotsam and jetsam. *Making* things . . . that was something else. It meant a workforce, a belief that you'd have people willing to buy. She said, "Do they have a good source of dilithium?"

"That I don't know," admitted Pa'Dan, "and I suspect that if they do, it's something they don't talk about in detail to their newest employees. They're certainly able to move around quickly."

"Is that what you are now?"

"What?"

"An employee?"

Pa'Dan laughed. "Well, I signed a contract! But I'm still independent. You know, I'm what I always was. Just trying to earn a living. And they do pay very well."

"I can see from the ship."

Pa'Dan leaned back in her chair. "I'm getting older, Burnham. A courier needs to be fast, needs to be able to adjust. Needs to be *young*. I'm not talking about settling down by a fireside, but the time is coming when I won't be able to compete. What do I do then? Starve? I need to put something away."

"No homeworld to return to? No family?"

"No," said Pa'Dan. "Not for a long time."

"I'm sorry," said Burnham. "I do understand. But these people you're working . . . With? For?"

"It's a good setup," said Pa'Dan. "They pay well, and they pay on time. You know, one reason I wanted to see you while I was back over here was to tell you about them. I think you should go and take a look. I think it might appeal to you."

"Appeal how?"

"They're organized. They have clear rules and regulations."

"Why is it," said Burnham, dryly, "that everyone thinks that what appeals to me most is rules and regulations?"

"That's what Starfleet was, wasn't it? A set of rules . . ." Pa'Dan's voice trailed off. She must have caught something from Burnham's expression. "Not that I'd know."

"Starfleet was more than that," said Burnham, softly. "It was a vision. An ideal. A way of life."

"But backed up by rules of conduct," said Pa'Dan. "Right?"

Burnham contemplated this. She had often wondered, over the last few months, why it was so hard to communicate to the people of this time what the Federation had stood for, what Starfleet had stood for. Sometimes, when she did try to explain, people looked at her in bafflement, as if the whole idea of a moneyless society, in which people were able to lead lives that allowed them to grow to their full potential, was simply unfathomable. They latched onto the simplest things, the outward signifiers. They put on the uniforms; they collected the artifacts; they obsessed about the regulations. But none of these were the Federation. None of these had made Starfleet. At the heart had been an idea, to which billions of sentient lives across hundreds of thousands of different species had willingly consented, deciding to lead their lives and organize their worlds according to a handful of principles. Mutuality. Tolerance. Diversity. This was what she found so hard to understand about the rapidity of the Federation's collapse. Had it all been no more than a fantasy, built upon dilithium? Sometimes she believed; sometimes she doubted. That double vision, once again.

"There were rules of conduct," said Burnham. "But they were not the whole."

"Well, I'm about ready to sign up for some rules of conduct," said Pa'Dan. "I'm tired of the game. I'm tired of finding myself in the middle of space, quarreling with some goon over who has salvage rights to some piece of junk, and hoping that my weapon has more charge than his. I'm ready to spend my days making sure I've got the right permit in place instead." She laughed. "But I'm making them sound like they're bureaucrats! They're not. It's busy there—lots of people passing through. Feels like a place where things are happening. A place where things are coming together. I think you should go and take a look, Burnham. I think you'll like what you see."

Burnham thought about this later, aboard her own ship. What particularly stuck in her mind was what Pa'Dan had to say about growing older. *I am going to be here for years. What if* Discovery *never comes, or comes in my old age?* What if she made contact with Senna Tal, and Earth, but only after many years had passed? She had never given thought to this in the past. In Starfleet, you risked early and sudden death, of course; but most Federation citizens lived out their old age in peace and comfort. That could not happen here and now. So how would she live in this time, this place, when she was old? She thought of Sahil, and Jeremiah, and the home they had on Devaloka. She thought about how vulnerable they were, how easily they could be displaced. Where would they go? What would they do?

Even after months here, Burnham thought, as she plowed her way through another set of calculations, she could still be caught by how much she had taken for granted in her old life. She wondered, now, whether those people who had drifted away from the Federation, who had not answered the call, might think differently, a century on, now that the old ways were gone, and this new, harsher, less-stable galaxy was now normal. Would they regret their choices? Would they have fought harder, cared more, done more, to keep the Federation alive? Would they have surrendered so easily? Had they simply not understood how much they had; how much there was to lose?

Burnham remained Starfleet enough that thoughts formed quickly into plans for action. She and Pa'Dan had joked about the rules and regulations, but the truth was that there was something about codifying transactions that gave a stability to everyday life, and meant people weren't always worrying about meeting their basic needs. A simple system of law, of governance, of codes of conduct. Even the couriers operated on some basic rules that meant they weren't permanently at each other's throats. Was there a way of formalizing this? A way to bring the couriers more closely together? She set a course back to Devaloka. Pa'Dan had left the previous evening, but she had sent a message before setting out again.

"I know you want to keep close to Sahil," she said. *"But I think it's worth your while to head over to the starbase and see how they work. I'm sure you'll like what you see. And I'll help—in any way I can—if it gets you started out there. Give it some thought, Burnham. The courier life can't last forever."*

Maybe, Burnham thought, but perhaps the couriers could be persuaded to change aspects of their way of life. She broached the subject with Sahil, once she was back.

"These people seem to be well organized," she said. "My contact out there, Pa'Dan—she says they even have access to some manufacturing facilities."

The relevance of this—and the stability it implied—was not lost on Sahil. His eyebrows shot up. "That is certainly a move in the right direction," he said. "But what is your aim, Michael? Do you want to go out there?" He studied her carefully. "That would take you farther away from here, for more of your time. I would . . . miss you, very much—but I would understand if you needed to be closer to something more organized. Closer to the center of things."

"I'm not sure there really is a center of things, beyond what we create for ourselves," Burnham said. "These people interest me—but I'd rather we did something on those lines for ourselves."

"Their resources must be much greater than ours—"

"Yes, but their resources seem chiefly to come from better organization. They've gained momentum, that's all. Got people behind them. I think we can do the same."

Sahil looked doubtfully around. His office was as calm as ever, but he knew as well as she did that it was a small haven in a space station that day by day fell further into disrepair. "What are you thinking of?" he said. "Have you discovered a lost legion of Starfleet officers and forgotten to mention them to me?"

"Nothing so helpful," she said with a smile. "But there is a small army of people operating around these sectors, with ships, and contacts, and even some camaraderie between them. The couriers."

He looked at her in disbelief. "The couriers?"

"I've met a lot of them in the last few months. Worked with some of them. Sure, had quarrels with a few of them. But they know me now, by sight or by name, and I have something of a reputation with them. They know I'm trustworthy. They know I'm smart. They know I get things done. They might listen."

"If you're hoping to make alliances, Commander, you might want to look elsewhere than to the couriers."

"I know you don't trust them. I know you don't like them. But some of them have saved my life. There's a code among them."

Sahil was shaking his head. "I strongly advise you not to romanticize the couriers, Commander. I know that you have a fondness for them, and for good reason."

A fondness? Burnham thought. *Is that what it is?*

"But you must surely be aware by now that a certain kind of person is attracted to the courier life. They prefer to work alone. They don't like to share. They might come to the aid of a confederate, but that is partly because they have a taste for adventure. A taste for risk. I hesitate to say an addiction to risk, but perhaps there is something of that. But what I mean is that they are not reliable when it comes to building alliances, or providing stable foundations for some kind of government."

"I'm not sure that's all entirely fair," said Burnham.

"But it is accurate." Sahil sighed. "I know how much you

long for a sense that we are making progress. Perhaps you should take Pa'Dan's advice—take a look at what her employers are doing. Perhaps you will find there is something a little closer to the Federation."

"I don't want to leave you undefended," she said softly. "When it comes down to it—this is all of the Federation, of Starfleet, that I've found. Other than shipwrecks, and one sole signal, years old . . . Let me give this a try," she said. "Let's see if we can make something, here, with what we have to hand."

He smiled back at her, ruefully. "In that case, you should probably talk to Book."

"I probably should," she said, and sighed.

"Is something not well, Commander?"

"It's . . . complicated."

"Couriers," he said. "It does rather come with the territory."

Donatu VII

Book woke to a fishy smell and hot breath upon his face. He lifted his hand and touched soft fur. "Grudge," he murmured. "Did you save my life again? Best of cats. *Queen* of cats—"

"It wasn't the bloody cat, you bloody idiot."

Book opened his eyes. Grudge's furry face was right up against him. He rubbed his cheek against hers. Next to the bed sat Brodie, looking at him with a mixture of fondness and exasperation. Book gathered Grudge into his arms and sat up.

"Hey, Brodie. What happened?"

"You nearly fell into a transwarp tunnel, you reckless bastard."

"A what now?" Grudge, squirming in his hands, escaped and landed softly in his lap. There she curled up and began to purr in contentment. Gently, he stroked her. Queen of cats.

"That cat deserves better than you."

"Never denied it. What's a transwarp tunnel?"

Brodie gave him an odd look. "You've not really heard about this before?"

"You're older than me, remember? Been around the block a lot more."

"Yeah, thanks. They're a kind of local wormhole. Some of the couriers used to use them to get around quickly."

"Yeah, I can see how they might have come in useful," Book said, irritated to learn there was a means of rapid transit of which he was unaware. "Did anyone ever think of mentioning these to me?"

"No, because they're not stable—increasingly not stable," Brodie said. "We think they're some leftover Starfleet project, trying to find another means of subspace travel that didn't rely on dilithium. Whatever they were doing, they left this mess behind, along with everything else. A network of unstable tunnels."

"So that's what the White Palm raiders are using to move around so quickly . . ."

"Seems that way." Brodie shuddered slightly. "They've got some nerve. I rode them once back when I was starting out. I won't do that again in a hurry."

Book eyed him. "How did I get out?"

Brodie looked past him at a point on the wall. "Tractor beam."

"You followed me? You didn't go in—?"

"I told you, I won't do that again in a hurry."

But he'd come damn close. "Thank you," said Book.

Brodie shrugged. *You're welcome.* "So can we close these tunnels?" Book said. "Stop the White Palm using them? What can we *do*?"

"I don't know," said Brodie. "I'm not going near them again." He stood up and made for the door. "There's one thing you can do when you've caught up on your beauty sleep."

"Uh-huh?"

"Stop that friend of yours from trying to turn us into her own private army."

Book blinked at him. "Excuse me?"

"Brennan, or whatever her name is—"

"Brennan . . . You mean *Burnham*?" said Book. Grudge, hearing the name, mewed. "Yeah, I know, puss, she really is trouble. What's she doing now?"

"Damned if I know. Thinks she's Starfleet or something. Wants to organize us. Anyway, tell her to back off." Then he was out of the door and gone.

Book looked at Grudge. Grudge looked back.

"Bloody *Burnham*!"

Pernilla Mercantile Exchange

Burnham did not contact Book. For one thing, she couldn't quite find the right words. She felt as if she ought to say sorry. But she wasn't entirely sure for what, or why. That made her feel angry, defensive, and then angrier that he was making her feel this way. Illogical, she knew. But then what about Book was remotely logical? She had arguments with him, in her head; she knew this was not helpful, but that made her fearful for how any interaction with him would go. She did not want their friendship—if that's what it was—to be damaged beyond repair. So she delayed getting back in touch, and instead she put out feelers to the couriers she knew. She suggested they might meet, and that she wanted to talk to them about working together. She was more or less universally rebuffed. Some were simply happy the way they were. Others didn't like the sound of someone else having a say over their operations. A few were outright hostile to anything that seemed like the Federation.

"Have you spoken to Book?" said Brodie, shutting down her suggestion in less than a minute.

"No."

"You should."

But still she didn't. She went back out to the Pernilla mercantile to look for work. It was more of a struggle than usual; she would bid for work to find herself outbid—someone swore they could get there quicker, or wanted less to do the same work. Too many people; too few jobs. All competing with each other. There was surely a much better way of doing this. She was about to give up for the day and go back to her ship, when she heard someone call her.

"Burnham."

She froze. *Well,* she thought, *one of us had to make the first move.* She turned to see him standing there. He was smiling at her ruefully. He looked good.

"Hey, Book," she said, keeping her voice steady. "How's Grudge?"

"She's fine," he said. "How are you?"

"I'm fine too." They stood and looked at each other. "I was stopping for the day," she said, just as he said, "Let's get a drink, hey?"

She wasn't sure it was a good idea. She wasn't sure she wanted to talk to him. Didn't their conversations always fall into the same pattern? She held on to her hopes; he thought her hopes were pointless. And then he smiled at her . . .

"All right," she said. "Just one drink."

———

They left the mercantile and walked through the streets of the makeshift town that supported the exchange. She had her arms wrapped around herself; he seemed to be walking slightly farther away from her than was usual. They had not spoken since their muted and awkward good-byes on Sanctuary Four. The awkwardness was still there but, at the same time, Burnham knew she was glad he was here. The first person she had seen in this strange new time. The one who had caught her as she was falling. Seeing him, she realized exactly how much she had missed him.

There was a bar she knew, run by an ancient Andorian woman. Quiet, not much used by couriers. The food was cheap but good and plentiful. As they went in, her stomach began to growl. It had been a long and fruitless day. She ordered *plomeek* soup, for comfort; he followed suit.

"I heard you're trying to make yourself boss of the couriers," he said.

She stopped with a spoonful of soup halfway to her mouth. She put it down again, and said, "You heard *what?*"

"That you're trying to make yourself some sort of local warlord."

She couldn't reply. She couldn't find the words to deny something so improbable, so ridiculous. She realized, after a moment, that he was laughing.

"No," he said, "I didn't think it sounded very likely."

"Not quite my style?"

"Not your style at all."

"I'd *make* a great warlord."

"I'm not denying that for one minute," he said. "You've already got the look—I really love that new leather coat, by the way."

"Thanks."

"All you need is a more considered strut—"

She thought of Her Imperial Majesty, Philippa Georgiou Augustus Iaponius Centarius. "I think it's more a swagger than a strut."

"One of them. Get yourself one of them," he said.

"You know, I think I'll pass."

They smiled at each other. How easily they had fallen back into their banter. She felt so much better after only a couple of minutes of talking this way. She couldn't understand now why she had put off talking to him for so long.

"Seriously, though," he said, "what's going on? Half my contacts are furious, the other half are baffled. And they all think you're out of your mind. What have you done to them?"

"Remember Pa'Dan?" she said.

He crinkled up his face, trying to place the name. "Was that the Cardassian woman on Atalis? The one that suckered you into picking her up and giving her a ride?"

"That's the one. And you've heard of these people operating out over in Sector 40?"

"Yeah, I've heard a few things," he said. Well, of course he had. Surely nothing got past him. "What about them?"

"Pa'Dan's been working for them," she said. "She's had good things to say about the way they operate. I thought . . . perhaps the couriers could do something similar, with Sahil's station at the center." As she spoke, and saw his expression, she felt less confident about the idea. "I was thinking about what you said—about how the sharks are circling around Sahil and the spaceport. About how they're waiting for their moment to move, when he can't run the place any longer. And I thought—perhaps we could do something about that." Her voice petered out. "Are they all furious?"

"Uh, they think you're pretty high-handed. You know, you've not been around for long. Some of these people have been flying up and down these routes for twenty, twenty-five years. Then you turn up and tell them you want to change the way they operate?"

"I can see how that might look bad," she admitted. "But . . . perhaps it takes a fresh eye to see what the problems are."

"I rushed to your defense, of course," he went on.

"Really?"

"Yeah," he said. "I said you weren't high-handed, just weird."

She burst out laughing. "Well, thank you very much!"

"You have to admit that's a fair assessment." He was smiling at her. "Time-traveling skydiving fast-talking Starfleet lady."

"When you put it like that." At the far end of the bar, someone had put on music. They moved closer, to be able to hear each other better. "But you think trying to unify the couriers is a bad idea?"

"As a matter of fact, no, I don't think it's a bad idea," he said. "But I've seen it tried before, and I've seen it fail before, and so I don't hold out hope that it will work this time."

"There's a difference this time," she said.

"What's that?"

"I'm here this time."

"That's true," he said. "And you're persistent, I'll give you that."

"And it's a good idea," she persisted.

"It's an idea whose time may have come." He lowered his voice. "I've been trying to find out about these White Palm raiders," he said. "Where they're coming from, who's in charge. What they want with this part of space."

"I didn't think you'd been on holiday," she said. "What have you learned?"

"They're organized. They're well equipped. They're led by a man called Leavitt."

"Leavitt . . ." She remembered Brodie telling her the name.

"It's him we need to get to if we want to fight the White Palm. But I can't find out his base." Book frowned. "There's a lot about them that I can't figure out. I don't like that. But I have found out how they move around so quickly."

He explained about the transwarp tunnels; how they were most likely a failed attempt by Starfleet to find a reliable replacement for dilithium-regulated ships.

"Did you go into one?" said Burnham, eyes wide open.

"Yeah . . . Brodie had to pull me out. Nearly lost the ship."

She reached to put her hand upon his arm.

"I'm okay," he said. "Everything turned out okay. But all of this is to say that these raiders have the potential to become serious players. And if the couriers operating around here don't want to find that this area of space has been taken from them, then you're right—they're going to have to band together. You need to make them see that they've got a common enemy."

"The White Palm."

"And you need to make a few more friends first. Earn a little more credit."

"I guess . . . But that's going to take years. I have a feeling we don't have years . . ."

"You might be right. I've got an idea."

"A job?"

"Um, don't hold your hopes out for much in the way of payment. But something that might further your agenda." He smiled at her. She smiled back. Damn, it was so good to see him. She had missed him.

"I'm listening," she said.

Donatu VII

Leaving her ship, Burnham stepped out into a small but well-kept spaceport, which she knew from her scans lay next to a settlement of about four hundred people. She had many questions about this world: it didn't appear on any of the charts she owned, and Book had given her a series of codes and encrypted channels so that she could gain permission to enter local space, and then to land. Someone called her name, and she looked up to see a short, stocky man heading toward her, palm up in welcome.

"Hey," he said, as he drew near. "You know, we've spoken a couple of times. My name's Brodie."

"Brodie!" She offered her hand; shook his gratefully. "You know, that ship you pointed me toward, she's been a marvel!"

He nodded, looking pleased, if a little gruff about the whole thing. "Did Book tell you what's happening here?"

"Book told me how to get here, nothing more."

Brodie puffed out a breath. "Very discreet of him. Well, you're here now. So I guess that makes you one of us. Let's head into town."

She followed him toward an ancient but well-maintained aircar. Two seats in the front; the back was packed up with crates and bags. She didn't ask—you never asked. He got the 'car moving, and they sped up and out of the port. The countryside around was green and pleasant; the weather was temperate. Questions, many questions, were now forming in her mind. They passed some traffic heading in the other direction; he waved a greeting at a few of them. After about ten or fifteen minutes, they came to the outskirts of the settlement. The houses—homes, indeed, since she saw kids here and there— were built from a rich yellow, almost honey-colored stone. Green trees; gardens. It was idyllic, in a quaint kind of way.

"Brodie," said Burnham, after a while, "is this a courier settlement?"

He gave her a sideways look. "Book said you weren't stupid. Yes, that's exactly what it is."

"Your homes," she said. "Your *families*?"

"All that lone gunslinger business," he said. "That's only true for some of us. Couriers are people, Burnham. People need a place to call home. They need somewhere they can go back to. They need a reason to be doing the work in the first place. And they need to know there's somewhere they can go, if they can't work any longer. That's what this place is."

"But you keep it secret," she said. "Off the grid."

"You make a lot of enemies in this game. Families are vulnerable. We don't want them getting used against us." He was slowing the 'car, and he brought it to a halt by the side of a two-story house with apple trees running along one side. "This is my place. I've got a few people coming over. They want to see you. Hear what you have to say."

"I thought you all thought I wanted to be some kind of local warlord."

"Book said not." He eyed her thoughtfully. "I'll listen—for Book's sake. But make your pitch good."

He led her into the house. It was timber framed, with whitewashed walls, pleasant and uncluttered. She imagined that if you spent weeks at a time stuck in a ship stuffed with crates, you might want your home to be pared back. They went through a well-stocked kitchen into a long garden, with green grass that led down to a river. There was a long wooden table out there, with several people already sitting around. At the head of the table was an elderly woman with cropped white hair, smoking a pipe. Brodie sat next to her, dropped a kiss on the top of her head.

Oh my, thought Burnham, *it's his mother . . .*

The old woman looked at her. "Michael Burnham?"

"That's me, ma'am."

"I'm Katerina. Take a seat."

She saw Book, two seats along, wave to her to come and join him. "Well," he murmured, when she was sitting next to him. "What do you think?"

"I can't quite believe this place exists," she said. "But it has to, doesn't it?"

"You've been let inside," he said. "Make the most of your opportunity."

She glanced around the table. As well as herself and Book, Brodie and his mother, there were maybe another half dozen people there. Someone poured her a glass of red wine. Someone took a plate filled with bread, cheese, and fruit and pushed it toward her. Conversation flowed past: business deals; what was worth someone's attention; what most certainly was not. Burnham kept quiet and listened. They all, really, had one thing on their mind. Eventually, the conversation ebbed, and everyone turned to look to the old woman at the head of the table.

"All right," she said. "You know why we're here. The White Palm. Somehow—we don't know how—they've become interested in Donatu."

"Do we know *why* that's happened?" said a younger man, sitting at the far end of the table. "Surely someone hasn't given us away?"

"Could simply be they've observed courier ships heading regularly this way," said Book. "Got curious. They might not even know what's down here."

"Hope so," said Brodie. "I'd hate to think one of us had given us away."

"Everyone's got a reason to protect this place," said Katerina. She looked Burnham in the eye. "And if what you've told me about this one is true, I don't think she'll give us away."

Burnham shook her head. *Never.*

One of the other women, she looked older than Book, not as old as Katerina, said, "You know, it might be that we're going to have to let a few more people in on the secret. If those raiders keep coming—we're going to have to ask for help."

Several voices came back at this: that this was too risky; that there were kids here, old people, sick people. Most of all, they doubted anyone would help.

"Who would come to defend a bunch of couriers?" said Brodie, bitterly.

Starfleet would, thought Burnham, but she said nothing, only looked down at the table. Book caught her movement. "I know what you're thinking," he muttered. "You're thinking that Starfleet would come."

"Well," she said, "they would."

Brodie, who caught this, said, "Yet I don't see your friend Sahil coming to help us if we asked."

"Only because he doesn't have the ships," said Burnham, firmly. "If the ships were there, they'd come." *I'd order them here*. Others around the table didn't look so convinced. "You said it yourself," she said. "There are children here, old people, sick people. Of course Starfleet would come."

"Which is rather beside the point," said Katerina, "given Starfleet no longer exists."

"Not here," said Burnham. "But there may be places where it does. I'm . . . I've been looking for that kind of thing. Trying to get in touch with people who have been successful in banding together. Who have managed to maintain more stability, more law and order."

"Any success?" asked the older woman, with some suspicion.

"Not yet," Burnham admitted.

"Thought not," said the woman.

"I live in hope," said Burnham. "But at some point, some-one in this part of space is going to make a move. Try to make a grab for power. The White Palm, whoever they are, have begun that process. I guess what you people have to decide"— she looked around at each one of them steadily, ending with

Katerina and holding her eye—"is whether you want to be part of making that happen, or wait until events overtake you. The White Palm are here. They'll be coming in greater numbers. You might already have lost your chance to reach out to other worlds, other people, to hold them back. Or maybe you're in luck—and it's still not too late."

Voices around the table sprang up after this; not hostile but taking her seriously. Burnham, having said her piece, kept quiet. The evening wore on. Lamps were lit, and more bottles opened. At length, Katerina stood and stretched and said, "I'm for bed."

Burnham was ready to sleep too. Katerina, seeing her stifle a yawn, said, "You're in the back room. Book can show you when you're ready."

Burnham nodded her thanks. She waited for Book to finish up his drink, and then followed him into the house and upstairs. The back room turned out to be small, but comfortable, and with a couple of crates stacked up in one corner. Burnham smiled. Almost like being on board *Alice*.

"You know," she said to Book, who was lurking at the door, "they should have reached out for help ages ago."

"That's easy to say," said Book. "But who would they turn to?"

"There's always someone," said Burnham. "But you have to reach out."

"I'm not sure that's true, Burnham," he said. "Maybe in the past. Maybe where you came from. But all we're doing now is trying to get by."

"And that's the problem. You can't get by alone."

They left it at that. He went off to his own room. She stood for a while by the window, the breeze on her face. She climbed into a soft, clean bed, and fell asleep listening to the voices and the laughter down in the garden.

—

She was woken, in the dead of night, by voices, but these were urgent, calling out. She guessed at once what was happening. She rolled out of bed, pulled on clothes, and hurried out into the corridor. Book was there, pulling on his jacket.

"Raiders?" she said.

"Raiders."

"I'll come," she said.

"I thought you would."

Downstairs, Brodie had personal transporters ready. Burnham grabbed hers and began to set the coordinates to take her to the *Alice*. Just before she jumped, she saw Katerina pull her son into a quick hug. "Come back to me," she said.

And then the three of them were at the port, pelting through the general bustle toward their ships, and then up, up, bursting through the planet's atmosphere and toward the six White Palm ships tearing through local space.

"All right," she heard Book say through the comm. *"Let's keep them busy until the others arrive. Burnham—watch your sensors and learn. Copy what I do."*

She watched as her sensors flickered, and then, where Book's ship had been were three lights. Two of these winked out, and then reappeared in completely different locations. One of the White Palm ships tried to give chase to one of these—and then the light winked out again, only to appear somewhere else. She got at once what he was doing: scrambling their sensors so that he appeared to be in several places all at once, while his own ship hopscotched around them. She followed suit. Brodie was doing something similar. Between them, they chipped away at the ships. One of the raiders limped away. Not long after, reinforcements arrived from the surface. A White Palm ship was hit and exploded; two more were badly damaged. Burnham heard Book speak.

"You've had your fun. But you've got to understand—this world is defended. Keep away from Donatu VII. And tell Leavitt—we're coming for him. You got that? We're coming for him."

The ships, pulling back, regrouped—and then they moved away, and were soon gone. Twenty-five minutes later, Burnham collapsed into the back-room bed and slept well into the following morning.

—

The next evening, the group met again, and Burnham heard the same arguments go around again. She kept quiet. She had, during the night, dreamed up what she thought might be a solution, but she had no idea how it would be received. Katerina, cutting her a slice of creamy white cheese, said, "You're quiet tonight. Nothing to say?"

"I do," said Burnham, "but you won't like it."

"You've earned your right to speak freely," the woman said. "Go ahead."

"All right." Burnham skewered the piece of cheese onto her knife and spread it over her slice of thick bread. "You know I think you should reach out. You can't defend yourselves against these attacks if they keep coming—and they will keep coming—and I don't think you can afford to bring people here permanently to defend you. Give them a reason to defend you."

"Oh," said Book, putting down his glass to put his hand to his head. "I think I know what's coming."

"Open a mercantile exchange," said Burnham.

There was a silence.

"No," said Book, "I didn't see that coming after all."

"Think about it," said Burnham. "You have the contacts and you have the expertise. You certainly have the space here, and I'm pretty sure you can lay your hands on what you need to build the place. You can build the damn thing halfway across the continent if you want to keep this settlement quiet—"

Voices were rising. "The whole *point* about Donatu VII is that it's safe," said Brodie. "Secure. Secret. A place for couriers and their people that nobody else knows anything about—"

"Sure," said Burnham. "That worked for a while. It's not working anymore. In fact, it's working against you. It stopped you bringing in help when the first attack came. You probably could have seen those ships off at the start, if you'd used a little money and credit to bring some people here. It's a liability. You need to change what you're doing completely. Look outward. Make this world somewhere people have a vested interest in protecting—not just you, other people. And what do people protect most?"

She looked at Book. He smiled at her, and said, "The chance to do business."

She nodded.

There was a short silence, and then a babbling of voices. She heard Book start to laugh softly. She looked at him, anxiously. Was this a terrible idea, after all? No, he was smiling, nodding. He thought she was right.

She took heart; gained confidence. She lifted her voice again and spoke with authority. "You can't stop people coming here," she said. "But you can change the terms on which they come. There aren't enough ships out there to defend you—and the White Palm will come again. But I've seen the exchanges in operation. We all have. People rely on them. They want them up and running. They're the most vibrant, most defended spaces I've seen in these sectors."

"Something like that will make us even more of a target!"

"But you stop being a backwater," Book said. "And the amount you make in trade—I reckon you'd make enough within months to be able to hire your own damn fleet to protect yourselves. So, what's it to be? Take the risk? Or wait for the White Palm to take this place by force? Because they will come back. And every time that they come back they chip away even further at your ability to defend yourselves."

There was more debate. Burnham sat back and enjoyed the rest of her supper. She had put the idea out there, that was the main thing. Now it was their choice. If they wanted to keep heading down the path to eventual destruction—well, there was little she could do about that. She had offered a solution. Would they take the risk—and look outward, to a possible better future? She couldn't force them. She could just hope.

A world like this, open for business, would go a long way to signaling to those White Palm raiders that this part of space isn't here for the taking, she thought. *I wish I could get more people to see this. Working together—even if, for now, it's just trading together—is the best way to protect each other. To build something better and stronger. People can't do this alone . . .*

The conversation, she noticed, had shifted from *Do we do this* to *How do we do this.* Book had noticed too. He caught her eye and winked. Eventually, she said good night to them all, and headed inside to go to bed.

Book followed. "You've certainly stirred them up."

"They needed stirring. They were paralyzed." She glanced back over her shoulder. "Think they'll give it a try?"

"They'd be mad to give it a try. And they'd be mad not to." He looked at her. "What is it about you? Everywhere you go, you bend people to your will."

"I see how much better things can be," she said. "I only want things to be better. Is that so bad?"

"Better?" he said. "Or how they were?"

"It *was* better under the Federation," she said quietly. "It just was. People lived long lives, in peace and prosperity. That's not something to dismiss lightly."

"No," he said. "I suppose not." Voices were still coming from the garden beyond. "Let's go for a walk."

———

They went down to the river, and sat together, side by side, looking up at three moons in a black and silver sky. *Whatever the time, whatever the place,* Burnham thought, *there is nothing to compare to looking up at the stars. They promise everything.*

"This was a good day," she said, at last.

Book turned to look at her. His face was in darkness, but she could see the gleam of his eyes. "I'm glad to hear that. I . . . hope you have more days like this."

"If they take this on," she said. "The mercantile—I think it could make a difference. Other people will think, 'Maybe I can look beyond my homeworld. Maybe if I reach out to help others, then they'll return the favor one day.'"

He turned away. "Oh," he said, "you were thinking about your alliance."

She felt a sudden rush of panic. Had she misspoken? Had she said something wrong? Had she missed something? "Why?" she said, in a quiet voice. "What were you thinking about?"

He didn't reply at once. He sat beside her, seeming a little more distant now, but, as she watched, he relaxed visibly, muscle by muscle. He stretched out onto his side, propping himself on one elbow. He smiled at her. "I was just thinking that it was nice to be sitting here looking at this beautiful view." He was looking at her. Not the view. Her. "But your mind, Burnham . . . Always strategizing. Do you ever stop?"

She moved to lean on her side, mirroring his position. "Sorry. Can't help myself."

"Don't change," he said. "Maybe a little? Not too much."

"I'm not sure I can," she said, and laughed.

His smile was warm. "I guess not. You know, I have to admit that despite my misgivings, I think a mercantile exchange here could make a big difference."

"It's a start," she said.

"But you know, part of the reason it worked is that you're the kind of person who turns up when other people ask for help. I'm . . . not yet convinced that other people would return the favor."

"Well, thank you," she said, "for that pretty damning assessment of my personality."

"It's not you I'm damning," he said. "It's other people. Besides—I'd come, if you called. Always. You do know that, don't you, Michael?"

First name, she thought. *That's something new.* "I know," she said. She turned her head to look back up at the beautiful view. She was glad of this warmth between them, this gentleness. She did not like it when they quarreled. No, that was not right. She *loved* it when they quarreled. She loved bickering with him, joking with him, firing off some sharp comment, waiting to hear his comeback. She loved the speed of his wit, the sharpness of his intelligence, the fact that he didn't allow her to resort to platitudes or sentimentality. Kept her feet on the ground. She liked their companionship. She liked their . . . compatibility.

"So what are you going to do next?" he said. "More of this?"

"I'm going to take a look across the sector," she said. "If I can't rely completely on the couriers, then perhaps I need to extend my networks. These people Pa'Dan has been working for—perhaps there's an alliance to be made there."

"What do you have to offer them?"

"Help negotiating with this part of space," she said.

"And what do they have to offer you?"

"Infrastructure. Protection? Someone has to look after Sahil." She looked at him. "Do you want to come?"

"I think . . ." She watched, hopefully. "I think I want to find out more about the White Palm," he said, and she hid her disappointment. "Try to track down their base of operations—there has to be one."

"Promise me," she said, "that you won't go into those tunnels."

"What? No, gods, no!"

"*Promise* me."

"I swear on Grudge's supper."

"That's a promise I know you'll take seriously. But take care."

"Of course I will. But . . . I need to know more about them."

"So do I. I think it's a useful task you're taking on."

"Think of me as your minister of defense."

She burst out laughing. "I'm not trying to make myself *president*!"

"Huh," he said. "Yet I wouldn't be surprised if that's where we ended up. Michael Burnham, First President, Reconstituted Federation of Planets."

She shuddered. "Sounds like *hell*."

———

Their good-byes, this time, were warmer, less fraught. As they parted company, Book stopped and pressed something in her hand. "Here," he said. "I found this a couple of months ago at one of the exchanges. I thought you'd like it."

She opened her hand and found herself looking down at a medal. It was somewhat tarnished, but nothing that wouldn't be helped by careful cleaning. The ribbon was rather frayed. Nothing to be done. She didn't recognize what it was—there had been a lot of history between then and now—but the face engraved on the front did look oddly familiar. She turned the thing over. On the back it said: *For remarkable leadership, meritorious conduct, and acts of personal bravery,* and there was a name on it.

"He got a *medal* named after him?" she exploded. "Jeez!"

He was looking at her in bewilderment. "What? What do you mean?"

"I knew Pike! I *served* with Pike!"

She watched his expression as he caught up. "I forget sometimes," he said. "You traveled in *time*."

"This future," she said. "It's *wild*." She reached out and kissed him quickly on the cheek. "I love your gift," she said. "But find the medal named after me, huh? Because then I'll be *really* impressed."

The Alice

In flight

Burnham hung the medal above the console on her ship, where it would swing gently while she was in flight. Every so often, her eye would fall on it, and she would start to laugh. Not just the whole idea of the thing, but the sudden, glorious, and joyful connection to her own past. Book's face as he realized how unexpectedly perfect the gift had been. He had taken the time to find something for her, and he had chosen this. That there had been such a twist. It seemed to her to encapsulate everything about the push and pull of their relationship.

Relationship . . . Was that what this was? Maybe this was what suited her. Someone who spent most of his time two sectors away on a different ship, and then, when they did meet, they spent their time running away from their mutual foes, and wisecracking. She felt her mouth curve into a smile. It was better, she guessed, than having her heart broken. It was . . . fun. *Fun,* she thought. *Am I allowed that? Is that an option for me?* She tapped the medal gently. Chris Pike's graven image looked back, solemnly, ridiculously. She burst out laughing. *Yes,* she thought, *perhaps it is.*

She flew directly toward her destination. Pa'Dan had given her a flight path that was guaranteed to draw attention. So she was not startled when she saw two ships come up on her sensors, the foremost hailing her. She had been expecting them. She had been intending to make contact with them.

"Courier ship. You're traveling without a permit. Will you identify yourself, please?"

She opened a channel back. "This is Michael Burnham, on board the courier ship *Alice.* I'm glad to meet you—and I'm here to find out more about that permit. Can you help?"

There was a brief silence, and then the comm crackled into life again. *"Sending you the flight path. We'll escort you to Starbase Vanguard."*

The last stage of the journey took no more than a couple of hours. She watched as flight traffic increased; sleek ships, well maintained, moving with surety of purpose. And when her guides announced that they were making their final approach to the starbase, and she looked out to see it—silver and gleaming and so pristine against the black night of space—she was struck with an overwhelming sensation that this was a familiar place. *Is this it? Is this civilization, at last?* She breathed deeply; held long-contained emotions still in check. *Have I come home?*

PRIYA TAGORE

PERSONAL LOG

I remember, as clear as if it were yesterday (But, really, was it almost forty years ago? How can that be?), when I was first elected to the Federation Council. Oh, how proud I was! How proud the whole family was! Prithvi had been a member of the Federation for less than fifty years. My own grandmother remembered joining! And now I was to become a councilor—and represent this world back on Earth!

I had only been to Earth once before. I had recently finished my studies at the university on Pernilla III, and, being the recipient of the highest honors for my cohort, I was invited by the current councilor for Prithvi at the time to an event for all high-flying recent graduates from across the Federation. And, oh, to visit Earth, at the height of its glory! That beautiful, historic world, from which my ancestors had set out hundreds of years ago. To see Mumbai, and Shanghai, and Djubuguli, and New Chinautla. Paris, gleaming under the stars. London, bustling and diverse. San Francisco, full of cadets. How great a place that world seemed to me! The beating heart of our great Federation.

I try to tell my grandchildren how it felt, to be there. To feel that a place that you had never seen before was— in such a meaningful way—still home. How connected I felt to this world. How much a part of it I believed myself to be. Later experiences as a councilor taught me a little more about disparities between the worlds of the Federation, but I have never stopped feeling that way. I am, in all ways, a product of that civilization. I will, to the end, hope that one day it will be restored.

But that task—that task is not for me. I have done all that I can. Prithvi will survive me. I have kept this world safe. But the day has come at last when I can do no more. The time has come to pass on the torch.

Somewhere, out there, I do believe there are flags still flying. Ships crewed by Starfleet officers. Perhaps, on Earth, a council sits in session—much depleted in number, but still working, in some fashion. Perhaps they have learned from their mistakes. Perhaps, next time, we shall do things right.

I commend this journal to history. Reader—do not judge me too harshly. I did my best.

8

Docking bays
Starbase Vanguard

Burnham came out of her ship into a familiar scene: a docking bay filled with a variety of ships, and the hustle and bustle
of pilots checking systems, engineers fixing systems, people
hurrying around checking inventories or ensuring the smooth
transference of cargoes. All this activity—which spoke of purpose, organization, stability—had, once upon a time, been so
routine that she would have walked past without notice. Now
she felt a wave of nostalgia for what she had once known, and
never realized could be irrevocably lost.

She looked around, taking in the layout and style of the
place. There was no doubt in her mind that this had once been
a Starfleet outpost. Even in the hundreds of years since her
own time, something fundamental had remained about the
design. Smooth uncluttered surfaces, technology that—while
vastly ahead of what she had known—combined elegance, us-
ability, and simplicity into something quintessentially Starfleet.
Pa'Dan had said she would like this place: she wasn't wrong.
But the differences from Sahil's base were all around her. This
place was busy, well maintained, and functioning. This was a
place where business was being done, things were happening—
not a quiet backwater falling slowly and steadily into decline.
Even the hum of instrumentation around her had a familiar

tone. She could almost believe that she was back in her own time, taking leave from *Discovery*. She could almost believe that she would walk out of this docking bay and find herself on a concourse filled with people in familiar uniforms, talking about familiar concerns.

She heard someone call out and turned to see a young woman approaching. She was wearing a crisp gray uniform, and on her left shoulder, like her delta badge, was a five-pointed black and silver star. Approaching Burnham, she greeted her with an open-palmed salute, and said, "Michael Burnham?"

"Yes. I'm Burnham."

"Welcome to Starbase Vanguard. I'm Senior Officer Nenee Raud. I'm the liaison for new arrivals here. I'm here to take you to the chief exec's office."

"The 'chief exec'?" Burnham raised her eyebrows. "Is that . . . a title? A rank?"

"Not a rank," said Raud. She gave a short, almost nervous laugh. "It's not as if we're Starfleet."

"No," said Burnham. "I guess not." It was a pretty good facsimile though. Raud gestured to Burnham to follow, and she fell into step beside the senior officer. She felt untidy beside this neat young woman, grubby from her long flight. She tugged at her jacket; smoothed her hand down the creases in her shirt. Raud did not miss this.

"I'll take you to your quarters later," she said. "But the chief exec did want to meet you and asked me to escort you to her office."

"I'd be glad to meet her," said Burnham. She was finding this welcome a little disconcerting, as if they had somehow been expecting her. Or did everyone get this kind of treatment? She recalled Pa'Dan enthusing about the care lavished upon her on arrival. The quarters, the living expenses, the upgrade to the ship. Maybe this was standard, all part of their recruitment drive.

They walked down a corridor, passing people in uniform going quickly but steadily about their tasks, and entered a turbolift. "Level four," said Raud. Burnham was by now beginning to find the cognitive dissonance very disconcerting. This place was so like the Federation, and yet so very unlike. She could almost be home—but there was no sign of Starfleet. How odd, she thought, that she had seen none of the familiar iconography. You would think something would have withstood the test of time. But then the Burn had been many years ago.

"Are you particularly busy today?" said Burnham.

Raud gave her a questioning look.

"The docking bays seemed very busy."

"A normal day," said Raud. "That's not a problem, is it?"

"No, it's good to see so much . . . purposeful activity."

Raud beamed. "Yes, it's great to feel that there's starting to be some order about the place again."

"Just like when Starfleet was here."

Was it her imagination, or did Raud's enthusiasm go slightly off the boil? "I couldn't say," the young woman replied, her smile fading.

Burnham did not press. She knew by now—had certainly learned the hard way—that there were plenty of reasons for people not to respond positively even to the mention of Starfleet. Perhaps this young woman did not realize exactly how closely she was following in their footsteps, how much her day-to-day life here depended on the work of those people who had come before her. And why should she? They were not even memory for her.

She asked a few questions—about how many people passed through daily, what kinds of cargo tended to come through—and received prompt and, she assumed, completely accurate answers. The turbolift came to a halt. Raud waved up a keypad and held up her palm. The doors to the lift opened onto a large room with a huge window taking up the wall opposite, giving a heart-stopping view of the stars. In front of the window was a desk, and behind the desk sat a dark-haired woman, wearing a smart gray suit. Burnham still found the ages of people in this time difficult to gauge. You never knew the kind of life they might have led. By her estimate, this woman was probably around fifty, maybe a little more.

"Thank you, Raud," said the woman. "You can go."

Raud nodded, and left, and Burnham heard the turbolift move smoothly into action behind her. "Michael Burnham," said the woman. "I've heard a great deal about you. I'm very glad to meet you at last."

Chief Executive Officer Remington's office
Starbase Vanguard

This, Burnham thought, looking around, could be any one of a hundred ready rooms or offices she had entered over her career, from commanders to captains to admirals. A clear, uncluttered space with a large desk. A few pieces of tasteful *objets d'art*. Collecting herself, she went farther inside, resisting the urge to stand to attention. *How should I play this? Am I an officer or a courier?*

"You know," said Burnham calmly, "I don't believe we've been introduced."

"My apologies, no, we have not. My name is Remington. I am the chief executive officer here at Starbase Vanguard."

"Chief executive officer?" Burnham still couldn't quite parse the title. It sounded part military, part civilian. Like the uniforms these people wore. "I guess that means you're in charge around here."

Remington smiled. "I'd like to think we were all in this

together." She gestured to a seat, inviting Burnham to sit. Tea was conjured up. "I'll be mother," said Remington, and poured. Burnham sat back in the chair and tried to look relaxed. Was the echo of her ritual with Sahil deliberate? How could that possibly be?

"Did Raud give you a good welcome?"

"She's been most attentive."

Remington smiled behind her teacup. "That's Raud."

"Your staff all seem very young, Ms. Remington."

"A conscious decision on our part. We've found that there are many young people without direction, without purpose, without homes. It would be easy for them to ruin their lives before they've even had a chance to start. So we give them a mission and a purpose. And they're loyal. Does any of this sound familiar?"

An image of the skill domes flickered into Burnham's mind. "I guess all cultures and organizations have their own ways of educating their young."

Remington smiled at her, a rather cool smile. *Red Queen,* thought Burnham; *off with her head!* And then: *I wonder why I thought that?*

"I'm interested to hear your first impressions of our base," Remington said.

Burnham thought of saying, *This place is so close to home that it's freaking me out.* She decided against. "I'm . . . impressed."

"I'm glad to hear that."

"This *was* a Starfleet base, wasn't it?" said Burnham.

"It was," said Remington. "I understand you have an interest in the history of the Federation. You deal in memorabilia, yes?"

"Some people like that kind of thing."

"And I gather you're very well informed."

"It pays to know your subject."

"I know less," Remington said, not giving the impression that she cared particularly about this gap in her education. "But my understanding is that our goals here are very close to those of the Federation in its early days. Trying to establish order."

"I believe that might be right," said Burnham, agreeably.

"But I'm correct that Earth was in chaos, yes? That there had been a collapse of order, of civilization there? And that the Federation was founded on those ruins?"

"It was a very long time ago," said Burnham, softly.

"Hmm," said Remington. She put down her cup and, with a wave of her hand, brought up a visual display that Burnham recognized immediately as sharing design and capabilities with the one that Sahil used. "Here," she said, "this is the area of space beyond here. This is where we come from. This is where we have been operating—so far."

She began to fill the display with details. A grid overlaid the whole, covering another four sectors. About fifteen systems. Primary worlds marked in blue. Two or three red dots. "What are these?" said Burnham, indicating one of them.

"Manufacturing," said Remington. "Oh yes, we have industrial replicators up and running again on a couple of these worlds. It took a lot of effort, but it's been worth it. The green lines, by the way, are the primary supply runs. This world here"—she displayed one system—"this is Sahnis III. A colony world of almost a hundred thousand. They had an outbreak of *vita* fever. It's easily treatable—with the right drugs. We were able to replicate enough and get them there in time. Stopped a pandemic."

"This is good work," said Burnham. "Very good work."

"I thought you might appreciate it." Remington played with the display over Sahnis. Burnham realized that she was seeing population statistics—had they taken a *census*? Surely they didn't have that much organization in place. "One of several examples of what we've been able to do. I could show you examples of bringing necessary parts for water-reclamation plants, or the right kind of grain for the individual climate, or repairs to subspace relays. I show you all this, because I believe it must appeal." She looked through the display directly at Burnham. The various colors flickered across her face. "Commander."

"Ah," said Burnham.

"That's correct, isn't it? Commander Michael Burnham, science officer. Serial number SC0064—"

"—0974SHN," Burnham finished along with her. "You know a great deal about me."

"Iliana Pa'Dan," said Remington, "has been very helpful recently."

Pa'Dan? Burnham concealed her surprise. Pa'Dan had told these people about her? She was starting to feel very uneasy. Was Pa'Dan *asked* to get her to come out here? Was she *paid* to persuade Burnham to come out here?

"You've seen a little of who we are, what we're doing," said Remington. "My hope is that it appeals. We have structure, Commander Burnham. We are organized. There was a great gap left when the Federation fell, and in all too many places, there's still chaos." She shook her head. "It's not good enough. The technologies remain to establish some order, some stability. But we have to work together to make this a success."

Burnham thought, *That's why I came here, isn't it?* But her unease grew with every new thing that Remington said. "What do you want, exactly?"

"I want the spaceport at Devaloka."

"Excuse me?"

"Aditya Sahil isn't as young as he used to be, is he? And he's all that's standing between that part of space and outright chaos. There needs to be a plan in place, Commander. There needs to be a smooth transition of power."

"And you want that transition to be to you?"

"Why not?" said Remington. "Who else? One of the gangs operating the mercantiles? Pumping people with truth drugs and destroying endangered species? The couriers? They're fractious, fractured. They fight even when they're friends."

Not entirely true, thought Burnham, but she was hardly about to reveal the ways in which the couriers worked together for a common good.

"You've seen this place. You've seen how we're operating here. And I've shown you what we've been doing back in the sectors already under our jurisdiction. The Federation's gone. Starfleet's gone. I'm sorry about that, Commander. They can't come back—but something else can replace them."

This, perhaps, was the moment when Burnham was most tempted. All she had seen here. If she closed her eyes, ever so slightly, looked at this place through a slight haze, she might almost convince herself that this was a Starfleet base, that these people were a good enough replacement for Starfleet. Drugs to sick people. Food to hungry people. Peace and stability for all. What would Sahil say, she wondered, if she arrived back at his spaceport with these people in tow? Would he welcome them? Or would he see this as the final defeat? The admission that Starfleet was gone for good, and that they would have to make do with some kind of new order? Burnham, sitting and contemplating all this, looked at the display. Four sectors. Nearly fifteen systems. What could they do, connecting these with the sectors under Sahil's purview? How far could they reach beyond?

"If it helps you decide," said Remington, "I can offer you something in return."

A small silver case materialized on her desk. She turned this around so that when she opened the lid, Burnham could see what the box contained.

A black cylinder, maybe eight inches long, gray caps at either end. A black box.

"You've been looking for these, yes?" said Remington. "They contain information that you want?"

Burnham looked up from the black box to consider the other woman. The smart, almost-uniform clothes. The palpable sense of purpose. She was so nearly right . . . But the truth was, she was subtly and profoundly wrong. She had mistaken Burnham's silence completely. She thought that Burnham was holding out for more. She thought that all she had to do was find the right price. But . . .

Moneyless economy, thought Burnham. *I'm not for sale.*

Her second thought was, *I wonder exactly how much Pa'Dan told her about me.*

Her third thought was, *How the hell do I get out of this alive?*

She looked up at Remington and smiled. "I am most certainly interested in this kind of thing," she said. "Is this the only one you have?"

Remington blinked. "Yes. The only one I've seen."

"That's helpful to know," said Burnham.

"So you're keen to work with me?"

"I'm keen to hear more about what's on offer."

Remington sat back in her seat. She looked surprised. "I'll be honest, Commander. I wasn't expecting—"

"You're very persuasive," said Burnham. "Besides . . ." She leaned in toward the display and put her fingertip up to Sahnis III. "Sick children."

"Of course," said Remington. "Of course. Well, if we're more or less agreed in principle, perhaps we should start to work on the details." She ran her hand over her desk, and a small companel came up. She spoke into this. "You can come in now."

The door opened, and a man in middle years came in. "Commander," said Remington. "This is Dell Leavitt, without whom none of this"—she gestured around the room—"would be possible."

Leavitt? Burnham concealed her shock—and the rising sense of fury. That she had been caught out. That she had not read the signs correctly. Of course. These were the people behind the White Palm. She rose from her seat. "I think we've met a couple of times," she said, and she could not keep the anger from her voice.

Remington and Leavitt glanced at each other. "I thought she knew," said Leavitt.

"So did I," said Remington. "Commander, is this going to be a problem?"

"A *problem?*" said Burnham. "Why ever would this be a problem?"

"I'm glad to hear—"

"Blockading worlds desperate for water. Threatening others with disruption to food and medical supplies. I saw your ships open fire on a vessel of six hundred people that had practically no weapons to defend itself! Do *you* think it is a problem?"

Perhaps, Burnham thought, Remington didn't know. The White Palm raiders were operating a long way from here, after all. Perhaps Leavitt had misunderstood how aggressively he was meant to act. Perhaps he had overstepped himself. Some part of her hoped this was true, that she could proceed, even now, to make some kind of arrangement with this woman, to use the infrastructure she had created. Then she saw the look that passed between them. Remington knew. She absolutely knew. There was not even plausible deniability.

"I see," said Burnham. "I think we're done here." She nodded toward the silver case. "I'd love to have it," she said. "I'd love to know what it could tell me." She shook her head. "But not at this price."

Remington, she saw, was becoming angry. "This attitude," she said. "It's typical of Starfleet! The moral superiority. The casual disregard for the lives of ordinary people. Yes, we've moved aggressively into places. Do you know what was happening on Sahnis before we intervened? Civil war. No wonder there was rampant disease. We arrived and both sides surrendered within a couple weeks. We saved *thousands* of lives there—"

"I've seen you attack defenseless worlds. Bring them to the brink—"

"Atalis? They'd brought that on themselves. We were about to make a deal with them—"

"Other places too."

"Donatu? That one's a puzzle . . . I bet you could tell me all about that . . . Never mind. We'll take the mercantile there, when it's up and running. We'll find out what they're hiding."

Burnham shook her head. "In the end, it all depends on threat, doesn't it? Coercion."

"It doesn't seem to have bothered your friend Pa'Dan," Remington said.

Burnham turned away. "It's time for me to go," she said. "I've appreciated your hospitality, and—strangely—I find that I appreciate your honesty. But we won't be able to work together. I guess all I can do is ask that you stop your incursions into our part of space."

"It's not yours," said Leavitt.

"I guess I have my answer," said Burnham. "I'll go."

"No," said Leavitt.

"We can't let you go," said Remington.

"I don't think you have any right to hold me here," said Burnham. "You can threaten me of course. But you don't want that. You want to win me over. You won't win me over. The best you can hope for now is to let me leave, and keep to these sectors already under your control—"

"No right?" said Remington. "Time traveler?"

Oh hell, thought Burnham. *Pa'Dan—I trusted you . . .*

"I have to wonder exactly how many laws you're violating just standing here *breathing*," said Remington. "You know, when we first heard about you, we thought—is this woman one of those reenactors? Dressing up and playing Starfleet, you know?"

"I know," said Burnham. "Don't knock it. At least they care about what it means."

"They can do what the hell they like," said Remington. "And then we started to realize—no, she means it. She thinks she's Starfleet. And then . . . Well, when we found out, it all came together. You really are a Starfleet commander."

"Yes, I am," said Burnham, wearily, finally. "Devaloka is under my command. And I have a sworn duty to protect it, and the people living there."

Leavitt laughed. "What, old Aditya Sahil and a handful of retired couriers?"

"If that's all that's left of the Federation," said Burnham, "then that's what I'll protect."

They were looking at each other in disbelief. "Commander, we are offering you the chance to build something. That part of space—it's chaos. Gangs of petty warlords, fighting over scraps. Desperate people on desperate worlds, hoping that someone will step in. You can make a real difference there—with our help. This isn't the past, Burnham. We do things differently here."

"So people keep telling me," said Burnham.

"We're building a lasting peace," said Remington.

"I don't like the foundations," said Burnham. "I'll go now."

Leavitt moved to put his bulk between her and the door. "Not so quick."

She eyed him thoughtfully. "I've put bigger men than you into intensive care."

She felt the nose of a weapon in the small of her back. "Not this time," said Remington.

Burnham smiled. "See? You can't win consent. So you resort to force."

"It's what the times need," said Remington. "Decisive action. Not committee meetings. We'll be keeping you here, Burnham. And when your ship arrives—*Discovery*, isn't it—they'll come to get you, and we'll welcome them with open arms. I'm looking forward to seeing your ship. I'm sure I can make good use of it."

She would, indeed, be delighted to learn about the spore drive. Burnham, swallowing, said, "You'll be waiting a long time."

"It will be worth it," said Remington.

That was where the conversation ended. Remington summoned up a couple of security officers, and soon enough Burnham found herself in a small holding cell. "Federation prisons," she murmured to herself, sitting down heavily on the narrow bunk. "I certainly haven't missed these."

She lay back and closed her eyes. She tried to still the tempest of her thoughts. She was angry with herself for being blindsided. She was disappointed, *hurt*, at Pa'Dan's betrayal. She saw now that she had misunderstood the basis of their friendship entirely. Everyone, in this damn time, corrupted by the need to buy their way to security. Pa'Dan had bought her own safety at Burnham's expense. She should have known better. And now—now people's lives were at risk. Sahil back on the base, and all those who looked to him for whatever aid and protection he could provide. And then all the worlds nearby. The people on Donatu VII, they would be targets. Was Remington able to take *Discovery*? Could *Discovery* be quickly overwhelmed?

Burnham raged at herself. She should not have trusted Pa'Dan so freely, so *guilelessly*. She should have learned the lesson Book taught her on that very first day: be wary, be careful. She should have seen this coming. She should have remembered what Sahil had told her—courier values were not Starfleet values.

She heard a soft movement in the room. Someone said, "*Ow!*" She opened her eyes to see Book standing there, rubbing his elbow. "Burnham," he said, and looked around her cell. "We must stop meeting like this."

———

Burnham pulled herself up and around to sit on the edge of the bunk. "How," she hissed, "did *you* get here?"

"What? How do you think? Personal transporter." He threw one toward her; she caught it deftly. "Give me a minute, mine isn't quite charged yet."

"Not *here*," she said, jerking her thumb around the cell. "Here! This starbase!" She waved her hand around more generally.

"Oh yeah. Here. You know those transwarp tunnels I absolutely promised you I wouldn't travel through?"

"I remember that conversation distinctly, yes."

"I may have traveled through them."

"Book!"

"I would say I'll never do that again, but we're going to have to do that again, aren't we? If we're going to get away."

"I said not to risk it!"

"I know. Worth it, though. I know something you don't know!"

"If you mean that this is where the White Palm raiders come from," said Burnham, "then I do know."

"Oh, you do know." He looked disappointed. "Anyway, it seemed the quickest way to find out where the raiders were coming from was to follow them." He shook his head. "They must have some serious shielding on their ships," he said. "Grudge is furious with me."

"Grudge is always furious with you."

"Not always. Our love is pure."

"I've never denied that."

He looked down at his transporter. "All charged. Shall we stay here chatting, or shall we make a move?"

Burnham shook her head. "Not yet—"

"Only, I'm using a fake courier code, and they do all these background checks, and I'm not sure it'll stand up to scrutiny, and also I had to search their databanks to find out where you were being held and I'm pretty sure they're going to track that back to my ship at some point, so the window of opportunity is rapidly closing . . . and you've got something you want to do first, haven't you?"

"Yes," said Burnham. "I've got to go back to the base commander's office."

Book gave her a look. "One question."

"Fire."

"Why in the *name of all that's holy* would we do that?" He was plainly furious. "Burnham, we've got to go!"

She held her hand up to placate him; to stop the flow; to explain. "There's a black box, Book . . ."

"What?" He shook his head. "Oh, of course there is. A bloody *black box*! I should never have told you about the damn things—"

"I have to get it." She spoke quietly, resolutely.

"You know, there'll be more black boxes. There are a lot of decrepit ships floating around out there."

"There hasn't been another in nearly a year! Please, Book! I must have it! I know we can get it!"

He threw back his head and let out an exasperated noise. "Michael Burnham," he said. "Michael *bloody* Burnham. Why do you do these things to me?"

"Why do *I* do these things to *you*? *I* told *you*," she said, "not to go down those tunnels. Anyway, we need a plan."

"The plan," he said, "is surely the same as every other plan."

"That's not planning," she said. "That's making it up as we go along."

He gave her his most ravishing smile. Damn the man. Why did he have to be *so* . . . Well, whatever he was, he ought to be considerably less of it. "Are we dead yet?"

"I guess not," said Burnham. She looked around the cell. "Though I hardly call this living."

He reached into his bag for a weapon, handing it to her. Their hands brushed together, lightly. "Michael Burnham," he said, "you wouldn't have it any other way." Then, suddenly, his eyes lit up. "Wait," he said. "I *do* have a plan!" Digging around again in his bag, he pulled out a couple of small devices. "Remember these?"

She looked at them. "The holoprojectors we used on Ikasu."

"Good work. Now, let me have a little look around their files." She watched, and waited, and then he gave a low, and rather evil, laugh. Suddenly, Dell Leavitt was standing in front of her.

"No way," she said.

"No? Prefer this?" He hit the holoprojector. Now Remington was there. "Take your pick, Burnham. Pirate—or bureaucrat?"

Burnham and Book walked purposefully along the corridors of the starbase, almost daring the staff to stop them. On the whole, people jumped back to let them pass; one or two nodded quick salutes. "So this is what it's like being at the top of the food chain," muttered Book. "I should have got myself a rank *years* ago."

"Let's not push our luck," murmured Burnham. "We need to find a turbolift—and I'm not stopping and asking for directions."

"As if I haven't already downloaded the base schematics," said Book.

There was a pause. "Where are they, then?" said Burnham.

"What?"

"The base schematics?"

Another pause while he busied himself. "Turbolift down this corridor and to the right."

"Thank you, Book."

"You are always welcome, Burnham."

Entering the turbolift, she said, "Level four." They were soon in motion. When the lift came to a halt, Burnham brought a keypad into existence.

"First stop," said Book grimly. "We don't have access."

"I have Remington's palm," Burnham said. "Or a hologram of it, at any rate."

"I got these holoprojectors from a drunk Lurian in a bar on Telsis V. I doubt they have the capability to do that fine-grained a re-creation of—" The door swished open. "Oh."

"Whatever you paid that Lurian," said Burnham, "you got your money's worth."

Weapons out, they went carefully inside. Remington's office was empty. Burnham shoved the weapon in her belt and hurried over to the desk. She conjured up an inventory and found the requisite nanocubes. Programming these, she made the silver case materialize. She opened it with shaking hands. She took out the black box, tenderly, and tucked it into her belt. Then she called up the visual display and began to rapidly scan through data.

"What are you doing?" said Book.

"I'm not leaving without taking some information about what they're up to," said Burnham. "Look, there's all *kinds* of things here."

"Are you looking for secret invasion plans, or something?"

"If they're anywhere, it's going to be where the base commander can read them . . . Oh, now, this will come in useful . . ." She programmed up a data crystal and began downloading information.

"What have you found?" said Book. "It'd better be good."

"Base logs, going back . . ." Burnham stopped short. She almost couldn't believe the vein of gold she had struck. "Book, they go back to before the Burn!"

"Burnham! This isn't the time to indulge a passion for history."

"It won't take long . . ." She bent over the display, trying to work out a way to speed up the rate of download. What else was here? She glanced up at Book. How far did she dare push his patience—and their luck?

"Have you thought," said Book, "what a *shitty* epitaph that would be? *It didn't take long.*"

"Hush," she said. "I'm working."

"Burnham," said Book, urgently, after a moment. "There's a turbolift heading this way."

"One more minute."

"I don't think you have a minute," said Book.

"Okay," she said calmly, "let's split the difference and call it forty seconds."

"I don't think you have that either. Dammit, Burnham, you have nerves of *steel*!"

Maybe, maybe not, but she still wanted the data. "*Come on . . .*" she murmured. "*Come on . . .*"

"Look, whatever there is, it's surely not worth dying for."

"You can leave now if you want, Book."

"Yeah," he muttered. "Like I'm doing that."

"Grudge is waiting."

"And she'll never forgive me if I come home without you."

Even as Burnham's heart flared up to hear that, she pushed it aside to focus on the task at hand. The download was nearly complete. "If you want to make yourself useful," said Burnham, "have your transporter ready to go the second I say now."

"As if that's not the case already."

Ten more seconds. Eight. Burnham heard the turbolift come to a smooth halt. *Five . . .* She pictured the keypad being constructed. *Four.* The palm being held up for identification . . . *Three . . .* The door opened . . . Burnham had just enough time to see Remington, staring in shock at her own self, before shoving the data crystal into her pocket.

"*Now!*"

Burnham was back on her own ship, leaping into her seat in front of the flight console, setting a course to get the hell out of this place. Her mind was crowded. *Can we fight our way out? How far can we get? We've got to get away, back to Sahil, let him know.*

She saw, across the docking bay, Book's ship, already in motion. Alarms were sounding. Airlocks were sealing. *Alice* began to move into place behind Book's ship. She wasn't fooled by the apparent ease of this exit. It was easier, safer, for the base and the base staff alike, to let them out, and pick them off once they were away from the base itself.

How the hell are we going to get away?

She increased velocity to keep up with Book. Could they outrun them? She doubted it. They were in enemy territory. There would be ships following them soon . . .

"Burnham!"

"What is it, Book?"

"I've got a way out of here."

"I was hoping you were going to say that, mister, because it's rude to invite someone on a jailbreak and not plan the itinerary in full."

"You're not going to like it."

Of course not. "Go on."

"Remember those tunnels I absolutely promised you I would never enter?"

Burnham closed her eyes briefly. "Yes, I remember those."

"I can open one."

"You can open one?"

"I think so."

"You want to try opening up a highly unstable transwarp tunnel next to a starbase full of people in the vague hope that we might be able to enter it and come out the other side intact?"

"Yep."

Her scanners were already showing three ships scrambling to follow them. "All right, then, Book," she said. "I guess we can call that a plan."

He whooped down the comms. *"Burnham! You beautiful, marvelous, wondrous woman! You queen! I knew beneath the Starfleet polish there was a true courier!"*

"Shut up and keep to the plan," she said, while thinking, *Beautiful?* She filed that away for later consideration. Book was transferring his flight plan to her; she plotted her own course to follow closely behind, increasing velocity to match his. One of the ships following sent off warning shots. "How long do these damn things take?" she said. "The White Palm can rustle them up from nowhere?"

"I don't know. Haven't tried it yet."

"What? I thought you used one to come here?"

"I followed the raider ships, Burnham!"

"Great," she muttered. An alarm sounded. On the visual display, the sensors were beginning to go wild.

"Here we go," said Book.

The heavens opened. It was like seeing a wound being torn open in space, Burnham thought, as if someone had slashed furiously at the dark night with a serrated knife. The gap opened, wider and wider, and there was a flare of blue light.

"You want me to go into this?"

"I'm going, and I'm taking Grudge," he said. *"You can stay and face those raiders if you'd rather."*

Hell, she thought. What other option was there? He'd come through. She kept her ship in line, close to his, and plunged into the chasm.

Her ship rocked violently. "Brave little ship," she whispered. "Hold on, *Alice,* hold on."

In her ear, she heard Book murmuring, *"Hush, Queen. We'll be fine, I promise."*

She struggled to keep the little ship steady. From the morass of data pouring from her scanners, she was able to determine that—incredibly—the three ships that had followed them in were still in pursuit. "Book," she said, "they're still after us."

Another voice crackled through the comm. *"Burnham. Book. This is Leavitt. This tunnel's in danger of collapse. Come back with us, and you won't be harmed."*

Burnham said, "Not the best—"

"—offer I've ever had!" finished Book. His ship was shud-

dering from the vast forces now at play. *"Burnham,"* he said. *"Get as close as you can."*

"I can't get closer! You're shaking so much you might send me into a spin."

"Do it anyway, Starfleet."

She did what she could, inching *Alice* forward as best as she could manage. Suddenly, ahead, she saw the black night of space—the light, paradoxically, at the end of the tunnel. She pushed *Alice* closer, closer, till she was hanging on to the coat-tails of Book's ship. *Alice* lurched; she felt her control over her slip away. She thought, *I'm done.*

But *Alice* was locked into place behind Book's ship. Relief washed over her. Book had caught her in a tractor beam. The two ships, locked together, shot out from the tunnel. She heard Leavitt say, *"What the hell are you doing!"*

There was a crackle of static, then silence. Book's ship, with *Alice* behind, slowed. Burnham saw the sensors begin to return to normal. *"Damn,"* she heard Book say. *"Grudge, we are* never *doing that again."*

"What happened?" said Burnham. "What did you do?"

"Sealed the tunnel behind us," said Book. *"Stopped them coming through after us."*

"Can they get out again?"

"Depends whether their navigation systems mapped their entry coordinates precisely enough. And how stable that tunnel is once the exit's closed. Otherwise . . ."

Burnham shivered. Two options, she guessed. Either the tunnel would quickly collapse on them, or they were lost, buffeted along the tunnels for as long as your air or your ship held out. She thought she might prefer the former.

"That takes care of Leavitt," said Book.

"Not a good way to go," said Burnham.

"I'd care more if he hadn't been holding whole worlds to

ransom. Perhaps you should stop worrying about the fate of a particularly nasty pirate and start worrying about getting the word back to Sahil about what Leavitt's cronies have in mind?"

He most certainly had a point. Setting a course for Devaloka, she said, "I'll see you there—you crazy, reckless flyboy."

"You're very welcome, Burnham."

Sahil's office
Former Federation Spaceport Devaloka

At the spaceport, Sahil received the news about the White Palm threat with equanimity. "Well," he said. "I suppose it was only a matter of time. How ridiculous that this poor base should be considered a prime location. But then we are strategically well placed to reach so many systems—one reason the spaceport was built here in the first place."

"I managed to retrieve a substantial amount of data from the base commander's office before we left," said Burnham. "I'm downloading it now. I'll start sifting through it tomorrow." She yawned hugely. "I'll send what I get that's useful to you and Jeremiah."

"Please do," said Sahil. He looked about his office ruefully. "Although I fear two old men are not likely to be able to put up much of a defense!"

"I'll be here," said Burnham, softly.

"Thank you, Commander."

"I would have got nowhere without Book," she said.

Sahil turned to Book, standing unobtrusively in one corner of the office. "Mr. Booker," he said. "Book, I am extremely grateful for your efforts on my behalf. I know we have had our disagreements in the past, and I have given you no reason to assist me. It seems I had friends I was not aware of. Thank you."

Book, Burnham was amused to see, looked quite taken

aback. "'S all right," he mumbled, and cleared his throat. "I'd say any time, but, well, perhaps not those tunnels again."

"These tunnels intrigue me," said Sahil. "I have heard nothing about such things in all my years here. Perhaps the data you retrieved will enlighten us. Speaking of which—we should take a look at this, Commander." He nodded at his desk, where the black box lay waiting for their attention, hooked up to the same panels that Jeremiah had used, the lights on it glowing gently. "Steel yourself," he said to Burnham, as she came to look. "I remember how disconcerting the last one was."

She nodded, recalling the crew of the *Yelchin*, how hard it had been to learn their names, their specialties, their worries, and their priorities. She watched the data scrolling from the box onto the panel. "A name," she said. "The *Starship Gav'Nor* . . ."

"Personnel files," said Sahil. "Captain Culbreath . . ." He glanced at Burnham. "Let us look into this later. It's the moment of the Burn we wish to find, yes?" He scrolled through the data. "Ah, this looks more like it. Logs of the final voyage. Ah, they were some distance from the *Yelchin*—a thousand light-years!"

Burnham looked over his shoulder at the display. "Back up," she said. "Here. The moment of the Burn." She stared at the numbers on the screen. "They're different."

"They can't be," said Book. "The Burn happened everywhere at once."

"I swear, there's a difference." Burnham reached for this panel, punched in some commands. "Here's the data from the *Yelchin*." Numbers came on screen: 80986 mark 272129. "Overlay that with the *Gav'Nor*."

"She's right," breathed Sahil.

Book was shaking his head. "That's one one-millionth of a microsecond later, Burnham—how did you *notice* that."

"Vulcan skill domes," she said, offhandedly. Her mind was rapidly processing the ramifications of this discrepancy.

"Vulcan what now?"

"Memory training. Intensive." She tapped the side of her head. "There's a lot going on in here."

"I did wonder sometimes," Book said. "So what does this one one-millionth of a microsecond tell you?"

"It tells me I need a third black box at least."

Book raised his eyes to the heavens. "Some people are never satisfied."

"If I find another, and there's a similar variance, then that will mean that the Burn didn't happen all at once." Excitement was rising in her. "That the Burn had a point of origin—don't you see?"

"I don't," said Sahil.

"I do," said Book, eagerly. "Because that would suggest that the Burn had a point of origin, a point of origin that—"

"—can be triangulated from the data from the boxes!" Burnham finished, and they leaned over the desk to high-five each other. "Look at you," she said to him, her eyes shining. "You're as thrilled as I am."

"Only because of the mystery," Book said. "I don't like a mystery."

"Sure," she said, raising an eyebrow at him.

"A point of origin for the Burn," said Sahil softly. "But if we knew that—"

"We'd have a chance at finding out *exactly* what happened. And if we know exactly what happened, we can start thinking about how to *fix* it!"

Burnham and Sahil talked on in this vein for a while, but

Book, she noticed, went quiet, all his initial excitement rapidly dissipating. Later, sitting in the empty concourse inside the otherwise empty bar, she put the glasses of Romulan ale down in front of Book, and sat down. "You're not happy."

He sipped the ale. "A lot on my mind."

"Mine too. But . . ." She leaned forward. She put her hand on top of his. "I would've thought that by now you would know you could speak your mind to me."

His hand twitched beneath hers. "I . . . I guess . . . You won't ever give up, will you?"

"That's not in my makeup, no. I'll protect this station from Remington and her raiders, or I'll die in the attempt."

"That's not what I meant, although I'm glad to be clear about that now."

She withdrew her hand. "What do you mean?"

"I meant . . ." He looked around at the decaying station. "I mean this. No matter how low it falls. No matter if all the lights go out, everywhere—you're not giving up on the Federation, are you? You're not giving up on Starfleet."

"I've tried," she said honestly. "You don't know how hard I've tried. And then something comes to find me. That message, from Senna Tal—"

"Twelve years, Burnham!"

"The black boxes."

"Messages from dead ships. The voices of *phantoms*! You know, for a long time, I thought what you wanted from this search was just knowledge, understanding. What went wrong. Why the Federation fell—"

"I think I understand that now," she said. "It became . . . not too big, but too disconnected. Smaller worlds couldn't compete with the larger worlds. The larger worlds became complacent. The diverse voices got drowned out. When the Temporal Wars hit, and Starfleet didn't always deliver, people began to disbelieve. But the big worlds were complacent. And when something really big happened—the Burn—there was little trust left. It had started to fray long before the Burn."

He sat looking at her. "Is the history lesson done for the day?"

"I'm sorry," she said. "I thought you wanted to know."

"All of this," he said. "When you talked about finding out about how the Burn happened, how the Federation fell—what you really meant, all along, was how to start the process of *reversing* what happened. You don't want to find a way to live in this place. You want to find a way to bring it back."

"It's not as simple as that."

"You dream, Michael, of seeing that flag of Sahil's flying everywhere again. Not just here at Devaloka but everywhere else. In Remington's office on Starbase Vanguard. Over Sanctuary Four, Donatu, on every world, at every mercantile you've ever visited—you see the Federation flag."

She drank some of her ale. "Would that really be such a bad thing?"

"I don't know," he said. "What I *do* know is it won't ever happen. It can't ever happen. People didn't want it, Burnham. They gave up."

"I know," she said sadly. "But I can't stop hoping . . ."

"Do you hope if you keep on explaining it to people, they'll change their minds? Become true believers?"

"Book," she said, shaking her head. "I don't want to quarrel with you."

"I don't think we're quarreling," he said. "I think we're finally making ourselves clear to each other. Making it clear where we stand."

She was tired. She was worried. She was still wired from the past few days. She was more than a little drunk. "Can't we leave this? Can't we just . . . carry on as we are?"

"What *are* we, Michael?"

"We're about to defend this spaceport from the White Palm."

He didn't reply.

"You're staying, right? You're going to help?"

He finished his drink. "I have somewhere else to be."

"You're *leaving*?" she said. He stood up. "You're leaving."

"I made promises to other people," he said. "I have to keep them."

She had things she wanted to say—angry things—but she caught herself and stopped them before they could come out. What right did she have to berate him? If he could not see that he had a stake in this, then what could she do? Keep explaining until he changed his mind? He had done so much for her already. Got her started here. Helped her learn how to navigate this time, negotiate it. Had thrown himself down transwarp tunnels to save her. Told her she was beautiful.

"Not going to try to talk me round, Burnham?"

She swallowed her disappointment. She laid her hands down, palms flat, on the table. She looked up at him and smiled. "I am grateful," she said, "for every single thing that you have done for me. You have gone above and beyond. I hope that one day I'll be able to find a way to show you how grateful I am."

"Okay," he said, and nodded. "Then . . . I'll be seeing you, Burnham." He flashed her his beautiful smile—and went on his way.

Slowly, Burnham finished her drink. She got up, slightly unsteady on her feet, and made her way back to her quarters. She sat for a while on her bunk, head in hands. Was she being unfair, feeling this disappointed? What more did she expect from him? Still, the sense of disappointment was real. She had trusted him—not only with her life but with intimate details

about herself. Perhaps that had been her mistake. This friendship . . . she had mistaken its foundations. It had always been
transactional. It had never been anything more.

She sighed. Book was gone now, and there was nothing to
be done about that. Once again, she would need to find some
well of stoicism to draw upon. She was used to that, to putting
aside emotions. She had no space for complications like this in
her life. She had to put aside distractions and work on defending this spaceport from what was coming. She needed to be
concentrating on concrete problems, resolving them with the
application of logic, intelligence, determination, and effort.
After all, hadn't that brought her to where she was today?

Burnham stood and stretched. Her eye fell on the data
download she had brought from Remington's office. This was
the place to start. There would be information about their
defensive capabilities, number of vessels at their disposal, ship
schematics. There was more than enough to keep her busy. She
constructed a visual display and began to scan through what
was there. There was a huge amount of data. She thought
about leaving it until the morning, getting some sleep. Instead
she got up and replicated coffee, added a measure of whisky,
and got to work.

She rapidly found the data she needed on the White Palm
ships, their weapons capabilities, speed, even some weak spots
in design. Good; that would help them defend the base. Less
positive was the news that they could most likely bring at least
two dozen ships to attack Devaloka. Burnham read this with a
sinking heart. How could she combat this? There were maybe
half a dozen ships here on a busy day, and not all of them
could be counted on to come to the spaceport's defense. Rubbing her eyes, she sent the data over to Sahil and Jeremiah.
They would think of something. They would *have* to think of
something.

There was much, much more on the data crystal, and she set up search terms to find immediately relevant information. Personnel files. They might come in useful at some point. If there was anything on Remington, it might be worth trying to get under her skin, work out what made her tick. Power, yes—but also some deep-seated need for order and stability. She would read them as soon as she had the chance.

A blue light began to flash, alerting her that something of interest had been found. She opened the file and began to scan through. The words *transwarp tunnels* immediately grabbed her attention. It would help to know more about these, even if it was simply to work on Book's method of closing the tunnels. Perhaps they could set up advance warning systems; close the tunnels even as they were opening.

She saw a file headed: *Project Rabbit Hole: Activation Test #109-11B*. Some information about what Remington's people had been doing to get the tunnels to work, perhaps? She opened the file. A hologram of a woman appeared before her. Burnham's breath caught. This was a Starfleet science officer.

"Science Officer Lorrah. Notes on test #109-11B. The most recent test of the tunnels shows the same problems as before—a fundamental instability in their structure and a frustrating tendency to tear starships apart."

As Burnham listened, realization dawned. The transwarp tunnels had not been created by Remington and her people. This had been a Starfleet project, one of those attempts to find an alternative to dilithium-regulated warp technology. Like the others that Sahil had shown her, it had not been a success. Report after report showed that the project team could repeatedly create the tunnels, but not safely enough for any large class of ship to travel them. Even ships as small as the courier ships that she and Book flew, or the White Palm ships, were put under considerable stress. She listened. People left the team; others arrived. How far had these new people gotten? How far had the project gotten, before the Burn?

Burnham moved to the last entry.

"Science Officer McIntyre. This really is a cursed endeavor. Every time I think we've made a breakthrough some part of the calculations turns out to be—"

The entry ended abruptly. Burnham frowned. Was this the Burn? She checked the date on the file.

Her heart nearly stopped. The year on the file was 3186. More than a hundred years after the Burn. Only two years before Burnham had arrived in this time.

This was surely a mistake. Murmuring to herself, she checked the timestamp. No, the year was right. She asked the computer to show her relevant files by date. And saw them all—the project files for Rabbit Hole, continuing from before the Burn to long, long after. Her voice shaking, she said, "Show me all files dated 3186 . . ."

The computer found them. All the data that she needed to piece together the story. A Starfleet outpost, cut off from the rest of space, connected to a few systems, trying to protect them with the small science vessel at their disposal. When the call came for them to return to Earth, some decided to stay to work on a project that might one day restore what was lost.

What happened?

In her heart, Burnham knew the answer; when she found the personal log of the last base commander, Commander Marshak, she got the full story. The woman's face appeared before her. The uniform—so achingly different, so tragically the same—still red, for command. The worried, exhausted face . . . *Ships with white markings . . . We won't be able to hold them back . . . I have tried to negotiate, but it's clear they want the base.*

The entry ended. With shaking hands, Burnham stopped

the holo. "They were here," she murmured, tears forming in her eyes. "Not even two years ago. They were still *here*." She thought back to that sense of homecoming she had felt, arriving at Starbase Vanguard. No, she knew the real name now, and she would damn well use it . . . No wonder Starbase 906 had felt so much like home. There had been people here, on an operational Starfleet base. One of those little beacons of light that she had been hoping beyond hope to find, that she had *known* must be out there, waiting to be connected up once again. They had been murdered. Remington, Leavitt, they had taken the base, and stolen their work. It was unbearable.

Operational before I arrived in this time, she thought, scrubbing at her damp cheeks. That would have been too much. To have to live with the knowledge that fellow officers had died, while she was here. She knew—rationally, logically— that it would have made no difference. She would not have been able to reach them, would not have had the resources to help them. But still she would have felt that it had been on her watch. *Too many died because of my decisions,* she thought. She knew that in coming to this time, she had saved countless lives. *I could not have borne the loss of any more.*

As she watched the holo once again, she felt a deep anger rise up in her. Remington was responsible for this. Remington had sat there, in her office, behind Commander Marshak's desk, and tried to cut a deal with Burnham. Knowing what she knew, she had tried to bring Burnham over to her side.

You won't win, thought Burnham. *You, and all you stand for—I shall* never *let you win.*

9

"It does cross my mind, Commander," said Sahil, ruefully, "that this would be an extremely good time for your ship to put in an appearance."

Burnham, eyesight blurry and head buzzing from caffeine, grunted her agreement. She could not deny that a *Crossfield*-class starship would come in handy right now—in fact, any kind of starship would come in handy. *Discovery* would surely swing any battle in their favor. The data she had taken had given them a good idea of what resources Remington could throw at them, but Burnham couldn't begin to guess what else the woman could draw on from the planets under her influence. Would she press an attack straightaway? Or would she gather forces to ensure her victory? What Burnham did know was that when the attack eventually came, it would be completely ruthless. Remington would surely not rest until this place went the same way as Starbase 906.

"If only, Sahil," Burnham said sadly. The previous night, she sent out another set of messages yet again, aimed at a new set of potential arrival points that she had calculated. While the presence of *Discovery* could be decisive, it could not be relied upon. That would be a sad bookend to her story, she thought, if they arrived too late for her and Sahil and Devaloka, just as she had arrived too late for the people at Starbase 906. "But we're going to have to hope for help from elsewhere."

"The couriers who were visiting here have mostly left," said Sahil. "Why would anyone want to be present when an invasion is on the way? I can hardly blame them."

No, she thought, but she could see he was disappointed. They had been happy to make use of the base when he could help them. Now they were gone.

"I've put out a general call for aid," he went on. "To the worlds that our two ships were supplying . . . The problem is, of course, that we prioritized those places that needed our help, and therefore they have very little on offer." He sighed. "You see how I am fixed."

Other worlds, those whom he had not aided, might have the ability to come to their aid, but no particular incentive. What did it matter to them who operated the spaceport, as long as it remained operational? Why should they put themselves in the firing line? That was what had happened, in the end, at Starbase 906, Burnham had learned. The small core of scientists devoted what they had to keeping their project alive. They had found themselves with few friends willing to risk themselves in the face of the White Palm's concerted attack. Burnham shook her head; tried to put the images from those last desperate holos out of her mind. The grief—the guilt, even, however irrational that might be, that she could have *done* something—was hard to shake off in her current state of mind. Sahil, she knew, felt the same way. As far as he had known, Starbase 906 had long been abandoned. He would have sent one of his ships that way—if he'd known.

"There might be more people I can call on," she said doubtfully. "Maybe some of the couriers." She had helped defend Donatu VII. Maybe they saw that as payment for being trusted with their secret? Maybe that was paying back

Brodie and his help with finding *Alice*? Courier values were, in many ways, a mystery to her. Pa'Dan had proven herself untrustworthy, and as for Book . . . Burnham tried to push that disappointment aside. He'd thrown himself down the transwarp tunnels twice on her account; helped her escape from Remington's clutches. What more did she want from the man? What more had she expected? "In the meantime, we should be focusing our attention on what we have to hand, and how we can improve that."

"There is one option we haven't considered, Commander," said Sahil, softly.

"Yes?"

"We could leave."

She stared at him. "Leave? You mean surrender?"

"A surrender, typically, means that a defense has been mounted in the first place. What I meant was that we leave before the White Palm arrive." He ran his hand across his neat desk. "If they are so intent on owning the place . . ."

"Where would you go, Sahil?"

"My homeworld, Prithvi, is not a long flight from here."

She studied him carefully. He was not a young man anymore, and today he looked tired and overwhelmed. "Sahil," she said, "is that what you want?"

"What?" he said. "No! Of course not! Commander, how could you think that! My whole life I've dedicated to maintaining this place! Upholding Federation values as best I could with what I had. To keeping the lights on here until the day Starfleet could arrive and resume their operations here. Of course, I don't want to leave! But perhaps we need to understand when we are defeated. That there are no Starfleet ships coming to help us, and—in the end—few friends."

She reached out to put her hand on his. "I told you," she said, "when I arrived, that you are as real a Federation officer as anyone I had ever served with. *I'm* here, Sahil. I'll stand beside you—until the lights go out."

"No surrender?"

She glanced over at the flag that they had lifted together. She said, "Never."

He clasped her hand and squeezed it. "Then let us make a final stand together, Commander. But we should not trust simply to our courage, I think. Would you perhaps go and find out how far that old rogue Jeremiah has got with boosting the capabilities of the defense grid?"

The Back Forty
Former Federation Spaceport Devaloka

Burnham had never thought she would see the day when her defensive strategy relied upon an elderly courier who owed her two weeks' back pay. Still, Jeremiah had worked wonders in the past. She doubted she could have retrieved the data from her old tricorder's chip so quickly. And she had seen the wonders he had worked on courier ships, nursing ailing systems back to health, fine-tuning others so that they found not only a new lease on life but, sometimes, increased capabilities.

He was bent over his table when she arrived. Hearing her approach, he looked up, and went back to work. She gave him a wry smile. That was about the limit of his emotional range. Jeremiah had never once said that he was pleased to see her, and she never expected he would.

"Hey," she said. "How's the defense grid looking?"

"It looks like the kind of grid you get at a place that once had a main reactor breach."

"Whatever you can do, Jeremiah."

"My suggestion is that you pack up and leave."

She shook her head. "That's not going to happen."

"No? Sahil won't have it?"

"Neither of us will have it."

"And so it falls to me to find a way to protect your stubborn asses?"

"I'd like to think this helps you too," she said, trying to keep impatience from creeping into her voice. She knew this was part of the dance with Jeremiah, but—damn, she was tired, and had so much on her mind. Couldn't he cut the crap and get to work?

"We'll see," he said. "At the very least, bring everyone onto one level. That way we really only need the shields to cover a limited space. Concentrate resources there."

"Risky, if they get through."

"You don't have enough people to defend this spaceport, Burnham."

That was certainly true. "We'd need ships ready to evacuate . . ." She could fit Sahil on *Alice*, but there were half a dozen other people to take care of.

"Sahil can see to that."

"Any chance of boosting our weapons, Jeremiah?"

He looked up at her. "There are physical limitations to what I can achieve given available resources, Commander. My professional judgment, based on the data you sent me about those ships, is that you and Sahil should get the hell off this station." He bent over once again. "I'll get back to work, if I may."

She sighed to herself and turned to go. The doors to the workshop had barely closed behind her when Sahil's voice came over the comms. *"Burnham,"* he said. *"I could use you here now, please."*

Sahil's office
Former Federation Spaceport Devaloka

Sahil was standing, arms crossed behind his back, looking at the visual display. Burnham came to join him. "What is it?"

"Over here," he said, pointing to a spot where Burnham could see some unusual distortion on the display. "From the information you brought back, I was able to develop what I think is a means of predicting when a transwarp tunnel may be forming—"

"That's clever!"

"Thank you, Commander—most of the work was done by the science officers on Starbase 906. But I think the distortion might be the first sign that a tunnel is forming. If that's the case, I believe we shall see White Palm ships within weapons range of Devaloka within the next ninety minutes."

Ninety minutes. "What will we have by then?" she said. "Ships, I mean."

"Four ships are due to arrive from Prithvi within the hour," he said. "Civilian freighters, I'm afraid, but with some defensive capability. One of the couriers who left this morning has returned—I find myself rather touched by this . . . I gather he has family on a world attacked by the White Palm. He said he may as well go down fighting now rather than later . . . That's the spirit that will help us win, surely!"

"Five ships," she said. "Plus my own . . ." She breathed out. "Well, let's see what we can do. With any luck, we can hold the station until . . ."

"Until what, Commander?"

"I've still got calls out for help," she said, doggedly. "We just have to hold on . . ." But she had to face the reality of their situation. They could not hold out for long against an aggressive and concerted attack. Turning to face him, she put her hand on his shoulder. "There'll come a point," she said, "when I ask you to leave."

"Oh, Commander!" he said, shaking his head. "I knew you were going to say this to me at some point."

"As your senior officer, I'll make it an order if I have to.

But I'd rather it was a request. I'll ask you to leave, Sahil, because I want you to take that flag back to Prithvi. I want you to take the knowledge of everything we've learned: about the tunnels, about the White Palm, about what happened on Starbase 906. The message from Senna Tal . . . The contents of the black boxes . . . Keep trying to contact Terralysium. Keep trying . . . *please*, most of all, keep trying to contact *Discovery*. Maybe one day they'll come." Her voice faded away. "In the meantime, someone has to keep the lights on."

"And, after all," he said, smiling at her radiantly, "*you* came. Commander, I shall comply with your request promptly, and to the very best of my ability. I shall try to keep the lights on." He looked back at the display, where the distortion was now more marked. "I have considerable practice in such things."

The hour crept by. The four little ships arrived from Prithvi, piloted by three achingly young and eager volunteers, and a white-haired older woman with a wearied but quietly indefatigable air. Burnham briefed them on their task; when she was done, she hurried away to get to her ship. She heard the older woman say, "All right, my loves, time for me to make you proud."

About fifteen minutes before the anticipated arrival of the White Palm, another courier ship appeared. Burnham recognized the pilot, Hambly: she had met her around Brodie and Katerina's table on Donatu VII. "I was passing when I heard your distress call," she said. "You didn't have to put yourself between us and those raiders. Thought this was the least I could do." Burnham was deeply touched—and hugely heartened to learn how well her ship was armed.

At last, Burnham took her seat in her own ship. She patted the control panel. "*Alice*," she murmured. "You've been a good home. You've been a good friend."

Her eye fell on her uniform, still folded, ready and waiting for a time she now believed she would never see. She reached over to rest the palm of her hand on it, to gather strength from it, and everything it meant to her. She reached for her delta badge and put it in place. As she started to move the ship into place, a medal—hanging just to one side, and above her head—twisted with the motion. She saw the familiar face, engraved on the medal's surface, and laughed.

"For remarkable leadership, meritorious conduct, and acts of personal bravery," she said to herself. "Thanks for that, Captain."

She was ready. Just the last few minutes . . . She took some deep breaths, calmed herself, and prepared to speak to the other ships with words of support. And then a message came from Sahil.

"Commander," he said. His voice sounded urgent and afraid. *"The defense grid has gone down."*

———

"What?" Burnham, scrabbling at the controls, looked at her own sensors.

"Our defense grid is no longer operational."

He was not wrong, she saw, scanning the data coming in from her own sensors. Where before there had been shields, now the spaceport lay open and undefended. "What's gone wrong?" she said. "What does Jeremiah have to say?"

"I can't locate him, Commander."

"What? Not at all? Has he been hurt?"

"I don't know. He does not respond to my communications."

"Can you locate him on Devaloka?"

A pause, then: *"No."*

"Can you locate him anywhere near Devaloka?"

Another pause, then: *"There's a ship moving away from the port—close to the Back Forty. He's on that."*

She located the ship and hailed it. "Jeremiah," she said, "what's going on?" Getting no reply, she moved *Alice* around the spaceport, until she could see the little ship. "Jeremiah," she said calmly. "Are you leaving us?"

"Yes."

"I don't blame you, given the odds, but any chance you could tell us what you think might have gone wrong with the defense grid? You're the expert—" She stopped short when she heard his laughter.

"Commander Michael Burnham," he said, *"all that knowledge of the past, and you're clueless when it comes to the future."*

Burnham went cold. Her first thought was: *He knows.* Her second thought was: *He's known for a long time, and we kept lying to him* . . . "Jeremiah—"

"I used to think Sahil was a fool. Waiting for Starfleet to arrive. And they did arrive! And they were the same as ever. Arrogant. High-handed. Superior."

"I know," she said, "that this seems as if I didn't trust you, but we told nobody."

"You told that courier of yours—Book. And the Cardassian woman, Pa'Dan! You were willing to tell them!"

Burnham stopped short. How the hell did he know that? Dots began to connect in her mind . . . Remington had known so much about her. She'd assumed it was Pa'Dan, trying to impress her new employers, but had there been another source? "Jeremiah," she said, urgently, "whatever you have against me, whatever you have against Starfleet, Sahil has been your friend for years. These White Palm raiders—they are vicious, and they are merciless. They murdered the Starfleet personnel on the base they hold now."

"Good," said Jeremiah.

"What?" she breathed.

"You think I care about Starfleet? I told you often enough—not that you listened. Starfleet never listens, not to people like me. Not to worlds like mine. Worlds like mine were thrown to the wolves. No hope. No aid."

"What aid could they bring, Jeremiah! There was no way of getting to you!"

"Before the Burn! My grandfather—he knew. Petition after petition. The Council didn't care. Not about the little people."

Burnham thought of what she had learned from Tagore's log. There might be some truth to this; she knew that this had been the source of many frustrations for Tagore. But to deny a world aid? That she did not believe. There would be some kernel of truth, she was sure, but the rest of the story told by his grandfather, misunderstood by a child living on a hard world, the embers of a grudge kept burning over decades.

"I'll be glad to see what's left of Starfleet go up in flames. And if the White Palm will do it, so be it. Good luck trying to fix that defense grid, Commander Burnham. You'll have one hell of a job cracking the access codes I've used, and I'm pretty sure you don't have enough time left to do it."

She checked the sensor readings. The tunnel was now mere minutes away from opening. She said, "Please, Jeremiah. Don't do this. If not for my sake—then for Sahil's sake. He does not deserve this."

"He lied to me, Burnham. After all this time, he thought I deserved nothing better than a lie. He can take his chances with the rest of you."

His ship began to move away. She thought, briefly, of firing on him—but what use would that be? What good was revenge? It would only deplete her already inadequate resources. Grimly, she began to move *Alice* back into position.

The tunnel opened. She saw, dark against its bright burn,

the raider ships. Her sensors told her there were two dozen of them. She thought, *Well, so this is it.* She thought, *I'm glad Pa'Dan didn't betray me.* She thought about everyone she had ever known and loved. She thought of her friends, on *Discovery*, and she wished them safe voyaging and a friendly harbor. She thought of Sarek, and Spock, and the strange bonds that existed between them. She thought of her daddy. And last of all she thought of the women who had in their various ways shaped her; she thought, *GabrielleAmandaPhilippa . . . Mommy . . .*

Shots were fired. *Alice* rocked. Then Burnham saw that her sensors were going wild. She tried to make sense of the data and, with horror, she saw that another tunnel was opening.

Damn you, Remington, how many ships exactly do you think you need to do this!

The new tunnel opened. Her sensors told her there were three dozen of them. One of them opened fire—and the nearest of the White Palm ships was blasted into pieces.

"What?" she said. "*What?*"

She heard a familiar, infuriating voice. *"Burnham! You know those tunnels I promised you I'd never travel down?"*

"Book . . ." she said.

"You're going to have to forgive me all over again."

They'd come from wherever he could find them. Couriers who owed him; couriers who liked him. A deeply interwoven and intricate web of mutual commitments and obligations. And then there were the people who were there on her account. Zuka had come with a handful of ships from Sanctuary Four. There were people whose families she had protected that day on Donatu VII. There was even someone she had brought from the generation ship, in a little courier ship. Pa'Dan? No.

The first few salvos took out Jeremiah's ship, as he tried to make it to the protection of the White Palm. Later, reflecting on the battle, Burnham wasn't entirely sure whether or not the fire that took him out had been friendly. Their numbers won the day. The White Palm raiders had come anticipating a straight-forward and easy victory, particularly once the defense grid was down. Instead, they faced an unexpected and vigorous fight. Burnham was able to pull back the weaker ships, using them as a second line between the fighters and the base, and the more experienced pilots took point. The White Palm was pushed back. Burnham's sensors showed the now-familiar readings, a tunnel was being opened. Reinforcement? But no—nothing came through. The remnants of the White Palm attack—eleven from the two dozen that had come—retreated into the tunnel, sealing it behind them. Devaloka was safe—for the present.

Former Federation Spaceport Devaloka

The pilots of the ships were congregating in the concourse, congratulating each other, congratulating themselves, checking details, swapping stories. Burnham, making her way through, guessed that this place hadn't seen so much life in decades. She was heartened by this. Something important had happened here today. Connections had been made; bonds had been forged. This might be the making of something else.

Burnham shook her head; tried to put this all aside. Through the crowd, she saw the man she was looking for, and wove her way toward him. Seeing her, he grinned.

"Burnham," he said, "some nice flying out there."

She stood with her hands on her hips. "I don't know," she said, "whether to hug you or to break your damn nose."

"Either way round seems to be how you say, 'thank you,'" he said.

"Thank you," she said. Then she threw her arms around him. "Why the hell didn't you tell me this was the plan?" she whispered in his ear.

"I don't plan, sweetheart," he said. "I make it up as I go along."

She thought: *Sweetheart?* And then she heard someone calling out her name. She turned to see Sahil, making his way toward them. She pulled back. Book murmured something— "Always interrupting"—but she couldn't be quite sure.

Sahil had no qualms about throwing his arms around her in a warm embrace. Then he turned to Book and did the same. "Thank you," he said. "Thank you."

"You're welcome, Starfleet," said Book. "Sorry I didn't let you know I was coming sooner."

"If you'd done that," said Burnham, "you wouldn't have got your dramatic entrance, now would you?"

"True enough," he said. "And . . . I'll be honest. I didn't know who would come. I didn't know if *anyone* would come. Looks like we've got a few people on our side over the years. Hey, what happened here?" he said. "Why was the defense grid down? If we'd been a few minutes later, they'd have taken the whole place out with a couple of shots."

"Jeremiah," said Burnham. She saw Sahil's expression. "I'm sorry, Sahil. Turned out he knew who I am. He knew from my data chip. And he wasn't happy that we hadn't trusted him."

"If he was willing to betray you for that," said Book, "it sounds like you made the right call."

Sahil was contemplating this news. "He did not have a happy life," he said. "I believe . . . perhaps there was more to his antagonism toward Starfleet than I understood."

"Son of a bitch," said Book, less forgivingly. "Did he ever pay you, Burnham?"

"He did not," said Burnham.

"Huh. Take what you want from the Back Forty, I'd say."

"Oh yes," breathed Burnham. "I will be. And we'll open

the place to these folks." She nodded around. "There'll be treasures in there that people could use."

"Good idea," said Book. He leaned in toward them both and lowered his voice. "We need to store up whatever goodwill we can," he said. "Because we're going to need it, if we want to pull off what we're going to have to do next."

"Next?" said Sahil.

"They're not gone," murmured Burnham. "They're just regrouping."

"I see," said Sahil. He looked old and tired again.

"Don't worry for now," said Burnham. "I'm going to get clean—get something to eat. But Book's right. There's a lot of goodwill right now. We need to move while we can."

Sahil's office
Former Federation Spaceport Devaloka

The three of them—Burnham, Book, and Sahil—sat together in his office. *A council of war. I would never have guessed,* thought Burnham, *when I walked in here all those months ago, that the three of us would meet again in circumstances like this. That we would be the ones taking command.* She smiled at these two men; her best friends here in this bewildering, surreal place.

"I know that today feels like a victory," said Burnham, "but we have to assume that the White Palm will be coming back as soon as they've had a chance to regroup. We need to talk about what we can do to stop them."

"Jeremiah's lock over the defense grid is proving trickier to break through than I would like," said Sahil. "But we'll get there. At least now we're not trying to do that under duress. And with Jeremiah dead, we're not at risk of such a betrayal again."

As long as Pa'Dan hasn't also switched sides. Burnham

pushed that thought away. She had no way of knowing, either way. For now, she had to focus on what she knew, and what could be done.

"Burnham," said Book, "I know we . . . well, we must have *pissed them off*, but do you think we should face up to the reality of this situation?"

"What do you mean?" said Burnham.

"The ships that came here today—that's pretty much the limit of what we can hope for. And not all of them are going to stay. They've done their job, they'll take a look around the Back Forty for payment, and then they'll be off. But we've shown Remington we can mount a defense if we have to. She'll be warier in future about trying to take this place by force. So why not . . ."

"Sue for peace?" asked Burnham. She shook her head. "No. That's not happening."

"All I'm saying is that it might be our best option. And if that's the case—we need to move now. We've got the benefit of a shock victory. If we let that pass, we might not get terms as good. Like . . . I don't know! Like looking for something for sale at a mercantile and watching the price hike up while you try to decide whether you want to buy."

"I understand what you're saying," said Burnham. "It's more complicated than that."

"Is it? Is it really though? From all I've heard, the sectors where they operate are doing well. They're stable. Wasn't that what the Federation was about? Stability? Law and order?"

"No, not entirely," said Burnham.

"But do you think it might be worth our while negotiating some kind of settlement?"

"Commander," said Sahil, softly, urgently. "I would not believe that any peace that Remington offered would be worth the paper it is written on. Given what we know . . ."

Burnham nodded. Book, glancing between them, said, "What? What gives?"

Burnham and Sahil shared a look. Sahil nodded his consent. "Listen," said Burnham, leaning forward. "We're going to share some information with you. What we know about Remington's base. I guess, strictly, it's confidential but . . ." She held up her hands. "I suppose I'm head of security here along with everything else."

"You've got my full attention," said Book.

Quickly, Burnham briefed him on all that she had learned. The project to create the transwarp tunnels. The work that had continued there after the Burn. The continuity with the Starfleet of old. And its sudden, terrible end. When she finished, Book stared at her.

"Two years ago?" he said. "You're sure?"

"I can show you the holos if you like—although it makes for grim viewing."

"Well shit," he said. "*Shit!*"

"I know," Burnham said softly.

"Burnham, I'm *sorry.*"

"Me too," she said. "I know, logically, that I couldn't have done anything. But it feels so . . ." She sighed. "I don't believe we can negotiate, Book. That's why I know they're nothing like Starfleet, they're all about coercion. The Federation was about consent." She rubbed her temple. "I think, you know, that's why it failed in the end. It was no longer able to deliver on its promise. But at its best . . ." She thought of her ship, her crew, her *friends.* "At its best, Federation values were constant. It was committed to peace, but it was prepared to defend itself when the need arose. I think that's what we need to do now."

"They will come back," said Sahil. "And they will lie and cheat and murder. It's only a matter of time before they try to take this place again."

Book sat back in his chair. "I think I know what you're going to say."

"Yes," said Burnham. "We have to take the fight to them."

Book looked at her. "You and whose army?"

The Alice
Approaching Starbase Vanguard

The transwarp tunnel opened and two little ships, buffeted by their passage through, came shooting out. *Last time*, Burnham thought, laying her hand against the console. *I promise, Alice—that's the last time* . . . Opening a channel to Book, she said, "Are you ready?"

"I suppose so . . ."

"Then let's go."

As the two ships drew nearer, Burnham hailed them. "Starbase 906, this is Commander Michael Burnham, science officer, *U.S.S. Discovery*. You are occupying a Starfleet facility. I'm ordering you to surrender control of this facility. Failure to comply—"

"They're scrambling their ships, Burnham."

"Failure to comply will be met with deadly force." Burnham waited for a response. All that happened was that the White Palm ships moved into formation. "Remington. You said you were looking forward to seeing my ship. Well, your wish is about to be granted. Because when the next tunnel opens, you'll see the *Discovery* coming through."

"Burnham—"

Book, she thought, *don't interrupt me when I'm extemporizing.* "That's right, Remington. *Discovery* has found me. They made contact. I told them what happened here. I told them you were responsible. They're not happy to hear about the deaths of their colleagues. I suspect they're ready to take this base with deadly force."

"Burnham," said Book. *"Check your sensors. Their defense grid is down!"*

She stopped. She checked the readings. He was right. *What the hell is happening?*

Then she received an incoming communication from the base—straight from the chief executive officer, no less, on all frequencies. *"This is Chief Executive Officer Remington, ordering all White Palm ships to stand down. Stand down and return to base immediately. Repeat—stand down and return to base immediately."*

There was a pause, and then, as Burnham watched, the ships began to withdraw. She murmured, "What the hell is going on?"

When the last raider ship was back at the starbase, she was hailed again from the base. A familiar voice came through the open channel.

"This is Iliana Pa'Dan, now in control of Starbase 906. Commander Burnham, I'm looking forward to welcoming you and your crew aboard."

Commander's ready room
Starbase 906

Iliana Pa'Dan was waiting to meet her in what had been Remington's office. However, she wasn't sitting behind the desk. Instead, she was sitting perched on one corner, arms folded, tapping the toe of her boot against the floor. When Burnham came out of the turbolift, she hopped up from the desk and rushed toward her. "I'm glad you've got here," she said. "I was starting to think I was going to be stuck in this room for good." She looked past Burnham. "Where's your crew?"

"It was a bluff," said Burnham, wearily. "I've no idea where *Discovery* is."

"Oh," said Pa'Dan. "Oh well, I suppose you can always take over."

"Pa'Dan," said Burnham, "what the *hell* has been happening here?"

"All right," said Pa'Dan. "Long story. But when I first came here—someone slipped me a message. Warning me about this place. I was just leaving—the most money I'd had in a long time. I tried to put it out of my mind. Then I came back, and I found out more. You know, don't you?"

"About the tunnel project. About how long Starfleet was here. Yes, I know," Burnham replied gravely. *The question is— what did* you *know about it,* Pa'Dan?

"I knew what Starfleet meant to you," Pa'Dan said. "I couldn't put it out of my mind."

"I came here," said Burnham.

"I know," said Pa'Dan. "I couldn't get to you. And you were gone again before I had the chance. Remington was furious—"

"She knew everything about me," Burnham said.

"I think she had a source at Devaloka," said Pa'Dan, and then she must have caught Burnham's expression, because she pulled back in horror. "You thought I'd sold you out, didn't you? Michael—you saved my life on Atalis. I would never have done that!"

Burnham nodded slowly. "I think," she said, "I understand that now."

"Things were heating up here. I'd been contacted by people here on the base. They were loyal to the Starfleet officers who were here. They wanted Remington gone. When she took the ships to attack Devaloka, we, er . . . We may have had a little uprising, yeah? Took the base back."

"I see," said Burnham. She began to laugh. How many emperors had found themselves deposed when they were away from the capital? Remington's empire might have been small, but she had made a fundamental error. "Where is Remington now?"

"In the brig. Her people too. There were only a handful loyal to her, really. They were just . . . *dedicated*? Anyway, once we got their weapons and pointed them back at them, they were less enthusiastic about carrying on the fight." Pa'Dan fidgeted. "Someone has got to think about what to do with them. Can I hand command over to you now?"

Burnham looked at the desk. It was a very good desk. She looked around the office. It was a very fine office. She looked at the view behind. The view was without doubt magnificent. Smiling at Pa'Dan, she said, "I have a better idea."

"Oh no," said Pa'Dan. "Whatever you're thinking—no."

Burnham put her hand upon her friend's arm. Gently but firmly, she maneuvered her around the desk. "For as long as I've known you," said Burnham, "you've been talking about finding somewhere to retire to." She pushed Pa'Dan into the seat. "You're going to make a very fine base commander."

En route to Devaloka

Burnham and Book had stayed for a few more days at Starbase 906, working with Pa'Dan and the remaining people there to ensure that the transition to their control would remain peaceful. Pa'Dan came down to the docking bay to see them leave. "I feel like I've been handed a massive and unexploded bomb," she complained.

"These are good people here," Burnham said. "The worlds in the systems have a vested interest in making sure that things continue to operate smoothly. I think you're not likely to see much trouble."

"Just . . . don't mess around with the transwarp tunnels," said Book. "I swear, I have made my last trip through them."

"Is this good-bye, then?" said Pa'Dan. "You're not coming this way again?"

"Perhaps, if *Discovery* does arrive, and we're able to make the trip rapidly. Otherwise . . ." Burnham shook her head. The transwarp tunnels were too risky. Burnham could not see when she would make the journey again. "You've got everything you need here. You're going to do a good job." Burnham stretched out her open palm, and Pa'Dan pressed hers against it.

"Good-bye," she said. "Good luck. I hope *Discovery* finds you."

She and Book were soon in flight, traveling, for the most part, companionably side by side. Sometimes she put her ship on automatic, let him use the tractor beam, and went over to join him on his ship. For a little company on the journey. To see Grudge. Nothing more. What more could there be?

A half a day from Devaloka, she sent Sahil a message, with a full report of everything that had happened over at Starbase 906. Not long after, his return message came, and Book played the holo-image. Sahil stood before them, hands clasped together.

"Commander," he said. *"I am so very glad to hear from you. I am so very glad to hear that both you and Book are safe, and that your efforts at Starbase 906 were successful. Please hurry back. Commander, I must tell you . . . I've received a communication—from Terralysium."*

Burnham turned to Book. "I know," he said, with a sigh, going over to the flight console. "Quick as we can."

Sahil's office
Former Federation Spaceport Devaloka

"We regret that there is nobody named Gabrielle Burnham here. We hope that your friend finds her mother in time."

In time, thought Burnham, her head in her hands. *Isn't that the problem? I am unstuck in time.*

"Commander," said Sahil, gently. "I am so sorry. I know how much store you had set in this . . ."

She sat up. Squared her shoulders. Tried to move on. "It's all right," she said. "I knew . . . I knew that this was a long shot. I knew, in my heart, that it was very unlikely that I would hear good news." *I lost you so long ago, Mommy. Perhaps it would've been better if you'd stayed lost, so I didn't have to go through this over and over again.* How many times, after all, could you grieve for someone?

I have to let go.

She took a deep breath and looked around. A cup of tea was cooling beside her. Sahil, in the seat opposite, was looking at her with kindness. "I wish it had been better news," he said. "I wish I could bring everyone you loved to you, here, now."

"I know," she said. "Thank you."

"I'm glad to see you," he said. "Your visits have become less and less frequent over the past few months, and last time there was hardly time to sit and chat like we used to. Perhaps there will be some quieter days ahead. The mercantile on Donatu is a good sign. People wanting to trade. That is often the start of something greater. Something better."

She drank her tea and listened to him talk. She felt soothed, but at the same time, rather melancholy. Perhaps it was because she had recently seen Starbase 906, so well maintained, so well organized, even under Remington. Now, this place looked sad, well past its glory days, locked in an inevitable decline. His talk of the possibilities offered by the exchange seemed misguided. Yes, there might be trade, and there might be some peace, but there would be no re-federation. The Federation was gone. Starfleet was gone.

He stopped and smiled. "Forgive me—I do go on. But you know my hopes. That one day that flag will fly again in many more places than here—"

"Sahil," she said, shaking her head.

"You know that I hoped that I might hand over this station to you in time. But I believe, Commander, that you might now have other plans. Am I right?"

He was so kind, she thought, so wise. He had been so very patient with her. "I'm going to move on," she said.

"I see."

"It's been a year . . . This message from Terralysium . . . I feel as if it's drawn a line for me."

"You might yet hear from *Discovery*."

"I've been sending messages from my ship too. If they come—big *if*—they'll find me. But . . ." She sighed. "I can't keep living this way. Pulled constantly to the past. Avoiding the future—*my* future. I have to give my life some direction. I've got a ship, I've got contacts—I know I can get work. I'll travel a little farther—look for more black boxes. There's plenty more to learn."

"What about all of this?" he said, gesturing around.

She was conscious of the flag—the flag that they had raised together, right behind her. "Rebuilding the Federation?" she said. "That's a task beyond me."

"All the more reason, surely," said Sahil, "for us to work together to achieve it."

She didn't reply.

"Michael," he said, and sat back in his seat, "do you no longer believe that's possible?"

Burnham found herself struggling to reply. Everything she had learned over the past few months—the worlds she had visited, the people she had met, the logs, files, and databanks she had scoured—they had all, in the end, told her the same thing. That something had gone wrong in the Federation well before the Burn. Whatever bound all those worlds together—it had frayed.

"After the Temporal Wars," she said, slowly, "there were worlds left to their fates. Nobody came, or not soon enough. You know from your own great-grandmother's account how frustrated the more distant worlds were. How the bigger worlds were no longer listening."

"But surely you don't mean that it was finished?" he said in alarm.

"No, no!" she said quickly. "I'm sure, given time, they would have figured it out. Worked out how to rebalance the laws and regulations. They would have found their way to their essential values. I guess all I'm saying is that it didn't *help*—"

"I am willing to concede that in its latter days it was no longer the beacon it had once been," said Sahil. "But what about what it was before? What it was in your own time? A brilliant, beautiful idea! Imagine what you saw on Ikasu! What we could all have at our disposal now, were the Federation still here!"

She shook her head. "What I saw on Ikasu was fear, Sahil, hostility to outsiders. That's not what the Federation was! The Federation was never simply the sum of its technological achievements! It was about open-mindedness, encountering something different and not seeing it as a threat but as an opportunity to learn and explore. I've seen that here and now, in many places. Take the couriers—"

"The couriers?" said Sahil. "Ah, you mean Book."

"Not just Book. But others too. Zuka wanted to leave Ikasu—the technology didn't matter to her. The chance to see other worlds, to learn what was out there. That was what she wanted. Binye too, in time, I think . . . If there are answers, Sahil, if there's a way to rebuild what we lost—it's going to be out there, I think. Not here.

"It's not the right task—not for me."

"Well," he said, with a sigh, "I can't exactly stop you. But I will . . . I will miss you."

"I'll come back. Not as often as I used to. But I'll come back." She stood up. "Thank you, Sahil," she said, "for everything."

She offered him her hand, and he shook it. "Where will you go?" he said.

"Wherever the answers are," she said, and laughed. "I guess what I'll find most is more questions."

"Commander Burnham," he said, "whatever you find—it has been my privilege to meet you, and to serve beside you."

They embraced, and she left. Outside, Book was waiting. "Ready now?"

"I'm ready." She followed him down the corridor. She felt light. She felt happy. She felt as if she had wings, and, at last, could fly free.

Who are you now, Michael Burnham? Who might you become?

The Alice
In flight . . .

Burnham sat in her little ship, flying alongside Book, on course for the mercantile at Donatu VII. There was word of some work there that would pay for her travel beyond her familiar routes. She was ready now to travel beyond familiar routes. To see how far she might fly.

She sat back in her seat and looked about her. Dotted all around the console were various talismans she had acquired over the year. Some were bits and pieces that had taken her fancy at the mercantiles, chosen to make this little space more livable, more *hers*. Others were more specific. Two black boxes, and all they contained. A holo-journal of a long-gone Federation councilor, who had shown courage and determination at a desperate time. A coral necklace from Ikasu that Binye had given her. A scratched emblem—like but not like Starfleet's—that she had put in her pocket from a generation ship. A *Kol-Ut-Shan* brooch. Ship relics and plaques that she could not bring herself to sell. A cube containing images of lost friends. A fair amount of cat hair . . .

Burnham picked up her delta badge and turned it around in her hand. This felt like part of the set now: a memento from a previous chapter in her life. Meaningful, important—but not of this time, this present. Still, she took it with her when, a little later, she transported over to Book's ship. She had brought her calculations too: he thought he might have some ideas, but she was in no hurry. She had sent out many messages already— and she had time now, after all, plenty of time. They didn't do anything straightaway. He had a new simulator to show her. He'd programmed it with some of the *Suus Mahna* moves she had shown him over the months.

Later, after they'd both worked out, and she stood sweating and smiling after her latest victory, Book threw her a towel and poured them both drinks. They sat and talked and drank and laughed. Between them, sprawled across the table, Grudge purred in contentment.

She raised her glass. "You know," she said, "when all is said and done—it's not such a bad life, is it?"

He smiled at her, like a proud teacher at the sight of a student who has come a very long way. "No, Burnham," he said. "It's not."

She could have sat there forever. But their peace was disturbed by a chime from the console. "Message for you from Sahil," said Book, and played it back.

"Michael," Sahil said, a quiet tremor in his voice. *"They're here. Sending coordinates."*

Burnham looked at Book. She knew, at once, exactly what

this meant—and she knew that he understood too. She said, *"Discovery—"*

He turned in his seat, his back to her, reaching for the flight console. "Where, Michael?" he said. No questions. No judgment. *You could love someone for that*, she thought, *given time*.

MICHAEL BURNHAM

PERSONAL LOG

It seems that my last set of calculations were more accurate in their predictions than I would ever have believed possible. I thought this was a long shot. Turns out my thinking was more rigorous than I could ever have hoped for.

Well done, past me.

Because they're back. My friends, my crew, my people. They're here. This changes everything.

Am I ready for this?

I guess I'm going to have to be ready for this.

This is all going to be very strange.

ACKNOWLEDGMENTS

Thank you to the truly wonderful Kirsten Beyer; superstars Margaret Clark, John Van Citters, Dayton Ward, Scott Pearson; and Max Edwards, agent and mensch.

And all my love to Matthew and Verity, who got me through this year.

ABOUT THE AUTHOR

UNA McCORMACK is the author of nine previous *Star Trek* novels: *The Lotus Flower* (part of *The Worlds of Star Trek: Deep Space Nine*), *Hollow Men*, *The Never-Ending Sacrifice*, *Brinkmanship*, *The Missing*, the *New York Times* bestseller *The Fall: The Crimson Shadow*, *Enigma Tales*, *Discovery: The Way to the Stars*, and the acclaimed *USA Today* bestseller *Picard: The Last Best Hope*. She is also the author of five *Doctor Who* novels from BBC Books: *The King's Dragon*, *The Way Through the Woods*, *Royal Blood*, *Molten Heart*, and *All Flesh Is Grass*. She has written numerous short stories and audio dramas. She lives in Cambridge, England, with her partner of many years, Matthew, and their daughter, Verity.